"FIRE!" BUCK CRIED SHARPLY. BROWN HELD HIS FINGER POISED ON THE FIRING KEY, THEN PUNCHED IT HARD. . . .

Back in the sonar shack, Schultz was watching the path of the torpedo. It curved to the right, speeding toward the spot occupied by the enemy submarine. It would run at high speed into the general area, then slow, make a circling search, finally go back to speed and home in on magnetic attraction. It was the best torpedo the U.S. Navy had, the product of years of research. Its record of successful firings was outstanding. It was fast, nearly silent, and almost 100-percent deadly.

But as they watched the sonar scope in disbelief, the spot the Russian submarine occupied became suffused with its own white light, a light which persisted. And when it was gone, there was not even a trace of the presence of another submarine. . . .

COLD
IS THE
SEA

Edward L. Beach

A DELL BOOK

Published by
Dell Publishing Co., Inc.
1 Dag Hammarskjold Plaza
New York, New York 10017

Dell ® TM 681510, Dell Publishing Co., Inc.

ISBN: 0-440-11022-X

Reprinted by arrangement with Holt, Rinehart and Winston
Printed in the United States of America
First Dell printing—November 1979
Second Dell printing—February 1982

There are some who go down to the sea in ships, and some who go under the sea. The causes of catastrophe can be subtle as well as manifold, but fortunately only a few fail to come back to port. To them and to their valiant memory, this story is dedicated.

COLD IS THE SEA

1

〜〜〜〜〜〜〜〜〜〜〜〜〜〜〜〜〜〜〜〜〜〜〜〜〜〜〜〜〜〜〜〜

To most of the outside world, the Pentagon is a huge five-sided pile of cement, looming squat and commanding on the Virginia bank of the Potomac River across from Washington, D.C. It contains the offices of the Secretary of Defense, the Secretaries of the Army, Navy and Air Force, the Chairman of the Joint Chiefs of Staff and the military Chiefs of the three Services. Behind their windows in the impressive, four-story, two-block-wide façade, these important personages can doubtless draw inspiration from the wide patriotic vista spread before them: it encompasses the mighty Potomac River in a single grand panorama from its confluence with the shallow Anacostia to Georgetown (the colonial "head of navigation"). The Lincoln Memorial on its banks, the spire of the Washington Monument and the Capitol dome all rise as if from a garden above the low screen of green bordering the river. One can visualize the high councils taking place behind those severe windows, the critically important, low-voiced briefings, the great decisions by which United States military policy is determined.

The Pentagon was built to be the world's largest office building, and it presides over the world's biggest parking lot. Some 30,000 people are housed in it from eight to twelve hours a day, more than eighty hours a week in many cases. Its life never ceases, for there are watch officers and duty sections all over it, most especially, but not solely, in the secure operational command areas. It is not one building but about fifty, all interconnected, and they actually form five complete pentagons, placed one inside another in a series of concentric five-sided "rings."

The outermost and largest of the five pentagonal rings, the E-ring, is sumptuously finished, with marble columns, terrazzo floors, escalators and even a private elevator serving the most high-level offices. The favored office suites are all on the E-ring, with outside windows looking to the west, north and east. The smallest ring, the A-ring, is favored in a different way by having its hallway along its innermost side, so that the passerby may enjoy the view of the pentagonal central court from its windows. Between these two extremes there are rows upon rows of hallways interconnecting, rows upon rows of identical doors opening into rows upon rows of cubiclelike interior rooms occupied by the owners of most of the cars in the parking lot. Some of the interior rooms have no windows. Most, of course, do, but there is very little to look at. Through these windows, the occupants of the warrenlike spaces—that is, most of the Pentagon's 30,000 inhabitants—have a flat view of the rough-finished facing of the outside of the ring opposite. They are given an excellent opportunity to inspect, in depth, the impressions of the wooden concrete forms which held the cement in its designed place while it was hardening and also preserved imperishably the shape of every board, the pattern of its grain, its occasional knotholes, nailholes and splinters, for the ages yet to come.

The window gracelessly lighting Captain Richardson's office faced more or less to the west, but except for the direction taken by the sun's rays it held identically the same view as all the other interior windows: the casemented window frame and venetian blind of the equally drab cubicle opposite. Rich had been gazing through it more abstractedly of late, and more frequently, now that he had relatively little to do. It was raining gently, a warm, flower-benefiting rain. Outside the Pentagon a presidential campaign was in its early flowering stages as well, with nominating conventions only a few months away, and the news every day was full of learned discussion as to who might succeed the war hero who had held the post for nearly eight years.

As was the case with the real flowers which Laura tended so lovingly at home, however, Rich had had little opportunity, until very recently, to follow the blooming, or nonblooming, of the national political scene. He had had no leisure time to follow anything else, either, including the growing needs of thirteen-year-old Jobie.

Now, for the past week and a half, it was different. Jim Barnes, designated by the Bureau of Naval Personnel to relieve him, had been aboard for a month. He had used the time under Rich's tutelage well, had formally taken over his job and, technically, his "desk" (although by courtesy he was temporarily using another) ten days ago, and was already enmeshed in the latest short-fuse requirement of the Navy Secretary. He had even showed some eagerness to take over the responsibility; well, he would soon learn, just as Rich had.

Three years in the Pentagon, in the office concerned

with Navy Programs and Plans, were about enough for any naval officer who would rather be at sea. Three years preparing specifications for the forces required to meet constantly changing national commitments, of endless weeks practically living in his office, responding desperately to the sudden demands of a Secretary of Defense whose habit, about 4:30 in the afternoon, was to say, "Have it on my desk at eight o'clock tomorrow morning," had given Rich a jaundiced view of Washington political officialdom and its inconsiderate demands on its minions. More than once he had worked all night because it would have been disloyal to the Navy not to, all the while wondering if the document being prepared at such personal sacrifice would actually be read by anyone, least of all by the minor official in someone's office up the line who had been the real source of the urgency keeping him there.

But all this was over now, had been for ten days, and there was nothing for Rich to do but catch up on personal business, lend a hand if his successor asked, in general try to occupy himself usefully—for the first time in his Pentagon career he was able to leave the office at the so-called "regular" hour—and wait. He was noticing, perhaps for the twentieth occasion during his three years in this particular cubicle but only now with genuine interest, that when it rained a regular river of water cascaded down the cement facing his window—when female footsteps approached his desk. Without looking, he knew it was the secretary he shared with another captain and two commanders, not to mention Jim Barnes, now, as well.

The rain did not continue down the outside wall of the building, however. Instead, much of it suddenly disappeared into the concrete through a hidden flaw in the structure. Doubtless some wretch on the floor below, perhaps an Army colonel also "program planning" for his own Service, was wondering what he had done to deserve this. If he didn't have enough sense to come up a flight and inspect the wall above his office, as Rich, however fortuitously, was doing at that very moment, he deserved to be flooded out once in a while.

"Captain, here's something from BuPers. . . ." Rich turned, his dampened opposite number in the U.S. Army forgotten, seized the bulky envelope.

"Thanks, Marie," he said, extracting a thick sheaf of paper from the envelope she had already slit open. It was immediately evident there was but a single typed sheet, with numerous copies clipped to it.

"From: Chief BuPers," the paper said—it was not a letter but one of those forms of official gibberish by which unnamed bureaucrats protect their jobs by confusing everyone else—"To: Captain Edward G. Richardson, USN. Subj: Orders. Herdet Prorep ComSubRon Ten Porich USS Proteus Delrep 10 . . ." There was more gibberish and a series of numbers that meant something to someone in the Bureau of Personnel, but for the moment he needed no more.

"Are those your orders?" Marie asked. "We know you've been waiting for them, but we'll be terribly sorry to lose you . . ." Her polite words trailed off. Everyone in the office had been painfully aware of Richardson's restlessness the past few days, and the reason.

"Yes, at last," said Richardson, unconsciously rising as though he might begin acting on them immediately. "I'm getting SubRon Ten in New London."

"Congratulations, Captain. That's the squadron you were hoping for, isn't it?" Marie, after many years in the Pentagon, had seen countless naval officers come and go. Orders to sea, she well knew, were highly prized. Usually they were received weeks, sometimes months, before they were to be carried out, and there was always a reason behind any break in this routine.

If no explanation was offered, it was tactful not to mention that one had noticed.

"Thanks, Marie. Yes, it is," Richardson said again, almost absently, toying with the paper. "But they've left something out, I think." He read the tersely worded document again, frowning. "I never could figure out this verbal shorthand. There was supposed to be something in here about nuclear training prior to reporting." He turned to look out the window, turned back to Marie, dismissed her with another word of thanks. He sat again at his desk, reached for the telephone. "Deacon," he said, "Rich Richardson. My orders to SubRon Ten finally landed here. It's been bad enough having to wait like this, and I know you've been doing your best to clear them through the bureau. But I've just noticed they don't say anything about that nuclear power training we were talking about. I've had my interview with Admiral Brighting, and that was all agreed. At least, that's what he said. Leaving it out was a mistake, I hope."

The voice on the other end of the line sounded slightly troubled. "It wasn't a mistake, Rich. I'm really sorry. I thought it was all set, too. But you know old man Brighting. There's just no figuring him out. The list for nuclear power he sent over last week didn't have you on it. We thought there might have been a mistake over there and called them up, but they wouldn't change."

"But dammit, man, is that why you've had me chewing my fingernails these last few days? Why didn't you tell me right away, instead of just sending over these orders after all this waiting around? When I went over there for my interview, he told me he was putting me on the list for the next class—that was the whole point of the exercise! The nuclear subs are all being assigned to Squadron Ten. I made the pitch that the squadron commander should also have a nuke ticket, and he agreed!"

Deacon Jones' voice lowered perceptibly, its unease emphasized. "Rich, I know how you feel, and you know all I can do is try to run this submarine assignment desk according to what is handed me. All I can tell you—and this better stay off the record, please—is that there was some kind of a flap up in the front office last week between the chief and Vice Admiral Brighting. It was all on the telephone, and we're not sure who slammed down the phone first, but I'm pretty sure it was over the nukey pooh list. Yesterday I got the word to send over your orders as is. Scott was so mad we could feel the walls shaking all the way down to my end of the wing here."

"What sort of a flap, Deac? Are you telling me there was a week-long flap over me in the front office between Vice Admiral Scott and Vice Admiral Brighting, and no one even told me about it?" There was a rasp in Rich's voice as he threw heavy emphasis on the titles of two of the most important officers in the Navy. "What sort of flap? Why did that take me out of nuclear training?"

"All I can say is if they didn't tell you it's because they don't want you to know. It went on more than a week, and I sure don't know what it was about. I didn't even find out this much until a couple of days ago. You know none of us can figure out how Brighting makes up his mind about the folks on that list when he puts it out. We even have to do undercover work to find out when one is about due, and I agree, it's no way to run a navy. Anyway, there's one bit of dope you'll be glad about. Your old exec, Keith Leone, is getting the blue crew in *William B. Cushing*. And another one of your old JOs, Buck Williams, is getting the *Manta* in your squadron. Both of them have orders to the next nuke school, and when they finish they'll be reporting to you in New London. Once in a while we try to do something right. That please you?"

"It's the greatest news I've heard for a year," Rich said fervently, then hung up the phone. But it was nevertheless a deeply troubled Richardson who shortly thereafter maneuvered his ancient automobile out of the Pentagon parking lot and, for once, beat the afternoon rush-hour traffic. The rain was abating at his rented house in South Arlington; Jobie would be delighted to bring out the newly purchased baseball gloves a little earlier than usual, and afterward he would have a word with Laura.

"Well, you just have to go and see Admiral Brighting," said Laura. "Whatever he has against you, he owes it to you to tell you, and I think he will. Then you'll know what to do." It was after dinner. Conscientious young Joe, known as "Jobie" because his middle initial was B, had gone to his room to study for his eighth-grade exams. Rich and Laura had made short work of the dishes and were now relaxing in the living room. Lately Rich had treasured this opportunity to look over the evening paper. It gave him a sense of returning to the real world, after a long absence. Not tonight, however. During the fifteen years of their marriage he had frequently taken his problems home to Laura, and he had learned to value the thoughtful insight she so often was able to bring to them.

"Brighting is a peculiar man, dear," Rich said. "You don't get to see him just by setting up an appointment the usual way. My interview with him in March was a set piece; all officers proposed for assignment to nuclear subs have to be accepted by him and go through his nuclear training instruction. He insists on interviewing every one of them personally, and he only takes about half the candidates."

"I know all that," Laura said. "The Navy's been talking about that for years. He's always been against protocol, I mean, the normal way of doing things, and he likes the unusual, especially if it's contrary to the system. You ought to telephone him direct, without going through any superior office or bureau—don't even tell them—and just ask if you can come and see him. If you do it on the phone yourself, instead of first having a secretary put the call through, I think he'll say to come on over. But he'll be expecting you, though, to try to get him to change his mind."

"He can't blame me for that!"

"Of course, darling. But he'll be ready to turn you down unless you can get him to listen to your side with an open mind. Do you know anybody in his shop who might tell him there's another side to the story beforehand?"

Rich did know somebody. He had been surprised to see her passing the admiral's office as he entered for his interview. He had not seen her since the war, had no idea she had become a Navy WAVE officer, not the foggiest notion in the world that she had been a member of Brighting's staff for several years already. "Joan!" he had muttered, when she suddenly appeared. Their hands had touched, a handshake. It was impersonal, a friendly warmth only, but even so, as there had been something unforgettable before, there was a strange awareness now. A conscious effort had been needed to put the awakened memories out of his mind, and he had not succeeded well.

"No," he said, answering Laura's question with the lie direct. He rationalized it by thinking he had no idea what Joan's status was in Admiral Brighting's group.

But he was vaguely conscious of another motive, its essence glimmering at the fringe of conscious awareness.

Joan had been out of his life since the war. He had made a decision then; so had she. It had been the right decision, difficult at the time because so abrupt and final, but for him it had not been hard to live with. Perhaps this was partly because the Navy moved one around so much anyway. That had been all right for him, but sometimes he had wondered about her. She had always seemed so self-contained, so undemanding. There had always been a private quality about her, some secret invulnerability. During the period of their intimacy she had somehow avoided telling him much about her background, what she had been doing before he knew her, what she was doing at the time. Then the war ended, and they parted. He would have liked to maintain some sort of contact with her, despite his approaching marriage to Laura—as one did with good friends in the Navy—but he could not think of anything but the wrong reasons for doing so. By consequence, he never had really tried. Neither had she.

Like so much that had happened during those strenuous, halcyon years, Joan, too, had receded into the never-never land. He knew her well enough to realize that was the way she wanted it. She had given him his freedom, and claimed the same for herself. Now, fifteen years later, she was back. But was she? Did he dare ask her to reenter his life, even in a small way?

2

~~~~~~

Despite Laura's misgivings about the lack of an inter-
mediary, her suggestion had been a good one. For all
Rich knew, Admiral Brighting had been expecting the
request for a second interview. His offices were located
in a separate, guarded, brick-and-concrete structure behind the "Main Navy" building dating from World War
I. Now the sharp-featured, hawk-nosed, wizened little
admiral peered across his book-and-paper-cluttered
desk at Richardson. His eyes were mild, expressionless,
slightly faded. He had been reading, but no glasses
were in evidence. As previously, he was dressed in civilian shirt, tie and trousers. His jacket was hanging
nearby. Two months ago, Richardson had come in uniform for his first interview, but today he had decided
to match the admiral's habitual attire. No one, however,
had invited him to remove his jacket. The room was
warm. The ancient air-conditioning unit in the window
behind Brighting was whirring, blowing an ineffectual
amount of humid, slightly cooled air toward him.

"Hello, Richardson. What do you want to see me
about?" It was hardly an auspicious beginning. Admiral

Brighting spoke in a monotone, barely loudly enough for Rich to hear him. He had the reputation of wasting no time in conversation, and in this he was running true to form. His eyes returned to the loose-leaf binder filled with pink flimsies from which he had been reading.

Richardson had carefully thought over how he would broach the subject of his visit, had decided to try as well as he could to fit the admiral's mood, whatever it might be; but he was already totally disarmed. His straight-backed wooden chair was as uncomfortable as it had been the first time, and he had long known the story about its front legs having been slightly shortened. Probably this was not true, but nevertheless it held him at an odd angle, and there seemed a tendency to slip forward. Determinedly, he planted both feet in front of him.

How to begin? "I came to try to convince you to reconsider, sir," he said. "I want very much to go to nuclear power school."

"Do you think just asking me will get you what you want?" Admiral Brighting's eyes remained on his loose-leaf binder. "Why don't you ask your friends at BuPers? They write the orders. They can send you to any university they want."

"Your training is the only one that can qualify me in nuclear power, sir. I'm to be responsible for administration, training and operations of the nuclear subs in the Thames River. It's going to be a big and tricky job, and that's why I want to know something about your submarines and your program, sir."

"Why aren't you wearing your Medal of Honor, Richardson? Are you trying to impress me with your modesty? Or are you ashamed of it?" The soft, monotonous voice had not changed. The admiral's eyes flickered, then once more fell to the notebook in his hand.

The pink sheets were all carbon copies, Rich noted. Brighting picked up a pencil, absently began to make little marks in the corner of the turned-over, left-hand sheet.

It had not occurred to either Rich or Laura that Brighting might make reference to the wartime decoration which was part of his uniform. Richardson nearly stuttered. "I'm not ashamed of it, sir," he finally said. "I just thought I'd come in civilian clothes today." His voice reflected his sudden defensiveness. He was trying to keep all emotion out of it, not quite succeeding.

Admiral Brighting made more marks on the paper. "You're a hero, Richardson. We don't need heroes in nuclear power. What we need is dedication, and workers who are willing to use their brains. We don't have any room for lazy naval officers. You go and be a hero in your new squadron. You won't have any trouble riding on your reputation there."

"I've never been afraid of work, Admiral," said Rich, fighting the urge to raise his voice. "All I'm asking is the same opportunity you are giving to others. I want to do a good job in New London, and it will be better for all the nuclear boats up there if I can talk to the skippers from knowledge instead of ignorance."

"Do you read any books? What books have you read recently?"

Rich was ready for the sudden shift in subject. "I've been interested in Napoleon lately," he said, "beginning a year ago with *War and Peace.* I've just finished General J. F. C. Fuller's *Military History of the Western World,* which I started mainly because he gives so much time to Napoleon."

"I've read Fuller, but his history is principally about battles. Have you studied Victor Hugo and Emil Ludwig? Ludwig is the recognized authority on Napoleon."

Brighting looked up at last. "Do you think Maitland was right to induce Napoleon to come aboard the *Bellerophon* with a promise of asylum?"

"Fuller says he only promised to bring him to England unharmed," Richardson said steadily. "Napoleon was lucky to get the protection of the British Navy at that point. The Germans would have killed him if they'd caught him, and the French royalists might have done the same if he'd not got aboard a big British warship."

Brighting's eyes dropped again to the notebook. He made another tiny pencil mark in the upper left corner. "You're wasting your time reading about Napoleon, Richardson. Nothing about him is relevant to 1960. He died nearly a century and a half ago. If you're so interested in nuclear power, why haven't you been studying some of the books on the subject? You're like all the others. You're not interested in nuclear power; you're only interested in furthering your career." He looked up. The pale gray eyes were now bleak. "No squadron commander is going to tell my skippers how to run my submarines, Richardson," he said, still speaking softly. "You operators have no idea of what's required, and you're not willing to learn."

"That's not true, Admiral," said Richardson. "I'm willing to give it all I'm capable of, if you'll let me have the chance. None of the nuclear power books gives the operational know-how needed, anyway. They're all theoretical. The only way anyone can get that is through your program. You're the only person or organization which has ever built an operational nuclear power plant." Trying to guess how the interview would go, he and Laura had decided that a little flattery would do no harm. "There's bound to be a lot of nuclear stuff in New London that I'll have to deal with. Personal ambition has nothing to do with it. With or without nuclear training, I'm already designated for the squadron up there. All I want is to be able to do a better job."

"All I've got to do to keep you from commanding Squadron Ten is to say I don't want you up there. What do you think of that? Did the Chief of Personnel send you over here to beg?"

There had been an ever increasing bite to Brighting's words, and now the insult direct. Rich could feel his adrenaline flow increasing. But he had anticipated this. He would not succumb to Brighting's famous baiting tactics. He was willing to become a supplicant, was one already. He had already decided he would beg, if necessary. If Brighting insisted on it. He would choke, but he would do it. "Admiral," he said evenly, as evenly as he could, "please! Nobody knows I'm here. I came over here on my own, to beg your help. I *am* begging. If you'll give me a chance, I guarantee you'll be pleased with my performance, both in training and in New London afterward."

"What makes you think your performance one way or the other means anything to me?"

There was pressure on the back of Richardson's neck. He would not be able to stand this much longer. "Admiral, when I first came over to talk about this, you told me you agreed that ComSubRon Ten should get nuclear training. What has happened, sir? Won't you at least tell me what changed your mind?" This would have to be his final effort.

"I don't have to tell you anything. I didn't ask you to come over here. You might consider that it costs thousands of dollars to put one man through my course. I'm responsible for the proper use of that money. You have only a few more years of service before you either retire or they make an admiral out of you. Either way, you'll have no further use for anything we could teach you.

After thinking it over, I decided it would be a waste of government funds."

"But Admiral," Rich began desperately, "you told me it was going to be your policy from now on that commanders of nuclear squadrons would be nuclear-trained—"

"Thank you for coming to see me," Brighting interrupted. He made one last penciled mark in the loose-leaf binder, put it down, picked up another book from his desk, leaned back in his chair and began to read.

"I don't know how I got out of there without saying something really disrespectful," Rich told Laura. "He was arrogant and contemptuous. I can't remember when I've been so mad!"

Laura was lying with her arms around him, her head pillowed on his chest. "He was brutal to you," she agreed, "but there's more to it than that."

"He had his mind made up before I got there, that was obvious, and it's pretty clear he doesn't have much use for me. After today, I don't have much for him, either. That won't worry him a great deal, but I sure agree with you. There's more to it, and he's a strange character. I wasn't even sure he was completely serious, at least not until near the end. For a while I thought he might be testing me somehow, sort of working me over to see how I'd react. That's routine, Deacon Jones says."

"Is there any chance he might still be playing some strange game with you?"

"Not anymore. I practically got down on my knees to him, and I think that's what he wanted, probably. But he turned me down flat, and he was pretty final about it. What I can't figure out, in spite of what he said, is why he changed his mind. He had plenty of time to think about me. My name was on his desk a month before my first interview with him."

"You don't really believe he thinks you're too old?" Imperceptably, Laura's arms tightened. Her head rolled forward, enough for a fluttered eyelash to tickle.

"He knows darned well I'm not too old, and so do you." He drew her face to his, kissed her full on the mouth. Her lips parted, opened wide and drew him in, as she kissed him back.

Later, when he was nearly asleep, Rich heard her whisper, "I know what the problem is, darling. He's afraid of you." She tenderly kissed the back of his hand, held it to her cheek.

"Rich," Deacon Jones said, "thanks for letting me bust in on you and your family at home like this. Don't let on I said this—you too, Laura—but I think I know what happened between Brighting and my big boss. Admiral Scott called him on the telephone that afternoon to talk about increasing the total number of nukey poohs. Scott's been big for this for a long time. He wants all submariners to be nuclear-trained as soon as possible. Eventually the same for all surface engineers, too. In a few years, he thinks, all our submarines will be nuclear, and so will most of our surface combatants. Brighting blew up, because when that happens he won't have control over who gets anointed, and he knows damn good and well that's exactly what Scott had in mind." Jones, in charge of the assignment of submarine officers, was a phlegmatic, serious individual who fit the characteristics imputed by his nickname. As was well known, he had had his troubles administering his job and keeping Admiral Brighting happy too. More than once, in frustration, he had threatened to quit and go back to the farm of his birth. His unhappiness had to be great at this moment, Rich knew, for him to unburden himself to this extent.

"I should think Brighting would want the whole

Navy to go nuclear, and the sooner the better. That would be a big personal triumph for him!" Rich said.

"You don't know Brighting, obviously. He's made a career of being opposed by the Navy. It's true that early in the game he had some tough times. Some of them were damn well deserved, too. But he's been king of the roost for years now, and he does it mainly through controlling the selection of those who get nuked and those who don't. Nothing else in the Navy has ever worked this way. Assignments are supposed to be the job of BuPers. They are, for everything else. He gets away with it because you can't have a nuke—you can't even be aboard—unless you're a nukey pooh. Also, he's a holy terror with the civilian contractors working for him, but that's not my worry."

"What does this all have to do with me, Deac? Even if it's all true, it doesn't affect me. I'm not fighting any personnel battle. That's up to the people wearing stars. I'm just a four-striper."

"Oh, for Christ's sake, Rich. This is what I'm trying to show you. You're already a captain. You could be an admiral and have your own stars in a couple of years, if the selection board is as smart as it's supposed to be. You're the senior person to apply for nukedom. Scott has been supporting your application for all he's worth. We all think it would be one hell of a great thing for you and the Navy."

"So what, dammit!"

"So you must be dumber than I thought. Remind me to make a notation on your detail card. You've got a Congressional Medal of Honor. You're a big hotshot skipper of the war. When your name came up for Squadron Ten, Scott personally checked your record from one end to the other before he let us go ahead. So, you're the chief's number-one spear carrier in this little fracas. And what do you think Brighting did when all of a sudden Scott's call let him figure this out?"

"Crossed me off his list?"

"He drew a line through your name that very minute and had the list retyped. That's one of the things Scott was so furious about. You did Brighting a huge favor, by the way, when you tried to wheedle him into changing his mind. If you'd told me ahead of time, I'd have broken your arm to keep you from going over there."

"How's that?"

Jones' tone of friendly exasperation grew more pronounced. There was a strange expression on his normally composed face. "You only gave Mr. Nukey Bumps his latest chance to show the whole U.S. Navy who its real boss is, that's all! You think your visit was a secret? I heard about it half an hour after he threw you out. On the carpet in Scott's office, by the way. That's why I thought I'd come over here on the QT. By tomorrow the whole Navy will know about it, and Scott is about ready to have you shot at sunrise!"

"It seems to me your chief could have left well enough alone, too, Deac. Calling up Brighting to talk about increasing nuclear quotas right then was not very smart. That's what did me in, and it also wrecked this little scheme that I was a patsy for. If he shoots anybody, he ought to shoot himself, not me!"

"Scott knows all that now, and maybe he will shoot himself at that. Don't blame him too much for using you for a patsy, though. You just came along at the right time. And, he's not really mad at you. He's mad as hell at himself for blowing the deal the way he did, and at us for not warning him. I'm the guy whose going to be shot at sunrise, more than likely. The flit has sure hit the shan around here—er, excuse me, Laura—and anytime they want to ship me back to Iowa, I'm ready."

Deacon Jones' information had been comforting, as was the fact that he had sought Rich out privately instead of using the telephone. But, Richardson decided as he reviewed the conversation afterward, Jones had told him nothing that could be of any value in furthering his hopes for "nukedom," as Deacon had colloquially termed it.

Laura had the same reaction. "He's a good friend of yours, and he was just blowing off some frustration. He's not really afraid of Scott holding anything against him, either, and you've been hearing about the corn in Iowa ever since you've known him. But he did clear up one thing. None of the reasons Brighting gave for turning you down are the real ones. It was entirely Admiral Scott's call. That triggered something. I think Brighting doesn't want anyone as good as you, and as senior, around him. Didn't he say something about you possibly having to retire in a few years?"

Rich admitted that he had.

"How old is Brighting? When do admirals have to retire?"

"When they're sixty-two, though special ones can be kept on to sixty-four. He's got three or four more years, I guess," Rich said.

"Maybe it's his own approaching retirement that's bugging him. Is there anybody he might be building up to succeed him that you might be getting in the way of?"

"Nobody," Richardson said. "There were a few earlier in the program, in fact some friends of mine, but they've all left. Some of them weren't too happy about the deal they had."

"Well, then, my guess is that your being taken in might set up a new potential successor, and he doesn't want there to be any successor. He's already gotten rid of the others. Why set up another one?"

"But that's crazy, Laura. All military organizations

provide for a succession to command. Whether it's engineering or operations, there's got to be someone to take over if and when the boss falls out, for whatever reason. It's a principle, a basic one. He knows that."

"Of course he knows it, darling. But since when has Admiral Brighting gone by the rules of any system except his own? You've had a great record in the Navy. People look up to you. They know you always do a top job on everything, and are fair and considerate besides, which he isn't. He's simply afraid that once you're in his business, you'll be the heir apparent. He doesn't want there to be an heir apparent. I think that's perfectly obvious. He wants to be the one indispensable man. When he finally leaves, he wants people to say there _was nobody who could take his place."

"Nobody could ever be a rival, or a successor, to Brighting. That ought to be obvious to him and everybody else. He's been in that business for so many years already that nobody will ever fill his shoes. But maybe Scott's phone call got him to thinking I was part of a Bureau of Personnel plot of some kind."

"That's what I'm saying. Taking you off the list was a way of getting back at Scott, showing him up. He thinks you were a full-fledged member of the scheme. That's one reason he treated you the way he did. Another thing, Brighting must have looked up your record too, and found out you're not the sort of person he would be able to push around easily."

"You're just being a loyal wife now. How can he not be able to push me around if Admiral Scott, who is a much nicer guy, seems to be able to do it so easily? He thinks I'm a patsy for Scott—"

"Don't be silly. Brighting has been pushing juniors around all his life, and lately seniors as well. That's something he's an expert at. Part of his game is to block in advance all those he might have trouble dominating.

Another part of it is to hit at one through another."
Laura smiled enigmatically. "But he hasn't really run
into you yet, my darling."

"There's not much chance he will, either," Richardson said morosely.

"If only there were someone on Brighting's staff who
could get the word to him that you hadn't anything to
do with any scheme BuPers—isn't that what you call
Admiral Scott's office—might have cooked up."

"Scott is the Chief on Naval Personnel, and BuPers
is the shorthand word for his whole bureau of a couple
of thousand people. . . ."

Laura knew the superfluous explanation was really
her husband's device to let him think over what she had
just said. She ignored it. "You must know someone over
there among all those people. You must have been with
some of them, men or women, somewhere. A lot of
them are submariners. During the war, maybe?" The
strange expression was still around Laura's mouth.

A thought was growing in Richardson's mind. Joan
had been moving in Navy circles ever since the war. It
was totally possible, even likely, that Laura and Joan
had met somewhere. Although he had never discussed
her with Laura, more than once over the years of their
marriage he had wondered if Laura knew of his wartime
affair with Joan. It was even possible she had heard of
Joan's early relationship with Jim Bledsoe, Laura's first
husband—for so tragically brief a time. Recognizing the
possibility made it harden into probability. Laura and
Joan might certainly have known of each other, might
even have met somewhere. If so, they had doubtlessly
been fencing, each uncertain how much the other knew.

Joan had been very much in his life, at a critical time.
Laura *must* know, or have shrewdly guessed, already.
But, womanlike, she must have it from him. He had al-
ready denied Joan once, would not a second time. He

could not, however, tell what he knew, or surmised, about her and Jim. That was not his secret. Nor need he distress Laura with any details of his own relationship (that word, again!) with Joan. Yet he would have to tell her something. That was clear.

"I do know someone over there, though there's nothing she could do. I ran into her by accident when I was over there. It's a WAVE lieutenant, Joan Lastrada. I knew her when she was in the intelligence business in Pearl Harbor, during the war."

Again that unfathomable ghost of a smile. "Good. Now maybe we're getting somewhere." (Could that simple statement have had a double meaning?) "How can we get Joan to tell Brighting you had no part in Scott's scheme?"

"We can't, Laura. Nobody has any influence over Admiral Brighting. She's only a lieutenant in his shop. I'm not about to go to her with any such idea!"

"I know you far better than you think, husband mine, and I wouldn't love you as much if I thought you would. But she might anyway, if she finds out what's been going on. . . ."

Something was going on in Laura's mind, all right. "We're not going to get Joan or anybody else mixed up in this," he said again, a little too loudly. As he pronounced the authoritative-sounding words, however, he sensed an unusual undercurrent. It was almost something one could touch. There was a fleeting, cryptic look in Laura's eyes, a general abstractedness, an attitude of listening to another tune entirely. For the moment, he had lost her.

The conversation, and the unusual note on which it ended, a note he could never before remember emanating from his wife, remained uppermost in Richardson's mind for days. There were the final details of turning over his office to his relief, the modest good-bye luncheon given by his office mates, finally the Friday morning arrival of a moving van at his house. Even the hectic activity of tearing up the home of three years and seeing it packed into the van, a routine gone through so very many times and yet always traumatic, seemed overshadowed by a quietness of waiting. Something was going on somewhere, out of sight and out of hearing. His sixth sense, whatever that might be, was whirling madly. Laura was no help, nor had she been, although on this moving day, when he asked her point-blank, she admitted to the same intuition. Even Jobie felt it. "It doesn't feel like we're moving to where we're supposed to be moving to," he announced with thirteen-year-old directness.

Late in the afternoon, the moving van was about to pull away from the empty house when the telephone, now on the floor in an empty hall, sounded its insistent tocsin. "Just a moment for Admiral Brighting," said a female voice.

There were no communication-establishing formalities. Brighting spoke on the telephone with the same expressionless monotone Richardson had heard in his office. "Richardson, there's a vacancy in the next class at Arco. It starts tomorrow. Do you want it?"

"Yes, sir!" Richardson could say nothing more. The unexpected words rang through his brain. Whatever it was that had changed Brighting's mind, it had indubitably happened. He had won! Euphoria flooded his body.

"You will bring no uniforms with you, and no rank insignia. You're to wear civilian clothes the entire time you're on the site. There are officers and enlisted men there whom I have put into positions of responsibility, and you're to accept orders from them as though they were from me. At no time are you to use your rank for any purpose whatsoever. I will not have my program and organization disrupted by the requirement of toadying to you by anyone, for any reason. You will be there for one purpose, and one purpose only: to learn what they can teach you. Is that clear?"

"Yes, sir," said Richardson again.

"Be in Idaho Falls tomorrow morning. There is a flight you can catch tonight, and I'll have the plane met on arrival in Idaho."

Richardson's elation evaporated. Even under wartime pressure, he had known of no case of such peremptory treatment of officer or man. Abandoning Laura and Jobie without warning could not be vital to any training course. Surely he merited more considerate treatment than this! "Admiral," he began, "the moving van is about to pull away, and our car is packed. We're within an hour of starting to drive to New London. May I have the weekend to get my family safely up there? I can be in Idaho Monday morning—" But Laura was frantically shaking her head and putting both hands over her mouth, as the flat voice cut in.

"Richardson, if you want nuclear power training, you'll be landing at Idaho Falls airport tomorrow morning. An officer as resourceful as you should have no trouble having his orders modified and arranging his personal affairs." The telephone clicked dead.

Laura was hugging him and kissing him, nearly crying her relief and delight. "Of course I can handle the rest of the move myself," she said. "Friends will help me if I need them. Jobie and I will repack you a suitcase right now, while you telephone Deacon Jones and get the paperwork started. Then we'll drive you to the airport. Jobie and I won't have any trouble driving through Baltimore to the motel tonight, and we'll roll into New London tomorrow just as planned."

There was an interval of furious activity. The car had to be partially unloaded and the two largest suitcases

packed for a lengthy stay in Idaho. Deacon Jones had
to be tracked down by the BuPers duty officer and
asked to return to his desk to prepare the new orders.
Airline reservations had to be made and tickets purchased. Admiral Scott's administrative aide had to leave
a party and return to the bureau to sign the modification
in orders drawn up by Jones. Finally the Richardsons
set off in their loaded automobile, not for the road to
Baltimore and the motel planned for their overnight
stop, but for Washington National Airport.

It was not until hurried good-byes had been said and
Rich was strapped in his seat in the airplane that he was
able to unwind enough to admit the thoughts which had
been knocking at the door of his consciousness for the
last hour.

What was it that had caused Admiral Brighting to
change his mind? What had happened the last few days?
What could lie behind the extraordinary order to leave
all rank behind—could this be a reaction against whatever it was that had brought about the reveasal?

Foremost of all the confused ideas spinning through
Richardson's head was one simple question which, he
sensed, might well remain forever unanswered. Could
Joan have had a hand in this? He had at least managed
to ask Laura this during a moment's breathing space.
But Laura's answer was totally unsatisfactory. "What
makes you think anyone had anything to do with it?
maybe old man Brighting just had a change of heart."

All the same, it was the first time, so far as Richardson knew, that Brighting had ever changed his mind,
and he wondered.

3

~~~~~~

Admiral Brighting's empire, carved out of an unlikely combination of Navy, industry and science, was the most complete and efficient Richardson had ever seen. A car met him very early Saturday morning at the Idaho Falls airport and took him immediately to "the site," as his driver-escort referred to it. The site was nearly one hundred miles away, and the station wagon hurtled along at top speed, accelerator pressed to the floor, over a flat, hard-baked plain which stretched in all directions, as level as the sea, to a horizon any seaman must know was false. The road was obviously built for speed, though only two lanes wide. There was hardly a curve and only a single intersection, and during the entire trip, which took just minutes longer than an hour, they saw only two other cars, both of them headed in the opposite direction.

The road had but a single destination, and it came in sight while still some twenty miles distant, a square white dot poised on the horizon at the base of glowering, slate gray mountains. "That's the prototype, or rather, the building it's in," said Rich's companion. "It's six stories high, and most folks can't believe it's that far away."

At closer range, the dot grew into a graceless, windowless, sand-colored cube, dominating a number of lower buildings of industrial character. A tall chain-link fence surrounded the complex, and a cloud of steam rose from a broad, squat structure alongside the boxlike bulk of the prototype building.

"That's the cooling pond," said the driver, answering Richardson's question. "We've been critical for three months. There's not much heat going into it right now, though. At full power it steams up a lot more than this." The speaker, who had introduced himself as Lieutenant Commander John Rhodes, officer-in-charge of the prototype, was a short, dark young man. He had not been talkative during the ride from the airport, and was clearly ill at ease. "Rhodes with E. G. Richardson," he said to the guard at the gate, and instantly Rich felt he knew at least part of the reason for his discomfiture.

"Here's where you'll be staying, Mr. Richardson." The car had stopped in front of one of a small group of quonset huts of wartime vintage. "I'll help you with your luggage, and then I'll take you over to the prototype and start you off. It's warm in there, so don't bother with a jacket or a tie." The speech had been rehearsed. Admiral Brighting's instructions must have been very specific. Rhodes tried to look squarely at Rich, but his gaze faltered. He was, clearly, having difficulty overlooking the thousands of Navy precedence numbers by which Rich was his senior. Until recently, his indoctrination had been all the other way.

"Fine, John," said Richardson, searching for the way to start off his study period on the right note. "Look," he said, "I'm here for one thing only, to learn everything you fellows can teach me. So why don't we just knock off the rates for the time being—that will make

things a lot simpler. My friends call me 'Rich,' " he
continued. "Is yours 'Dusty,' like all the Rhodes in the
Navy?"

"Right—uh—Rich. Nobody calls me 'John' anymore. I guess I sort of like 'Dusty.' "

"Okay, and don't forget that 'Rich' business."
Rhodes' handshake contained considerably more
warmth than at the airport. "That goes for everybody
else here, too, Dusty, and now that's settled, is there
time for me to shave before coming over?"

"I really don't think so, Rich." This time Rhodes'
eyes were unflinching, and again Richardson had the
sense of a hidden message, some concealed urgency,
behind the words.

Once in the prototype building, however, Richardson
was surprised to discover only a duty section, a very
small percentage of the total force, present. Rhodes had
a small office suite opening directly into the cavernous
interior housing Mark One, as the prototype reactor for
the *Nautilus* was known, and there were desks for an
assistant and two secretaries, all three vacant. The main
room of the building, occupying almost all of its interior from concrete floor to metal roof, had the air
of being full of activity even though few persons were
present. Toolboxes, workbenches, storage lockers,
equipment bins and boxes were everywhere. Mark One
was festooned with steel ladders, catwalks, wire cables,
steam piping and waterlines, the ordered confusion of
the paraphernalia of many functions and many workers.

And, of course, Mark One itself, a horizontal cylindrical section of a huge submarine's pressure hull projecting through the side of a tremendous circular steel
tank the size of a big swimming pool and filled with light
green seawater, instantly captured Rich's attention. He
had already read of the pool and seen a photograph of
it, but the reality of the beige-colored pool walls, green

seawater and dark gray hull cylinder was breathtaking.
The purpose of the salt water, he knew, was to duplicate the radioactive shielding effect of the sea around
the simulated submarine's reactor compartment. The
submarine hull section was identical to the *Nautilus'*
reactor and engine compartments, except that, for
economy, only a single turbine and propeller shaft had
been installed. The water level in the pool surrounding
the reactor compartment was the same as it would be
with *Nautilus* fully surfaced, since that was the condition of least shielding.

"There she is, sir—Rich. You're to be here fourteen
weeks and learn all about it. Then we'll give you an
examination, and if you pass it you'll be a qualified reactor operator." Dusty Rhodes was looking with pro-
prietary satisfaction at the surrealistic monster. It was
humming softly. Richardson thought he could detect the
noise of ventilation blowers buried amid the other
sounds, but the rest meant nothing to him. Rhodes answered his unspoken question. "We've been keeping her
self-sustaining for the past couple of weeks. What you're
hearing are the electric turbo-generator sets, one of
them, that is, and the main coolant pumps in slow speed.
The main turbine isn't running."

Rich nodded his acknowledgment, though he was far
from clear as to the information imparted. But it was
then that Rhodes, his guard let down perhaps because
of his companion's ready acceptance of his role as a
student, forgot himself. "You'll have two days' head
start on the others," he said. "The class won't really
begin until the other students get here Monday morning." The moment he spoke the words Rhodes realized
they were beyond recall, and the consternation he felt
reproduced itself on his face. Richardson struggled to
keep his sudden anger from showing.

Dusty Rhodes' slip regarding the other students made

little difference, Rich assured him. He would have known soon anyway, and he was too grateful for Admiral Brighting's change of heart, whatever the cause, to quibble over his pettiness. Rich kept a second reason for silence to himself: whatever or whoever had changed Brighting's mind—Joan maybe—was owed something too. But the internal anger remained until it was replaced on Monday by the pleasure of welcoming Keith Leone and Buck Williams. It had been years since they had been in the same duty area as Rich. Despite occasional correspondence, the closeness brought on by wartime service together had begun to dim. Now, magically, it was all restored. All three felt it, and Rich was forced a few times to emphasize that, as students under Brighting's control, the old official relationship had no place on the site. Not until Richardson had spent several hours guiding his newly arrived friends in a thorough inspection of Mark One did he realize that there were no other new students. Keith, Buck and he were the entire class. It must have been organized and scheduled just for them.

"You're here to participate in the actual operation of a submarine nuclear reactor," Dusty Rhodes told them that first day. "The whole function of all this machinery is to turn that propeller shaft." The four were standing on the floor of the mammoth enclosure—"room" was hardly the proper word—in which Mark One rested. "As I guess you know, we call this Mark One because Mark Two is the *Nautilus* herself. They were building her in Groton at the very same time they were building Mark One here out in the desert. Only, Mark One was kept a few months ahead. Everything was tested and proved out before its duplicate was allowed to be installed in the ship. All changes that were found to be needed here were automatically done there, too."

It was obviously a speech that Dusty Rhodes made

to every new group of trainees, but there was also a note of pride in his voice. It had been one of the extraordinary engineering feats of the time. Mark One was a monument to the genius of its designers and constructors, particularly that most demanding and irascible construction engineer of them all, Admiral Brighting. And now he, Lieutenant Commander Dusty Rhodes, had been entrusted with its total and exclusive charge.

"I don't see any propeller, Dusty. How do you simulate the resistance of the water? Just turning a big thing sticking out of the end of a fake submarine hull isn't the same. To get horsepower you have to do work." Keith's question was one he knew Rhodes would have the answer for.

"We thought of that, all right," said Rhodes, picking up the cue. "When you get into your schedule, one of the things you'll be learning about is the water brake. It duplicates propeller resistance. Makes the turbine think there really is a propeller out there—even puts thrust on the thrust bearing. There is some trouble with it, though. Since we're not really driving a ship, what we really do—the work we do—is make heat. You'll be calculating the BTUs before you're through here. We make a lot of heat, and this damn things heats up too easy. We have to have a garden hose spraying water on the outside casing of the water brake whenever we stay at full speed for long."

The others nodded their comprehension. One of the fine points, obviously, was that since the water brake was not an integral part of any submarine, a permanent and "engineered" solution for its overheating was not a matter of urgency or even concern, so long as the jury rig, the garden hose, solved the problem. After a moment, Rhodes went on. "What we do here is operate Mark One just like a submarine underway for a long cruise, and the trainees stand all the watches, along with the instructors. There's usually several classes going on at the same time, in various stages of the program, so there's trainees on nearly all the billets. The instructors fill in the rest of them. The only exception we make to shipboard routine is that the watches are eight hours long instead of four. Everything else is exactly like on board ship. We go through all the evolutions of starting, running, maneuvering and stopping, cope with simulated or real casualties to the machinery, do everything the *Nautilus* could do.

"We'll put you fellows right into the system. The only thing different about you is that the normal trainee is here for a year, sometimes longer. So he drives in from Idaho Falls, or maybe Arco, wherever he lives, stands his eight-hours' watch every day and goes home. Some of them have to be on night watches, but we keep most of the activity for the eight to four shift and leave things pretty quiet during weekends. You three are going to have to cram the whole year's training program into the fourteen weeks you'll be out here. So my orders are to fix you up with a place to sleep right here on the site, and you're to spend all your time in Mark One, as if you actually were at sea." He paused. "That doesn't leave you much time free. You didn't have any other plans, did you?"

"Nope." Rich answered for the three of them.

"Good. You won't find this site the most comfortable place in the world to live. The quonset huts aren't bad, but we don't have a mess hall. You'll have to get your meals from the slot machines they have around, and things may get pretty stale for you, I'm afraid, but that's the way it has to be. I even got vetoed on the idea of having you out to my place in the Falls some weekend, just for a change of scenery and a decent meal."

"Thanks, Dusty," Rich said, again instinctively speaking for all, "but really, we'd rather just stay right here.

I've already had the benefit of one weekend all to myself wandering all over the machinery, and that's the most valuable time. When there's practically nobody here you don't have to worry about interfering with others." One of the things they would have to do, clearly, was to make their presence as easy for Rhodes as they could. His position under Brighting's difficult leadership, subject to that prickly personality, must have its problems. No doubt he had already spent time wondering whether his three new trainees would add to them.

"Well, that's good then," Dusty was saying. "I'll just give you our regular training schedule for our one-year course. Maybe you'll want to shift some things around because you'll only be here a quarter of the time, but you're supposed to complete the entire program, stand all the watches outlined and turn in all the drawings of systems, just like the regular trainees. At the end, after you've finished all the requirements, we'll give you a comprehensive test. If you pass it—you'll pass it, all right, if you do everything on the training schedule— you'll get a certificate of qualification as a nuclear operator. That's the ticket everybody's after. You can ask any questions you want, and we've got plenty of copies of the operating manual. The only rule is you've got to do all of the things, each one of you, yourself."

Inside the building housing the prototype there was neither night nor day; electric lights kept the windowless cavern bathed constantly at the same level of illumination. The passage of time became a factor of how often one's wristwatch had been around all the numbers, punctuated periodically by a weekend. Not that a weekend provided relaxation, except in a very particular way. Saturdays and Sundays, when there was only a duty section at the site, were the most valuable times of all because of greater freedom from interference. Gradually a routine emerged. Living on the site, never leaving it, the three trainees easily could be working in the prototype before the day's workers arrived from Arco or Idaho Falls, and they always remained there until well after the second shift departed at midnight. Meals were haphazard, only a hasty sandwich or can of soup obtained from one of the many food dispensers for whose slots a ready supply of quarters was required. There was no time for relaxation; nor were there any diversions, not even reading material—except for the engineering manuals and operating instructions for Mark One. The best times were the short nightly conversations the three shared in their quonset hut, but even these had a tendency to become curtailed after a succession of eighteen-hour days spent crawling through the cramped innards of the submarine hull, or poring over blueprints.

Afterward, Richardson had trouble distinguishing any chronology pertaining to his time at the site, or the many memories which remained. Everything was compressed into a set of kaleidoscopic impressions. With no day and no night, there were only work periods and short hours of exhausted sleep. Since there were no women present during the evening and morning watches, it was possible to confirm the suspicion, after a few days, that the ladies' rest room probably contained a cot. Here a person could lie down between particularly interesting evolutions of Mark One, or when he was totally beat, provided only that he was gone before any early arrivals for the day watch. And so, fortified by a few hours of fitful slumber (for fear of an unaccounted-for female), Keith, Buck and Rich often skipped their quonset hut bunks entirely.

Frequently, toward the end of their stay, they were not even aware of the change of shifts, except that new faces were at the various posts. Once, during a test for flux density under a new control rod program, Keith noted with mock dismay that they had not been outside the windowless prototype building for two and a half days, or even looked out an opened door, except to determine whether it was day or night (i.e., whether it would be safe to use the cot in the ladies' room).

Through it all there was the uncomfortable realization that Admiral Brighting must have ordered Dusty Rhodes to make a daily telephone report on their activities. More than once, Rich saw Rhodes' honest face become troubled when they unexpectedly observed him speaking into the equipment, and invariably there would follow an episode of exaggerated warmth and high spirits which confirmed the idea that Rhodes was trying to square his conscience.

Midway through the time at the site, Richardson got into a telephone conversation, and therefore an angry exchange, with Admiral Brighting. The subject was the proposed construction of a cafeteria near the Mark One building, so that on-site subsistence would not have to depend on lunches and dinners brought from home or, as in the case of Rich, Keith and Buck, who never left the site for any reason, from one of the many sandwich-and-soup dispensing machines which must have been a bonanza for their concessionaire. The cafeteria had already been authorized. Dusty Rhodes had circulated a request for opinions as to the most desirable location for it. The three trainees, whose ideas Dusty had solicited as representative of one of the groups affected, had all responded with suggestions. A building contractor from Idaho Falls had appeared, and Rich had been one of several who had talked with him.

The denouement was begun by Rhodes, who appeared suddenly, on his hands and knees with an unusually long face, alongside the spot where Rich was lying on his back, under the outside skin of the Mark One simulated submarine, tracing one of the nonconforming hydraulic supply lines. In the *Nautilus* the line had, of course, been inside the submarine. For Mark One it had apparently been deemed unimportant that actual submarine practice be followed to such a degree of detail, an execrable decision which Richardson had decided was surely never made by Brighting.

"You're wanted on the telephone in my office!" Rhodes shouted above the roar of the turbine in the hull overhead.

"Who is it? Tell him I can't talk to him now!" Richardson had already spent hours tracing this particular system and understanding its function. He was out of sorts because of its inaccessibility, angry at the design stupidity revealed, furious at the necessity to inch his way on his back along the dirty, oil-soaked, evidently never-before-visited concrete underlayment beneath the engineroom.

"It's the boss! He wants to talk to you right away! He's already on the line, and he's mad about something!"

"What's he upset about, Dusty?" Rich had begun worming his way out of the corner into which he had wedged himself. "Is he mad at you or me?"

"Don't know for sure, Rich. Both of us, probably." Long since, Dusty Rhodes had become accustomed to using Richardson's nickname. "It's something about the cafeteria, but I don't know what."

"Well, nothing like finding out," said Rich, brushing his coveralls and striding toward Rhodes' office. "Richardson here," he said on the phone.

"Please hold. The admiral wants to talk to you." A female voice. Joan! But the line was open, no one on the other end. Protocol required a junior to wait on the telephone for the senior, and well-indoctrinated aides accomplished this automatically. Joan had gone to have Admiral Brighting pick up the connection. Too, she was doubtless carrying out careful instructions, for she had not tarried even for a moment's personal greeting.

Brighting's familiar expressionless voice, as usual, did not bother with salutation or any other of the ordinary preliminaries. "I thought you understood you were to keep your nose out of everything but your studies. Can't you carry out a simple order, Richardson?"

"In what way have I not carried out all your orders, Admiral?" Rich knew enough about his difficult superior by this time to speak up directly. Failure to do so would be equated to acquiescence or confusion.

"Don't try to play innocent. I hear you want to install a cafeteria at the site for the convenience of you and your friends."

"Not so, Admiral!" Richardson was speaking rapidly. Admiral Brighting would not be listening long. "The cafeteria was approved last year. I was asked where I thought it should be located. So were a lot of others."

"I don't need any suggestions about the site from you, now or any other time! You'll have your opportunity to give orders when you're on board the *Proteus*. You have only one job out there, and I expect you to give it your full attention!" Richardson found himself holding a dead telephone.

Two days later, a downcast Dusty Rhodes handed Rich an official flimsy. It was a carbon copy of a one-sentence order canceling funding for construction of a cafeteria.

Vice Admiral Brighting's arrival, several weeks later, was apparently part of a pattern long set. That is, it was unexpected. Rhodes was late driving in from Idaho Falls, the first time in Rich's memory, and the reason became known when the passenger beside him was seen to be Brighting. Rhodes had received a telephone call at home the previous evening, directing him to be at the airport next morning.

All this, Rich learned later. His own awareness of the admiral's arrival came from a sudden appearance in the lower level of the engineroom during a cold start-up procedure being carried out by Keith. Rich's duties were to draw a steam bubble in the pressurizer in response to Keith's instructions: a critically important function that allowed him only a brief surprised nod of recognition as he concentrated on his task. When Richardson straightened up, satisfied that the bubble had formed and was in accord with the specifications, the admiral had gone on.

There was, however, an atmosphere of approval left behind. Rich was grateful, as he thought about it later, that he had been observed carrying out an important evolution instead of, as so often happened, merely monitoring some static condition. Not until that evening did it occur to him that Brighting might well have timed his trip so as to be able to make a personal evaluation of a significant part of the training schedule.

Neither Keith, Buck Williams nor Rich had paid much attention to the other two quonset huts in the tiny complex of wartime surplus buildings. One of these, it developed, had been designated for Brighting's exclusive use, and it was here that the three trainees found themselves summoned. To Rich's surprise, there was no one else present. Not even Dusty Rhodes was there. The day shift had long since ended, and, no doubt carrying out specific orders, Dusty had climbed into his station wagon and driven off at his usual time.

The routine developed over the weeks by Rich and his companions involved spending all the night shift, a portion of the morning watch after midnight, and full time over weekends actually in the engineroom or reactor compartment of the prototype. At these times the reduced manning level made possible thorough and even leisurely study of the fascinatingly intricate mechanisms. During the day watch there was a steady schedule of operational drills to participate in, with result that there was little time for investigation of the "why" as well as the "how" of what was going on. This had to be done at night. Early in the game it had become necessary to set up a rigorous schedule of work and sleep if they were ever to be finished. Admittedly ambitious and several times revised, this schedule was now so tight that interruption of even a single night's work would be directly reflected in a reduction of the six hours of sleep they had allotted themselves for "regular" nights (defined as not having critical evolutions forcing emergency use of the cot in the ladies' lavatory). Admiral Brighting's invitation was welcome but, like everything else about him, not without its cost.

Never had any of the three seen their chief so relaxed. The flat monotone speaking voice was unchanged, but now there was added a subtle difference, a puckish quality never before evident. "Now do you see what I'm trying to do?" he asked, looking mildly and yet shrewdly from one to the other.

"Yes, sir," said all three together. Keith and Buck glanced toward Rich, willing him to continue the response.

"I think we do, Admiral," Rich said. "None of us has ever been through a training period this tough, nor this satisfying."

"It's doing you a lot of good, is that what you're saying?"

"Yes, sir. We're learning the operational concepts of a totally new source of power, and a totally new engineering development. And we're learning them more thoroughly than we've ever learned anything."

"You admit all the training you've had before was wasted."

"Not wasted, Admiral, but clearly not on a par—"

"You know it's been wasted. You could have learned twice as much in half the time if you had been forced to put your mind to it. That's the trouble with our Navy. People are more interested in organization charts than they are in what really counts. That's why so many things break down. The designers and operators are all incompetent!"

Richardson felt they were being baited. There was a set to Admiral Brighting's mouth, the manner in which he pursed his lips, that conveyed as much. But he could not be certain, decided to try another tack. "There's one thing sure, and that is your nuclear power plants have been making records for reliability ever since the *Nautilus* went to sea. That ought to prove something."

"They've been making records like that ever since Mark One went critical in 1953!" The words were words of pride, but the puckish look remained.

"Of course, but it's when the *Nautilus* began to operate that everyone recognized it," Rich began. As before, Brighting interrupted.

"That's exactly the point, Richardson! You're like all the naval officers. You're not interested in real performance. What good is a four-hour full-power run? A twenty-four- or forty-eight-hour run would mean something, but what naval battle is going to be decided in four hours these days? A four-hour run doesn't mean a thing!"

Richardson was about to expostulate that he had made no reference to the regular engineering performance standard, a four-hour run at full power, that in fact he had been about to point to the *Nautilus* as having far exceeded this on her first day at sea, but Brighting swept on without pausing. "Before *Nautilus* was even launched, her prototype, right here, made a full-power run the equivalent of crossing the Atlantic Ocean. No new power plant has ever been put to this sort of a test before. If some of them had, perhaps we'd have had fewer problems with some of our ships!"

The simulated transatlantic trip was, of course, well known throughout the nuclear power program. Every four hours the theoretically attained position had been marked on a chart. Mark One had been relentlessly kept at full power, her single turbine screaming its high whine, her reduction gears roaring, clouds of steam rising from the cooling pond, the water brake steadily rising in temperature so that it had to be bathed continuously in a spray of cold water to prevent failure of the simulated propeller, the enthusiasm of the prototype crew building to an emotional crescendo as the regularly plotted line on their chart approached the coast of Ireland. Some of the more conservative engineers, worried about breakdown of turbine, water brake, main bearings or the steam generators themselves, had counseled shutdown once the ability of the plant to attain its designated operating characteristics had been demonstrated. It was Brighting, monitoring the test from his Washington office, who had refused all such requests, assumed all responsibility, insisted the run be carried through to completion.

Predictably, Brighting's detractors had pointed out that a breakdown at this early stage would have delayed the entire program, that such a severe test of new machinery was not good engineering practice under any circumstances. Some whispered their belief the test run was more for the personal aggrandizement of Brighting than for any other reason. No one mentioned the fact that the nuclear reactor, the heart of the entire nuclear power effort and the only really new, innovative item in all of Mark One, had flawlessly provided the energy source for the entire "trip" without difficulty of any kind. It had been fear for the other machinery, all of it standard off-the-shelf items, even the main turbine and the water brake, which had caused the concern of their manufacturers' representatives.

Much of this Richardson had heard before, although without emphasis on the extraordinary performance of the nuclear plant. The familiar story as told by Brighting now sounded a different note. For the first time, Richardson was able to savor fully the vitally important view Brighting and his assistants took of their tests, their refusal to accept a halfhearted trial as adequate witness of performance to be expected or, realistically, to be demanded during the exigencies of war. Had submarine torpedoes been properly tested, the course of the war in the Pacific would have been vastly different, especially in the early stages. This was something no submariner who had lived through it could ever forget, or forgive. More recently, proving that not all designers in the Navy had learned the lesson, the new fleet submarines built during the early 1950s had been a hushed-up scandal; their diesels had been undependable, their torpedo control input erratic, their freshwater distilling apparatus farcically ineffective, their torpedo tubes a maintenance nightmare. The skipper of the first one to go to sea, an experienced wartime submariner, had furiously radioed in during her shakedown cruise that his new boat was a travesty not fit for service—with the shattering result that he was severely dressed down, nearly relieved of command, for excessive forthrightness. Many submariners, Richardson among them, had been incensed at the refusal of the Bureau of Ships to accept the obvious fact that the new class of submarines was a failure, and to move heaven and earth—or at least bestir itself—to fix them immediately.

But here, in the person of Admiral Brighting, was proof that with nuclear power old mistakes would not be repeated. And the three submarine officers learned also of another aspect of Brighting's approach to engineering: like the commander of a ship at sea, he accepted full and complete responsibility for everything connected with his charge.

Admiral Brighting spoke for some time. Richardson was entirely unaware of the expressionless monotone he usually noticed, and certainly one would never have guessed that this articulate, actually eloquent person was renowned for his taciturnity. The strange, naïve expression, the one he had earlier termed "puckish," was still there. Only now Richardson thought of it as a look of exaltation, something he might have expected of a passionately idealistic young man. A flash of insight tugged at his senses, and suddenly Brighting was talking about the central question of all. "Have you figured out what you're here for?" he asked.

"Sure," said Buck. "We're here to learn how to handle nuclear power."

"That's only part of it."

Rich began, "Nuclear power in the years ahead—"

Brighting interrupted impatiently. "You're like all the rest. You see everything as just small improvements on the stuff you're used to. What do you think the Navy will be like in the years ahead?" He answered his own question. "This is the program for a totally new navy. We're starting over. Suppose we had the *Nautilus* in World War Two—what do you think you could have done with her?"

"With the *Nautilus* and good torpedoes," began Rich, "one submarine could have taken on the whole Japanese

Navy. We'd not have had to worry about recharging our batteries, or evading at slow speed. We could have outrun almost any antisubmarine ship—" He would have gone on, but Brighting again broke in.

"You're a piker, Richardson! Who cares about World War Two torpedoes? Did you ever think of a submarine that could stay submerged weeks or months? Or one that could blockade an entire nation by itself? How long could you stay submerged in the *Eel?* Twenty-four hours?"

The shift from weaponry to endurance to a global concept and then back to endurance had come rapidly. "Seventy-two, with everyone except a minimum watch turned in to conserve oxygen," said Rich, "except I don't think the battery could make it that long."

"How long on the battery? And how far could you go?"

"We figured forty-eight hours at minimum speed, maybe a little more, if you started with a full charge and had all nonessential services secured. About a hundred miles."

"What would you have done if you could stay down six months and go twice around the world without coming up? What if your submarine had been the size of a cruiser, with a load of missiles that could hit any target in the world from any position in the sea? What if your submarine could outrun any surface ship ever built?"

"We could have ended the war a lot quicker," said Keith.

"We're not talking about the last war!" A note of triumph, his own inconsistency brushed aside, sprang into Brighting's voice. "Can't you get that through your head? That's the trouble with all you people. You can't see beyond your previous experience. You have no imagination. We're not even talking about the next war, either, or the one after that. We're talking about the prevention of all war by total control of the sea! All of it, from above the surface down to the very bottom! We're through with the Mahan concept of big fleets maneuvering around trying to outguess each other!"

The three submariners sat silently. Rich could feel the mind-expanding impact of Brighting's vision. From the rapt, fascinated expressions on their faces, it was clear that Buck and Keith did too.

"We're only in the early phases of the history of man," Brighting went on, "and the key to development has always been the availability of power. But all power has always required consumption of oxygen, combustion somewhere in the process. With the exception of hydroelectric power, that is. The key to control of the sea in a manner similar to the way we control the land is to have adequate power. Mobile power, for the time being. The sea is the last and most limitless resource of man. It's three-dimensional, and so is the air above it. For all these years, the surface of the sea has been the prize we were after, because it provided cheap transport, and livelihood. That's what navies have been built for since year one. But not forever. The changes are coming fast. First mobile power, for new and wonderful ships. Then stationary power, with fantastic capability, on the land or in the sea, wherever power is needed."

"You're talking about an entirely new and different kind of a navy, aren't you, Admiral?" said Richardson.

"Not just a new navy, Richardson! A whole new type of civilization! How long do you expect the world's stocks of fossil fuels—oil, gas and coal—to last?"

"In 1945 I was reading that oil would last only fifty years or so, but we seem to be finding more oil all the time. . . ."

"That's true. But have you any idea of how much

energy we are using, in just one year, just in the United States?"

"A lot. . . ."

"A hell of a lot, Richardson. That's something people aren't thinking of these days, but one of these days they're going to have to. Since 1957 the United States has expended more total energy than the whole world used up to then, ever since the beginning of time! What do you think of that!"

There was no answer expected. Rich, Keith and Buck merely stared at Brighting.

"Besides, do you know what's happening to world population? Man's been around for thousands of generations, but five percent—that's a twentieth—of all the people who ever lived are living this minute! Now do you see what I'm trying to do?" The puckish look was gone. In its place were the pinched nostrils, the rigid posture, the glaring eyes of the zealot. Only the flat voice was the same. The whole bearing of the man had changed, almost instantaneously, without visible movement of any sort.

Later, Rich would wonder if Brighting had been acting a part. At the time, however, he could only notice the metamorphosis with anstonishment, as Brighting continued. "The Navy is just the beginning. War, as you and I have known it, is over. Out the window. What will come next is a struggle to survive on earth. In a hundred years all the oil will be gone. That's only three generations away. In ten generations all the rest of the fossil fuels will be gone." The manner in which Brighting pronounced the words "fossil fuels" gave no doubt of the contempt in which he held the ordinary energy sources.

"What about tides, solar energy and the internal heat of the earth?" asked Buck.

The disdain in Brighting's face was palpable. "Sure!" he said. "We've only been talking about all those great things for years. Where are they?" Again it was only a rhetorical question. He gave no time for an answer. "Nuclear power is here now. But it has its own engineering problems, like anything else. So people are afraid of it. They lack confidence in their own ability to control it. And they're right. Most people are nice. Nice and friendly, like big puppy dogs. And they'll never do things right if it's easier to do them wrong. Nobody does things right unless he doesn't dare do them wrong. He's got to know he'll be called to account."

The pinched nostrils tightened another notch. No one spoke. "You fellows are supposed to be the best submariners in the Navy. That's rot! Maybe you can handle diesel submarines, but they're nothing. You're worthless if you can't discipline yourself to handle a nuclear power plant. That's what you're here for. This program is a lot bigger than just submarines or the Navy. Now do you see why I have to do things the way I do?"

There was a moment during which no one spoke. There was nothing to say. Again Brighting seized the initiative. "Good night," he said, as he rose to his feet.

Buck Williams put the cap on the evening, as the three officers thoughtfully walked back to the prototype and their interrupted study program. Buck was always the irreverent one, the one given to the apropos comment which tore through obfuscation to expose gobbledygook, the non sequitur or the stupid—or, alternatively, to put things into balanced context. This time, after a minute during which the only sound was their own footsteps on the graveled walk, he did it with a single statement that encompassed what all three were thinking. "No wonder the Navy hates him," he said, "and still lets him get away with it all. He's a bully and a genius at the same time. Tonight we saw his genius side. We're damned lucky to have him in our Navy, and we three are lucky to be working for him."

The others said nothing. The crunch of their footsteps was loud in the chill desert night.

4

~~~~~~

"Captain! Wake up, Captain!" The voice using the unaccustomed salutation came from far away, from far back in the past. He was sleeping on the stool in *Eel*'s conning tower. The hand shaking him was Keith's. The voice too. Richardson must have fallen more soundly asleep than he had expected. He rolled upright on the cot in the ladies' room. "How long have I been out?" he asked, groggily.

"Not long. Probably only fifteen minutes. Buck and I were going to let you caulk off another half hour at least, but we think there's an emergency on its way."

"That's right, sir! It's a big one, I'm afraid, and you're the only one here . . ." Buck was speaking from the other side of the cot.

Richardson's mind subconsciously recorded the fact that both former subordinates were putting him into the role of years ago. Simultaneously his own habit asserted itself, framed the words for him as his quickening pulses for a precious second drove the blood into his brain. "Yes, what is it?"

"Reactor casualty, I think! There's steam in the lower

level, and all the dosimeter readings are climbing fast. Buck's and mine have already gone way up the scale." Keith pointed his pocket dosimeter, a penlike instrument with a frosted glass lens at each end, to the overhead light, squinted through it. "It says I got more than three-quarters of my allowed weekly dose of roentgens during the last half hour!" Hurriedly, he clipped it back into his shirt pocket as he followed Richardson and Williams to the door and down a steel stairway to the main floor.

"Why couldn't this have waited a few more days," Buck was saying. "Two weeks ago Brighting was here and everything was fine. Next week we're supposed to take our end-of-course exams, and then we're through, finished, on our way back to New London. After that the whole place can go to hell, for all we care!"

"Sure," said Richardson, "except you're not fooling anybody. You know you're not going to let anything happen to our reactor if there's anything you can do to stop it."

"That's why we were in such a hurry to call you, Skipper," said Keith, catching up. "You're senior man on board. If something is really out of line, it will be up to you to take charge."

"Not so fast." Richardson paused at the watertight door leading to the engineroom. "Old Brighting was pretty clear that when we came here we left our Navy rank somewhere in the Idaho desert. The regular engineering watch officer is in charge until Dusty Rhodes or somebody else shows up. We're under his orders. There can't be two bosses here." He jackknifed through the steel doorway.

There was a crowd at the other end of the engine-room, around the watertight door leading to the reactor compartment. To Richardson's surprise, among them were the three members of the reactor duty section and the engineering watch officer, a young-faced red-haired civilian employee named Baker. Baker was staring through the glass peephole in the steel door as Rich pushed his way through to him.

"What's happened, Red? Did you abandon the reactor compartment?"

"Had to, Rich! All our dosimeters were way up! Couldn't take a chance on staying!"

"Any idea what happened?"

"There's steam in the lower level. I saw it through the periscope myself. Something has given way down there, is my guess!"

"Did you scram?" Richardson hissed the question to Baker alone. He already knew the answer, for the turbo-generator sets which provided power for the simulated submarine were still running. Unless the reactor had been shut down only during the past few seconds, less than a minute, they would no longer be getting steam.

"Not yet. Maybe I'd better. It just happened less than five minutes ago. Somebody noticed his dosimeter had climbed, and then we all checked our own and saw the same thing, and about the same time somebody looked in the lower level through the periscope and saw steam. But everything's still running okay."

"But Red, we can't leave the reactor untended."

"I know," said Baker uncertainly. "I guess we should scram, but we were hoping to finish this test run tonight. . . ." His voice dropped. He had been recently put in charge of a watch section and was known to be a good technician. Clearly, however, his training had not yet equipped him to make a decision of this magnitude.

Richardson dropped his voice to a low note meant for Baker only. "Have you called Dusty?"

"Uh, no. I guess I should. . . ."

"Better do that right away. How long did it take your dosimeters to rise, and how high did they go?"

"Maybe five minutes, and they're all pretty near the top. So it was a pretty healthy dose we all got."

"If they didn't hit the peg you didn't get much radiation, Red. Have somebody collect the film badges and get them checked. That will give you a better idea of it. Tell someone else to call Rhodes. He's got the responsibility for the plant and will have to take charge of this. It will take him more than an hour to get here, though, and we've got to decide what can be done before then." Richardson still spoke in a carrying whisper. Unconsciously he had been giving orders, and equally unconsciously, Baker moved with alacrity to carry out the only sensible program that presented itself.

Richardson was staring through the glass eyeport in the door. It was not possible to look into the lower level of the reactor compartment where the steam leak existed, for that could be seen only through the two "periscopes" which penetrated the thick lead-and-plastic-shielded deck between upper and lower reactor spaces. There was a hatch in the deck, but no one could go into the lower level until the reactor had been shut down, and then only after residual radiation had died away. Everything that could be seen in the upper level was as it should be. Clearly, the only way anything could be discovered was to reenter the upper level and look through the two periscopes.

He had felt the quickened pulse before. There were chances to be taken, a risk for what might be gained, the problem of attaining the objective with danger to the fewest number of people. Or, what was the same thing in a different sense, how to use the maximum number of people with the minimum exposure to each individual. And suddenly, there it was. An idea. But first, something more had to be known about the problem.

"Baker," he said. He nearly barked the name, realized too late he had reverted to type and used the man's surname. Baker had been seeing to the film badges which, upon development in the lab, would accurately measure the degree of radiation received by each person.

"Yessir!"

"Red, I wasn't aboard when the trouble started, and my dosimeter is still on zero. I'm going into the reactor compartment to take a good look through the periscopes, and I'll watch my dosimeter at the same time. I'll come back out here before it hits the peg at the top. We've got to find out where the steam is coming from."

"It's got to be in the primary loop, Rich. The radiation level went up at the same time as the leak was discovered. In fact, that's how we found it."

"Where in the primary loop? That's the question. If we can find out which line is leaking, perhaps we might be able to do something about it."

"Maybe we should scram out anyway. I hate to think of anyone going in there. . . ."

"You told me you were in the upper level for five minutes yourself, just now, and your dosimeter didn't even peg. You didn't get as strong a dose as from an ordinary radium-dial wristwatch!"

Radium-dial watches had been banned from Mark One because their presence set off all the delicately tuned warning devices. Richardson could tell from the look on Baker's face that he had got in a telling point. "Okay, sir, maybe we'll have something from the film lab by the time you come back out."

"Good, Red. Ask them to send down a new film badge for me, too, and we'll send up the one I've got on to see how badly it got fogged." Richardson spun the dogging handwheel, pushed open the submarine-style door, stepped inside. Directly in front of him, dominating the compartment, was the tall, cylindrical

stainless-steel shell, on top of the reactor, which protected the control rod drive mechanisms and the tops of
the control rod housings. On either side of the reactor
compartment two large, heavily insulated domes projected through the floor and nearly touched the curved
overhead. These were the steam generators, corresponding to boilers in a conventionally powered ship. From
the tops of the two domes a pair of large insulated pipes
passed through huge steam stop valves and then joined
together in a single larger pipe which led aft to the
engineroom. A profusion of smaller equipment, mostly
control and monitoring panels, filled the remainder of
the space except for the narrow walkway in the middle
and around the reactor top.

Richardson's first move was to inspect his dosimeter,
which he held up, telescope-fashion, to the nearest light.
The index was moving, but not perceptibly. That was
good. The radiation level was at least well within human
tolerance. Clipping the device back into his shirt pocket,
he grasped one of the periscopes and looked down into
it. Unlike a submarine attack periscope, which went up,
had two magnifications and could measure range, this
one went down through the deck and had no magnification at all. It combined all its far simpler controls in a
single handle by which it could be swung around to permit inspection of about half the space beneath the deck,
where the reactor itself, and all its principal components,
were located. He had expected to find the place foggy
with steam, but there was only a slight mist issuing from
somewhere on the other side of the tremendous steel
pressure vessel housing the reactor proper.

He moved to the other periscope, looked a long
searching moment through it. The point of issuance of
the steam, a tiny stream of vapor, could not be directly
seen. There must be the tiniest of cracks in one of the
auxiliary pipes, not a main one. The wisp of steam was

issuing from its other side. It was what he had hoped to find. A leak in the primary loop itself could not be repaired without completely shutting down and draining it. Since it was a small subsidiary line, there might be some other way.

He seized his dosimeter, held it in his hand while still looking through the periscope, straightened up quickly to peer through it: good! It had mounted only about a quarter of the way up its scale.

Back to the periscope, twisting it slightly, focusing as carefully as he could set the eyepiece, following the faulty line as far as the instrument would let him see. At one point he crossed over again to the other periscope, identified the line he was inspecting, following it further. There was indeed a way!

"Red," said Rich, once again back in the engineroom, "it's a very small leak, a pinhole, and we can fix it."

"How? How are we going to fix it without shutting down?"

"We'll have to shut down, but not for long, and we can make a hot start. So we'll not lose the test. The leak is in the demineralizer bypass. We'll put a freeze on both sides of the leak, cut out the faulty piece of pipe, and cap both parts of the line. It'll be out of commission, but we don't need that by-pass line much anyway. How many stainless-steel welders are on tonight with you?"

"Three, I think. Maybe now there's a couple more qualified."

"Okay, here's what we do. As soon as the radiation in the lower level gets down to ambient we can go in there. Once the reactor is shut down we'll have an hour or so to wait, and we'll need that to get organized. By the time Dusty gets here we'll be all ready to go, and if he okays it we'll have her back on the line in a couple of hours. We can keep the pressurizer hot and keep the bubble in it. It'll be hot working alongside it, but nobody will be in there more than about three minutes, and nobody will receive more than the allowable week's radiation. The main thing to be really careful of is to stay out of the path of the leak. That's hot in more ways than only one!"

Rich spoke swiftly and, as before, in a low tone. He could see Baker's discouragement vanishing, his confidence and enthusiasm mounting. A period of hyperactivity came over the crew of Mark One. The entire group was assembled for a briefing on the procedure to be followed, and each individual's part in it was assigned. A plan of the compartment, showing the line to be cut, was procured and posted. Each of the men designated to enter the lower level studied not only his own operation but those of the persons preceding and following him as well. Liquid nitrogen bottles were made ready. Molds were prepared to hold the frigid liquid around the faulty pipe at the selected points. Tools, clean coveralls, shoe covers, gloves and masks were taken from storerooms and laid out. Supplies of salt tablets were procured, to be swallowed in advance by those designated to enter the lower reactor compartment.

When Rhodes arrived at the site, after a high-speed dash over the lonely highway from Idaho Falls, he required only a briefing prior to putting through the obligatory telephone call to Admiral Brighting in Washington.

Richardson, following a brief but detailed conversation with an anxious Dusty Rhodes, was first in the lower level, his job to mark the point of the leak he had spotted and the locations of the two freeze points. Maximum ventilation had been on for some time, exhausting the hot, confined air of the lower reactor compartment.

Cool air, streaming through the hatch in the insulated deck separating the two levels, flapped the legs of his heavy white canvas coveralls as he descended the hot steel ladder, but, once inside, the heat of the steel surrounding him penetrated swiftly through his baggy coveralls and his shoes, gloves, cloth helmet—actually a hood covering his entire head—and his face mask. He had been prepared for it, knew what to expect, carefully breathed through his nose only and through the gauze with which his mask had been stuffed. Nevertheless, he nearly lost consciousness when the wild, searing heat first went down into his lungs.

The piercing, high-pitched shriek of the main pumps, no longer shielded by the heavy deck through which he had descended, tore at his eardrums. He could feel the delicate membranes of his ears reacting, toughening, screeching their protests into his senses, bruising themselves, swiftly dulling their ability to respond. Too late to do anything about this now. It should have been foreseen. The hood and mask were not enough. He must specify earplugs for all those who followed him.

The hot air shriveled the tender mucous linings of his nose and throat with every breath as he drew it in. Instantaneously he could feel the droplets popping out of his sweat glands, collecting, trickling down under his armpits, down his chest and backbone until absorbed by his clothing. Quickly his undershirt, and the civilian sport shirt, were sodden, as were his trousers along the front of his thighs and at the top of his buttocks. His feet felt tight in his suddenly moist shoes. He was grateful for the warm sweat. It would help keep his body temperature down.

There was no time to lose. His part was vital. So were all the other parts, so carefully rehearsed, to follow. He must do precisely what had been scheduled; exactly that, no more, and certainly no less. The pain

in his ears was less. Thank heaven for that! To reach
the faulty demineralizer bypass he must crawl over a
portion of the main coolant piping. An insulating mat
had been dropped down the hatch before him. He
gripped it, struggled upright, draped it over the nearly
incandescently hot, foot-diameter pipe. Sliding over it,
he crouched on hands and knees to crawl under a heavy
cable channel, squeezed upright between the reactor
pressure vessel and a smaller duplicate, the pressurizer.
The heat from both, reflecting from the curved steel
plates forming the bottom of the cylindrical hull, radi-
ated through the thin asbestos lining of the work clothing protecting him. Down on hands and knees one more
time to crawl under the thin bypass line itself (very
carefully, so as to avoid passing before the crack with
its still-issuing steam), he finally was able to sit upright
facing the defective pipe, on the hot curved bottom of
the reactor compartment. (This, at least, was at a more
normal temperature, thanks to the tank of salt water
on the other side of the simulated submarine hull.)
Working rapidly, he removed two sections of colored
tape from a coverall pocket and fumblingly, but very
carefully, wrapped them around the pipe, two feet apart.
This would mark one of the freeze points. He crawled
under the bypass line once more, around to the other
side of the pressurizer, again positioned himself before
the pipe, this time on the other side of the leak, marked
the other freeze point with two more pieces of tape.

By this time, Richardson was totally bathed in perspiration, his body as wet as if he had jumped, fully
clothed, into the cooling pond. He had heard old Navy
tales of men crawling into the firebox of a steaming
coal-fired boiler to make emergency repairs. What he
and the others were undergoing—or would soon be—
was at least as severe a physical test, he thought, as he
tortuously retraced his path through the packed com-

partment. It was only Admiral Brighting's insistence that all components be accessible which had made it possible to reach the bypass pipe. Otherwise, left to the standard designers and contractors, it would not have been. But, even so, there could have been more than the barest minimum of space. . . .

The upper reactor compartment was a cool heaven, and so was the engineroom, where Rich ripped off his mask and hood and then, more slowly, removed his wet coveralls. A lab technician seized his dosimeter and film badge, hurried them away for immediate inspection. Red Baker, several turns away from his own descent into the lower compartment, handed him a glass of cold water and another salt tablet. "Get earplugs!" Rich gasped to Dusty and to the man next scheduled to go below. Then, in greater detail, he began to describe to both what he had seen and done. The man, who by pre-arrangement had been watching through the periscopes, appeared to understand. But Richardson, who could feel himself talking, could hear nothing as he carefully mouthed the words.

Dusty Rhodes was swearing, the dead telephone handset still gripped tightly in his hand. "Damn him!" he spit out. "He's the most inhuman human being I know! Here we've made an emergency repair to keep his re-actor running, with his approval, mind you, and you know what old man Brighting just said to me?" He slammed the phone into its cradle. "He said we should have properly inspected that line before starting up this series of tests. Three weeks ago! How in the hell am I supposed to have done that? Maybe he's a superman, but we're not! We're just ordinary naval officers trying to do a job right. He's responsible for faulty construc-tion, not me!" Rhodes' voice trailed off. His trembling fist slowly unclenched.

Richardson grinned. "Did you tell him my ears are a lot better now, thank you?" he said. "The old man must have been a little tensed up himself."

Rhodes slowly smiled back. "Maybe you're right, Rich. Anyway, it does me good to yell back at him sometimes. After he hangs up the phone, that is. But seriously, what more does he expect of us? We went over the whole plant four months ago, just before you came. Every weld was radiographed. So was every pipe more than an inch in diameter. Those are his standing instructions, and we did it very carefully. But that steam leak wasn't at a weld, and the pipe is less than an inch in diameter. It was a faulty piece of half-inch pipe, and it finally just gave out. Could have happened anytime!"

"I know," nodded Richardson, "and you know how he's always harped on manufacturer's quality control. That crummy piece of pipe just plain rotted out. It should never have got through the vendor's inspection. It might even be made of the wrong material. You're going to send the piece we cut out back to Washington, aren't you?"

"It's gone already. He just now told me to send it, and I had the pleasure of telling him it's already on the truck and gone. A little piece of pipe in a big lead box. That was before he began to chew me out." Rhodes' grin now matched Richardson's. "I see what you mean. The old man was just warming up, I guess. I'd hate to be president of that pipe company, about now!"

Privately, Richardson had been mentally preparing himself for the telephone call from Brighting, who, reputedly, had spies everywhere in his organization, and throughout the Navy as well. Inevitably, the wizened admiral would discover Richardson's role in the emergency, and no matter how Rich's participation was described, it would be interpreted as a violation of his instructions. There would be one of those sudden summons to the telephone, the even-toned voice demanding an explanation to which its owner would not listen, the receiver crashing down, some sort of retribution exacted. Rich found himself thinking through the short speech he would be permitted. The admiral might not listen, but he could not avoid hearing. Perhaps a telling point could be forced into his consciousness.

But nothing happened for three days. Daily routine went back to normal. The emergency was relegated to its place in the machinery history book, reflected only in the procedure changes necessitated by the cut in the demineralizer bypass line. When the call came, Rich could feel his nervous system gearing up for the quick conflict—and was totally unprepared for the direction Brighting took.

"Richardson"—Rich thought he detected menace in the expressionless voice, afterward could never be sure —"do you know what the NEPA project is?"

"Why, yes, it stands for Nuclear Energy for Propulsion of Aircraft . . ."

"Is that all you know? I thought you had an inquiring mind." This, at least, was according to form. Rich had had ample training in how to handle it.

"I've not had any time to think of anything except Mark One since I came here."

"You're a Captain in the Navy. You're supposed to have initiative. Do I have to hold your coat for you, too, besides telling you how to do your duty?"

"No, sir." Anger bubbling to the surface.

"Rhodes will set it up for you. You and your friends go over to see it. Maybe you'll learn something." The telephone went dead.

"Why did he send us there?" asked Buck. The question had been hanging during the whole of the return trip.

The drive to the Air Force site had been a welcome interlude, even though the hours involved would cost further curtailment of sleep from their schedules. It was the first time outside the compound for any of them since their arrival. "What did he send us for?" Buck repeated. "There's nothing those guys could show us. They don't have a reactor, or even a design for one that's light enough for an airplane. They'll never get their thing going. It's a waste of time!"

"Maybe that's what we were supposed to find out," said Keith.

"They've done a lot of theoretical study and made a mockup of a lightweight reactor," said Rich, thoughtfully, "and even that's too heavy for an airplane. They can't compare with Mark One, which is like a part of a whole operating submarine. I think you're right, Keith. He wanted us to see the difference."

"And see what a great person he is!" exclaimed Buck.

"It's more than that," began Richardson. "Maybe he was trying to do something for us. . . ." But then he could not find ready words to articulate the unformed thought, left it uncompleted as they rode across the desert toward the looming windowless cube which housed Mark One.

5

~~~~~~

"Well, Rich," said Keith, "we're nearly at the end of our stint here. Tomorrow is Monday, and we're as ready as we'll ever be for that exam. I'll be glad to get back home, even if I do have to start calling you 'Commodore.' I think Peggy is a little tired of doing everything herself, back in Groton."

"Cindy too," Buck said. "She's trying to keep a stiff upper lip, though. I've been writing her that it's the same as when I'm at sea, except that then she'll not get this many postcards. All the same, this is the longest cruise I've been on since we've been married, and it'll be good to get back."

The three submariners were wearily trudging the hundred yards to their quonset hut sleeping quarters, oblivious to the sparkling early morning darkness, the canopy of brilliant, unblinking stars over the entire sky and the nearly full moon gleaming high in the west.

"A lot of ships have been underway a lot longer than this," began Rich, "but I feel the same. First, though, I hope all three of us hit that exam really hard. We need to show Brighting. . . ." His companions knew well what Richardson felt it was necessary to show Admiral Brighting. It had never been far from any of their thoughts. In this instance, however, they were to receive no new iteration of it.

There were hurrying footsteps behind them, a recently arrived trainee. "Rich!" he called, slightly out of breath. "Rich! —Captain! There's a telephone call in Dusty's office for the senior man on the site. That's you, sir! He said it's urgent! It's some kind of emergency in Arco!"

The voice in Dusty Rhodes' desk telephone spoke hurriedly, its deep masculine timbre obviously unaccustomed to pleading. "Captain Richardson? I'm Doctor Danforth at Arco Municipal Hospital," it said. "We've had a power failure. There's an operation going on. It's an emergency operation, and the patient will die if we can't get some help!"

"I'm not in charge here, Doctor. I'm only a student," said Rich. He felt he should go on, not leave the doctor with only this negative information, but his thought was interrupted.

"I know you're not, but you're a Navy Captain, and you're the senior person around. I was a Navy medical officer during the war, so I understand what you're saying, and I know Admiral Brighting has forbidden what I'm about to ask. I've already tried to call Commander Rhodes in Idaho Falls, but I can't reach him, and I can't reach Admiral Brighting, either. We don't need much power—this is a small town and a small hospital —but the woman will die if we can't get some electric power fed to us right away! There's no time to spare!" The doctor's resonant voice rose as he spoke. "Our emergency generator has been broken down for a month. We've had new parts on order, but they've not come. Now the whole town's gone black. She was already in the operating room, and she's in shock, and all we have are flashlights! Even this telephone is running off the phone company's emergency batteries!"

"What do you need?"

"Electricity. Right now! There's a line from our power company into your place for emergency power in case you need it. Now the emergency is the other way. If you'll close the switch and put on your generators, your power will flow to us. Everybody is sound asleep in Arco, and the power company has already open-circuited all its lines except the one to us. So all the juice you can pump into that line will come right to the hospital. It was an emergency when the patient came in here. Now it's life or death! We have three surgeons in town, and all three of them are with her in the operating room this minute. If the lights and power come on soon we may be able to save her. Otherwise, she's gone!"

The doctor's voice bespoke a condition of frantic urgency, of a critical concatenation of circumstance in which, suddenly and shockingly, unforeseen technological failure had brought human efforts to a standstill. This could not be a fake. The unworthy thought flashed into Richardson's mind, was cast aside. The speaker's distress was too genuine. In tiny Arco, he probably knew the patient well. It was not only a professional but a personal thing.

Richardson could feel a quickening of attention, the heightened awareness of imminent action, and, down underneath, the unmistakable scent of danger. It was a different sort of danger, but otherwise it was all so much like a few days ago, with the steam leak, or many years ago, with the enemy lifeboats in sight. Rich paused only long enough to get the doctor's telephone number.

"Keith!" he barked. "Find the shore power switch. You can trace the line in from where it enters our compound. Figure out how to transform our four hundred and forty volts into whatever they need in Arco. Maybe the Arco power company can step it down. If not, maybe we can give it to them direct from the hundred and twenty volts AC end of our motor-generator sets. Take half of our electricians on watch to help you!"

"Got it, Skipper," said Keith. He had been standing beside him during the whole of the telephone conversation.

"Buck, we've got to do this fast. Keith can't do it all from that end. You take the rest of the electricians and start from the turbo-generator sets. Find out what's the best way to pump power into that shore line, and meet Keith halfway!"

"Right!" Like Keith, Buck dashed away.

"Dan"—to the new trainee who had called them back from their hut—"you get on another phone and try to find Dusty. Maybe he's gone somewhere for the weekend. Keep trying until you get him. He's got to be somewhere near here, even if it is Sunday morning. Someone must know how to get in touch with him!"

The task of finding and communicating with Admiral Brighting, in Rhodes' absence, Richardson had allocated to himself. But in this he was unsuccessful. There was no answer at Brighting's Washington apartment; several hours would elapse before even the Sunday duty officer would be at his office. True to form, there was no executive officer or second-in-command, nor home telephone numbers of any of those in Washington who might be expected to have some useful information as to where Brighting was. Between efforts somehow to get in touch with him, Richardson lost himself in the welter of reports, impediments, suggestions and counter-suggestions, interspersed with increasingly urgent calls from Dr. Danforth.

Three moments—two decisions and an instant of warm satisfaction—stood out. Wiring had to be improvised to bring the output from the turbo-generator sets around to the transformer; this took several hurried conferences with Keith and Buck, and their electricians, to determine the circuit. Then there was the decision to close the emergency power switch and build the paralleled generator sets to full power, so that current could begin to flow into the Arco line. As Rich gave the order, it was suddenly with much the same sense of commitment he remembered from combat long ago. This was the point after which there could be no turning back.

The instant of satisfaction occurred when he told Dr. Danforth there was now power on the line, and heard the gratitude in the doctor's voice reporting that the operating room lights were functioning at last, the operation was proceeding normally, and the patient's life would be saved.

"Everything's fine now at the hospital," Richardson reported to the nucleus of his working group. He was in the process of describing Danforth's final call as Keith and Buck entered Rhodes' office.

After all the others had left, Keith and Buck put into words the shadow lying in the back of his mind, the one flaw in the success. "Boss," Keith said in a low tone, "did you ever get in touch with Brighting?"

During the months in Idaho, Richardson had many times pondered the clear dictum in the standing instructions for the site that under no circumstances whatever was power to be provided off-site. It might be brought in, in emergency, but never sent the other way. Dusty Rhodes' explanation had been unilluminating: "Far as anyone knows, he figures there'll be a temptation to count on us as an area resource if we ever do anything like that. Then sometime when we might want to go down for overhaul or a drill or something, we might not be able to without their okay. It would cut into his complete control of this place."

A life-or-death emergency clearly lay outside the scope or intent of Admiral Brighting's instructions. Could he have been reached, he most certainly would have authorized provision of emergency assistance to the Arco hospital. Rich had done only what Brighting himself would have done, he mused uncomfortably, realizing the while that, unquestionably, he had disobeyed not only the written standing orders of the training site but also the personal order about leaving his rank and title outside the chain link fence enclosing the complex. He had done this twice recently, in fact. But Rhodes' telephoned report of the repair of the steam leak under the hot reactor had not mentioned Richardson's part in marshaling the repair effort. Likewise, no one (he hoped) had told Brighting yet that those present that night, at least the Navy people—and tonight as well—had automatically reverted to old training and addressed him as "Captain."

This had not happened through any desire of Richardson's. It had been a subconscious wish for and acceptance of leadership on the part of everyone. But in responding to one of Dr. Danforth's anxious telephone calls before the power hookup was complete, Richardson had himself used his title as the quickest and simplest method of indicating his acceptance of responsibility. He was as guilty as the rest. More so. With the town of Arco and its power company involved, there was no way Brighting could fail to learn all the details almost immediately, wherever he was.

Rhodes, when he finally came to the telephone after being rousted from the duck blind in which he had barely settled for his first try at duck hunting in Idaho, was incredulous when he learned what Rich had done. "You know I'll have to tell the old man," he said unhappily. "There's no way I can not tell him. Arco's been trying to get us to agree to do this for years. They've even gone to the State Power Commission to try to force us. Now this will be all over the papers."

It was a badly shaken Dusty Rhodes who greeted Richardson Monday morning. "He chewed me out all over the Bell Telephone System," he said. "He already knew all about it. He must have spies everywhere. I didn't even get a chance to talk at all. The way he carried on you'd have thought I had done it myself, instead of being off in a duck blind. Even early on a Sunday morning, I've got no right to be in a duck blind. Said I'm in charge and should have been here. So now I've got to move into the quonset alongside yours and be on board whenever the reactor is critical. To hell with family life. We're critical for months at a time, and I'll just have to stay on board. And the Navy calls this shore duty!" Rhodes audibly expelled his breath. "Also, I've got to tell you you can't take the exam. It's okay for Keith and Buck, but not you. He won't even listen. Twice I tried to tell him how it was, and both times he said you were like the gunner of the *Claymer,* or something like that. What's this *Claymer* business? And what's it got to do with knocking you out of taking the operator's exam? That's all he'd say, except that he doesn't want to talk to you."

"It's a famous story by Victor Hugo," said Richardson, thinking of something else, almost absently answering the question. "A gun broke loose on a ship named *Claymore* during a storm. It rolled around on deck smashing things and killing people and nearly sinking the ship, which was carrying some big general back to France during the French Revolution. The gunner risked his life to secure the gun, and after he finally got it lashed so it couldn't move, the general gave him a medal and then had him shot. Some say the general was supposed to be Napoleon, but I'm not so sure."

"What did he have the poor guy shot for?"

"The medal was for heroism in tying up the gun again. He was shot because he was responsible for it getting loose in the first place. I get the message all right, mainly that Brighting won't listen to my side of the story. But his analogy is mixed up. I didn't let any guns get loose!"

Rhodes looked curiously at Richardson. "You're awfully calm about it," he said. "I thought you'd be mad as hell."

Rich grimaced. "Well, I'm not happy about it," he said. "That make you feel any better?" He had not been able totally to keep the bitterness out of his voice, even knowing that Dusty Rhodes had been a very unwilling bearer of bad news. He had expected something like this, had spent a good portion of the past day considering the manner of his defense during the telephone conversation with Brighting which he believed to be inevitable. The unfairness of the summary decision cut deep. He had been denied even the opportunity of saying a single word in his defense, as if he counted for nothing. The effort he and the others had made, the good accomplished, the life saved, the agonized decision to proceed in the emergency without permission which was, in the circumstance, unobtainable, all were being treated contemptuously. Fury suddenly boiled within him. Brighting had no right to do this to him!

But the inner rage could not come out. It would be unseemly. More, it would be stupid for him to let Brighting goad him into saying or doing something which could be construed as disrespectful. So far, he was morally certain of the right of his position and the support of the Navy. He must not forfeit this by losing control now, no matter what the provocation.

With Buck and Keith, however, both of whom announced they would also skip the exam, he could be less reserved. It was almost a relief to shout at them.

"Certainly not!" he blazed. "You two damn fools get in there and take that exam! And you'd both better come out with damned near perfect marks, both of you!"

But then, as the morning wore on to noon—a can of soup warmed by the vending machine while he waited—and the afternoon turned into evening, it became too painful. The study program had all been directed to the end of taking the qualifying examination for reactor operator, one of several qualifications it was possible to attain. All three men had already done all the physical testing and watch-standing work, had passed all the practical factors required for qualification. Remaining was only the theoretical test, the examination. Mark One was already programmed for a following study group, this time prospective engineers instead of skippers. Even in Mark One there was nothing for him to do except observe some other students follow the same learning path, make the same mistakes, learn the same basics. Reading for relaxation or trying to occupy himself in some other way did not work. He found a magazine which someone had surreptitiously brought in, threw it down after only a few minutes. The operating manuals were hopeless. His eyes glazed over the words.

As he paced restlessly about, conjuring up new errands, torturing himself with his inability to control his bitter emotion, wishing he were anywhere but where he was and yet not able to go away for more than a moment at any given time, Richardson could not help occasionally seeing Keith and Buck, sitting on opposite sides of the examination room, concentrating on the question sheet before them, scribbling madly on pads of ruled paper, drinking cup after cup of coffee. In this, at least, he could participate; getting coffee for his friends was one of the ways his life could be meaningful. Frequently one or the other, sometimes both at once, cast him a quick glance of gratitude for the coffee, of sympathy for the pain he was feeling, of worry for their inability to help assuage the anguish. But the demands of the test were primary. For the most part they kept their eyes on their papers, their pencils in ceaseless motion.

Several doors away, in the officer-in-charge's private office, the same which Rich had commandeered for a command post only thirty-six hours ago, an associated drama was taking place. Rhodes' telephone rang more often than usual, and most of the time it must have been Brighting.

At least, Rhodes' alacrity to answer, the somber sympathy of his secretary or the hurried search organized when Rhodes happened to be absent could spell no one but Admiral Brighting on the other end of the line. Once Rhodes spoke louder than usual, and Rich heard him say, "No, sir, he's not. He's not in there." The negatives were emphatic. "He's down in the prototype somewhere. Do you want me to get him to the phone?"

Evidently Brighting did not, for no one came for Rich. It was not his intention to eavesdrop, but Rhodes might have realized he was only a few feet away and could not help overhearing. Maybe this was a hint. Perhaps Rhodes was more subtle than he thought. Anyway, he would take it as such, would force himself to find something of interest in the drills down in the prototype.

Keith found him in the reactor compartment, two hours later. "Well, we're finished," he said. "Buck's winding up his last question right now, so that's done. He'll be here in a couple minutes. Boy! That was some exam!"

"How did you do?"

"Oh, I'm sure I did pretty doggone well. It was fair enough—it just asked me everything I ever knew. That's why it took all day. They've already started to grade my paper, and we'll know pretty soon what Dusty's crew thinks of it. I've got a great case of writer's cramp, and a permanent dent in my finger where I held the pencils, and I'll bet Buck has, too! But what a lousy deal this is for you! I wish there were some way we could square this!"

"We can't help that," said Richardson, speaking as normally as he could. "Don't forget I learned what I came out here for, nuke ticket or no. I'm just glad he didn't lay on you and Buck for helping. You're the guys who will really need the tickets on your records with your nuke boats."

"Ships, you mean," said Keith, sensing that Richardson would like to change the subject. "Some of us have been calling them 'ships' ever since the *Triton* went in commission—about time, too. She's as big as a cruiser. I suppose we'll be heading home tomorrow. Dusty's already cut our orders, I think, and I'm anxious to get back to Peggy and the *Cushing,* both."

"Spoken like a true sailor," Rich began, glad for the chance to take up a new topic. "I've got interest in New London, too. . . ."

"I don't know which needs me the most, *Manta* or Cindy," said Williams' voice behind them, "but I know which one I need most, and she's no damned submarine!"

"You young bucks are all the same," growled Richardson with mock disdain. "Can't keep away from women!"

"You just now said something about New London yourself, Skipper," said Buck mischievously. "Is there anyone there in particular . . . ?"

Someone was approaching rapidly on the other side of the reactor housing. Rhodes. "Rich," he said,

Brighting's changed his mind! Can you take the exam right away?"

"You mean right this minute? You bet! What's happened?"

"Damned if I know," said Rhodes. "He suddenly called up again, and out of the clear blue he said to give you the test immediately. Now. Then he hung up. It's now or never, the way he said it. He's not even willing for you to wait till tomorrow morning. Can you start right now?"

There was neither disrespect nor lese majesty in the blows Keith and Buck were suddenly raining on his back, and their delighted exclamations. Dusty Rhodes joined them after a moment and in a somewhat more inhibited fashion, and within minutes Rich found himself seated in the same examination room lately occupied by his friends, fortified by a cup of black coffee and staring at his first question.

"There's no time limit, but you have to do it all at one sitting," said Rhodes. "Just work till you finish, and then lay your papers on my desk. I'll get them in the morning. I couldn't give you the same test as the others, though. Brighting's orders. It's a little tougher, so it won't be lying on my desk very long, I don't think. This is the one for reactor supervisor, which we normally use to qualify top-grade technicians who've been out here at least a year. I'm afraid you'll be working pretty late."

After Rhodes had left, Keith said quietly, "If this exam is tougher than ours, it's going to be a long night for you. Buck and I will go watch-and-watch on you, so there'll be one of us around for moral support and coffee. We've got plenty of quarters for the soup machines, too; so all you have to do is yell when you need something."

The examination taken by his two friends had contained thirty questions, they had said, and it was with some dismay that Rich found forty-two in his. Dusty's sure not going to find all these finished and on his desk when he gets there tomorrow morning, that's one thing certain, he thought. It took Keith and Buck nine hours to do theirs, so they averaged ten questions every three hours. At the same speed this one will take more than twelve hours. He put his wristwatch on the table in front of him, picked up the first of a boxful of sharpened pencils and began.

"Sketch and describe the control rod configuration in Mark I," the question read. "Show the relationship between control rod geometry and the fuel element geometry. Explain the effect on nuclear flux. Draw a three-dimensional sketch of the flux density at various control rod positions, describing the theoretical considerations pertaining to each. . . ."

What could have caused Brighting to reverse himself? Or had he been hazing him the entire time? This special test was certainly far more difficult than the one for which he had prepared. And he had been forced to begin it at the end of an already long and emotionally exhausting day. Maybe this, too, was part of the hazing.

No matter. Whatever the cause, or causes, he had been given his chance. There was no time limit; so he could work as long as necesary, or as long as his brain could function. He would budget twenty minutes per question, three questions per hour. It was now just seven o'clock. With luck, he might be dropping the completed examination on Dusty Rhodes' desk sometime in the late morning, about fifteen hours from now.

6

wwwwwwwwwwwwwwwwwwwwwwwwwwwwwwwwwwwwwwwwwwwwwwwwww

It was nearly noon of the next day when Richardson carried into Rhodes' office ninety-two sheets of ruled legal-size paper, closely written with pencil and ball-point pen. "Here it is, Dusty," he said. His mind was still awhirl. Sometime during the all-night grind there had come on him some inner strength, an increased alertness, a mental second wind. He had been sixteen hours at his desk, except for necessary trips to the head, had used up all the pencils provided—and faithfully sharpened—by Keith and Buck, and had drunk many cups of coffee, also brought by his two friends. True to their word, they had split up the night so that one of them was always there. Shortly after midnight a large mug filled with hot soup had appeared, and at eight, wonder of wonders, a plate of scrambled eggs.

"Compliments of Mrs. Dusty Rhodes," Buck had said, "only she doesn't know it yet. Now that Dusty has to stay on the site she fixed him up with a hot plate in his quonset and will keep him supplied with stuff. He's not allowed to do anything for you, you know, but he can't help it if I swipe a couple of eggs while he's shaving."

Richardson had expected to be exhausted, physically and mentally. To his surprise, he felt positively ebullient. He wanted to talk, could not sit still, paced up and down in front of Rhodes.

"You'd better turn in, Rich," said Rhodes. "You're so wound up right now you'd go *boing* if I tapped you with a pencil. We'll start marking your paper right away; so when you get back over here we'll have your grade for you. The old man will be pleased, I know. He's called a couple of times this morning already, and I told him you were still hard at it. We'll have your orders ready so that you can start for New London by the night plane out of the Falls, if you want."

"The admiral must figure he's doing us a favor," grumped Buck from beside the driver of the Twelfth Naval District sedan. "There's just no other explanation. First he treats Rich worse than a plebe at Annapolis, and then he sends us all three on a joyride to Mare Island, California. It doesn't make any sense. We don't even know what we're supposed to do, except inspect the reserve fleet subs. Inspect for what? We've got no instructions at all. He must figure we need a vacation for a day in California, before heading back to the rigors of New England. If he'd sent Cindy out here and given us a week, maybe I'd feel different."

"Mare Island is where we left the old *Eel* after the war, you know," said Keith, thoughtfully. "I've not heard of her being moved or anything. Wonder if that might have anything to do with it."

"No way, Keith. You know the last thing in the world Brighting is is sentimental." Williams tossed his head as if to lob the words over his shoulder to Keith, in the back seat. The sedan, moving at only moderate speed, lurched frequently on the uneven asphalt road.

"The only thing everybody always agrees on about Brighting is that no one has yet figured him out, or ever will, probably." Richardson, sitting beside Keith, spoke for the first time in several minutes. "I've been thinking maybe Keith's right. I'm sure the old boat is still there, and our orders to come out here so suddenly just might have something to do with her. We'd all have known if she'd been put back into commission, and I'm positive we'd have heard if they'd scrapped her or used her for a target or something. So this will at least be a chance to look her over for a few minutes, anyway." He paused. "There may be something going on, too. This car and driver were waiting for us at San Francisco airport. No word about that, either. He just met the plane. Driver"—addressing the uniformed sailor behind the wheel—"the Reserve Fleet Admin Office is back there in the shipyard, isn't it? Why aren't you taking us there?"

"Dunno, sir. My orders was to take you right to the reserve fleet berths. It's upstream from the yard."

"We have to catch the night flight out of San Francisco for New York. Are you going to wait for us and bring us back?"

"Nosir. I'm supposed to start right back for District Headquarters. Those are my orders, sir. I don't know how you're supposed to get back, sir."

"We'll have to work on that," muttered Rich half to himself, as Buck turned around and Keith leaned forward the better to look at him. "We're not going to have much time to inspect if we have to spend some of it scrounging up a car to take us back to South San Francisco."

Ahead and off to the right, a large ship bulked high above a forest of masts. The car reached the end of the road, turned to run along the waterfront. "That's the mothball fleet," volunteered the driver. "There's the tender, I don't know its name, and there's all kinds of old ships here, mostly little ones, like DEs and such. There's a bunch of subs just beyond them, all moored together. They should be waiting for us on the tender, but if we don't see anybody there I'll run you down to the subs."

The repair ship, or tender, floating extremely high in the water, loomed above the sedan as it passed. Ahead, a group of people stood in the road. There were about a dozen men, some in civilian work clothing, some in naval uniform, one showing the four broad stripes of a captain. Behind them a dozen old submarines were moored to heavy wooden pilings. Serried ranks of gray had faded to a ghostly white. The rounded hulls were streaked with dirt and rust, and rubbing scars showed where the paint had scraped off against the pilings. In two groups of six each, they floated so high that the curve at the bottom of each bow, where it turned aft to join the keel, was visible above the water. Torpedo tubes, normally below the surface, were totally exposed, bow and stern. The effect was incongruous. If submarines could fly, this was how they'd look just before lift-off.

Prominent on the deck of each of the submarines was a large silver dome about six feet high with a thick, stubby projection on one side and curved vertical ribbing intersecting at the top like longitude lines on a global map. This was the protective covering over a mothballed deck gun. One submarine displayed two such domes, one forward and one aft of the bridge. With a pang of sentimental attachment, Richardson recognized the *Eel*. This was where she had been left, abandoned, fifteen years before. This was exactly the spot, unchanged, except that now there seemed to be fewer ships of all kinds around. *Eel* was fourth boat out in a nest of six, exactly as she had been. She had been carefully prepared for the mothball fleet. All deactivation instructions had been meticulously, even lovingly, carried out. Her machinery files were complete; her spare parts were as up to date as they could be, with requisitions to fill deficiencies already prepared. Her batteries, ammunition, torpedoes, fuel and provisions had been removed, her propellers detached from their shafts and securely stowed on deck. Her interior compartments had been scrubbed clean, painted where necessary, at the end—just before the dehumidifiers were turned on and the hatches locked.

Her crew had gradually been diminished during the deactivation period, until only a few were left. Then these also departed, leaving *Eel,* covered with gray preservative paint, tethered with heavy lines through bow and stern chocks, floating a full ten feet above her normal waterline. And there she lay, now, exactly where she had been waiting all these years.

Could inanimate hulls that once were living ships have a personality, could they think in fact as sailors are accustomed to credit them in fancy, *Eel* might have spent the intervening years grieving for the masters she had once served. The thought was maudlin. Richardson had felt no compulsion to revisit his old ship. Yet now, the first time back, the forgotten emotions were with him, as if they, too, had lain dormant awaiting his return. He recalled that he himself, citing the tradition that the captain must be the last to leave his ship, had shut the last hatch, been last man over the side, on that final day of abandonment. It had been done as a matter of course, not with any show of emotion, but symbolic nevertheless. *Eel* was not, after all, to be done away with. She was not, like the *Walrus,* gone forever. She would someday be returned to the active fleet, to resume the glory of a free being in the limitless sea. And yet, there had been a feeling of abandonment. He had imagined her crying not to be left alone. There was the memory of a lump in the throat, a voice not quite ringing true, a hand secretly caressing the bridge rail and periscope supports as he took his final leave.

Much had happened since then, but he had not been back. Until now; and suddenly it was all alive again.

The man wearing the four-striped uniform came around the car to Richardson's side as Rich stepped out the door. "Captain Richardson?" he asked, dubiously eyeing the civilian suit. "I'm Jim Boggs, reserve fleet commander. This is sure good of you. I can appreciate why you wanted to do this, and it solves a problem for us, too. Great idea, but why the civvies?"

"They're all we had where we were. But what's this about this being our idea? We were sent here to inspect something. That's all I know. I figured you'd brief us on what it's all about, and we'll look over what we can while we're here, but we have to catch the night flight to New York. So we'll not have much time. . . ."

"Oh, getting to San Francisco airport is a breeze from Hunter's Point. They'll run you over there in a car in fifteen minutes. You'll have plenty of time to party with the Brazilians in the club before you have to leave—ah . . . What are you supposed to inspect?" The puzzlement on Boggs' broad face was genuine.

"We thought you'd be able to tell us. All I know is that our original orders were modified by telephone. We're to report to you, inspect the reserve fleet subs, and leave San Francisco tonight."

Boggs' face was increasingly clouded. "Nobody not in my own chain of command can give me a surprise inspection. Something's funny about this. I got a telephone call last night, too, telling me that you three were coming and had volunteered to ride the *Eel* down to Hunter's Point. We're turning her over to Brazil, you know."

"The *Eel?* To Brazil? We volunteered?" Rich was conscious of sudden acute interest on the part of his two car mates.

"That's right. We were going to turn over the *Orca,* but she wasn't in too good condition, and the Brazilians refused to accept her. So the *Eel* was picked to take her place. She was being saved in case our own Navy wanted to put her back in, and we know she's in top shape. Whoever put her out at the end of the war did a good job."

"We put her out ourselves, you know," said Rich, "and I guess we were sort of proud of her. Some of the boats weren't that lucky."

"That explains it. Some of the relief crews didn't care very much, I guess. Anyway, ComSubPac was so embarrassed about the *Orca* he wanted to send someone over with the *Eel* to present her, to square himself, like. I naturally thought that's what you'd volunteered for. The Brazilians are going to meet her when she gets there, and I expect they'll want to look her over before the yard begins ripping her apart. The best presentation committee ComSubPac could put aboard would be her old skipper."

"I guess she'll be a lot different when the yard gets through with her," said Rich. "Snorkel, new radar . . ."

"And new sonar, new radios, streamlined bridge, take off the guns. You'll not recognize her. She'll be a brand-new submarine."

"When are you shifting her across the bay?"

"That's the whole point of this exercise, or at least, I thought it was. ComTwelve phoned that you were in and would be here as quick as the car could bring you.

Otherwise we'd have sent her an hour ago. The tugs are here. We're ready to break the nest and snake out your old ship as soon as you're aboard."

"Skipper," said Keith, "this has got to be what we were sent here for. There's no other way it make sense." Buck, standing beside Keith, nodded his agreement.

"Captain Boggs," said Rich, "did your information say we had *volunteered* to do this?"

"Sure did. What's more, I got a dispatch last night from ComSubPac authorizing me to turn the *Eel* and tug both over to you. The tug skipper already knows he's to take orders from you."

"What about charts, lights down below, people to handle lines, a below decks watch, interior communications, emergency gear . . . ?"

"It's all there. We've done this lots of times, remember. We have responsibility for safe passage, not you, even though you'll be in nominal charge. The tug-master's spent his whole life on this bay. It's his job to get your old boat over there and dodge the mud flats en route. He has the charts in his pilothouse, but we put a set aboard the *Eel* for you also. There's binoculars, a big thermos of coffee, plenty of box lunches, portable hand lanterns if you want to go below. Matter of fact, you can make the whole trip down below if you want; all you really have to do is receive the Brazilian Navy when they meet the boat at Hunter's Point. We checked out the sound-powered telephone system, so you do have interior communications. You won't have any power, that's all. No rudder, no anchor, and of course your propellers are just where you left them, on deck secured with welded straps. *Eel* is only a barge so far as this little trip is concerned. Your job is to show the Brazilians that we're not passing off another crock to them."

It still seemed unreal that the well-organized U.S. Navy bureaucracy could have been toying with them to this extent, but Richardson allowed himself to be convinced. Maybe Admiral Brighting had had something to do with this, too, along with everything else that had happened to him lately! "Okay," he heard himself saying, "it will be our last trip in the old *Eel,* and we may as well enjoy it."

"It's a lovely time of year to be on the bay, Rich." The puzzlement on Boggs' honest face had cleared, and its broad features now held a cherubic smile. "You'll find it full of sailboats. San Francisco will be a sight, too. I wish I could go along with you, but I'll phone Hunter's Point that you're on your way. I'll have to tell them that you're not in uniform, anyway. They're expecting you in all your official glory."

The tug skipper, a heavyset warrant boatswain with a red face appropriate to the years he must have spent at his profession, extracted the quiescent *Eel* from her berth as soon as the two submarines moored outboard had been pulled clear by the assisting tug. With professional aplomb he put his bluff, heavily fendered craft on *Eel*'s port quarter, made fast, and with no ceremony whatever swung the submarine's bow downstream and increased speed on his engine.

"It's amazing how simple they make it seem," said Buck Williams, as the three officers stood on *Eel*'s bridge, watching the maneuver. "I wonder why they call this 'towing,' though. 'Pushing' is more like it."

"They do call it 'pushing' some places," said Keith, "like the Mississippi River. You ought to see those Mississippi towboats. They can shove a couple of dozen big square-ended barges upstream, against the current, and maneuver them besides. Sometimes they handle more cargo in their barges than a big freighter could. A lot of the Mississippi is too shallow for a seagoing ship, and the big towboats are the answer."

"Why don't they just put a towline over their stern and pull the barges? Wouldn't that be easier?"

"They do in the open ocean," said Keith, "or anyplace where it's rough. But in smooth inland waters this gives the tug better control. Did you ever steer a ship while towing something big, like a barge, astern? This way he can handle us as though his tug and whatever he's pushing is simply one big ship."

"That's right, Buck," said Richardson, joining the discussion. "Why don't you visit over there before the trip's over? Even though he's pushing from alongside, you'll see he doesn't need any rudder to keep us going straight ahead. The way he's made fast, his helmsman steers for us both."

"Then that's why he was so particular with his bow and stern lines, slacking them and heaving them in?"

"Sure. He's got his bow toed in toward us just a little, just enough to balance the turning effect of pushing from the port quarter instead of from dead aft. That's the whole secret."

Keith grinned at Rich as Buck raised his binoculars and inspected the tug and its lines with renewed interest. "You should have been a schoolteacher," he said. "You never could resist teaching a little whenever you got the chance." Richardson grinned back. "You're another," he said, raising his binoculars.

A new thought struck Keith, and a slightly more serious expression settled on his normally open countenance. "You know, I guess all three of us agree that old man Brighting must have been the source of our 'volunteering' for this little chore. And I've got to admit I probably would have volunteered if I'd known about it. But isn't the whole thing rather peculiar? I mean, keeping us in the dark the way he did?"

"I've been thinking the same thing," said Buck. "This is sort of a surprise bonus. All the way out here, until around an hour ago when we found out, I've been cussing him for not letting us go right home after that sweatshop time in Idaho. Now I'm glad we're here, but mad because he made such a secret of it."

"The way I see it," said Rich, "he well knows we were once together on this boat. So when BuPers wanted to know if one of us could come out here, he volunteered all three of us. Not telling us what he was up to is simply his way of doing things. He's trying to do something for us. It's like that time he sent us to look over the NEPA project. It's a day off, a holiday trip, sort of."

"Then he must be trying to make up for his bitchiness to you more than anyone," said Buck, "and he must think you come pretty cheap. He knows doggone well it was you who kept the reactor running that day, and that it was you who saved that woman's life in Arco, whoever she is. Both of these things make him look pretty good, you know. So, he holds up your exam long enough so that you had to stay up all night to do it, and on top of this, even though it was a tougher exam than ours and you got almost a perfect mark on it, he made Dusty hand you a lower-grade nuke certificate than we got. Don't tell me what a grand old guy he is."

"Maybe there was a little hazing going on," said Rich, "but it didn't hurt us. Don't forget, he's the source of our nuclear submarines, and we ought to overlook about anything because of that."

"How about that telephone call after we finally got you to turn in?" said Keith. "Dusty tried to talk him out of it, but he said you had no business sleeping in the daytime when there's work to be done. He knew our work was finished, and that you'd been up all night because of him besides! And then after he made Dusty get you to the phone, all he wanted was to say he'd decided to build the cafeteria after all! That had to be deliberate. He knew exactly what he was doing!"

"The main thing is, now all three of us have our nuclear ratings. I'm lucky he even let me join you two. He wasn't going to at first, you know." The look on Richardson's face signaled his two juniors to leave the topic. Experience had taught them that his thought processes could not always be predicted. Something, perhaps their arguments, perhaps his own greater awareness of the political structure within the U.S. Navy, perhaps something totally unrelated to anything they had been doing, caused him to want to close it off. They would have been astounded could they have known they had evoked the memory of Joan. Might she have caused Brighting to reverse his initial rejection of Rich? Could she, just yesterday, have had something to do with his relenting on the business of the examination? Could it have been she who had suggested this last visit to their old wartime submarine? After all, she too, had had her connection with the *Eel!*

Boggs had certainly been right in his characterization of San Francisco Bay as a most pleasant place to cruise in. Smoky brown hills teeming with life surrounded it, a warm sun turned its mud-gray waters iridescent, great bridges vaulted across it, and in the distance the tall buildings of the fabled city of the hills beckoned. Nearer, like disorganized flocks of wild birds, the sails of countless pleasure boats followed their own aimless quests, some in a cohesive pattern, perhaps a race, others without discernible motivation or objective except that of simply being there.

The combined ambience of industry and pleasure

could be both seen and felt. A group of cylindrical white tanks to port, marching away from the water in stubby silhouettes up a steep brown hillside, marked a refinery. Trim white sails, tiny in the distance, softened the outline of the land, disappeared against the white oil tanks and the nearby buildings, and stood out, etched in slowly moving white silhouettes against the salt-streaked hulls of two oceangoing tankers anchored in the distance. To starboard an old freighter, her broad bows pushing a bulging wave despite her slow speed, was heading for some unknown destination up one of the rivers feeding Carquinez Strait at the north end of the bay. Beyond her, another cargo ship, newer, a moving forest of masts and booms, was heading away, probably bound out the Golden Gate for a distant and foreign shore. A white-sided passenger liner, suddenly visible against the exotic spires of San Francisco, was also steaming toward the Golden Gate Bridge, and thence to Acapulco, Honolulu, Seattle—or anywhere. And the shores to starboard were pocked with the evidences of people: houses of many differing colors, glints of glass windows, shifting flashes denoting the speeding windshields of automobiles. Great numbers of small boats, both sail and power, clustered along the benign coast.

The sight of some member of the mothballed fleet being ignominiously barged through San Francisco Bay was probably a familiar sight on its waters. The tug skipper, indeed, had boasted having made the same trip countless times, sometimes to deliver a well-scavenged hulk to the wreckers, sometimes, as now, to start a discarded lady toward a new and different life. For the three submariners, once they had assured themselves that all was proceeding normally, that *Eel* was not unexpectedly taking water into her bilges, that the tugmaster's charts of the navigation hazards agreed with theirs and the course he had laid out was to their liking, it was a pleasure trip with overtones of nostalgia.

Richardson found it was easy to stand on the bridge where he had stood so many times, shoulder hunched into one of the TBT wells (the target bearing transmitters themselves had been removed) and imagine *Eel* moving under his direction in enemy waters, responsive to his will, alert, alive, alive to the quintessence of being alive in the face of mortal danger. The pleasure boats, the friendly shores, even the distant ships on their peaceful missions, could fade out of consciousness. It could be a bright moonlit night; strange how well he used to be able to see at night, without lights of any kind to bother his eyes. More than once *Eel* had been in waters far more confined than this, had seemed to be hemmed in by the forbidding hills of the seacoast of Japan. More than once he had, somehow, summoned up the necessary—it seemed only days ago, instead of years—on this very bridge, at this very spot.

That tanker, now, about a mile ahead, crossing from starboard to port: were she an enemy he would have by now opened the torpedo tube outer doors. A small order to the rudder to reduce the angle between the torpedo course, controlled by its gyroscope, and that of the submarine (the less the gyro angle, the more accurate the old torpedoes); Keith would be giving the bearings, Buck running the TDC, the torpedo data computer, and shooting the fish at his command. The setup was so similar to one he remembered from *Eel*'s third patrol: the tanker, unescorted, moving confidently in the shallow waters where no enemy submarine had ever dared to enter; the submarine, keyed up, but equally confident because of past successes. Except that it was just before dawn, instead of broad daylight, as now. The ship, in fact, had looked almost exactly like this one. You had to hand it to her skipper. When he saw the submarine, he had instantly turned to ram. Stupid of Rich to have tried a surface attack with daylight so near! With the U.S. Fleet pressing ever closer to the mainland of Japan during those closing months of the war he must have forgotten the caution he had learned during previous patrols. A routine approach (no approach was ever "routine," but this one had seemed simple, uncomplicated) had been suddenly converted into near catastrophe. The ships speeding toward each other, bow to bow. Too close to shoot! Get everybody below! The tanker opening fire (how had he been able to get his guns going so quickly?)—large-caliber shells whizzing overhead. Desperate maneuvers to avoid. The ships slipping past each other, the tanker swinging toward, trying to strike the submarine's side, *Eel* turning toward the tanker, swinging her stern clear. Enemy machine guns spitting, striking the bulletproof bridge bulwarks (a good thing they were made of special armorplate); Rich ducking at the last minute, just in time, as the *Eel* rocketed clear.

Looking through his binoculars at the approaching tanker, musing at the coincidental similarity of ship and situation to the one creased in his memory, Richardson saw the curved front of her bridge growing wider. The tanker should be passing ahead; soon it ought not to be possible to see the front of her bridge at all—but instead the curved surface was becoming broader. Then it hit him. Were this war, were he on the alert for changes in enemy course and speed instead of in a nostalgic reverie, he would have seen it instantly. The tanker ahead was turning toward! Her rudder must have been put hard over left! This was exactly the way it had been! The bearing must soon become steady, a collision situation! Rich drew a deep breath to begin the maneuver to avoid, order the watertight doors shut through the boat. It was so much the same, but there was no one below to shut the doors, no one steering in the conning tower to handle *Eel*'s rudder and annunciators. In the binoculars the oncoming bow was tremendous. Somewhere behind—he had forgotten the tug—a series of angry blasts on an air horn. *Eel* began to vibrate as the tug's engine went into full reverse. More blasts from the tug. Now some answering blasts from the tanker. What could they be thinking of, over there?

Swiftly, the distance narrowed. *Eel*'s speed, never great in her captive condition, was decreasing. She had almost come to a complete halt, was swinging left, the wrong way. Her whole fragile side would be exposed to the collision. If the loaded tanker could not stop her forward motion she would plow into the submarine's starboard ballast tanks, surely rupture her pressure hull as well, ignominiously sink her in the middle of the ship channel.

Now it was clear the tanker had also gone into full reverse. Her bow was swinging again, away, to her own left. Her way had hardly reduced—a laden ship is very hard to stop—but her engines were thrashing water up under her counter. Her bow swung away more. No danger of a bows-on collision now, but she's going to sideswipe us. *Eel,* now dead in the water, began to gather sternway. The tug captain had slacked his stern line, was now nearly perpendicular to the submarine's side, backing frantically, as powerfully as he could, trying to drag *Eel* bodily sideways out of the sweeping path. One hundred yards—fifty yards. People staring over the tanker's side, from her bridge, her bows.

The onrushing tanker's bow was now abeam, no longer headed straight on, but close! The flare of the great profile overhung *Eel*'s deck, so far below. If that huge anchor nearly directly overhead were to be let go, it would land right on deck, crash clear through and carry *Eel* on down with it. Ludicrous for *Eel,* after all the dangers she had been through, to meet her fate here, in a well-known American harbor, at the hands of a lubberly U.S. tanker skipper! That must be he up on the bridge, or maybe the pilot—if he had a pilot— peering over at the wreckage he was about to cause. The wash from the tanker's single propeller was up along- side her after deckhouse, reaching along the rusted slab- sided bulk of her gigantic hull. Her bridge was now abeam, and still she moved sideways under the impetus of her rudder. The turbulence from her screw began to reach *Eel*'s side. This might help to lessen the impact. Less than twenty-five feet between the ships now. May- be the thrust of water from the tanker's propeller would help to push *Eel* away, form a cushion between them.

But the huge vertical side of the tanker was also coming sideways. If it continued it would inevitably strike. No danger of being pierced by her stem now, but the whole side of the submarine, her light tank structure, would be bellied in, ribs crushed and bent, its clean symmetry ruined, *Eel*'s ability to float upright destroyed. She would be brought to the dock at Hunter's Point listing to starboard, her side smashed, instead of clean and straight as she should be. Hunter's Point could fix the damage, could build a new side if neces- sary, or replace the wrecked portion. But this was not the way the U.S. Navy had wanted to deliver the re- placement for the *Orca*. Maybe Rich could reach the tanker skipper, or pilot, that seemingly impassive figure almost directly above. He, or whoever that was in some kind of uniform coat, looking as if mesmerized by the approaching collision, had not uttered a word, given an order, that Rich could see.

No megaphone. There should have been a mega- phone. No doubt the tug carried one. Rich cupped his hands around his mouth, bellowed with all his strength. "Shift your rudder! Put your rudder right full!" Several times he repeated the words, pitching his voice at what he considered to be its best carrying level, straining neck, jaws and lungs to force the maximum response from his vocal cords. Once the pitch rose almost to a scream. No matter. Most people, except perhaps Keith and Buck, would call it a scream anyway.

There was some wind. The tanker's engines must be making noise. The tug's diesels were rumbling loudly behind him. The splashing of the water between *Eel* and the tanker was louder still as it was driven forward by the big backing propeller, was forced in white turbulence between the ships. The tanker was deep in the water, still moving forward with speed hardly slackened. The edge of her rudder post was barely visible under the counter stern. Her rudder was fully submerged, could not be seen. Had the tanker helmsman gotten the word? Had Richardson been able to reach through the noise and confusion? Again he shouted through cupped hands, his voice cracking with the effort.

A wave of the arm from the man on the tanker's bridge. He turned, shouted something toward his enclosed pilothouse. Richardson had to hope it was an order to his helmsman. Was the rudder post turning? It was wet, gleaming. Rust-colored. No seaweed or bottom growth; a tanker's waterlines are much too variable for anything to attach itself this high. Because of the slick shine of the round vertical forging, it was not possible to tell if it was turning. Even if the rudder was now at last reversed, put hard over right toward *Eel,* there was little effect it could have in the time remaining. Stopping the slide to starboard of that tremendous bulk, with its 50,000 tons of momentum, would take several hundred yards of forward motion. She was still crabbing sideways, would hit *Eel*'s thin ballast tanks soon.

Ten feet—five feet—separated the low-lying submarine from the overbearing steel cliff that was the side of the tanker. A huge, obscene, rust-streaked monster, nothing but an oil tank formed into a blunt bow at one end with an engine tacked on at the other, she towered shapelessly over the submarine and extended probably at least twice as far below the surface as above. From a fisheye view, Richardson thought, *Eel* must resemble a lifeboat just launched alongside. The thin canal of water between the two ships was insane with turmoil. Frenzied currents boiled to the surface, whipped themselves into frothing waves, surged into the narrow crevasse.

Because of her light condition, floating high, *Eel*'s rounded sides were essentially vertical where they entered the water, but beneath the waterline, as above, they curved away from the tanker. The point of contact would come right at the waterline, right where the screw wake thrown up by the other ship's beating propeller would exert its greatest effect, obviously was doing so, for the water level between them was now raised, "bunched," if such a word could be used to describe a fluid condition lasting only a few moments.

The tanker's bridge and her unconcerned skipper were now well past. Her speed had not perceptibly slackened, despite the thrashings of her propeller. Perhaps her crabbing motion had somewhat reduced, if indeed the rudder had been shifted, or maybe it was only that the tug was at last beginning to drag *Eel* sideways and away from the approaching bulk. That big single propeller, now. Good thing this tanker had only a single screw. Twin screws were more dangerous, because they usually projected beyond the side, but the single propeller was bigger and would not be far below the surface, even with a deeply laden ship. And the tanker's stern was still swinging toward, although more slowly.

The water channel between the two ships had widened toward *Eel*'s stern, but was correspondingly narrower in the vicinity of her bridge, *Eel*'s widest point, where Richardson, Leone and Williams were standing, helplessly watching the oncoming catastrophe. No longer, however, did it appear the ships would strike broadside to broadside. Now, the rounded portion of the tanker's stern, where her ungainly middle section began its compound curve to meet the rudder and propeller cavity, would be the point of contact.

"Better step back, Captain," said Keith suddenly. "There's a lot of overhang coming our way." Rich felt two pairs of hands gripping his shoulders, physically pulling him to the port side of the bridge just before the overhanging stern quarters of the tanker swept through the place where his head had been. There was a scraping, grinding, metallic crunch, oddly similar to the noise of a cardboard box being crushed, and then a higher-pitched sound of sheet steel being dragged over a rough surface. *Eel* heeled far over to port, heaved sideways, stayed there. Towering overhead, her stern quarter projecting into the airspace above the submarine's bridge, crushing in its side plating, the huge ship scraped and ground past. In a moment she was clear, leaving a last indelible impression of the big letters emblazoned on her stern: *Forward Venture. Monrovia.*

Eel lurched back to an even keel. The three officers dashed back to the now ruined starboard side of her bridge. There was still a tiny water channel between the two ships, and the submarine's rounded side was well into the concave space under the tanker's quarter. Richardson wondered why he could not hear, or feel, *Forward Venture*'s big propeller blades slashing into the ballast tanks, instantly saw why. Water was no longer being churned up. The tanker had stopped her engine. *Forward Venture*'s skipper, evidently not quite so heedless as Rich had been willing to believe, must have ordered engines stopped just before contact.

A quick evaluation. No visible dents or even scratches on *Eel*'s smooth rounded side. With the tanker propeller stopped as the two vessels ground past each other, it was even possible that momentary contact with the propeller had merely rotated it slightly to where the blades cleared. At worst, a single blade might be bent near the tip, and there might be a dent in the corresponding part of the *Eel*'s underwater surface. The only visible damage was on the submarine's bridge, where the side plating had been smashed in and the TBT cavity crushed out of recognizable shape.

"Good thing he hit us on the bulletproof steel bulwark," said Buck, grimacing. "That's pretty strong stuff. With the tug pulling, that bump pushed us out of the way. I don't believe we hit at all, down below, so there's really no damage."

"That's what I think, too. This whole bridge is going to be ripped off in Hunter's Point when the snorkel is put in, you know. So, far as Brazil's concerned, there's no damage at all. Looks like old *Eel*'s luck is still good." The unalloyed relief in Keith's voice matched Buck's. Richardson also felt it. It would of course be necessary to alert the Navy yard people to check for underwater scrapes and dents, but the danger of crippling damage had passed.

Behind them, to port, a great froth of water continued to boil up along both sides of the tug. It had swung around so that the full power of its engine at Emergency Astern was pulling *Eel* away from the tanker. The tug's bow was high, unnaturally so. Its stern squatted under the pull of its big tugboat propeller and the strain of the

towing lines. *Eel* was moving sideways in a fairly satisfactory manner—and the tug's diesels would need an
overhaul when it got back to Mare Island. Now, the
crisis past, Rich could see the tug skipper fumble with
his engine annunciator. A moment later the wash from
astern subsided. The man made a show of mopping his
face, then picked up a megaphone near his feet.

"Any damage over there?" he yelled. "You look okay
—any injuries?"

"We're all right!" Richardson yelled back through
his cupped hands. "He hit us up high. No damage to
the hull!" He paused. Now that the emergency was
over, another emotion was sweeping through his body.
The adrenaline which had been commanding him was
still surging through his system. He could feel the hot,
impotent rage. "You get his name?" he yelled.

"No! Too busy!"

"Well, I did! I'll file the report! That incompentent
bastard ought to have his license lifted!" Rich could
feel his hands trembling against his cheeks. Pilot or
skipper, whoever had been conning the loaded tanker,
should not get away scot-free. He should have known
that his deeply laden ship could not have turned inside
the approaching tug and tow, that the rules of the road
required him, as the privileged vessel in a crossing situation, to hold his course and speed!

The tugmaster waved his megaphone in acknowledgment. Two men appeared on his forecastle and another
pair aft to handle his lines as he began to maneuver
back to his original position on *Eel*'s port quarter.

"He sure belongs to the Don't Worry Club," said
Buck after a moment. "Me, I'm mad as hell at that
tanker. What in the devil was that son of a bitch over
there thinking of? Who taught him to handle a ship?"

"He was a fool, that's for sure," said Keith. "Maybe
we looked farther away than we were because we're so

small compared to him. That's no excuse, though, even if he didn't have a radar."

"He had a radar, all right," Buck said. "I saw it turning on top of his bridge."

"At least he reversed his rudder in time," said Rich, the fury still strong in him. Then he added, "Good thing he had the sense to stop his engine, too, when he saw we were going to hit aft." He could feel the anger leveling out, the hot blood cooling into more professional indignation.

"I'll bet he was thinking more of bent blades than the damage the spinning propeller might do to us," said Buck, angrily. "Besides that, some of us could have been hurt. You were right alongside the periscope shears. You could have been squashed between them and the overhang of that big tub of his."

The thought of personal danger seemed suddenly calming. The determination to make an official report of the incident was still fixed—it was his duty in any event, and the Brazilian Navy would no doubt want to know. So would the commander of the shipyard at Hunter's Point, who would have to allocate funds for whatever repairs were thereby necessitated.

Rich realized he was hungry too, as he heard Keith say, "Me, I'm all at once hungry. Do you think we might drop below and have one last meal in our old wardroom? Things look pretty clear now."

The prospect of leaving *Eel*'s bridge unwatched went against the grain, but a short shouted conversation with the tugmaster from the main deck abreast his pilothouse took care of the matter. His instructions punctuated by massive bites from the spread of sandwiches before him on top of the binnacle, the warrant boatswain sent one of his crew members over to the submarine, where he could relay immediate information below by telephone. Once this was arranged, the operation of the ship's phones explained, Rich climbed down the familiar ladders into the control room, ducked through a watertight doorway and joined the others.

Keith and Buck had arranged lanterns in the corners of the tiny wardroom—strange how small it looked—and they had spread a white tablecloth on the green linoleum of the tabletop. The cloth had seen better days. It was yellow around the edges and along its prominent creases. "Where did you find this?" asked Richardson, surprised.

"We were wondering if it was still here," said Keith. "Remember our last meal aboard, back in '45? There weren't many of us left, then, just a couple of the chiefs and two other sailors, plus Woodrow and the three of us. So all of us were around this table for that last breakfast. The lights were already out, too, just like now, and we had to use the battle lanterns. Anyway, after it was over we cleaned up, and I folded the tablecloth and stuck it in a drawer under my desk. That's where I found it, right where I left it."

Keith's words loosed a compartment in Richardson's mind. Some locked door, as yet only imperfectly opened, suddenly flung itself wide. A naval career always involved leaving behind old friends, and old ships, and moving on to new ones. Knowing the day was coming when it would be necessary to turn the key on the ship and crew which had meant so much to him, knowing that things could never be the same anyway, he had nerved himself to go through the ritual. If he had been the only one to consider, he would simply have gone away. But there had been a decommissioning ceremony, a required inspection in company with the reserve force commander who was about to add *Eel* to the list of ships of which he was nominally commanding officer. There was completion of the machinery history and the deficiency list, and a hundred other items invented by Navy bureaucracy for the better administration of its ships. All were now unnecessary, outmoded, no longer relevant. They were required because some regulation, or some senior officer, somewhere, said so. But few were actually of any earthly significance in the particular circumstance of the postwar decommissioning and mothballing of the *Eel*. The last thing of all was the official terminal entry in the log, which he had made himself.

He had submerged himself in these details, railed at them because they could not be avoided, spent his time accomplishing them because some amorphous, unidentifiable authority, unnamed, unknown and probably nonexistent behind the myriad façade of Fleet Orders, Force Instructions, Navy Department Orders, Bureau of Naval Personnel Letters and rules and regulations of every conceivable kind, simply prescribed them. Now he realized he had secretly been glad they existed.

The reality, he had frequently reminded himself—it had been something like a placebo for his mixed-up feelings—was in that quonset hut in another part of the Mare Island Navy Yard, where he had brought Laura. Where, like a hundred other wives in like circumstances, she was struggling to create a home inside the curved walls and rudimentary facilities which were all the Navy could provide for seagoing personnel. He would never have believed, then, what he knew now, that even Laura's gentle ministrations had not been adequate to assuage his depression, that he had welcomed the mountain of meaningless detail because it gave a sense of accomplishing something for the *Eel* (inanimate steel that she was) and her steadily decreasing crew. It was almost as though the Navy understood that wartime skippers of small, tightly knit ships like submarines or destroyers might need something to keep them from going mad during the enforced dissolution, and had deliberately provided it.

Buck Williams' voice cut through, started a new train of thought. "We sure used to spend a lot of time thinking up big schemes in this little place. Remember the rockets we took on our third patrol, and how we finally used them on the emperor's palace?"

"Getting there was really something," chimed in Keith. "Those rockets had just one range, you know, and we couldn't train the launcher, either. So we had to get to the exact spot we picked, and lie to there with the boat exactly stern-on to the palace. That's when I earned my navigator's merit badge. If old Doherty hadn't been helping me we'd never have made it."

"That was just one of the good jobs you did for us, Keith," said Richardson. "More power to Doherty, too. He was a sharp navigating quartermaster. Wonder what he's doing now—but it was really you, you know. Remember how you found our carrier? The ultra message was wrong, and you were the one to realize it. If you hadn't made me change position at the last minute we'd not have found him."

"Sure, Skipper," said Buck, "and if you hadn't got the damned torpedoes squared away earlier she'd never have sunk, either. We only had four fish left, remember."

"Admiral Small gets the credit for the torpedoes in my book," said Rich. "He's the man who fought that fight all the way to the top. Joe Blunt was his honcho for the experiments, and I was lucky to be around with my bum leg after the *Walrus*. That was right before the *Eel* showed up needing a new skipper."

"And crew, too," said Keith. "That was some training period you put us through. After that, there wasn't anything we couldn't do. I guess chasing that convoy out of Tsingtao was the toughest thing, ending up in the fight with the *Mikura* tincan. But getting those Chinese coast watchers right out from under the Japanese Army on our next run was no picnic either. I'm still envious of Buck, too, for having the most fun of all, going ashore to blow up that train in the tunnel."

"The British did the same thing in World War One," said Buck. "Do you still have that book of yours, Skipper? We all read it for ideas. That Sea of Marmara submarine business of theirs was wild, the way they went through nets and minefields with those old simple boats. They didn't have any of the special stuff we had for our Tsushima caper."

The conversation was animated, each bringing up his own memory nuggets, each reliving the exciting days, hardly waiting for the preceding episode to be savored before claiming attention for his own latest recollection. They had, as a matter of course, ranged themselves in their habitual places in the wardroom. Richardson could almost imagine all of them turned back in time, himself included. All were fifteen years older: Keith and Buck designated to command new submarines the like of which had not even been dreamed of when last they had sat here; himself, now nearly as old as Joe Blunt had been, named to be their squadron commander. Yet, in Richardson's eyes, all looked the same. Buck's hairline had receded a trifle, lines had become permanently etched around his mouth and eyes, and he was a little heavier, though still the wiry, humorous activist. Keith looked precisely as before. His shock of brown hair was as full as ever, the wide-spaced light gray eyes looking as directly and sincerely as always from a still youthful, though more mature and self-confident, face. If anything, he was even more trim than before. Only his capable hands and stubby fingers, slightly more wrinkled, betrayed that he must be nearing forty years of age.

Richardson himself looked no different in his own eyes, certainly felt no different, although he had had to make the usual adjustment to growing astigmatism: glasses for reading in artificial light. His two juniors would have testified that the intervening years sat lightly on him, forgetting that the change in their own perspectives worked both ways. The sandy hair was farther back over the temples, the nose with that strange crease in it was slightly heavier, the skin under his chin a little more lined, looser. He, too, had kept his weight, although (his own confession) it had been a battle because of Laura's good cooking.

The lunch, despite coming out of boxes, was excellent. All three were ravenous, ate swiftly. There was a tacit understanding that they could not stay too long below. Besides, San Francisco Bay had too much of interest.

"I wonder what Furakawa is doing now," said Keith, pouring himself a second cup of coffee from the thermos jug. "He was one of those dedicated naval officers. Samurai, I'll bet. Actually I rather got to like him, even though I was certainly afraid of him for a while."

"Yancy said none of them would have lasted another day in the water," said Richardson. "They were in a pretty bad way at first. But I agree with you. After he got back on his feet, he was a menace until the surrender."

"Lining them all up outside the wardroom, in the passageway, to hear the surrender broadcast was a stroke of genius," said Buck. "Remember the look on their faces? I'm sure it was old Hirohito himself, because they all bowed down to our radio. That was the day we realized for sure they were planning something really desperate. Old Furakawa had the oddest expression when we paraded him through the boat and showed him the stuff we had laid out to clobber his people with."

"That was after his personal surrender, wasn't it, Skipper? Didn't he personally tell you the war was over so far as he was concerned? But I can recall being petrified when you let him come into your room alone. What if he'd tried to attack you right then?" Keith frowned at the memory.

"Well, I was ready for him, and we knew he had no weapons," said Rich. "Besides, he was a man of honor, and I figured he'd keep his word. If it had been Moonface, now, from our second run, you can bet I'd have been a lot less accessible. I'd like to see Furakawa again, too. Someday he may be running the new Japanese Navy. He was an honest, dedicated man, as you said, and an enemy to be respected, even while he was a prisoner. I learned a lot about his country from him while we were waiting to get out of the Sea of Japan." He glanced at his watch, lifted his cup for the last gulp of coffee.

The others were torn between the desire to preserve a delicious nostalgic moment and the need they all felt to go on deck again. Twenty minutes below, now exceeded, was long enough for almost anything to happen. But Buck tried to hold the magic an instant longer. "Speaking of Moonface," he said, "makes me think of poor old Commodore Blunt. What a shame no one realized how sick he really was. He should have been in a hospital instead of being sent to sea as our wolf-pack commander. I don't suppose any hospital could have helped his brain tumor, but if you hadn't had Yancy put him out that day . . ." he stopped uneasily. Something, a shadow intensified by the dim light, had crossed Richardson's face. Keith's smile had changed

to a thundercloud. He should have remembered that
Jobie Richardson's real name was Joseph B., and that
the middle initial stood for "Blunt." "Sorry, Skipper,"
he muttered, thoroughly abashed. "That was dumb of
me. I know how much you thought of him."

Richardson was looking at his watch again, rising
from the table, his countenance expressionless. "That's
okay, Buck," he said. "Joe Blunt was my first submarine
skipper, and I wish none of that had happened, that's
all. But I think we'd better go back topside. Seeing San
Francisco Bay like this is too good to pass up." He
strode purposefully into the passageway, did not hear
Keith's savage, low-voiced comment to Williams as they
busied themselves with the cleanup Richardson had
forgotten.

"What in God's name made you bring that up, Buck?
Both of us know it was about the only thing we could
do, but I bet he's been killing himself over that ever
since. We never made any official report about giving
Blunt that mickey, you know, and haven't you heard
some of the weird stories on the wives' circuit?"

"No. What stories?"

"Peggy says the rumor is he didn't die of a brain
tumor at all!"

"What did he die of, then? That's what the doctors
found when we brought him back!"

"That's what they *said* they found, Buck. Some folks
will see dirt anywhere. You know that!"

"Like what, for Christ's sake!"

"Like maybe someone did him in, if you want it
cold turkey! We were pretty desperate during that
depth charging, remember. He damn near got us sunk!
Rich saved us. No one else could have. The whole
crew knew it. The way we all felt after that, maybe
someone could . . ."

"That's crazy, Keith!"

"You know that. We all know that didn't happen. But don't forget, we were in damn bad shape. The idea must have crossed quite a few minds, about then. A lot of rumors get started that way. After the fact. And when did the truth ever stop one? It's been fifteen years, and Peggy said some gal whispered it to her a while ago. I just hope it never gets back to Rich or Laura!"

"Do you think there's a chance of that?"

"How should I know? I just know nobody better say anything like that around me. But I thought you must not have heard it."

"Thanks, Keith," said Williams somberly, as the two friends reached the watertight door leading to the control room. "Depend on me to keep my smarts from now on. This is plain sick—" They ducked through the door.

Richardson was standing there, one hand on the ladder leading to the conning tower, much as he had been accustomed to in times past. "I thought you might have gone up ahead of me," he said. "I just took a quick turn through the after compartments. The dehumidification machinery did a pretty good job. She looks clean and neat, just the way we left her. I didn't see any rust or moisture stains."

"We'll probably have one last tour through with the Brazilians, won't we?" said Keith. "Isn't that what ComSubPac wants?"

"No doubt, but this is our last look while she's still ours." Rich stopped. "You know," he said after a moment, "I don't know what I expected to find, or feel. It was good to sit in the wardroom and talk, and think about things that used to go on. For a minute it almost felt like those old days. But it isn't the same to stand here and look at all this cold equipment. Even when we walked off the last time, back then, it didn't feel like this. Up to now, I've always thought of this control room as being full of people, with plenty of room for all of them to do their jobs. Now, I can't see where we put them all. It's exactly the same place, and yet it isn't. And I don't think it ever will be again. It's the same with the galley and crew's mess hall, the whole after battery, and the engineroom. She's a dead ship, and you can feel it."

Keith and Buck nodded their understanding. Much the same thought had occurred to them as well. It was not something one could lay one's hands on. The old atmosphere was gone. Their attempt to revive it in the wardroom had succeeded only for the instant, had collapsed because there was no way it could be perpetuated.

Richardson broke the silence. "Maybe this is why Admiral Brighting sent all three of us for this job that any one of us could have done. Matter of fact, anybody at all could have done it. I'm sure the Brazilians won't really care very much who presents the ship to them, and I'll bet ComSubPac doesn't care either, just so it's done right. That's why we're down as volunteers, so they couldn't turn us down. This is Brighting's way of showing us that you can't live in the past." He swung up the ladder, disappeared. Keith found Buck staring at him, unblinkingly.

Topside, a brilliant sun bounced countless glitters from the tall shafts of San Francisco's skyline, accentuated because many of them stood on hills already high above sea level. To the right, high enough for the tallest ship to pass beneath, gleaming red above the infinite western sea, a great bridge leaped from promontory bluff to promontory bluff. The swooping curve of its suspension cables, the delicate traceries of wires supporting the roadbed, the complex steel structure of the span itself, all resembled an extraordinarily well-ordered spider's weaving. The Golden Gate Bridge.

This was the Mecca of the war years, that one thing, above all others, which symbolized coming home again. Violently opposed before its building by claims it would disfigure one of nature's masterpieces, when complete this bridge over the spectacular entrance to San Francisco Bay came to epitomize the meaning of the land. Men had died to build it. Novels had been composed around it. Movies had been made of it. Daredevils had dived from it, and some had lived to tell of their feat. Suicides had jumped from it. Ships had collided under it, or with its concrete piers. Songs had been written expressing the yearning for which it stood. It was the gateway to adventure and the all-embracing arms of the motherland welcoming home the traveler, at one and the same time.

To the left, the silvery suspensions of two more great bridges, end to end, spanned the bay from San Francisco to the mound of Yerba Buena Island with its flat, man-made beaver's tail, Treasure Island. A tremendous truss-and-cantilever structure, tailing off to a long curved causeway, spanned the distance from Yerba Buena to Oakland, on the east side of the bay. Silent for long minutes, the three naval officers stood absorbed in the grandeur and the beauty, each feeling a stirring of the spirit within himself.

The tug, phlegmatically puffing along, was aiming to pass to the left of the tremendous block of concrete which joined the two Bay Bridge suspensions. Rich, Keith and Buck inspected them with interest through their binoculars as they drew nearer. Autos were crossing on two different levels, those traveling toward San Francisco on the upper level, those going to Oakland on the lower. The ceaseless movement of multicolored machines was steady, regular, as though they were connected by some invisible linkage. It wasn't so, of course, for each car was driven by a different set of compulsions. But from the distant perspective of the water surface far below, the only impression that could exist was that of order, not the hurly-burly of highway traffic that must be there.

Not all was motor cars and traffic, however. There were workmen on scaffolds, painters carrying out the ceaseless maintenance the tremendous structure required. There was something else, too, and the three pairs of binoculars on *Eel*'s damaged bridge focused almost simultaneously on it. "Something's wrong over there," said Keith.

There were red lights flashing, a crowd gathered along the bridge rail on the lower level. At least half of them were in blue uniforms. Police. As the submariners watched, the blue uniforms gathered together, wedged what were evidently onlookers away from their focal point of interest. Then Richardson saw it.

"There's a man down there," he said. "He's sitting out on the edge. Just sitting there. It looks like the police are after him, but they can't reach him without going out there too."

"It's a suicide," said Keith.

"The cops are getting a man out over the rail with a rope around his waist," said Buck, "but it's pretty far, and they're moving slowly. They're afraid he'll go ahead and jump if they get too close too fast."

"We're heading to pass about underneath him," mused Richardson half to himself. "If he jumps at the wrong time he might land on deck. That wouldn't be very pretty to see." Irresolutely, he lowered his binoculars, looked at his companions, put them back up again. "I suppose we ought to stand by to help the police pick him up if he does do it," he said. Still no answer from Keith or Buck. The submarine and tug drew nearer to the span. So far as anyone on *Eel*'s bridge could tell, the tug skipper, still steering his craft himself, was paying no attention to the drama taking place high above him.

"At least, we ought to alert the tug to what's going on," said Keith. "He'll probably alter course to pass under the other span, well clear of where the man might hit the water."

"If I were going to jump off the bridge, I'd want us to get out of the way too," said Buck. "Landing on a steel hull with hard-looking things like hatches and girders wouldn't be quite as clean a way to go as dropping into the bay. I guess the cops hope he'll wait until we're clear. The extra time might be just what they need to reach him, or talk him out of it, or something."

"That's it!" said Rich, impulsively snapping his fingers. "Buck, you get down on deck to relay word to the tug! Tell the skipper to put us right under that fellow up there. I'll help him conn from here and pass any changes to him via Keith and you." Startled, both younger officers glanced away from their binoculars, still holding the glasses up as before, stared at Richardson. Buck recovered first.

"I've got it! Great! This may give them some time!" He swung himself through the bridge railing, climbed down to the main deck, ran aft. In a moment he could be seen talking earnestly through cupped hands to the tugmaster, who had placed his megaphone to his ear the better to hear over the noise of his diesels. Buck ran back alongside the submarine bridge. "He says okay, he'll do it. But he can't see straight up out of his pilot-house, so he'll need you to tell him which way to go. Also, maneuvering sideways will be tricky with the current through here, so try to anticipate your orders as much as you can."

"Tell him to put a line on his best swimmer and be ready to send him after the man if he does jump into the water!"

"Roger, Skipper!" Buck ran back to his station.

The welcoming committee at the San Francisco Naval Shipyard, Hunter's Point, was within minutes of becoming vocally impatient when *Eel* and her tug finally appeared off the designated berth. There were some quizzical looks cast at her smashed bridge bulwark and the new scratches in the weathered gray paint as the tug brought her in starboard side to the pier. The ComSub-Pac representative on the scene was nevertheless able to report by telephone to the Twelfth Naval District Commandant, and by official letter to the Submarine Force Commander in Pearl Harbor, that the aristocratic Brazilian naval officers had been well impressed with the condition of their newest acquisition. They had felt particularly honored, he said over the telephone, that her wartime commanding officer and two others of her wartime complement, albeit in civilian clothes, had been on board to assist in the arrival inspection. And they deeply regretted that the unexpected lateness of the hour had made it impossible for Capitao-de-Mar-e-Guerra Richardson, Capitao-de-Fragata Leone and Capitao-de-Fragata Williams to attend the reception they had arranged in honor of the transfer of the *submarino Eel* to their Navy.

Richardson, Leone and Williams were in the landing pattern at Idlewild International Airport as the morning editions of the *San Francisco Examiner* and *Chronicle* came off the presses. They never saw the little articles on the third and eighth pages, respectively, of the two newspapers, detailing that rescue of a would-be suicide from one of the main spans of the Bay Bridge had been possible because of the curiosity of a tug and decommissioned submarine which had stopped to rubberneck directly beneath her. The woman, who gave her name as Mrs. Susie Glotz of upper Geary Street, said she had prepared for the attempt by dressing in trousers and a jacket belonging to her estranged husband, but had lost her nerve for fear she would be horribly mangled upon striking the ships beneath. While she was thus delayed, a minister who happened upon the scene was able to dissuade her from her purpose, and police took her into protective custody.

The *Chronicle* also carried a short editorial in the same issue, decrying the morbid curiosity of those who would go out of their way to see someone commit suicide. It noted that in this instance at least, as a sort of poetic justice, the lugubrious onlookers below had unknowingly prevented the very tragedy they had stopped to watch.

ww

"No one's ever figured out Admiral Brighting, Peggy. You're wasting your time." Laura had not intended to speak sharply, instantly realized her impatience with Peggy Leone's growing obsession had shown in her voice. She tried to smooth over the momentary awkwardness. "Now that our husbands are nukes, I guess Brighting is just someone we'll have to learn to live with. Rich says he's a totally dedicated individual, one of those people who put their whole personality into what they're doing."

"Keith says the same thing." Peggy raised her cup to her lips, thoughtfully sipped the hot light brown liquid, looked appraisingly at Laura. "He told me some of the things that went on out in Idaho, though, and I'm surprised you can defend him after the way he treated your husband."

"Maybe Keith took more offense than Rich did. He's one of Rich's best friends, ever since the war. Anyway, the big thing was to be nuked, as they say. They all got that, and they think the training was great. I'm like you, though, I'm glad it's over and finished." Laura consciously kept her voice light. Peggy's single-minded concentration on finding fault with the Navy was becoming vaguely unsettling. She changed the subject. "When does Keith get in with the *Cushing?* Have you gotten any letters from Cape Canaveral?"

"He's been so busy with those ship qualification tests he's only written a couple of times. They'll be back next week. I thought you would know that."

Again there was something accusatory in Peggy's comment, some fine edge of feeling not yet out in the open. The warm midmorning sun streamed through the kitchen windows, dappled the floor with the pattern of lace curtains. Peggy was a small, intense, very pretty woman, apparently immune to the large quantities of sweets she habitually consumed. Her increasingly frequent arrivals at Laura's door were always preceded by a polite phone call citing an errand bringing her across the Thames River to New London, and initially Laura welcomed the resulting morning coffee break. Lately, however, she had begun to realize that the growing regularity of Peggy's visits must be more than mere happenstance. "I guess I did know it," she carefully replied. "Rich says Keith's got his crew very well checked out. The *Cushing's* flying through her tests and he doesn't think there'll be any holdups. But it is a pretty strenuous time for them. It ought to be easier—more regular, anyway—when they finally start going on patrol."

"I don't think I'll like it any better, to tell the truth. The missile boats stay away so long. . . ."

"Sure, Peggy, but they have two crews, don't forget. Two skippers and all. Except for the turnover period, either you or Nancy Dulany will have your husband at home. He won't even have the ship around to worry about. You're luckier than Cindy Williams. The *Manta* doesn't have two crews. Buck's the only skipper she's got. Even in port, there's no relief for him."

"Somebody was figuring out that because of the slow training program for replacements, a missile boat sailor would have to stay continuously on sea duty for thirteen years. That's Admiral Brighting's fault."

"There's always somebody talking that way at the beginning of anything that's new and big," said Laura. "It's only last year the *George Washington* went to sea for the first time. You can't . . ." The conversation was right back in its old track. Peggy was not looking at her, was staring out the window instead. Laura felt rising resentment at the U.S. Navy for putting her in the position of having to defend it, then realized it was exasperation with her visitor. She fought down the ire, made her voice gentle. "Come on, Peggy," she finally said, "with two crews, the blue crew and the gold crew, Keith's going to be home half the time, maybe more, counting overhauls and such. Besides, he's barely begun with the *Cushing*. It hasn't been too bad yet, has it? How was it with his previous boat?"

"Just the same," said Peggy. "He was married to it, too."

"Well, you're not blaming Brighting for that, are you? Anyway, how long was he skipper of it?"

"About two years. That's when the baby was born. Even then, I hardly saw him."

"Has he had any shore duty since you've been married?"

"Yes, sure. He was in the Pentagon just before he got the *Dogfish*. It was nearly as bad. Sometimes he stayed nearly all night there. It's just not fair!"

"What's not fair, Peggy?" Despite Laura's resolve, she sensed asperity creeping back into her voice, had to make an effort to will it out.

"The Navy. The way it treats people. Especially the ones like Keith who didn't go to Annapolis!"

"That's not true, Peggy. The Navy isn't that way at all. Keith's been treated exactly the same as everyone else."

"Then why does he always get these tough jobs?"

"He doesn't. At least, they're not only tough jobs. They're also very good jobs. Keith's reputation is tops in the Navy. Look at the *Cushing*. She's the newest and the best of the big new missile subs. Don't you think every submarine skipper around would like to take Keith's place? Or Bud Dulany's in the other crew? Why do you think Keith was picked?"

No answer from Peggy. Again she was staring into the distance. Laura had the feeling that nothing she was saying, or could say, would change Peggy's determination to find fault with her situation.

Proteus, a floating machine shop built during the war to tend diesel submarines, had been modified by the addition of facilities for the servicing of nuclear submarines and Polaris missiles. She was, by consequence, some forty-five feet longer than her sisters, but the extra length was indistinguishable except for the huge pair of gantry cranes that surmounted it. What was noticeable about the ship was that she looked more like an ocean liner than a warship. She had two promenade decks from bow to stern, two large smokestacks for appearance only (since she, too, was diesel-propelled) and she had many portholes along her sides. Only the anti-aircraft guns, still mounted, though seldom exercised, her coat of navy "war color" gray paint, and the cranes—far heavier than any liner would need —testified to her military purpose. That, and the fact that she seldom moved from her berth alongside a pier on the New London side of the Thames River. No ocean liner in service to an active shipping company would have been allowed to remain so immobile.

But *Proteus* was actively carrying out her primary function, although her propellers hardly ever turned, for there was always at least one and sometimes as many as four submarines alongside. The whaleback hulls, dull black in color, lay very low in the water. Only a tenth of their structure showed above the surface, and were it not for a prominent protuberance amidships vaguely resembling a sail, their presence would be easy to overlook.

Not that the residents of New London and Groton were likely to overlook anything. The easiest way to keep aware of what submarines were alongside the *Proteus* was to look southward over the rail of the high arched bridge across the Thames River as one drove eastward from New London to Groton. To the initiated, the white block numbers painted on the respective sails translated automatically to an intimate communication of the myriad of details beneath.

To be sure, the submarine nearest the bridge obscured the numbers of those between her and the tender. But such details presented little difficulty to residents of the area, who had long since become nearly as adept as any members of the U.S. Navy at checking out the submarines alongside the *Proteus*.

Rich's office, as Commander Submarine Squadron Ten, or ComSubRon Ten, was at the forward end of the topmost "promenade deck" of *Proteus,* with large circular ports opening out upon the forecastle which lay two decks below. There was a watertight door to the side, backed up by a light wooden screen door, giving access to a verandalike extension of the covered promenade. Aft of his main room Rich had a private bedroom with a standard civilian-type metal bed bolted to the floor, and a private bathroom. The suite had a twin, on the other side of the ship's centerline and easily accessible through a door, assigned to her skipper. Over the years it had become customary for the captain and commodore to mess together in the captain's sitting room, thus leaving the squadron commander's sitting room available for discussions and conferences. It was an arrangement dictated by necessity, for these seemed always to be going on.

There was a desk flush against the slightly curved forward bulkhead of the space, upon which rested a standard dial telephone, supposedly plugged into a special dock connection when the ship moored. It had been so long since *Proteus* had moved from her accustomed berth, however, that, for all Rich knew, the wiring might have been run directly to the nearest telephone pole. Attached to the bulkhead were the standard ship's telephone, a gyrocompass repeater, a voice tube with swing cap leading to the bridge and, prominently centered, a bows-on photograph of *Proteus* with ten tired diesel submarines alongside. The caption read, "Tokyo Bay, 1945."

Richardson had swiveled around to face Keith Leone, who was slouched in an armchair.

"You must really have pushed your gang on the *Cushing,* Keith. All the tests down at Canaveral were perfect, and you got away three days early. Now what can we do for you up here?"

"The usual, I guess, Commodore. Get us ready for the next drill. My crew is tired, though, and I am too, after the pressure they put us to down there. We'll be glad to turn the ship over to Bud Dulany and the gold crew next week." In what was an unaccustomed gesture for him, Keith passed his hand wearily across his face.

"After that welcoming committee I saw on the dock

yesterday I thought maybe you'd been gone on a regular deployment, instead of only a month." Richardson grinned.

Keith grinned back. "It was the longest we've been away yet, so I guess the families were pretty glad to see us. How did you get the word to them all that we were coming in early? I don't think there was a single individual on board who didn't have at least someone waiting on the dock for him. Having the gold crew set up the security watch so we could all get ashore was a great idea, too. Who thought of that?"

"They did, so far as I know," said Richardson. "Are you on holiday routine today?"

"Yes, we sure are. Till noon, that is. We couldn't pass up a chance like that."

"Well, I'll not keep you long, Keith. You deserve some time off too. My apologies to Peggy and little Ruthie for asking you to come over this morning at all."

"What's up?"

"We've got to lay a special mission on you. If you want it, that is."

"On me? You mean on the *Cushing?*"

"Right. Washington has delayed *Cushing's* deployment. They want you to do something else first."

"But it won't be us, you know. The gold crew takes over Monday. Bud Dulany's the one." There was disappointment in Leone's voice.

"That's why I had to send for you, old man. The powers-that-be down there must have been impressed with what they were hearing from the missile-testing range. They want you and the blue crew for this one."

"Gee, that's great, Rich—I mean, Commodore! But won't that mess up all the Polaris scheduling? I mean, I thought that was supposed to be inviolate!" Keith's tiredness seemed to have disappeared. His posture was now animated.

"That's not our worry, Keith." Richardson felt himself reacting to his friend's enthusiasm. "If the Joint Chiefs tell the Navy, and the Navy tells Special Projects, and Special Projects calls ComSubLant, and his operations officer calls me, we can assume that's already been covered. The big question now is if you can do it." Richardson rose, swiftly shut the door between his room and the dining area. He started back to his chair, reversed himself, closed the door to his bedroom also. "Keith," he said, "it's a top-secret mission. There may be danger—in fact, we know there will be. You don't have to take it on. If for any reason you'd rather not, you can say so and that will be the end of it. They'll send another submarine, one that's already got a patrol or two under its belt, as soon as they can fit her with an ice suit. The reason they picked you first is that you're not yet deployed. Your operational routine will suffer less. The record you turned in at Cape Canaveral with your firing tests and the other readiness inspections is what convinced them. But there'll be no prejudice against you or the *Cushing* if you feel you should decline."

"We'll not decline anything," said Keith. "What is it? Is it something only a missile submarine can do? Tell me more."

"All I personally know is in this folder. It was sent by messenger from Washington a week ago, but I thought I'd hold it until you'd been in overnight. No need to spoil your first night in port." As he was speaking, Richardson took a large, already opened manila envelope from the top drawer of his desk, held it in his hand. "You'll want to study this privately, in your own stateroom in *Cushing*, Keith. Come back before you talk to anyone about it. You'll have a lot of questions. I've already read it three times. Don't let it out of your possession."

"What is it?" Keith asked again. He restrained his eagerness to reach for the envelope. Richardson had not yet handed it to him, obviously wanted to say more.

"It's an under-ice mission. Being the newest missile sub, *Cushing* is better off than the others in under-ice capability, and that's another reason Washington picked you. Basically, they want you to make a test deployment in the Arctic Ocean. The mission is to see if it's feasible to fire missiles through the ice. If we can do it, the whole capability of the missile system will be radically improved." Rich could recognize the look on Keith's face. He had seen that contemplative evaluation many times before.

"I guess we've all done some reading about the Arctic lately," said Keith. "Probably it is possible in some areas up there at least part of the year, when the ice cover is less." He spoke slowly, his brow creased in concentration.

Rich said, "You'll see in this set of papers that what we're looking for is a year-round capability. In other words, a certainty. That's another reason for sending you right now. We're about to come out of winter into spring here in Connecticut, but the ice is thicker now in the Arctic Ocean than at any other time of the year."

"Do they expect us to shoot missiles up anywhere, no matter how thick the ice is? There's no way! They're pretty impressive coming out of the water, all right, but the launching system has nowhere near enough power to break through heavy ice cover. If there are enough polynyas maybe we can always stay near one. In winter most of those are also pretty heavily iced, though."

"Well, read the operations proposal. They've thought of that, and they have a couple of things they want you to try." Richardson thrust the envelope toward Keith.

To reach his ship, Keith had to climb down three decks and walk through *Proteus'* big machine shop to the cargo door in her side, through which a portable walkway, a brow, had been laid over to the *Cushing*. To his surprise, there was another submarine outboard, much smaller, lacking the raised deck over the sixteen missile tubes which were *Cushing's* total reason for existence. She must have come in during the night or early morning. The number on her sail was a familiar one: Buck Williams' boat, the *Manta*. Keith felt warmed by the thought of the proximity of his friend. Before he left for home he must see him. His own gangway watch was saluting, but he was a stranger. One of the gold crew. There was a second brow directly opposite, leading to *Manta's* much narrower deck, and a second gangway watch was visible standing nearby.

Manta and *Cushing* were totally dissimilar in design, save for the nuclear power plant, and already *Manta* was outmoded by the more powerful whale-bodied *Skipjack* class now coming into service. Buck would probably have the *Manta* for only a couple of years and then, in his own turn, shift over to one of the much faster *Skipjacks* or *Threshers,* or even directly to one of the new ballistic missile ships like the *Cushing*. Keith toyed with the idea of going on over the second brow and surprising Buck down below. No doubt he had long since finished breakfast, but he might catch him drinking a second cup of coffee while going over some of the never ending paperwork.

But that would have to wait. The large, slit-open envelope in his hand—from the feel of it there might be anywhere up to two dozen sheets in it, lying flat, plus some pamphlets—had a magnetism he had felt before. Keith returned the salute of the watch. "Is Captain Dulany aboard?" he asked, to ascertain in advance whether his stateroom was free down below.

"Nosir. There's just us standby gold crew here, sir. Lieutenant Ridgely has the watch. He's down below. I didn't see you coming, so he don't know you're here, sir." Good. He would make himself known to Ridgely of the gold crew, then lock himself in his room. By noon the changeover back to the blue crew would be complete and *Cushing* entirely his once more. Bud Dulany, knowing that the presence of another skipper must halt all productive activity on Keith's part, would probably not appear at all.

The ladder leading below was inside a vertical tube, with a watertight hatch at each end. Its inner surface was lined with shiny sheet metal, stainless steel (officially, corrosion-resisting steel, or CRS, in building-yard jargon), and its diameter was such that a person could ascend or descend the ladder with his back sliding against the slick smooth surface, thus with his hands free. Negotiating the twelve-foot distance to the linoleum-covered deck below was second nature. Keith stepped swiftly through the maze of instruments in the control room, allayed Ridgely's embarrassment at not having been topside to greet him, and retreated with a cup of coffee into the sanctuary of his own tiny stateroom. There was an aluminum door as well as the traditional green baize curtain at the entrance. He gently closed the door and locked it from the inside. Each of the thirty heavily typed sheets of bond paper in the manila envelope bore a stamped notation in large red letters: TOP SECRET. EYES ONLY. So did the two printed pamphlets.

This is not an Operation Order. Conditions are not yet clearly enough defined to permit definitive treatment. An Operation Order for conduct of this mission will be prepared later, after consultation. Whoever undertakes this mission must be prepared to improvise according to conditions and circumstances found. The purpose is to investigate the

Arctic Ocean as a potential area for SSBN strategic operations and to determine appropriate tactical and materiel adjustments as may be necessary. Safety of ship and crew is paramount, but certain potential hazards must be recognized from the rigorous environment and from possible interference by unfriendly powers.

The most favorable entry for a submarine into the Arctic Ocean basin is via the Greenland or Barents sea. Entry may also be made from Baffin Bay via Barrow Strait, or via Smith Sound and the Lincoln Sea, but neither of these routes offers assurance it may not be totally choked by layers of rafted ice. Entering through Bering Strait presents even greater difficulty because of the extremely shallow water, lack of deep channels and near certainty of heavy rafted ice. *Nautilus'* first attempt to transit the Arctic Ocean failed through inability to penetrate this barrier. Ice cover is heaviest during early spring, in both extent and thickness, and during this period it must be assumed that entry will only be possible via the Atlantic Ocean (i.e., Greenland or Barents sea). Undetected submerged entry should be possible here at any time of year.

The Arctic ice pack generally retreats north of Spitsbergen during summer, reducing in size through surface melting and wave action. Warm water from the North Atlantic Current assists in pushing it back. During winter it has on occasion been solid well south of Spitsbergen, and may extend as far as the north coast of Iceland. Iceland's south coast, however, is generally ice-free. The edge of the ice pack is always marked by block and brash ice which has broken loose from the parent floe. Occasional icebergs of much greater size may be encountered frozen into the ice cover,

and they will, of course, survive much longer in
the sea, drifting to a far more southerly latitude
in the process. . . .

Keith was surprised to find he had been reading for
most of the morning. He had covered only part of the
material when his own exec, Jim Hanson, knocked on
the door to announce lunch. Carefully, he locked the
refilled envelope in his desk and composed a plausible
story of his morning's activities. He would have to confide in his officers in due course, for there were many
preparations which must be made, but this could wait.
For the time being it was best they not even know something was brewing. Besides, he had promised Richardson. . . .

8

~~~~~~

The promises of eventual spring were freshening along the banks of the Thames River—what there could be of the signs of spring among the few forlorn plants able to exist amid the obscene ugliness placed there by man. A few buds were beginning to become evident, still wrapped tightly in their protective sheaths. There was a slightly warmer flavor to the still, cold air; for two days it had come from the south instead of the north. It was a lovely morning for late February, 1961. Richardson had just shaken hands with Keith and crossed the brow from the *Cushing* to the *Proteus*. The huge, delicately balanced crane with which the submarine tender was fitted had already been attached to the long brow bridging between her cargo port and the flat missile deck of the big submarine, and he had to duck under the wires. The brow was gone by the time the squadron commander of Submarine Squadron Ten reached the upper deck of *Proteus*.

The shorter brow between the *Cushing* and the *Manta* had already been removed. *Manta*'s own crew was at mooring stations, ready to cast off the *Cushing*'s lines and allow her to back out. Then she would wrap herself in alongside the *Proteus,* bringing in with her the submarine outboard of herself, the *Swordfish,* which had arrived a few days before. The heavy mooring wire from the *Cushing*'s bow had already been shifted to the *Manta.* High on *Proteus*' forecastle, the inboard end of the wire cable had been led to a hydraulic winch. All this was routine preparation for letting an inboard submarine out of a nest. Once the *Cushing* was clear, the *Manta*'s line-handling crew would pass their own lines around the heavy bitts built into the tender's sides and then, with bow and stern capstans, gently bring her, with *Swordfish* clinging outboard, into the *Cushing*'s place alongside the wooden float—the camel—which served as a fender to keep steel from grinding on steel. In the meantime the cable to *Manta*'s nose would be heaved in by a capstan on *Proteus*' forecastle, until *Manta* was located in precisely the desired position along the submarine tender's starboard side.

It was a carefully orchestrated maneuver, one which had been done many times over and was consequently second nature to all those involved. Richardson saw with approval that Buck Williams was on the bridge of his ship, alongside his in-port duty officer, whose responsibility it was to supervise the line handling. A few feet beyond, on *Swordfish*'s identical bridge, the same situation existed, and there were men on deck at her mooring lines standing by in the event action was needed. Down below, in both ships, there would be an engineering watch on station ready to respond to orders to the propellers, should such be necessary. The reactors of both submarines had been shut down, however, and all maneuvering would have to be done on the much lower power available from their batteries. Because nuclear submarines are underpowered on battery alone, the squadron tug was lying off, ready to assist with her big, slow diesel. A couple of times in the past some unexpected current in the river, a poorly executed maneuver in one of the submarines alongside or inexpert handling of the wire cable had caused the tug to be called into use. A gentle shove at just the right place had prevented bent propellers or other expensive damage.

But there would be nothing of this sort today. Keith and Buck, the principal actors, would make no mistakes. The state of current, tide and wind would have been thoroughly considered. Orders to the lines and to the screws (if necessary) would be timely and forehanded. Only the most unexpected of situations—a sudden line squall, a ship passing too close aboard, at too high speed—would disturb the deceptive simplicity and ease with which the complicated maneuver would be carried out. Watching, so far as Rich was concerned, was purely ceremonial, a way of saying good-bye, a private farewell.

A regular mooring line already had been led from the *Manta* across the *Cushing*'s bow to one of the bitts in the tender's side. By heaving in with her bow capstan, *Manta* had eased her stern clear, so that *Cushing*'s rounded belly would not brush against her vulnerable inboard propeller. Two sailors with coiled heaving lines appeared on *Manta*'s forecastle, two more on deck aft of her sail. Their presence was precautionary; they would probably not be needed. Rich glanced at his watch. It was precisely ten a.m., the agreed-on time for getting underway. Both Keith and Buck had grown up with Rich's method of line handling, to pass all routine orders by telephone to the various stations. Except in emergency, there would be no frantic-sounding shouts from the bridge of either ship. Evolutions would be done quietly, in virtual silence, the better to be heard if voice commands became necessary. Watching, Rich-

ardson realized that these two skippers whom he had
known so long were maneuvering their ships almost as
though an extension of himself were doing it. In effect,
they *were* extensions of himself, for he had trained
them. And there was another ingredient, in a way much
like the war days—and suddenly the old tense miasma
enveloped him in clammy vapors: a gut feeling of unspoken anxiety. The ship getting underway was going
on a special mission, into danger above and beyond
that usually associated with a submarine voyage. As in
the war years, she might, indeed, never return.

Richardson's reverie was broken by the blast of a
foghorn. One long blast: the *Cushing* was backing.
Water surged gently up from abaft her rudder, swept
forward until it lapped the rounded hull where it
emerged from the water. The remaining lines attaching
the departing submarine to the *Proteus* on her port hand
and the *Manta* on her starboard were cast loose, swiftly
hauled in: *Cushing*'s which had held her alongside
Proteus, to be quickly stowed in her deck lockers; *Manta*'s to be merely kept on deck in readiness to be put
over to the tender as soon as the missile submarine was
clear. Movement was now evident. *Cushing*'s sail was
slowly drawing aft. As it passed clear, heaving lines
were flung down from the tender to land their weighted
ends on *Manta*'s deck. At first they were merely hand-
held until danger had passed of inadvertently snagging
someone or something on the departing *Cushing*. As
soon as she was clear they were successively attached to
Manta's mooring lines and the lines dropped into the
water, so that unseen hands on board the tender could
haul them in. By the time *Cushing*'s bow had passed
from between the ships the space between *Proteus* and
Manta was already spanned by four mooring lines. Two
of them, powered by capstans on *Manta*'s bow and
stern, were slowly hauling her and her immobile sister,

Swordfish, across the intervening water preparatory to reestablishing the cobweb of lines and communications which had been broken only minutes before.

Now clear in the Thames River, *Cushing* had the problem of turning around in the relatively narrow channel. Of a later design than *Manta, Cushing* had only a single propeller, necessarily behind the rudder instead of ahead, as in the more conventional configuration. She had been able to turn slightly while backing, now lay almost exactly across the channel. Backing and filling was possible with a smaller ship, and could also be done with *Cushing*'s ponderous bulk and great length, but there was an easier solution at hand. The tug carried out its second mission of the morning by putting its heavily fendered nose against the missile submarine's bow and pushing it downstream. After a suitable interval, screw turbulence showed astern, the topside section of the *Cushing*'s rudder indicated it had gone to full left, and the sleek whale-shaped form began to gather headway.

There was a wave from the departing submarine's bridge. Richardson could not from the distance identify who this was, but it must be Keith. He waved back. Someone on the *Manta*'s bridge did the same. The tiny microcosm of the world which she and her crew constituted was now cut off, an entity all its own, a totally independent spaceship coursing toward the opening vastness, leaving behind the infrastructure that had created her and sent her forth. Save for the vital linkage of the radio, from this moment the *Cushing* and her crew were alone. The world was water, the land merely markings on a chart to be avoided as her navigators plotted the directions and distances she was to go.

Richardson stood watching until the submarine had passed Southwest Ledge lighthouse, at the mouth of the Thames River, and was lost to view. Disquietude possessed him as he finally turned to reenter his quarters. This was certainly not the first time he had watched a departing ship until she was out of sight, nor the first time he had thought of the ridiculous old nautical adage that doing so brought bad luck. Why, then, did it rest like a weight in his mind?

Buck Williams' normal combination of jocular seriousness was for once totally absent. He was seated facing Richardson in the Commodore's Office on board the *Proteus,* fingers holding the porcelain handle of a cup of black coffee in one hand, its saucer palmed in the other. There was a look of honest bewilderment on his features.

"What I can't understand," he was saying, "is the priorities. The *Manta*'s a good boat. We don't need much of a refit. I know you couldn't give us priority until the *Cushing* got underway, and even though Keith never said a word I've got a pretty good idea of why. But that was three days ago. What's holding things up now? We can easily finish our refit in the ten days we have left alongside. All we need from the tender is a little help with some of the bigger jobs. The *Proteus* can do it with her elbow."

"I know, Buck," said Richardson.

"That's what I can't understand. Yesterday the squadron engineer said he didn't know when we'd have all our work done, but then he clammed up and wouldn't talk. I was fixing to come up here anyway when you sent for me. We've never failed a commitment yet. We're all keyed up to get into that North Atlantic barrier exercise we're scheduled for. It's the first time the Iceland-Faeroe barrier will have nukes in it, and I want to show what we can do!"

Richardson was looking steadily at Buck, listening. Williams sensed he might be getting through to him, warmed to his topic. "We can make a whale of a difference," he said. "Our assignment is to be the barrier backup, sort of like a safety man on football defense. The diesel boats in the barrier will be vectoring us to find the transistors. It will be easy to find the diesel transistors—they'll have to snorkel and that's when we'll get them—but nailing the old *Seawolf* is going to be a problem, even if she is a mite noisy for these days."

"How do you propose to do it?" Richardson's eyes had not wavered. There was an expression of ineffable sorrow on his face, something behind the shadow in his eyes that could not be stated. But Buck could not be sure, was in any case so wrapped up in his schemes that the question was irresistible.

"Radio communication between barrier submarines has always been a big problem, and now that we're in it the problem will be bigger. When you're down listening below the thermal layer you can't be at periscope depth transmitting information. So you have to break off listening and come up to where you can get a transmitting antenna out of water. By the time you've gone through all the procedural business to get a message off, half the time your contact is gone when you get back down there. It isn't so bad with snorkelers, mainly because they have to move so slowly. But the *Seawolf* is as fast as we are. She's a different story altogether. Ultimately we're going to have to figure out a better way to make tactical contact reports. Maybe by releasing something through our signal ejector that floats up and broadcasts a taped message. Right now, though, we've been working on Keith's old idea."

"Keith's?"

"Sure. Don't you remember the communication procedure Keith and I worked out back during the war when you had to run that wolfpack for Commander Blunt? It cut out a lot of the excess transmission so that we could put out the important dope in a hurry. Well, before he left on this secret trip of his, Keith had some free time, and he and I dragged it out again. It's perfect for what we need, and he helped me work up a vocabulary for the BarEx. There's been a lot of changes in submarines and in communications too, since the war, but for fast passing of tactical dope between subs in a barrier . . ." Williams hesitated, stopped uneasily. The grave look on his superior's face was disquieting. "What's the matter, Rich?" he said, after a searching look.

The two sat in silence for a moment. Richardson leaned forward with a decisive motion. "Buck, I've been doing a lot of thinking in the last few days, especially since Keith shoved off. I'm worried about him, because nobody knows what he might be getting into. If he runs into any kind of trouble up there under the ice"—Buck's eyes flickered—"we've got to have a way to help."

"Under the ice, eh?" said Williams. "Keith never said, but I guessed that was it. *Cushing* will be the first missile ship up there, won't she?"

"Yes."

"Pretty rugged for a shakedown cruise."

"Yes."

"This is the worst time of year for ice, too. The greatest coverage. There won't be many potential missile launch spots, if that's what he's supposed to look for."

"That's part of it, Buck, but this is all classified stuff, so I can't talk to you about it."

But Buck Williams was not to be put off. "I know he has a special bottom mapping rig attached to his fathometer, and that new bump on his forecastle has to be a closed-circuit TV. He might even have some of these new navigational beacons to drop here and there.

The main thing, though, is whether he really could launch a missile on demand. He'll have to have some way to clear the ice overhead, maybe a vertical running torpedo, or a mine that would float up and go off on hitting the ice. . . . What do the Russians think of all this? Or do they know about it?"

Richardson's face had, for the first time, the faintest suggestion of a smile. "Damn you, Buck, you always ask too many questions. I don't know if the Russians know or not, and we can guess what they'll think. But that's not what's worrying me. Suppose Keith breaks down up there? What can we do to help him?"

"We'd have to send another submarine—Keith's not in trouble up there, is he?"

"No trouble so far as we know, Buck. But right now there's nothing another boat could do if he did break down for some reason, except surface through the ice—assuming he could, too—and pick up his people. That's why I asked you to come on up here today, and that's why I think we should send the *Swordfish* on that barrier exercise in your place."

Williams stared, wordless for once. "Now wait a minute," he finally said. "Of course I want to be ready to help Keith, if he needs it. But he isn't in trouble, and the chances are that nothing at all will happen. If something does, there's a lot of submarines you could send. You could send planes with skis to land on the ice— that would be a lot faster than going up by water anyway. What can we do that some other nuke can't do? Why scrub us from the BarEx just on the off-chance something might happen?"

"We're not scrubbing you, Buck. I was sort of hoping you'd volunteer. . . ."

"Goddammit, Commodore—Rich, dammit—stop playing games with me. There's something going on. What's it got to do with us?"

"Buck, I'm sorry. I'm asking you to take a lot on faith, and to give up something you've obviously put a lot of time and effort into already. It may all be for nothing, but if we're needed, we'll be needed badly, in a hurry. It's true that another boat could probably do the job, but, frankly, I'd rather have you, because it's Keith we're talking about."

"Can't you tell me anything at all? I've got so many clearances now they'd have a time squeezing another one in. . . ."

"You'd be surprised, Buck. They can think up new classification categories anytime. Ever hear of the TPBR category?"

Buck shook his head.

"It means 'Take Poison Before Reading,' and it's supposed to be funny. Anyway, maybe I can make you feel a little better about the rest of the mystery. How many nuclear submarines are fitted with stern torpedo tubes?"

"Not many—now that you mention it there're only the five in the *Manta* class, and the *Triton*. You can't put stern tubes in a single-screw submarine. They'd have to shoot between the propeller blades, and that won't work."

"That's right. World War One airplanes had an interruptor mechanism to fire machine guns through their propellers, but a torpedo is too big. So none of the new single-screw boats have stern tubes. Have you ever towed another submarine?"

"Once, in the old *Sennet,*" said Buck, "for a couple of hours. It was easy, after we got coordinated."

"You had to make up the tow rig to *Razorback* while lying to on the surface, start towing her and then dive together, right?"

"That's right. You read our report, then. I was exec, and that was the tricky part. We passed the 'execute' for diving and surfacing on the radio, and had to relay the rest of our messages on sonar through our escort, riding abeam. We couldn't hear a thing astern on our sonar set." Williams deliberately did not ask what his superior was leading up to. He could afford to be patient, now that Richardson was talking at last.

"How would you take the *Cushing* under tow from under the ice pack?"

This was it! This must be the problem! Buck could feel his excitement mounting, but he knew Richardson too well to let it show. At least, not just yet. "You mean without surfacing? I don't think we could. We'd have to use divers, locking them in and out through the escape chambers, but I don't think there'd be a Chinaman's chance to rig the towline. It would be a bitch of a job, even in warm water, and even if everything was ready on deck before we went under the ice."

"Without surfacing, and without sending anyone out of the ship," said Richardson. "I suppose we'd have to have some cold-weather divers along, just in case of absolute need, but the way to do it, if at all possible, is to make the contact submerged, hook on, and then drag her out all in one motion."

"Why not break through the ice and do it the regular way?"

"Sure, if the ice is thin enough, but it's not apt to be. Besides, that would be a mighty chilled working party. You've read Jim Calvert's reports of his trips with the *Skate*, haven't you? He said his crew just wasn't acclimated to the cold. Their effectiveness was cut in half as soon as they got outside the ship, and got worse minute by minute. Your working party would be frozen solid in an hour."

In Williams' eyes, Richardson seemed to have reached a decision of some kind. He rose to his feet, led

Buck into his sleeping quarters in the adjoining compartment, unrolled a blueprint on the bed. "You may as well see this," he said. "It's designed for one of your after torpedo tubes. We're building two of them in our machine shop right now."

Ever afterward, Buck Williams would remember this moment as one of the climactic ones in his relationship with Richardson at this period, rivaled by only one other, of very different character, a few weeks later. He studied the blueprint in silence, bending over the bed, aware only of Richardson's measured breathing as he stood beside him. The open inner door of the torpedo tube was familiar enough. The side view of the tube was equally clear, but the rest was totally new to him. There was a circular steel thing labeled "Anchor Billet," evidently sized to fit into the breech of the open torpedo tube and lock there. There were two lengths of chain, one with a heavy grapnel-like hook on one end, a tight coil of eight-inch cable, a strange football-shaped object with stubby wings labeled "Floating Paravane," all shown separately in detail. And there was a composite sketch showing all the parts put together, the anchor billet at one end and the paravane at the other, with dotted lines around it to indicate the dimensions of the torpedo tube into which it would fit.

Buck finished his inspection, turned to Richardson. "What is it?" he asked. "I see it fits our stern tubes— they're shorter than our bow tubes, you know—but what does this thing have to do with Keith?"

"It's a contraption we hope will snag his anchor chain if he has it hanging down. You take off the inner door of one of your after torpedo tubes, slide this into it, and lock the anchor billet in place of the breech door. It's watertight, of course, and will take full submergence pressure. When you open the outer door, the paravane streams out and upward, dragging this first chain with the hook and six hundred feet of premium nylon hawser. The other end of the cable is attached to the center of the anchor billet via the second chain. We've set the paravane vanes so that it will tow off to the side and a little above the submarine."

"Anybody ever use this before," asked Williams.

"Nope. We've only just now invented it. That's where you and your ship come in. I've convinced ComSubLant that we need this capability, and we've been putting a lot of steam behind it these last few days. It'll be ready for a trial in a couple of days more. We'll do our first experiments with our own squadron rescue vessel, the *Tringa*. That way it will attract the least notice. She'll lie to in deep water with her anchor hanging down twenty fathoms or so. You'll come along underneath and off to the side just enough so that the paravane streams across her chain and snags it with this hook. This eight-inch cable hardly looks strong enough to tow a big ship like the *Cushing,* but the figures say it will, so long as you don't go too fast. Probably there should be a strain gauge on the line, anyway. The main thing I'm worried about is the initial jerk." Richardson was talking rapidly, with certitude in his voice. The speech had evidently been made several times already.

"It's time you were brought into this, anyway. I was about to ask permission to brief you. You'll have to have the right amount of way on for the paravane to stream properly, and that's a point we'll have to check. Maybe that will be too fast, and the line won't take the jerk when you make contact. However, picking up the catenary of the other ship's chain will ease the shock. Nylon line is very elastic, as well as being the strongest line there is. Also, it floats and doesn't absorb water. That will help. Since you'll both be submerged there'll be no wave action to worry about while you're towing.

That much we do know. But we have no experience in any of these other factors at all. This is what we have to find out."

Buck Williams' puzzled look vanished as the idea sank in. "What a terrific idea!" he exclaimed. "Of course, if *Manta* or any older submarine were in trouble they'd have to have men topside to handle their anchor gear. . . ."

"But all new submarines use a mushroom anchor operated from inside the hull. They can lower and raise it while submerged," finished Richardson with a grin. "You want to give this rig a try?"

"You could make a dozen passes and miss contact," said Buck, "but once you do pick up the other ship's chain you have only one shot. That's the weak point in the scheme. There'll be no way to rig a new line or make repairs. If you break the line, you're dead."

"You won't be able to take this anchor billet out of your torpedo tube breech if this hunk of chain is lying in the way of closing the outer door," said Richardson. "But you'll have another whole rig for your other stern tube. If you break that one too, it's the other fellow who's just found out he's dead. It's Keith up there, and if he gets into any trouble you're the one who should go to help him."

Williams saw the smile slowly vanish from Richardson's face, to be replaced by a look he could only describe as foreboding.

9

~~~~~~

Montauk Point was well astern when Keith climbed down the ladders from *Cushing*'s narrow bridge, through the watertight hatch, and descended into the control room. "We'll be diving in a minute," he said to the men on watch. "What's the sounding?"

"Just on the fifty-fathom curve, Captain," said one of them, his eyes close to the fathometer window through which could be seen a stylus tracing an exaggerated profile of the bottom. "Mark; fifty fathoms," he said.

"Control, this is bridge! Sounding!" the control room speaker blared the order from the officer of the deck above. The chief of the watch reached up to the speaker-control panel mounted above his station, pressed one of the toggle switches. "Fifty fathoms, bridge," he called.

"Is the diving officer ready in the control room?" said the loudspeaker.

Lieutenant Curt Taylor leaned across the chief, pressed the toggle, spoke into the microphone. "I'm here, Howie. Ready below!" He turned to Keith. "I have the first watch, Captain. I'll relieve Howie of the conn after we're down."

Keith nodded. Jim Hanson had arranged all this several days ago. The report was unnecessary, and both of them knew it; but regular ship's routine required the report to be made, inasmuch as the captain was in the control room. The control room watch, already on their stations, had gradually assumed an aura of expectancy. Keith could not have specified any particular attitude, but he had seen it many times. The way the men lounged at their stations told its own message: an orderly, professional readiness, apparent in the certitude with which they eyed the controls and gauges occupying every available inch of space on the compartment's bulkheads and the curved skin of the ship as well.

There was a bustle in the hatch trunk leading to the bridge. A pair of dungaree-clad legs appeared, quickly followed by a second pair. Two men wearing foul-weather gear jackets, the hoods drawn tightly by the drawstrings around faces reddened and slightly swollen from the cold wind into which they had been peering.

"Lookouts," one of them said through stiffened lips to Taylor. This too was part of the regular routine.

"Okay," responded Taylor. "Get your coffee and come on back here." The two men shambled stiffly off in the direction of the crew's mess hall, fumbling with parka strings and zippers.

Again the loudspeaker blared. "Clear the bridge! Dive! Dive!" Almost simultaneously the diving alarm sounded twice: two raucous blasts transmitted on the ship's general announcing system to all compartments. The chief of the watch, now standing before his diving control console, had forsaken his built-in stool. Alongside him stood Curt Taylor. Both of them kept their eyes fixed on the hull opening indicator panel, which showed two red circles and a series of dashes. This was the successor to the old "Christmas tree," with its red and green lights, which could never be positively and clearly interpreted under conditions of night adaptation when the only light permitted was red. The chief, fingering a switch on his diving panel, glanced inquiringly at Taylor.

"Shut the induction," said Taylor. The chief flipped the switch. One of the two circles vanished, was immediately replaced by another of the dashes. The two men continued to watch the panel, relaxed ever so slightly when the last circle changed to a dash. "Straight board, sir," said the chief to Taylor, unnecessarily loudly because Taylor was standing right beside him, and unnecessarily in any case since Taylor was also looking at the board. But again, this was part of the routine. Not only was Keith in the control room, so were a dozen other members of *Cushing*'s crew. All of them were vitally interested in the proper conduct of a dive.

"Open the vents," said Taylor. The chief's practiced fingers flew across another row of switches on his console. A series of red dashes in a second indicator panel changed to circles, and simultaneously a faint noise of rushing air could be heard. A pair of khaki-clad legs appeared in the bridge access trunk, followed immediately by dungaree-clad legs. Their owners, similarly garbed in dark green foul-weather parkas, with faces reddened from the exposure to the elements like those of the lookouts preceding them, stepped into the operating area around the diving panel.

"Hatch secured," the one in khaki said to Taylor.

"Aye," responded Taylor. "I'll take the dive, Howie."

"All right. I'll pass the conn over to you after you get her under." Turning to Leone, the officer of the deck said, "Bridge secured, Captain. All clear topside. We're still on the same course, one-two-five true, speed fifteen.

I'll pass the conn over to Curt as soon as he's ready."

As Keith acknowledged the formal report from Lieutenant Howard Trumbull, officer of the deck, he could feel the slight downward inclination of the submarine. Bow and stern planesmen were sitting in their seats near the forward bulkhead of the control room, facing an impressive array of dials in their carefully designed instrument panel. Extending from the floor between the legs of each was a stubby column topped with a steering wheel minus its top quadrant, patterned after the control columns in aircraft and designed to fill almost the identical purpose except that they could be, and frequently were, operated independently. The man on the left, in fact, had already pushed his control column forward. "Stern planes on fifteen dive," he said to Curt Taylor, who had moved over and was now standing behind him.

"Three degree down bubble," said Taylor. He turned to the man operating the right-hand column. "Put your sailplanes on full dive," he directed. Obediently, the man pushed his control stick all the way forward, held it there.

The deck tilted farther under Keith's feet. There was more sound of air venting from the ballast tanks. The depth gauge quivered, began to show increased depth, and the log speed indicator remained fixed at fifteen knots as the steady throb of *Cushing*'s single propeller drove her mighty hull down and forward.

Keith's mind flipped backward. In some ways this was so much like going to sea on a war patrol. But yet so different, and in the space of only fifteen years! In departing from Pearl Harbor, *Eel* had traveled almost entirely on the surface to her operating area. Except for daily drills and the ever present necessity to dive on appearance of a patrolling aircraft—all the more likely to be encountered as she approached enemy waters—

she tried to stay on the surface in order to make more speed. The *Cushing,* by contrast, could make higher speed submerged. Furthermore, she could manufacture her own atmosphere from seawater, and dispose of unwanted gases, such as carbon dioxide and carbon monoxide, overboard. She was totally divorced from the surface, had no need for it, except for entering and leaving port. She could do everything she had to do submerged, far better than on the surface. She would dive as soon as she cleared the shallow water, and remain submerged until return. She would surface only if necessary.

Eel had been a much smaller ship than *Cushing,* but she had dived and surfaced more frequently, and her dives were more complicated to execute. There were diesel engines, up to four—five counting the dinky, or auxiliary charging engine—to shut off; for each, as it rolled to a stop, there were two exhaust valves—one hydraulic and one hand-operated—to be closed before the submarine went under (but not before the engine stopped revolving). And there were two big spring-loaded air inlet ducts to be closed in each engineroom with a great clang of metal.

Shutting the even bigger air intake valve, hydraulically operated, was one of the principal control room functions, to be accomplished after the engines had stopped and before the valve itself, located as high as possible under the after part of the bridge deck, went under. Then, as soon as the last hull opening was closed, usually the bridge hatch, there was always a great whistling and roaring as the control room bled high-pressure air into the submarine to confirm that she could hold air pressure and therefore was indeed watertight. A logical practice for a slow dive, right out of overhaul for instance, when some overlooked repair or some shore-based workman's carelessness might have left an important hole unsealed. But in a fast dive the ship was half under before the last closure, the hatch or the induction valve, was shut, and there was no way to stop her downward momentum. If there were in fact a large hole, such as an open and unnoticed torpedo-loading hatch or a stuck-open air induction valve, the first sign of danger would be an increase in air pressure as the sea came in.

An artificial increase in air pressure during the act of diving would only delay detection of the first sign of danger, not help reveal it. But this had apparently not struck the submarine force authorities of that time. The whoosh of air, accompanied by pressure on the ears, had become part of the symphony of diving, welcomed uncritically by all because it signified orderly accomplishment of an orderly procedure.

In the *Cushing* things were much simpler. Air bleeding, with its attendant noise, had been abolished. Not only had the disadvantages been at last recognized, there were many fewer hull openings to close and hence less reason for a last-minute air test. There were no air-breathing diesel engines to shut off, no switching to electric motors for submerged propulsion, no haste to get down before an enemy aircraft could get on top of her with a bomb. In her engineroom a dive caused no change of any kind, except that the ship tilted very slightly downward for a short time and then leveled off again. To maintain the ordered speed, the engine throttleman might have to adjust steam flow to the turbine, that was all. If she went deep enough, he would have to close the throttle slightly, to match the reduced resistance to *Cushing*'s forward motion.

Something all submariners know: the laws of physics hold immutable, even though sometimes they seem to place effect before cause. A great deal of the power necessary to drive a ship through water is wasted in turbulence, visible in the form of wake astern and waves radiating outward from her passage. When a modern submarine is operating at shallow depth with any speed at all, there is nearly as much water disturbance as if she were actually on the surface, an incongruous and startling thing to any observer in the vicinity. But as the submarine depth increases, there comes a point when the pressure of the sea no longer allows turbulence to be formed. At this depth, and deeper, there is no surface evidence of her passage. The depth at which this occurs is dependent, of course, on speed; the faster the submarine is going, the greater her depth must be.

Several other things happen at about the same time, among them a sharp reduction in propeller noise, but most noticeable of all is a sudden increase in speed. The engines now have but one outlet for their horsepower: driving the submarine forward. She is no longer creating waves or turbulence. She has been freed from surface effect, which means there is now reduced resistance to her forward motion. And so she speeds up. To the throttleman in the engineroom, this is evidenced by an increase in propeller speed, and he automatically closes the throttle slightly, reduces the flow of steam to the turbines, holds the rpm to the ordered figure.

Another factor is propeller slippage. Defined as that percentage of propeller revolutions not converted into forward motion, slippage is essentially another measure of power wasted in turbulence. Designers have long known that the deeper a propeller can be, the less its slippage (another reason why the paddlewheel lost out). A deeply submerged submarine experiences virtually no slippage at all. Her propeller speed becomes precisely a measure of her speed through water. The distance she travels over any given time may be calculated with almost mathematical exactitude by multiplying the pitch of her propeller by the number of revolutions it has made, as shown on the revolution counter in the engine-room. For all these reasons, a deeply submerged (and properly streamlined) submarine can go faster than she can on the surface. This is true despite her larger displacement when submerged.

"Make your depth two hundred feet," said Keith to Curt Taylor. It was an unnecessary order, but part of the ritual. Diving officers (and all planesmen as well) had already been instructed to keep the ship one hundred feet off the bottom, slowly increasing depth as the bottom fell away until ordered cruising depth, four hundred feet, was attained. The drumming noise of the surface had ceased. Air was no longer venting from the ballast tanks. *Cushing*'s speed stayed rock-steady at fifteen knots, her angle downward at a comfortable three degrees, her depth gauges slowly creeping upward toward the ordered depth. As they neared it, the planesmen without orders pulled back on their control columns, the ship leveled out, and Taylor turned to Keith.

"Two hundred feet, Captain," he reported. "Fifteen knots, course one-two-five true. There's a hundred and five feet of water under our keel. I have the dive and the watch, and will take over the conn as soon as Howie is ready to turn it over."

"You've got it, Curt," said Trumbull, who had been standing unnoticed in the background. "Course one-two-five true. Speed fifteen. Ordered depth two hundred feet, increasing to four hundred cruising depth. There is one ship in sight, well clear to port. No land in sight."

"Aye, Howie." To Keith, "I have the conn, Captain."

It was all so businesslike, so controlled, so routine. There was very little of the thrill of the old-time dive, the split-second timing. Nor was there any need for a stop watch in the hands of a quartermaster to monitor the time it took to get under.

Fast dives had been necessary in the old days, because a plane coming at two hundred miles an hour could bring disaster in a very short time. *Eel* had regularly submerged in less than thirty seconds. It had taken the much larger *Cushing* twice or three times that long, but diving from under aircraft attack was no longer the problem it used to be. In 1961, with a ship like the *Cushing,* cruising on the surface was for leaving and entering port.

With *Cushing* once more on even keel, Keith left the control room, walked thoughtfully forward to his own stateroom. He would keep *Cushing* on course one-two-five until clear of the hundred-fathom curve. Then he would change the ordered course to due east, and in about three days more, when clear of the Grand Banks, he would order it changed again, to northeast. *Cushing* would find her way by sound alone, probing constantly by fathometer and forward-beam sonar against the possibility of an uncharted bottom anomaly, or another ship. It was another ship which worried Keith the most. The ocean floor had been well enough charted of recent years to assure against sudden surprises standing on the deep seabed, but the possibility of another ship—a submarine—was a different matter. No U.S. or NATO submarine would be routed through the vicinity of *Cushing*'s plotted positions, but there was no telling what the submarine of another nation might do. Which was another way of saying that a Russian submarine, routed by its own navy department without relation to anything planned by that of the United States, might conceivably blunder into *Cushing*'s path. And if the other sub happened to be at the same depth—another remote chance in the huge world ocean—the collision could be catastrophic. But this was not something one worried much about. The mathematical chances against such an incident occurring were astronomical.

In the event of war, of course, it would be different, but even so the main danger of collision would be with submarines on one's own side. Enemy convoys or task forces could be considered a magnet drawing all submarines in the vicinity. Even as far back as World War II, when diesel-driven submarines pursued enemy convoys on the surface and dived for attack after having attained a favorable position, the problem had been recognized. Coordinating operations so as to avoid the danger of collisions while submerged, or—even more to be dreaded—accidentally torpedoing a submarine on one's own side as it also sought a favorable attack position, had occupied much thought and careful planning. Ultimately, if submarines continued to increase in number, there might come a time when the danger of collision would require measures similar to those controlling airplanes in the sky. But this time was far in the future. Keith gave it only a second thought, shrugged his shoulders, opened the letter from Peggy. As he read it, his forehead furrowed.

Darling,

I know this trip isn't going to be as long as most of the trips you will probably be making on the *Cushing* and I know how busy you've been getting ready for it. So I didn't want to bother you with this before you left, and would like you to think about it so that we can talk it over when you get back. I know it's not supposed to be the code of the Navy wife to lay a problem on her husband just before he gets underway for a long cruise, but I'm sure it has happened before. The fact is, I wanted your last days in port to be as pleasant as possible, and I want to confide in you too. But I want to give you the whole story so that you can think about it, and then we need to have a long talk after you come home.

I love you very much, Keith, and when we are together everything is just swell. But you have been away for so many long absences. You couldn't even be with me when Ruthie was born, because the Navy had you out on some sort of a long deployment or exercise or something. I'm afraid this is going to be the way our whole life together will be. We have never really been able to establish a home. We've bounced from one place to another. Even Ruthie, at age five, is beginning to notice something. "Where do we live, Mommy?" she said the other day, and I almost broke down because I couldn't answer her.

I'm worried about the future, Keith. I know how much the Navy means to you, but remember, it's really the only thing you have ever known. You got in it right at the start of the war when you were very young and have been in it ever since. But there is a lot more to living than just being in the Navy. This year you'll reach twenty years' service (why doesn't the war count double? It should—) and become eligible to retire. This is what I want you to think about. We could move anywhere in the country, have our own little place, and live a normal life. You could easily get a good job, and with your retirement pension we'd never have to worry.

Keith turned the paper over. Although Peggy had digressed into a discussion of the idyllic joys of a permanent home, the flower and vegetable garden she proposed to start (she could have done that anywhere!)

and the general peace and contentment long-term permanence seemed to spell for her, his brow remained furrowed. The letter was four pages long, closely written on two sheets of paper. Midway through page three his frown deepened.

It's different with someone like Laura Richardson, Nancy Dulany or Cindy Williams, you know. All three of their husbands are graduates of the Naval Academy, and that means that the Navy will look out after them. You're not. Someday the Navy is just going to drop you when you least expect it. I've been seeing quite a bit of Laura lately, as I told you. Sometimes I even make up excuses to go by, even if she sometimes seems so smug because of her husband. Sometimes I think he's the one talking to me instead of her. I know he was your former skipper and all that, and you think the sun rises and sets in him. So does she, even though she was married once before and she must have heard of that Joan person he had the wartime fling with.

She never has said much about the war, but I'll just bet she knows about Joan. One time it nearly came up but somehow she sidestepped it, and I didn't have the nerve to come back to it. Laura is a pretty cool number, not like Cindy Williams. Cindy is just a sweet kid. I wonder if Laura's heard that story going the rounds about how maybe the Commodore's old friend, Joe Blunt, didn't die of a tumor on board the *Eel* after all. We've talked about this, and I know you don't believe it, but a lot more people are talking about it now than before. The way I hear it now is that somebody got to him in the middle of that depth charging when you all must have been half crazy anyway, and the Navy just covered it up with that business about his dying from a brain tumor.

Keith clenched his fist, slammed the opened desk top in front of him with it as he turned to the last page of the letter.

She probably has heard it, too—like I said, she's a cool number—but it doesn't seem to faze her a bit. Even so, I like her. Maybe I can get her to unbend a little bit while you're away. It would be interesting.

There was a little more to the letter but Keith hardly saw it. "Stay away from Laura, Peggy," he muttered under his breath. It was like her to say nothing to him of all these thoughts she had been having, to hold them within her and then lay them all out when he was unable to answer, unable to prevent her from doing whatever it was she had in mind to do about it. *Cushing* was already well at sea, deeply submerged. In emergency he could transmit a message, but not about something like this. Even if he could send Peggy a message, what would he say? He felt himself trapped, powerless, his comfort and security at home suddenly destroyed, or, at least, endangered. "Damn Peggy anyway!"

Running deep beneath the surface, her main coolant pumps at half speed, U.S.S. *William B. Cushing* effortlessly put 360 nautical miles behind her per day. She would make a landfall at Spitsbergen—if indeed a "landfall" was the proper terminology—for the latest report of ice reconnaissance by air had placed the edge of the late winter ice pack well to the south of that frosty land, and the confirmation of position would have to be by sonar and fathometer. Even this, while good conservative practice, was probably of little real use compared to the phenomenal accuracy and dependability of the two inertial navigation sets with which the *Cushing* was equipped. After Spitsbergen, at the reduced speed required by the operation order upon going under the ice, the North Pole would be some four days' steaming away.

Normally, the ice would be only a few feet thick at the edge of the pack, gradually—but fairly rapidly—increasing to the average winter thickness of about twenty feet. An iceberg, however, could be much deeper. Granted, bergs are not very apt to be encountered in the pack ice, the frozen surface of the Arctic Ocean. Icebergs come from glaciers on Greenland, which break off when the glacier hits the sea. As they slowly drift southward, they can be a fantastic hazard to navigation until they have slowly melted into the sea. Generally they stay close to the shore of Greenland, but occasionally an errant one may unexpectedly be caught, like ships of bygone years, in the middle of the ice pack. There, its behavior would be controlled by the circular motion of the drifting ice in the Arctic basin rather than the southbound currents which affect most of them, and it would be carried down into the Atlantic Ocean with the ice pack.

Encountering an iceberg at sea in northern latitudes, or in the ice pack, was, Keith knew, of far greater concern than encountering another submarine. For one thing, it would make no noise, unless wind or sea conditions were heavy, causing it to grind against surrounding pack ice. It would simply lie there, a stone-hard cliff hundreds of feet in depth, hanging in the midst of watery space like a gigantic trap for an unwary submarine. Keith saw to it that several hours a day were spent studying the ice patrol reports and the reference material with which he had been provided. Although the packet was a thick one, he took the time to read it all twice, and hold wardroom seminars in addition.

Contrary to popular belief, a submarine crew underway is at least as busy as the crew of any other type of ship. In the first place, the ability to submerge makes the submarine infinitely more complicated than any surface ship; and in the second, the submarine crew is smaller, for her very nature requires the minimum practicable crew, in the most confined of quarters. While underway, everyone except the captain, executive officer, ship's doctor and the cooks stands two four-hour watches per day. Regular drills, exercises in the many evolutions of which the ship must remain capable, come out of the off-watch time of two-thirds of the ship's company. So do cleaning the ship, routine ship's work, repairs to machinery or—the more usual case—regular maintenance. The idea that a submarine crew finds time hanging heavy on its hands while their ship drives her way submerged across an ocean or halfway around the world is unrealistic. A submarine does not even float without attention, like an ordinary ship, but maintains a specific depth at the will of her masters. The days pass swiftly. The pressure of day-to-day routine is inescapable. Keith made the most of the time he had.

The ice pack appeared on schedule. Keith had instructed Jim Hanson to adjust speed in order to reach it during the daylight hours. At the proper time he brought the ship to periscope depth so that those of the crew who were interested could look at it through the spare periscope while the *Cushing* approached at slow speed. He himself spent long minutes inspecting the thin white line which appeared on the horizon just at noontime, interspersing his own looks with letting an eager sailor have a turn. *Cushing*'s other periscope had been turned over to the crew entirely, but it soon was apparent that a single 'scope could not suffice for everyone to have the long look he obviously wanted. And Keith had to admit to himself that he was in truth exercising a skipper's privilege with the other, that a major portion of his own interest was purely personal curiosity.

Seen from a distance, the ice looked like a heavily demarcated horizon, a solid white line between the gray of the sea and the leaden blue of the sky. As the *Cushing* drew cautiously nearer it was evident that it was not solid, for what appeared to be the edge was a mass of broken blocks, crumbled off the solid ice behind by the combined action of sea movement and the weakening effect of melting. Most of the pieces nevertheless were of quite respectable size, several tons in weight and many feet across; and when Keith decided he had approached as close as was prudent he turned to a course parallel to the putative frontal edge for a close and leisurely inspection, all the while maintaining a continuous and careful watch ahead. It would not do to damage valuable periscopes by ramming them against a miniature iceberg during a quixotic rubberneck tour for crew members!

The coloration of the ice and ice blocks was fascinating, even though he had been prepared by his reading. White on top, of course, and white on the broken-off edges, down to the waterline. But where the ice entered the water it assumed a greenish tinge. Some of the blocks were wallowing gently in the nearly motionless sea, enough that he could see a foot or more below their normal waterlines, far enough to note that the light green shaded swiftly to almost black. Some of the pamphlets he had read had explained it: This was the norm for much of the Arctic, though not for all of it. The discoloration was the combined result of normal sea growth and water action on tiny organisms frozen into the ice when it was formed. These organisms, and growth on the ice under surface, formed much of the food for the wildlife—the seals, porpoises, whales and fish—and through them for the bears and man himself. The white mass was essentially snowfall over the frozen sea ice, built up during the years it had slowly circulated around the Arctic basin.

Ice, to Keith, should be white; or at least clear, like frozen water. But he had learned it could be a number of other colors, the slimy blue-green of the undersides of these blocks being only one of several manifestations. It was also hard, both from the cold and from the compression to which it was so often subjected, and deserving of respect. *Cushing* had been built with an ice suit, one of the reasons she had been chosen for this mission. Her sail was specially strengthened, as were her propeller, hull and control surfaces. In addition, her sailplanes were designed so that they could be put on ninety degrees rise, straight up and down, to facilitate breaking through the ice if necessary. She could cope with the ice, if handled intelligently, but she could not ignore the facts of physics, either. For the next few weeks he and his ship would be spending all their time in intimate relation with this common, yet most unusual, substance. It behooved him to learn what he could of it at first hand.

Sunlight was waning when Keith decided that his crew and he had had enough opportunity to inspect the ice under which they would henceforth be operating. He housed the periscopes, retracted the radio antenna masts, ordered deep submergence and set the course due north. Jim Hanson had obtained several Loran fixes, and the next thing would be to detect the nearest part of Spitsbergen, Prins Karls Forland, on sonar and Fathometer, in the place where it was supposed to be. This would confirm the practicability of avoiding unwanted shallow water should there be difficulty with other navigational equipment. From this time onward, except for occasional tests of missiles, *Cushing* would be divorced even from periscope view of the surface of the sea, confined—except for thinner ice in a rare winter polynya—beneath a virtually impenetrable layer of ice twenty feet thick.

In obedience to his operation order, Keith set a slower speed of advance than before, and when the upward-beamed Fathometer showed that block and brash ice had given way to solid cover he doubled the sonar watch. As the *Cushing* drove ever northward, her echo-ranging sonor probed ahead, on a secure and varying frequency, listening for the somewhat mushy return which would spell danger. If there were a return echo, any attempt to halt *Cushing*'s forward progress would be useless. Like all nuclear submarines, however, especially the whale-shaped ones, she turned on a dime, far more sharply than any surface ship could possibly hope to match. Here lay her safety. Keith's orders to his officer of the deck and helmsman were simple and direct. "If deep ice is contacted ahead, immediately put the rudder hard over away from it, and then call me."

It was not, however, Keith's intent to proceed directly to the North Pole. If there were time, he might do it later. Likewise, the slow counterclockwise rotation of the ice pack had long been plotted by explorers and scientists. This was a factor of interest, not of immediate concern. *Cushing*'s mission was to proceed to several specified geographical positions and determine if she could depend upon being able to fire her missiles within a given radius of each as the ice slowly drifted overhead. The operation order said she was to be the first of a number of submarines sent to determine whether the possibility of firing missiles in the Arctic Ocean could be guaranteed during all periods of the year.

Of all the navigation instruments with which ships

have been fitted since the beginning, the most important has always been the compass. The early mariners had nothing else. But a compass in the Arctic Ocean is essentially valueless, a fact dramatically brought out when one contemplates that at the North Pole all directions are south. The rotation of the earth no longer gives any directive force, and the gyrocompass, that marvel of the industrial age, wanders at will. A magnetic compass might theoretically be able to point to the nearby north magnetic pole, which ever so slowly drifts around among the icebound islands of Canada's northern archipelago, but at this close range the magnetic pole is very broad and very weak. Inside the steel hull of a submarine a magnetic compass, moreover, is not dependable.

This problem had presented itself with the voyage of the *Nautilus* across the top of the world, not quite three years before. It had been resolved by installation of the guidance system of an early missile, and by redrawing the map of the Arctic so that *Nautilus'* northward course, as she headed toward the Pole, continued to be "north" after she had passed through it and was heading in a southerly direction—and remained so until normal functions of the gyrocompass could be restored. The grid system resulting made it at least possible to orient one's location in relation to navigable water and land masses. Three years later, *Cushing* had a much more sophisticated system designed specifically for submarines and useful anywhere in the world. A good segment of Keith's training and that of many of his officers and crew, before ever reporting to the Electric Boat Shipyard, had been devoted to learning the intricacies of the Submarine Inertial Navigation System, which, inevitably, became known as SINS.

Now they were using their SINS for real, in the trickiest of situations, the high northern latitudes, and applying it to the same old grid system. Even though he had been well prepared for it, both in briefings and in his studies of previous northern voyages, Keith felt a surge in his adrenaline when *Cushing*'s ice detector showed that the ice above was solid.

There was an underwater television transmitter mounted on the main deck several feet forward of the sail, controllable in train and elevation from a small console located near its receiver in the control room. Two strong searchlights had also been installed, synchronized in direction with the television head. It was hard to see far underwater in the best of conditions, but the water was at least clear, the lights powerful. Keith estimated that he could see for about a hundred feet in any direction. The only things visible, however, were *Cushing*'s rounded bow, if one trained the head down and forward, and bumpy ice overhead.

The comparison to the plastered ceiling of a room flashed into Keith's mind. Surprisingly, despite the fact that his research into previous under-ice voyages had prepared him for it, the undersurface of the ice was far from smooth. Great rounded projections extended downward, reflecting additional thickness above. From his reading, Keith knew that such projections usually resulted from jamming together of the ice floes and the consequent rafting, or piling up, of broken segments of the once smooth surface when they did so.

One of the books had been written by survivors of a whaling ship which had been caught in the Arctic and had had to spend two horrible years there. It told how their ship had ventured into a wide lead at the edge of the ice pack, how it had unwisely gone too far between solid floes, how the lead began to close at the same time as the wind died, so that finally, in desperation, the crew had tried to tow her by getting out on the ice and pulling on hawsers.

Two or three times the lead reopened, bringing hope and causing renewed effort, but finally the ship was caught fast. Efforts to keep the ice broken up around her waterline were totally unavailing, and the squeeze began. Driven by far-distant winds and currents, the ice floes between which she was caught pushed inexorably together. Great blocks of ice popped up from the pressure, lying askew on top of those below. Many more were driven below the surface. A regular pressure ridge formed where the original lead of clear water had been, and the poor whaler was part of it, embedded in it.

The grinding pressure was slow, but irresistible. The ship's wooden ribs bent, finally broke in a number of places. At the same time, by good fortune, she was heaved up, out of the worst of the pressure, so that her hull, though dangerously wounded, was still sound. Listing over heavily on top of the ice hummock created by the rafting together of the floes, she remained in this situation for two years, her crew suffering unbelievable privation from lack of food and the fierce cold. Ultimately this particular ship was fortunate. She had been stove in, but not excessively so. Her crew had been able to make the most critical repairs. When the ice floe released its pressure, which luckily for her it finally did, she was able to remain afloat and sail home. Most ships in her situation were not so fortunate and sank as soon as the ice opened up again.

The Norwegian explorer Fridtjof Nansen had deliberately taken advantage of these circumstances when he made his exploratory voyage across the Arctic Ocean in the last years of the nineteenth century. His ship was specially built, so designed that when frozen in the ice and subjected to the squeeze of the ice floes, she would rise up on top rather than be crushed. The little *Fram* endured a three-year freeze in the ice during which she actually did slowly progress across the Arctic Ocean, and finally, when the ice let her down once again into the free sea, sailed home to Norway, triumphant.

All of this was history; but now Keith was seeing the same situation from underneath. Although ocean currents and slow melting gnawed at the bottom side of the rafted ice floes and blunted their initially jagged edges, the hummocks nevertheless projected far deeper into the sea than their corresponding grinding edges extended above it. And in the water, as Keith well knew, the floes he was observing were teeming with life —primarily microscopic life—so that, even under the *Cushing*'s pair of powerful searchlights, the undersurface was dark.

But, though rafting was frequent, particularly in the area near the edge of the ice pack, it was by no means consistent. Most of the ice was a broad, thick sheet, solidly covering the surface of the sea. This was what Keith expected, having read all the accounts of the early under-ice explorations. As long as *Cushing* remained submerged in deep water, and barring the possibility of an iceberg frozen in the vast expanse of sea ice, he need fear no danger. In an apt analogy, one of the accounts had compared the Arctic Ocean to a huge room full of water, with a submarine the size of a matchstick suspended from the ceiling. On this basis the ice would be the thickness of the paint on the ceiling of the room, and the occasional rafting could be compared to carelessly laid or cracked plaster, bulging it downward.

Indeed, one could include polynyas in the metaphor by suggesting that the plaster had cracked open in several places—and icebergs by comparing them to occasional walnut shells, glued to it. In any case, in the deep Arctic Ocean basin, actually two basins, the only problems were those associated with its ceiling.

Next day, with the ice solid overhead, Keith ordered *Cushing's* speed slowed to the minimum creeping speed and gently planed upward, raising a periscope long before there was danger of contact with the ice above. This permitted him to see the ice directly, from a much closer range, to confirm the reports he had read and the visual impressions given by the television transmitter. There was danger to the periscope, of course, should *Cushing* inadvertently come too close to a hummock. In one of the early explorations *Nautilus* had bent both of hers in such an accident.

To maneuver the ship into the shallowest portion of the ice floe, however, to find a polynya (inevitably frozen over in winter) and surface through it, or fire missiles through it, use of the periscope was imperative. It was as much for drill as for anything else, but it was nevertheless with extreme curiosity that Keith followed his periscope up from the floor. He put his eye to it as soon as the eyepiece came out of the periscope well, almost as though he were making an observation during a wartime approach of an enemy ship.

By careful calculation, the top of the 'scope was no closer than twenty-five feet from the bottom of the ice floe. Nevertheless, Keith had momentarily forgotten that even in low power it had a magnification of one and a half times, and his first reaction was alarm as the huge menacing cover filled the delicate lens. He had deliberately chosen the time of maximum daylight, and there was a moderate lighting of the nearly impervious ice. Except for color, it looked much like the frosted glass viewer upon which people spread their colored slide transparencies for comparison. Training the periscope forward he could see the powerful rays from the searchlights of the television set beaming upward through the water and reflecting upon the bottom of the ice, giving it an eerie surreal effect. To either side, with less benefit from the searchlights, the ice appeared like heavy green-tinged rain clouds, except much closer and more menacing. The best view was dead ahead, where he had the most light, and he could see, as the television had shown from farther below and with less resolution, that while it contained many small bumps and a few large ones from rafting, the undersurface of the ice was relatively free of jagged edges. He would never dare run at more than creeping speed this close to it, however. An unseen hummock of deep rafted ice, detected too late by the upward-beamed fathometer, could easily destroy a periscope and even damage the tough steel of *Cushing*'s sail.

Cushing had only just entered the ice pack. Perhaps there were thinner patches of ice ahead. Perhaps a polynya, or a lead, more thinly frozen over than the main floes. But already the vista was discouraging. Fifteen or twenty feet of ice were far too much to shoot a missile through, no matter what stratagems were employed. *Cushing* would have to break through and launch her test missiles in the surface mode. And, so far, the ice detector had found no areas of thin ice at all. Thoughtfully, Keith motioned for the periscope to be lowered. The entire time it was up had been one of tension. He was afraid of damaging the delicate instrument, but mainly his tension was due to the menace of the ice cover.

With a sense of concern, Keith ordered *Cushing*'s depth increased. His mission was going to be more difficult than he had imagined. There were millions of square miles of solid ice in the Arctic Ocean. This reality brought home the implacability of the environment against which he was pitted. On his side, he had a fine ship with a sturdy hull and a magnificent, ever supplying heart, the reactor. But compared to the vast expanse of solidity under which he must maneuver, *Cushing* was indeed a matchstick, suspended by an infinitesimal thread, under a flat ceiling of ice. And the ice stretched as far as the eye or the imagination could reach, in every direction.

10

wwwwwwwwwwwwwwwwwwwwwwwwwwwwwwwwww

Peggy Leone's almost twice-weekly drop-in visits had
become a real bore, but maybe her pattern was beginning to change. If so, Laura was grateful she had not
yet shown any of the impatience she had been beginning
to feel. Maybe the problem was starting to solve itself.
So far there had been but one subject on Peggy's mind,
worked over interminably, through infinite variations:
her desire that Keith exercise his option to retire from
active duty at the completion of twenty years of com-
missioned service in the Navy. His retired pay would
be fifty percent of his active-duty pay (she hardly
acknowledged Laura's comment that the allowances for
subsistence and quarters, a substantial part of the total
pay package, would not be included in the computation,
nor would submarine extrahazarodus duty pay). He
could easily get a job paying him at least that much
again. They would buy a home somewhere, have a
flower and vegetable garden, plant permanent roots.
Ruthie and any later little brothers and sisters would
grow up in a stable home environment. They would no
longer be gypsies, traveling hither and thither at the

behest of BuPers. They would at last be the same as
other people. Keith had already made his contribution
to the country and the Navy; not only during the war,
but afterward. The twenty-year retirement option had
been created for dedicated people like Keith. He should
exercise it. Now that he was a commander, he had advanced in rank about as far as the Navy would allow
a nonacademy graduate to go. (Laura reminded her
that the highly honored first skipper of the first nuclear
sub, the *Nautilus,* had not been an academy graduate
either. Commander Wilkinson was now a captain, with
every prospect of becoming an admiral in a few years.
This, too, was irrelevant to Peggy's thesis.)

Laura was bone weary of citing the holes in Peggy's
arguments. It did no good. Like Peggy, she was only
repeating herself, but unlike her, she was tired of trying
to think of new verbal clothing for the same old facts.
Keith's prospects were every bit as bright as Wilkinson's, or Rich's, for that matter. Besides, he so obviously enjoyed what he was doing. The *Cushing* was one
of the best commands in the Navy. Bud Dulany was
three years older and a couple of years senior to Keith,
and he had campaigned with every means at his command for the assignment to one of her two crews.
Cushing, a standard Polaris submarine in all respects
otherwise, had been built with a strengthened sail and
superstructure designed to take far more than the usual
impact with hard sea ice—everyone in the New London–Groton area knew that—and by consequence was
expected to be a candidate for all sorts of special missions. It had been a feather in Bud's hat, and an even
greater one in Keith's, to have been ordered, respectively, as skippers of the gold and blue crews of this somewhat special ship. But Laura might as well have been
talking to herself. None of her arguments made the
slightest impression. Peggy simply was not receptive to

anything which, in the slightest way, contradicted her already cemented preconceptions.

But for the better part of a week now, Peggy had not called. Laura was beginning to hope the careful speech she had planned might not be necessary. She hated the idea, had finally nerved herself to do it. There was no way out of it. She just had to tell Peggy that she simply could not discuss the subject of Keith's possible retirement anymore. Merely saying this would be sure to offend the woman, possibly have repercussions on Keith's relationship with Rich also, but this she would have to risk. "Look," she would say, "I've told you all I can tell you. It's Keith's future, and yours. No one can make this decision for him." She would enlarge on this theme briefly, then conclude, "Please don't ask me about it anymore. Keith would resent it, I'm sure, if he knew, and so might Rich. And please don't talk to Rich over Keith's head. Rich would be furious if I did anything like that, and it must be the same with Keith!"

This morning, however, after a gap of five days, there had come the usual telephone call. Could Peggy stop in on the way over or back from her doctor in New London? This in itself was a variation; she had never mentioned a civilian doctor before. Perhaps she was seeing a private psychiatrist. Most Navy wives, Peggy included—up to now, at least—went to the infirmary in the base on the Groton side of the Thames River for ordinary ailments. Until now, Peggy had cited a shopping visit across the river, or a sick friend whose existence Laura had begun to doubt. Or maybe she had been seeing a "pysch" all along, and only now was coming a little closer to telling the truth. If so, perhaps he was doing her some good.

Instead of offering morning coffee, as had been her habit, Laura changed the signals by inviting Peggy to a cup of tea in the late afternoon. Rich's return automatically would put an end to the visit. Now they were sitting in the Richardson's small living room, a pot of tea and some cookies on the low coffee table between them.

"Keith's been gone three weeks," Peggy was saying as she replaced her cup on its saucer, "and already it seems like a year. I don't think I'll ever get used to having him away at sea like this."

"You know the old Navy story, don't you?" Laura said. She was determined to keep the conversation light. "It's a fair deal if you're happy half the time. So in the Navy you get a sure thing, because your husband is at sea half the time. One way or the other, you can't miss."

"It's all right for the men," Peggy said, after a pause barely long enough to acknowledge the ancient joke. "They're so wrapped up in their boats they can't think of anything else. It's the ones who have to stay home who suffer. The wives and kids."

Laura recognized her inability to deflect the direction of her guest's thought. Different pattern or not, Peggy was the same. With an inward sigh, she decided her next half hour would be dedicated to providing what solace she could. Perhaps that really was what Peggy needed. The speech, perhaps, could wait. The necessity to prepare for Rich's return home would give her an excuse gracefully to extricate herself. "Nothing is perfect, Peggy," she said. "At least our husbands have an exciting life and we share some of it. Just living in the same old place and doing the same thing over and over again for years can be pretty dull, too. I've read somewhere that there are far fewer divorces in the Navy than anywhere else, for example."

"But that's not the point. The point is that some people are ambitious, and that's fine. The Navy needs them. They go to the Naval Academy, and then they're in. They get promoted, and when they're admirals they're in charge. But people like Keith don't have a chance. He'll never be an admiral. He'll be lucky if he makes captain!"

"That's ridiculous, Peggy!" The flat statement would do no good. It got out before Laura could stop it. As she said the words, Laura knew she had already failed her earlier resolve. This was not the way she had planned to begin that speech.

"That's all right for you to say, Laura. Your man is an Annapolis graduate. They look out for each other. Keith's always going to be an outsider."

"Are you trying to say you think Rich or anyone else in the Navy would count four years of undergraduate study at Annapolis as more important than the many more years of service since?" Laura put down her tea, leaned forward. There was no help for it. Maybe going over it one more time would do some good. Anyway, it would be mercifully short. "I happen to know Rich thinks Keith is tops. You've heard him say so, too. Many times. Keith can go as far as anyone else in the Navy. It's really up to him, his ability I mean, and you, because you're his wife and have a greater effect on him than anyone else."

"I know you believe it's all fair, Laura, but I've heard different from a lot of people."

"What sort of people? In the Navy?"

"Sure. In the Navy and out of it. In the sub force, too."

"The people who count aren't saying that."

"Are you kidding?" Peggy's eyes were turned unblinkingly on Laura. "If you mean the admirals running the Navy, of course not. But they're not the whole Navy anyhow. There's a lot more of it out there, a lot more than some of those admirals ever heard of. You learn a lot from just listening to those others." Peggy's whole expression was triumphant. She had found her entry point. When Laura did not immediately reply, she pressed her advantage. "I'm not saying this kind of thing doesn't affect the Annapolis boys, too. Ever hear of the Green Bowlers?"

"Sure," said Laura, "but that was years ago, before the war, and its importance has been blown up a lot. The membership was secret. That's why there's been so much talk about it."

"Right, except there's more to it than you think. It's not the only one, anyway. Most of them never did get found out. The whole game was to help each other, the other members of their own private little club, I mean. What I'm saying is that with in-groups like these looking out for each other inside the big Annapolis in-group, how can Keith ever make out when he's not in any of the groups at all?"

"Look, Peggy, if you want Keith to retire from the Navy, that's your business. Yours and Keith's. I can't help, either way." Laura's impatience showed in her voice and manner. It must have given Peggy exactly the opening she had been waiting for.

"Joan. Joan Lastrada. She helped Rich. Didn't she, Laura? He knew her pretty well during the war, you know. She was in some kind of intelligence work then. Now she's with Admiral Brighting. Didn't Rich tell you he'd seen her there?" There was a silence in Laura's mind, a blockage in the conversation process. There was a full tick in time before the words fell into place and conscious reaction was possible.

Peggy's large, innocent eyes were turned full on. Laura saw the pupils dilate. There was the breath of unknown danger. Fight for control. Show nothing. Keep her own pupils from dilating. Another tick and tock of time. "Oh, sure. Joan was a wartime romance of Rich's, before we were married, but of course I've never asked about her. He'd lost sight of her entirely, and then she turned up in Brighting's office. But why bring her up? She can't help Keith with this problem."

"No, but you could. That's what I mean." There was something furtive, veiled, in Peggy's expression. Her eyes were hidden now, her hands—the manicured fingers suddenly resembled red talons; perhaps she was pressing them together with greater than usual force—clenched together in her lap.

Danger. Treacherous path ahead. Caution flags flying. Forget what you'd decided to say. Don't make any positive statements. Ask questions. At least, asking a question doesn't commit anything. "What do you mean, Peggy?" Smooth, that's it. Stay cool. This is a fencing match.

"It's just—you know—he thinks so much of Rich. I'm sure the only reason he's still in the Navy today is because of Rich. He wants to be like him. Probably he wants me to be like you, too, though he's not said so."

"I've already told you how much Rich thinks of Keith. But what does this have to do with me?" Laura was genuinely puzzled.

"Maybe Rich could talk to Keith when he comes back from this trip and explain how the Navy really works. Keith will believe it, then. He'll have his twenty years this month. He should retire while he's still young." Peggy's eyes were lifted, bored into Laura's. "We women have to stick together," she almost whispered.

The words were distinct, and they were said with deliberation. Suddenly Laura realized she knew nothing whatsoever about the mind behind Peggy's too smooth face and studied demeanor. Peggy had controlled the conversation, driven it in the direction she wanted, and there was a clear hint of some kind of a threat behind her sudden words. Why had she brought up Joan so unexpectedly?

Laura had never told Rich how much she really knew, how well she actually understood the forces driving Joan, Rich and Jim Bledsoe, her first husband, during those tense war years. He had never discussed that phase of it, had never mentioned Joan. It was one of those basic understandings between men and women that have existed since the beginning. Intuitively, Laura knew his reticence was at least partly because of Jim, just as hers was. She would never forget how hard it had been to keep silent after that busybody wife of a senior officer, shortly after she and Rich had been married, told her that Joan had been involved with both of them.

Thankfully, she had managed it, and Rich had never suspected. Then, a few years later, she had got on a train alone in New Haven and found herself by chance sitting alongside Joan, of all people. There had been some strangeness at first, but that passed, and Laura evermore treasured that fortuitious, completely private, encounter. Years, prejudices and misconceptions had fallen away, and although their paths had not crossed again, she knew it sufficed for both of them for all time.

Not so with Peggy Leone. More properly, just the reverse. Something was wrong with her, with her thinking. Laura was secure with Rich, had always been. Why had Peggy brought up Joan. What lay behind her strange words about women sticking together? How much did she know or imagine of Joan's wartime romance with Rich? Did she know there had also been an affair with Jim? What was she saying now?

". . . thought a lot of Captain Blunt to name his son after him—why do some people say it's because of his guilty conscience? I don't see anything for Rich to feel guilty about. People ought to be forgetting those old rumors after all these years. . . ."

Something congealed within Laura. "What are you talking about, Peggy?" Her voice was deeper than usual, nearly throaty. Of course she had heard the rumors about Blunt's death aboard the *Eel*. There were always rumors when something unusual happened to people. Blunt had been Rich's idol as a young naval officer. During Rich's first years of submarine service in the *Octopus,* then later when Rich commanded the *S-16* and the *Walrus,* and finally when he was given the *Eel,* Blunt had been strongly supportive. Rich had told her all about it. Then, during the latter stages of the war, Blunt had inexplicably changed. He had behaved irrationally, endangered the *Eel* during a near disastrous depth charging, had hurt his neck and then had suddenly died while inactively sitting in the wardroom during a furiously fought surface gun action. The *Eel* had brought his body back to Pearl Harbor, and the autopsy disclosed a brain tumor, aggravated by the injury and the stress of combat. The neck injury itself had been ruled out as the proximate cause of death, but there were those who said the Navy might have been covering up the true cause. Someone aboard the *Eel* might have done something to him during that terrible depth charging. Perhaps even Rich.

"Of course, I don't believe a word of it, Laura. Nobody could who knows Rich even a little bit. But I thought you ought to know what they're saying. . . ." Peggy's voice was pitched low, barely audible. "Most people won't tell you this sort of thing," she said. "That's why I felt I had to . . ." again she let her voice trail off.

Beware the bearer of evil rumor under the guise of friendship! There lies the quicksand! Peggy herself might have revived that old story. But why? What does she want? If she wants my help in her campaign to get Keith out of the Navy, this is not the way to go about it. I'll not help her after this. All I want is just to get her out of here. Far away from here. Maybe that's it. Get her out of New London, out of the Navy, that is, and Keith too, of course. But that's stupid. She's a stupid woman. This conversation is insane. Maybe she's not right in the head. I'm the wife of her husband's senior officer. I don't have to listen to this drivel. Especially day after day, as I have. How to turn her around without activating her implicit threat? How to stop her without risking the intensification of rumor, the spreading, even the creation, of destructive, titillating gossip? Can she have the slightest idea of how harmful this could be to Rich, at this time of all times, with an admiral's selection board in the offing?

She must. Obviously, she must. This must be her game. But it won't hurt much if it comes only from Peggy. More people than I must know her for what she's turned out to be. Cool head. Don't show that it stings. Play it down. Don't let her see how she has suddenly scared you. Don't give her anything she can use. What to say?

"Don't worry yourself about any of that idle talk, Peggy. Rich and I have heard it all, and so has the rest of the Navy. It doesn't amount to anything. Commodore Blunt's death" (for some obscure reason she felt his title should be attached to his name) "grieved Rich deeply. That's why he decided to bring him back to Pearl instead of burying him at sea the usual way." That's enough. Now get off the subject. "And don't concern yourself about Joan Lastrada, either. She's a fine person, and a good friend of both of ours." Enough of that subject, too. There's sufficient truth in what she knows or guesses to keep the gossip mills grinding endlessly. Even Rich doesn't know what I know, and I may never tell him. "But I can't influence Rich's official Navy actions, about Keith or anything else. He wouldn't let me if I tried. What Keith does is only his business, and yours, of course." Best hand her this placebo. "He'll have plenty of chances to talk all this over with Rich if he wants to after the *Cushing* gets back from this trip. Keith will have to bring it up, though. Rich sure won't. He feels very strongly about this sort of thing. If Keith wants to talk about it, he'll tell him the very best he knows and thinks. But it will be up to Keith.".

"But you will speak to Rich, so he'll know what Keith's thinking." It was an assertion of fact, not a question. "Keith sets a lot of store by his advice. This will be a very big decision for him." Peggy was still looking at her with intensity. There was something she was trying to project without saying it. Laura could only interpret her manner as a nervous challenge.

With a decisive motion, Laura rose to her feet. "I'll tell him what you've told me. What he does about it is up to him. He'll be home in half an hour, and now I've got to get ready." Peggy remained seated. Would a stronger hint of dismissal be needed? But Laura was saved from the necessity by the sight of a familiar auto entering their driveway. "Rich is home early," she said with a mild note of surprise.

A moment later he came in through the back door, and she knew something was wrong, that he was upset to see Peggy, that, whatever it was, it would preoccupy him all evening to the exclusion of everything else, and that if it had to do with naval operational matters, he would tell her nothing.

The slight bustle attendant upon Peggy's departure provided a respite. Laura could sense his urgency for her guest to leave, hoped Peggy did not. "What's the matter?" she said as soon as they were alone.

"Nothing that we can't fix, I hope," he said. "That's why I came home early. There's nothing I can do on the *Proteus* right now, but there may be later tonight. I'll probably have to spend the night aboard, so I'll throw a few things in a suitcase. . . ."

"Can you tell me what's wrong?"

Rich's answer was proof that he could not. "What were you and Peggy Leone talking about?" he asked. To Laura's sensitive antennas, tuned as she was to her husband's sometimes uncommunicative moods, there was the slightest—barely the slightest—emphasis on Peggy's married name, almost as though Peggy were the last person in the world he had expected, or wanted, to see.

"Just girl talk," Laura said lightly. "She's not been over for some time, so I asked her to stop by for a drop of tea." Sometime soon, Laura knew, she would need to discuss the problem of Peggy and Keith, but now was not the time. There was a familiar look of concentration on his face, a preoccupation she had experienced often enough to have evolved her own method of dealing with it. Then intuition flooded her mind. "Is something the matter with Keith and the *Cushing?*" she said before she could stop herself.

The look on Rich's face told her she had hit close to the mark. It also told her to ask no more.

It was quite dark as Richardson parked his car in the designated space near the *Proteus'* forward gangway. He had succumbed to Laura's suggestion of a hastily prepared supper before returning. The lights of the submarine tender were blazing brilliantly, especially those associated with her machine shop and the submarine service areas. The cargo entry ports had large soft lights rigged on a small boom projecting out over them, casting a diffused yet penetrating glow around the area.

Similar lights were burning on the other side, where the submarines lay, encasing the entire ship and the sleek low-lying hulls she mothered with a small cocoon of brilliance which fought unsuccessfully against the surrounding night. From the distance, as his car approached New London's State Pier, alongside which the tender was moored, Richardson was conscious of the general impression that the entire combined structure of tender, submarines and dock area was magically incandescent. As he approached, however, the lights divided into their individual sources, each causing the outlines of a portion of the component structure of the ship, the covered dock on one side and the submarines on the other, to stand out against the pressure of the supervening blackness as though, somehow, each possessed its own internal source of light instead of being only a reflection.

It did not seem real. There was a mystery to the entire scene. *Proteus* was moored bow in, the customary way. Her masts disappeared into nothingness overhead, her hull stretched out to nothingness alongside the deck. The submarines on her starboard side floated on nothing—which reflected shimmering light in certain places —and the sleek superstructures rising from their rounded hulls had their own forests of shiny retractable masts extending upward into black nothingness.

Reflections from the slab-sided *Proteus* and the rounded hulls of the submarines contrasted strongly with the dullness of the large wooden warehouse which dominated the pier. Yet, though the profusion of luminescence seemed to spring from inexhaustible energy, and the large lights glowed everywhere, it was not enough to drive the blackness very far. It hovered above, on both sides, and ahead and astern. It seemed poised to close back in, and its gloominess seized Richardson as he approached the accommodation ladder, returned the sentry's salute at its foot, and heard *Proteus'* loudspeaker system announce his arrival: "Squadron Ten! Squadron Ten!" Slowly, his suitcase in his left hand, he climbed the twenty-seven varnished steps to the gangway opening in the ship's rail. Buck Williams, alerted by the speaker, was waiting.

"We'll be fully provisioned and ready to leave by day after tomorrow if you need us, Commodore," said Buck.

"Are there any problems? What about the two rigs?"

"No strain there. Your *Proteus* gang will have them both made up again and ready by tomorrow night. They'll make that change in the hook by then, too."

"Good," said Richardson. The two had disengaged themselves from the obligatory attentions of *Proteus'* officer of the deck, were walking toward Richardson's cabin. The gangway messenger had already disappeared with the suitcase in that direction. "I'm sorry to have to do this to you, Buck," he went on, "but there's not much choice after that message from Keith."

"Thank God we got this little invention of yours built, Commodore, and a chance to try it out. At least there's something we can do. But maybe there won't be any need. Maybe it will all turn out okay after all."

"Maybe," said Richardson. "I don't suppose there's been any new message."

"Not from *Cushing*. There's one from ComSubLant, but all it does is confirm what he told you on the telephone, that you're operational commander."

The two officers reached Richardson's door, with "ComSubRon 10" emblazoned over it on an engraved brass plate. It was ajar. His suitcase stood in the center of the floor. Wordlessly he pushed Williams inside, shut the door, began turning the combination on his desk safe. He opened it, pulled out an unfolded message flimsy, laid it on the top of his desk. Williams closed in beside him, also reading it. For a moment neither spoke.

It was as if, by the intensity of their concentration on the paper, they could elicit some additional word, some further meaning, that Keith might have put there.

URGENT FOR COMSUBLANT AND COMSUBRON TEN [the preliminary procedural letters indicated] FROM CHARLIE JULIET X POSITION GOLF NOVEMBER TWO NINE X NO POSSIBILITY LAUNCH EXCEPT SURFACED THROUGH MINIMUM THREE FEET ICE COVER X ONLY FOUR POLYNYAS FOUND DURING WEEK IN OP AREA CMA ALL ICED OVER TWO DASH THREE FEET AND SMALL X TOP SECRET X COLLISION WITH FOR-EIGN SUBMARINE WHILE SURFACING X PROPELLER DAMAGED X TOP SECRET X

Williams broke the silence. "When it first came in, both of us said that message isn't like Keith. It tells us practically nothing about his propeller, except that it's damaged. He's left out everything we need to know."

"I've been thinking about that too," said Richardson, "but that's not quite true. The information about the collision came at the end of the message instead of the beginning."

"That's what I'm talking about," said Buck. "You'd think the dope on that would be the first thing on his mind instead of the last thing."

"How about an add-on."

"Add-on?" Buck was incredulous. "What do you mean, Commodore?"

" 'Rich.' We're by ourselves."

"Okay. Rich. But what's this about the collision being an add-on?"

"It's a guess. Encoding a message is the hard part. That and writing it as carefully as you can. The cipher system Keith used is designated for operational situations and generally calls for simple operational precedence. Operational Immediate at the most. If there's anything secret in a message, the whole message is supposed to be ciphered in a secret code. Keith goes even a step beyond that. He labels the last part 'top secret.' But this message isn't in a top-secret code. It's in an ordinary code. But he sticks the words 'top secret' on both sides of the secret part, right at the end of the message, and sends it Urgent, the very highest priority."

"That's true," said Buck very seriously. "A collision with a foreign sub is a pretty obvious top-secret thing, and pretty urgent, I'd say. It's enough to spoil your entire day. . . ."

Richardson did not even notice Buck's characteristic frivolity. "Keith would have had plenty of time to get the message ready before trying to break through. He and his coding board probably spent half the day getting ready to broadcast the minute the *Cushing* got her antenna above the ice. It would have been all encoded and sitting in the radio room. The first part is a routine report on conditions. Then suddenly he breaks into something really secret and really urgent. I think he added on that last bit hurriedly. The collision could have happened a very short time ago, maybe only minutes before that message got on the air!"

"You think that's why he made it so short?" Buck's seriousness was genuine now.

"That's what I'm guessing. It's the first thing we've got from him since his report that he was about to go under the pack. You'd think he'd have had a lot more to say. It's my guess he scrubbed at least half of what he had there at first."

"Why shorten an already written and coded message, though? Why not just add on what he wanted, or make up a whole new one?"

"Time. That's got to be the reason. It's much quicker to crank up a coding machine that's already set up with the original code than to break out a different code book and set it up with a whole new one. And he made it short because he didn't want to transmit for very long."

"But why not, boss? The other sub must be damaged too. It's probably trying to surface to get off a message to its headquarters too. Just like Keith. What difference does that make? Keith doesn't have to bother them, and they don't have to bother him, either. In fact, they should help each other."

"Not so fast, Buck. Two boats have collided under the ice. That's a lot of bother, right there. It's bound to annoy that Russian skipper a little."

"So, he's unhappy. So's Keith. So's everybody."

"Maybe he's not all that unhappy?"

"Who's not? Keith? . . . Oh, you mean the other skipper. How do you know he's a Russian?"

"All I'm doing is guessing. The Arctic Ocean is as big as the whole United States. If the only two subs tooling around up there have a collision, that's one hell of a big coincidence. One sure thing is that Keith's doing a lot of guessing too. One of the instructions in his operation order was to remain undetected at all costs. Another was a warning to be alert for possible unfriendly reaction to his presence there."

"What right do the Russians or anybody else have to object to his being there? It's international waters, just as much as any other ocean!"

"Sure. But one whole half of it borders on their country, and they've been running ships through it along their northern coast for a long time. They've got the biggest icebreakers in the world keeping the channel free in the winter." Richardson turned suddenly, picked up his suitcase, walked with it into his sleeping room, opened it decisively on the bed, began to transfer its contents into a drawer.

"So you figure they think they own it?" said Williams, following.

"They might. Nobody has ever competed with them. The *Nautilus, Skate* and *Sargo* have been up there, we've sent some exploring teams out on the ice and nowadays we fly over it all the time. But that's about it. It figures they won't like our putting a ballistic missile submarine up there."

"If that's the way Keith's thinking, that would account for his trying to be on the air as little as possible, I guess," said Buck. "At least, that would make it harder for the Russians to locate him by DF-ing his transmission, if they have a direction-finding station up there. Do you think he'll send another message?"

"Yes, I sure do. Another short one, and he'll send it at the best radio propagation time. That's why I'm sleeping aboard tonight. Another message would add a lot to what we know, and he knows that, too. But he'd like to avoid as much as possible of the preliminary procedure signals." Richardson abruptly changed the subject. "Did you find out how this message was routed?"

"Radio Asmara. Relayed on landline to Washington. We got our copy from the Pentagon and had it decoded even before ComSubLant, down in Norfolk. What difference does it make how it got here?"

"None. But remember, with a message this important, Keith was probably in his radio room when it was sent. Radio Asmara, eh?" The cadence of Richardson's sentence slowed perceptibly.

"It's one of our main communications stations serving the Sixth Fleet in the Mediterranean," ventured Buck, aware that Richardson knew this as well as he.

"It's a quarter of the way around the world from

here. Keith must have had the devil of a time getting through," said Richardson musingly, as he closed the empty suitcase, shoved it into a corner.

"Is that why you think he made the message so short? But he couldn't have known it would have to go through Asmara before he opened up!"

"Maybe he did at that, Buck." The younger officer felt his senior's measured gaze. "He knew he'd have to raise some very distant station and start with a lot of procedure signals. So there would be a lot of lost time before he could even get to the main part of the message."

"So?"

"So maybe someone might try to jam his transmission! That would be another reason to make it short!"

Comprehension on Williams' face, but still a question. "Why didn't he say so, then? He'd want us to know that, if he expected it, wouldn't he?"

Richardson's voice dropped a half-octave, as he answered. "Security, Buck. They didn't get that submarine up there overnight! This wasn't all just an unhappy accident. I'm guessing it wasn't, and I think Keith is guessing the same thing. At least, it might not be. If it isn't, they've been reading our mail for a long time. And it stands to reason, if the collision was deliberate, that was no ordinary submarine!"

"Good Lord." Buck expelled the words not as an exclamation but almost as a sigh. "So you figure maybe they sent whatever is up there because they knew Keith was coming into the Arctic Ocean?"

"Only a guess, I said."

"You're reading an awful lot into this little message, Rich."

"The next installment from Keith will tell a lot more. That's why I figured I'd better spend the night aboard. He's going to send another message, and he'll time it for when we're in darkness. If we can intercept his transmission direct, instead of depending on some shore station to relay it, we might learn quite a bit just from the way he sends it."

Buck was silent for a short moment, then said musingly, "He'll know we'll be anxious for his follow-up message, all right, but why should he wait with sending it? We'd get it sooner with another relay through Asmara or Guam, or somewhere, than if he waits till we're in darkness and there's a chance of giving it to us direct."

"Sure. But it's Keith up there, and he knows we're down here. What would you be thinking, right now, if you were in his shoes?"

"Well, I guess it's obvious I'd be hoping my friends in New London would rally around."

"You know damn well they would, Buck. And you'd also know that Keith and I would be having this very talk, right about now, and would be sitting in our radio room when your message comes over the air. And you'd also know that we'd figure you'd be in yours."

"I see what you mean," said Buck, slowly. "That's just what he'll do." Then a thought struck him. "Do you think we could talk to him by voice?"

Richardson hesitated before answering. "No. At least, not for anything really important. Maybe our single side-band set can reach him, and hear his, but what could we say that's worthwhile? Any real information he wants to send will come coded, in the right code this time, and by CW."

"Coded dots and dashes are fine, Rich, but just think what it will do for Keith and his whole crew if we can talk to him by voice!" Buck was speaking rapidly now, throwing all he had into it. "We don't know anything at all about what kind of shape he's in. He'll tell us in his next message. He's probably already got it drafted.

What he and his whole outfit want to hear is that we're right in there with them, and using every resource the Navy's got. There's no rule against voice, is there?"

"No—voice doesn't have the range CW has. But you can't encipher voice. No voice code is secure. If our guess is right there's bound to be an army of unfriendly communication types monitoring everything that goes on the air in that area."

Buck could sense his superior's desire to be convinced, could hardly wait to press the argument. "I'm talking about morale, boss, not security. We don't need to say anything at all that refers even to where they are, or what they're doing. Don't you think Keith knows us well enough to read between the lines of whatever we say to him?"

Weakening, Rich nodded at the justice of this point. However, he persisted. "The problem is that we'll be making him transmit a second time. If they're monitoring the Arctic, maybe with direction finders, we're making it that much easier for them to locate him. We've no idea what they're up to. I agree it will be good for his morale—and ours, too—if we can come up on voice with him. And he is in international waters, and has every right to send anything he wants. But if there's something funny going on it would be wrong to make him send a lot of procedural transmissions to establish the voice contact."

Satisfied that he had won, Buck nodded in his turn. "That's no problem, boss. The call-up procedure and all that, I mean. We can get around that easy. We'll use our old wolfpack code. He'll be sitting there in his own radio room and hear it himself, and it'll work like a charm!"

Richardson felt his own enthusiasm beginning to match that of his junior. "You did say that you and

Keith had resurrected that old wolfpack code of ours. How would you use it?"

"We wait for him to send the next message, right? We hear it come in, right in our radio shack. The minute he gets the receipt from the shore station working him, we break in with the wolfpack code and tell him what we're up to. He won't have to come back at us on CW, and there'll be no prelims on voice either. Then we shift right over to the single side-band set and talk to him. He won't transmit one single syllable until he opens up to answer, and he'll not have to do that if he doesn't want to."

"Looks like you're planning for us to break a couple of our communication rules, Buck, but it sounds good. The most important thing of all, though, will be that message he'll be sending. No interference with that, and no making him repeat on voice what he's already put in the message!" He stopped, then continued, "I want to get on top of that right away, as soon as it comes in. Do you want to help me be the decoding board?"

"You know you couldn't keep me away, Skipper," said Buck with a warm smile. "But do you think a broken-down old submarine skipper and squadron commander will be able to run one of those new coding machines?" The smile of anticipation on his face belied the words.

"Then you'd better take over one of the division commanders' staterooms and get what sleep you can. When the message comes in we'll be up for quite a while, working on it. Maybe you should tell Cindy you'll not be home tonight."

Buck grinned. "I did already," he confessed.

* * *

The ship intercom phone buzzed on the bulkhead above Richardson's steel bed. He reached for it swiftly, alertness awakening throughout his body.

"Commodore, this is Radio. We're intercepting a message from the *Cushing* to NSS Annapolis. He's in loud and clear."

"Call Commander Williams in ComSubDiv One-oh-One's room. I'll be right up!" He slammed the telephone into its cradle, jammed his feet into slippers, ran out the door in his pajamas.

Buck, barefooted, carrying his shoes, arrived in the radio room only seconds after he did. Evidently he had been sleeping in his underwear, had delayed only to pull on his trousers.

There were three crewmen there, one a supervisor. "I called you as soon as the message started coming in, Commodore," the senior said with a hint of pride in his accomplishment. "We're copying it at two stations." He indicated the two radiomen seated at their typewriters, earphones on their heads, clacking the keys with measured simultaneous cadence as their eyes stared miles beyond the radio receivers banked directly in front of them.

"Have you another set of earphones?" Richardson knew there must be, automatically reached out his hand. Buck Williams, he saw, likewise could hardly contain his eagerness.

"Yessir. But we can only plug you in at one station." The supervisor handed Richardson a single set of earphones, swiftly plugged in the other end of the six-foot cord. Rich fumbled with the headpiece, detached one of the earphones from its clip, handed it to Buck, put the headpiece with now a single earphone to his head. Buck, crowding close to be within range of the wire attached to his earpiece, held it to his near ear. The earpieces were fitted with earmuff-type coverings to cut out extraneous sound. Both men cupped their hands over their unused ears, strained to blot out all other sensation.

XVTMW, said the radio waves. PLTMV ZAWLN MMPTL XZBKG—the rhythm was steady, hypnotic. Glancing over the shoulder of one of the radiomen, Williams could see the encrypted message forming before his eyes. There were already three lines of type, ten five-letter groups per line, all neatly columnar, the letters coming one by one as the distant operator hammered them out with his radio key. Like many officers, Williams had learned Morse code early in his career. He had never become as good at it as the radiomen who dealt with it every day, but he could recognize the letters, although not fast enough to receive a message at normal trans-mittal speed.

"Dash-dot-dash-dot," went the faint signal. The let-ter C. C appeared on the paper as the radioman hit the typewriter key. Then a single dash, the letter T. Then three more: O. Holding both hands, one with an ear-phone, to his head, Buck could visualize the distant operator, far to the north, beating out the dots and dashes as rapidly as he could, yet well aware that a rhythmic swing, and steady, precise formulation of the letters was vital to accurate receipt. He was obviously a professional. Buck would have described him as hav-ing a "copperplate hand," meaning that the dots and dashes were crisply distinguishable, the spaces between them always the same, the spaces between letters slight-ly longer but also exactly the same, the spaces between groups longer yet but still unvarying. Keith must also, at that very moment, be hunched in a chair alongside his radio operator, a spare set of earphones on his head, following his radio transmission with his ears and with his mind. He would hear the signals streaming out from his ship, imagine them crossing the frozen ocean, bouncing at least once off the ionosphere and finally coming within range of the tall, huge antennas across the Severn River from the Naval Academy. There, the so-carefully-tuned receivers would amplify them back into the audible range to be copied. In his own receivers he would hear also the much fainter notes of the distant station as Annapolis responded to his call and indicated readiness to receive the message. He would listen as his radio-men confided his enciphered letters to the aether, hear the procedure signals calling for repeats of doubtful passages if any, finally hear the R for receipt that indicated the shore station now assumed responsibility for the message and its delivery to the addressees. Not until a message of this importance had cleared completely would Keith himself—short of urgent matters elsewhere—leave his radio room.

But would Keith know that his two closest friends were similarly occupied, that they had lain in wait to intercept his expected second message, had carefully planned to be in the *Proteus'* radio room to hear it directly, from his own transmitters? It was what Keith himself would do were the situation reversed, and if he was anywhere within reach of the proper receivers. But there was no way Keith could be sure that Rich and Buck, his most immediate associates, had monitored the ship-to-shore frequency and were taking his message directly, that they were at that moment directly connected to him by the tenuous, invisible, fragile radio waves emanating from his own radio room. For that matter, he expected Buck to be at sea in the already-begun barrier exercise.

But, beyond doubting, the hope would have been in his mind. Positive confirmation would be a tremendous booster to morale. If possible it should be done. How to alert him?

"Chief," Buck said to the radio supervisor, speaking

in a low voice so as not to interrupt the concentration of the men receiving the message, uncovering his left ear as he did so, "Chief, is your transmitter on this frequency?"

"Yessir. The Commodore had us do that this afternoon—I mean yesterday. But we don't have the power to reach the *Cushing* where she's at."

"You mean we don't have the power of a big shore station. We can hear *Cushing* okay, and we have bigger transmitters than she has. So she ought to be able to hear us."

"Sometimes it works," said the supervisor doubtfully, "but the *Cushing* didn't know which shore station in the whole world would be the one that could hear her message. You never know that."

"Sure, but maybe she aimed it at us, Chief. She picked a time when we'd be in darkness. Maybe she's hoping we would think of putting this watch on her frequency."

"Annapolis answered her call-up, sir," the chief radioman said earnestly. "All we're doing is copying her message. There's no way she could know we're on the circuit. Since we're in port, we're not allowed to use the ship-to-shore frequency. Even if we did open up as soon as she's finished with NSS, we might be just enough off-frequency from her that she won't hear our weak signal."

"I know," Buck said, containing his impatience. "But if we can hear him, isn't right now the best chance we'll ever get for him to hear us?"

"Where is he at, sir?"

"Oh. Sorry, Chief." Buck quickly covered his near breach of security. "Anyway, he's in about the same longitude as we are, and so is Radio Annapolis. So that means the radio conditions in this north-south line right now are at their best, and we ought to be able to work

him direct ourselves." Richardson had become an interested and approving onlooker, Buck noticed.

It would be necessary to disregard the rule against
transmitting while in port. *Proteus'* transmitter, already
on the frequency, would be fine-tuned to Annapolis'
transmissions. Then, as soon as Annapolis receipted to
the *Cushing*, *Proteus,* acting as though she were another
ship at sea waiting for the circuit to clear, would open
up with the cryptic call signs of the old wolfpack code.
These would mean nothing to anyone, not even *Cushing*'s radio operator (unless Keith had prepared him
for this eventuality) but they would to Keith, if he were
there and heard them, or even if he only saw them appear on his radioman's typewriter log sheet. Keith *would*
be there. He might even be hoping for something like
this to happen.

The problem was whether Keith could afford to stay
on the surface long enough for more messages. He had
to have surfaced through the ice to transmit this message
coming in. Those were his own beeps and key clicks
they were hearing, faint and weak because of the distance but clear and distinct, nevertheless, and they
proved that at that moment, at least, he was on the surface. Unless *Cushing* was in immediate danger, he would
stay surfaced long enough to hear the receipt signal
from Annapolis, probably would stay longer if not under pressure to submerge again. On the other hand, he
might have to go down immediately—if the damaged
Cushing was able to dive—and if that happened the
only way to get a message to him would be the one already used: the long-wave low-frequency radio transmitter system based at Cutler, Maine, designed for communication with submerged submarines.

Richardson had uncovered his free ear also. "We
don't have much time," he said. "What do we send
him?"

Buck showed him the message he had written. "Here it is. He'll spot this for the wolfpack code as soon as he hears it."

"KE RI BU C5," read Richardson aloud. "I remember the code was in two-letter groups. But why do you think he'll be able to decode it on sight? He won't have the code with him in the radio room."

"He won't need it. That's the beauty of it. It's designed to be used between people who know each other well. The first three groups are the first two letters of the names we use for each other. For Keith, just that much will do a lot."

There was pleasure in Richardson's voice as he acknowledged the truth of Buck's statement. Then he asked, "But what's this C5?"

"Once Keith catches on that we're trying to communicate something via the old wolfpack code, he'll know it means crystal system number five. Single sideband is frequency-controlled by crystal. So this whole message tells him we're here in the *Proteus* radio room —somebody's radio room, anyway—that we want to talk to him on single side-band radio, and which sets of crystals to use. He and I spent quite a bit of time working these out for that barrier exercise. He'll understand exactly what we're saying to him. We'll be using one crystal, on its frequency, and he'll be using a different one and come back at us with a different frequency."

There was a drop in Richardson's voice. "Remember, Buck, voice isn't secure. Don't get your hopes up too high about what we can tell him. Any ideas about what we can do to help him from down here will have to go in a classified encoded message. Matter of fact, we told him about your towing hookup rig in our answer to his first message. We're monitoring the scheds right now to pick up the transmission."

"I know, and I checked on that too, a little while ago." Buck had moved closer to Richardson, dropped his voice until he was practically whispering. "Our answer hasn't been sent out yet. That's one of the troubles with our system. There's so many messages to send that they haven't got to it yet. It's been hours since he sent his first message, and now here's the second, and still he's not received an answer to the first one. When it does go on the air, it will take him an hour or so to decode it, besides. It's just too slow!"

Richardson said nothing, and after a pause Buck went on. "You're boss, and you'll do the talking, but we've got to tell him something! Just say we're not sitting here on our ass while he's got a problem! You don't have to say anything classified!"

Williams' entreaty was having its effect, bolstered by Richardson's own natural desire. "The Russians might be able to find Keith's transmissions if they're continuously searching the entire spectrum. If they hear us down here they'll have no idea who we're talking to." He was talking to himself. "But if they've got a frequency scanner anywhere near where he is, when he opens up they'll zero in on him right away."

"And a lot of good may it do them! Keith has all the right in the world to use his radio!" Buck waved the message pad. "They're nearly finished transmitting. The group count's solid. Can I give the chief the go-ahead? I've already briefed him. We've got to break right in on CW before the *Cushing* closes down." With Richardson's nod of assent, Buck handed him the earphone, seized the chief radioman by the arm, began talking earnestly to him.

"He's already got his transmitter on the frequency," Buck reported a moment later with a smile of pleasure, "and he knows exactly what to do. Says every time he's listened on a circuit he's thought of how he could get something across to one of the other operators, if only he'd be allowed to try. He's getting set right now. As soon as NSS sends a receipt he'll zero beat with them. That will put him exactly on with NSS, and therefore with the *Cushing*. They'll hear him, too, and out of curiosity they'll listen to see what's coming off. Then they'll hear the chief send our little message five times and shut down. Keith will both see it on paper and hear it in his earphones, and that ought to do it."

"You're sure he won't answer and alert anyone listening that it was meant for him?"

"He won't answer," said Buck with a confident grin. "That's not in the code. I mean, it's in the code not to do that, ever. He invented it, remember. He won't send another thing on CW. 'c5' gives him both crystals. We wait a little while, then open up on voice, that's all. If he heard our CW transmission he'll simply set up his own radio, and wait. The next thing we hear from him will be his own voice, with no warning to anyone, when he answers us."

There was a change in the smooth cadence of the incoming message. The last few letters were drawn out, lengthened by the tiniest of fractions. Then the distant transmitter fell silent. Rich, Buck and the chief swung simultaneously to the two operators. Both were counting the coded groups they had been receiving. The chief seated himself at a third operating station, fingered the transmitting key, looked inquiringly at Richardson.

"Go ahead," said Rich. "Open up as soon as Annapolis sends the R. I'll take responsibility for breaking the rule."

"Whoever Keith had on the key was a damn good operator," said Buck. "I'll bet NSS doesn't need many repeats. Maybe not any. Our men seem to have it solid.

NSS should too." He put both hands to his head, pressed the earpiece hard against one ear. Richardson, he saw, was doing the same.

W7ST 130642 DE NSS went down on two radio typewriters. The signal was much louder than the one they had been hearing. There was a slight pause, then a prolonged, positive, dot-dash-dot, the letter R, sent with all the finality that could be mustered in a single monosyllabic note. Instantly they heard a faint tap from the distant station. *Cushing's* operator had barely touched his key, acknowledging, in the unwritten code of professional radiomen, that he had been fully serviced. His next move would be to turn off his transmitter. His message had been sent and receipted for, and there would be no further use for it.

Proteus' chief had, however, swung into action himself. One hand on his turning dial, the other on his transmitter key, he sent a single long dash, varying his frequency slightly. It took only a second or two, but it was already beginning to seem too long to Buck when the man released his key, apparently satisfied. Then, without preamble, he began to send the eight letters, four groups of two, over and over without pause. Five times Rich and Buck mentally recorded the four two-letter groups. Five times the radiomen at the receiving stations typed the short message. Then, as unceremoniously as it had begun, the transmission was finished. The chief was already looking for the next order. Buck made the sign of cutting his own throat, the chief reached into the recess of his operating station, and with a loud *cachunk* the transmitter power hum abruptly stopped.

AA DE NSS, the radiomen typed, and a moment later, K. "Unknown station using this net, identify yourself." There was a faintly querulous note to Radio Annapolis' normally steady tone. AA DE NSS, it sent again, and then, after a nearly imperceptible pause, ZKA ZKB. One of the radiomen jerked out a well-used pamphlet which had been stuffed between receivers at his station, flipped it open. Rich and Buck crowded to read over his shoulder. He ran his thumb down the margin. ZKA first. "I am net control," read the procedure signal entry. Immediately below, ZKB—"You are required to request permission to use this net."

Buck and the chief were smiling. There was an upward twitch also to Richardson's mouth as he said, "Don't answer. I suppose we'll have to confess someday, just to keep them from apoplexy down in Naval Communications in Washington. But we'll worry about that some other time. What now, mister communications wizard?"

"We wait long enough for Keith's people to set up his SSB set, and then we pick up our hand mike and start talking. If he heard our wolfpack transmission, he'll be there." Buck's pleasure at Richardson's compliment was evident.

The radio supervisor and one of his assistants were bustling about one of the radio sets ranged on the shelf above the operation positions. "Do you want to take it here?" he asked, addressing both Rich and Buck. "We can pipe it either to the bridge or to the Commodore's Office."

"Here's fine," said Rich. "If we have any problems, we may need your help."

"Okay, sir," said the chief, handing a microphone on the end of a wire to Richardson. "You can give me back that headset. You'll not be needing that. Just press this button on the mike and talk across it, not directly into it. You'll hear him on our speaker when you let go the button. Use normal voice procedure."

Rich fingered the microphone, looked it over carefully. The button was on the side convenient to his thumb. "Are we all ready? Has he had enough time?" he asked.

"Yessir. Go ahead." The chief still had his eyes on his equipment. Buck only smiled, nodded his head.

Richardson pressed the button, let go. A faint buzz came from the bulkhead-mounted speaker above the radio set. He could sense the powerful carrier wave emanating from the antenna on the tender's foremast, spreading instantaneously, in a huge ellipse oriented north and south up to and partway through earth's Heaviside Layer. A portion of it, now much weakened by distance over the frozen Arctic, would come within reach of the *Cushing*'s antennas and thence to the receivers in her radio room.

This had, in fact, already happened, and with the speed of light. Keith's receiver, if turned on and properly tuned to the right frequency, had already heard the unmodified note Rich had transmitted by pressing the button.

He pressed it again, held the microphone to one side of his mouth. "Keith," he said, "this is Rich. Buck is here too. Do you read me? How are you, old man?" He released the button, heard the squelch come off the bulkhead speaker.

The chief radioman had his fingers on the receiver dials, sensitively and carefully moving them. There was a faint crackle. He turned past the spot again, more slowly yet. There were words, high-pitched, faint, surrounded by static, but words nevertheless. More gentle adjustment of the dials.

"—and clear," the distant voice, suddenly distinct, said through the speaker. "How me? Over." It was Keith. Richardson felt a peculiar sensation on his skin. Keith was speaking slowly, distinctly, to give his words maximum readability over the thousands of miles of frozen sea, tundra and ordinary land it must cover. He must be in his own radio room, therefore well below the ice even if *Cushing* were somehow entirely surfaced.

Richardson squeezed the mike button. "We hear you the same, Keith. Buck's here with me. There's an answer already on the way to your first dispatch, and we've just intercepted your second. Can you stay up on voice? Over."

"Negative, Rich. There's too much activity over the equator." Rich caught the sharp glance from Buck, grimaced understandingly in return. "Our second message explains it better. It's great to hear you, though. Over." Keith spoke rapidly, now that communications had been established. There was just enough emphasis on the word "great" to accentuate the undercurrent of anxiety in his words.

"That's okay, Keith. We just want you to know we're with you, and will keep this circuit up on our end. Anytime you want to use it, open up and we'll be here. Over."

Keith evidently had begun talking even before Rich enunciated the final word. "—help a great deal," his voice said. "There's not much time—" There was a short pause, someone saying something in the distance, words unintelligible, then Keith's voice again, speaking even more rapidly. "Got to go. Thanks for calling. I'll come back to you when I can. Out." There were both urgency and finality in his voice.

"He's under a lot of pressure, Buck," said Rich gravely. "Something's really wrong up there."

"We hardly got a chance to talk at all. I was hoping there'd be enough time to say more than just 'hello,'" said Williams, betraying his own concern by speaking nearly as rapidly as Keith. "Should we tell him we're on our way to help him? He might be able to hear us even if he can't answer."

"No. He's signed off. That's telling us something, right there. Probably he's already retracting antennas and flooding tanks. No point in adding any more complication to his life right now. Let's take this message of his and decode it. That's the most useful thing we can do."

Buck hesitated an instant, then said, "Shall I leave instructions up here about guarding the voice frequency? I'll join you in a minute."

"Okay, Buck, thanks," said Richardson. "I have the key to the coding room down in my safe. Tell the chief to set up a continuous watch on voice and CW both, and call one of us if they hear anything. Also, they should record all transmission on tape, especially if we're not there to hear them. The squadron office has a tape recorder. Have them get it up here and be ready to use it."

Setting up the coding machine was an unfamiliar exercise for both officers, although both had been well versed in an earlier model. An added complication was the necessity of implementing a totally new top-secret code, extracted from the code room safe. Much reference to the printed instructions and many false starts were necessary before the machine finally began to type out intelligible copy. Richardson and Williams, their heads nearly touching, read the words as they appeared from under the typing bar.

"This CHARLIE JULIET business is silly," muttered Buck as the first words appeared. "What good is a code name in a ciphered message?"

Rich did not answer. The next few words engaged his full attention. He could feel Buck Williams' heavy breathing, only inches away.

FROM CHARLIE JULIET X SECOND REPORT FOR COMSUBLANT COMSUBRON TEN X MAX SHAFT SPEED TWENTY RPM WITH HEAVY VIBRATION X PROPELLER STERN PLANES AND LOWER RUDDER DAMAGED COLLISION SUBMERGED OBJECT BE-

LIEVED TO BE SOVIET SUBMARINE X SECONDARY
PROPULSION MOTOR WIPED OFF X NO SERIOUS
LEAKS X NO PREVIOUS SONAR CONTACT X MILITARY
TYPE AIRCRAFT APPARENTLY SEARCHING AREA X
UNABLE INSPECT SCREW WITHOUT RISK DETECTION
X ICE COVER FIFTEEN DASH TWENTY FEET EXCEPT
POLYNYAS AND LEADS FEW AND FAR BETWEEN
WHERE FROZEN ONLY THREE DASH FOUR FEET X
INSPECTION MANDATORY BEFORE PROCEEDING DUE
HEAVY VIBRATION X REMAINING IN POLYNYA PO-
SITION GOLF NOVEMBER TWO NINE AWAITING OP-
PORTUNITY USE DIVERS X SUSPECT BENT SHAFT X
WILL REPORT RESULTS ASAP X IN VIEW APPARENT
DAMAGE BELIEVE MUST ABORT MISSION BUT UN-
ABLE ESTIMATE ABILITY YET TO CLEAR PACK X

Richardson broke the silence. "Buck, this is a real
emergency! I'd call Norfolk right away, but there's only
a duty officer and a communication watch on, and anyway they'll not have Keith's message decoded yet. How
quick can you pull your ship together and get out of
here?"

"Tomorrow, like I said. But we're not on any emergency basis."

"Go down right now and check the critical items. Be
back here in an hour. We can have a quick breakfast
while we talk it over and get ready to phone Norfolk.
Put your crew under emergency notice, but don't tell
anyone why. I'll see what the *Proteus* can do to speed
up getting the two towing rigs ready. By that time
they'll have decoded the message and rushed it to Admiral Murphy, and he'll be anxious to talk to us and
Washington both."

Reveille was sounding aboard the *Proteus* as they
locked the steel door of the coding room behind them.

11

~~~~~~

There had been no warning whatever of the presence of another submarine, or anything else, for that matter, until too late to avoid. It *must* have been a submarine, running silent, close to the underside of the ice. Nothing else could have produced the sudden, disconcerting heave of *Cushing*'s big hull, the metallic grinding sound as her propeller mangled its seven exotically shaped blades into twisted bronze, the shriek of tortured bearings in her engineroom as the propeller shaft bowed in the middle and then returned to normal. The initial shock had thrown the big missile submarine heavily to starboard. It was followed by a series of smaller, more scraping blows. The *Cushing* heaved upward from the stern, and suddenly it was over, the noise gone, leaving only reverberations in the water and slow-growing appreciation of disaster.

An inspection of the turbine mounts and the propeller-shaft steady bearing, carefully conducted later, confirmed that these massive mechanisms had been displaced as much as half an inch, and had then returned to their normal positions. The findings had been greeted with incredulity by *Cushing*'s engineering officer, Curt Taylor, and by all the enginemen and machinists who had made the measurements; but the proof was there, marks in the machinery foundations themselves. Only Keith, when he saw them with his own eyes, could accept the undisputable evidence. Some years previous he had viewed remote-control movies in slow motion of what actually happened when a sister ship of the old *Eel* had been subjected to a test depth charging. The veteran hulk had been depth charged to destruction, but the cameras, specially protected, had been brought back by divers who had carefully entered the shattered and flooded old hull after it was all over.

Keith and the other viewers of the film had had it run several times, at both fast and slow speeds, before they could believe what they saw: steel forgings stretching like rubber, snapping back to their original configurations; pieces of heavy equipment moving radically, sometimes as much as a foot or more, in relation to each other; more slender rods and pipes bending and springing like so many thin rubber bands, and then, after the shock, looking as if nothing had happened—except for a cloud of paint particles which had flaked off and, for several seconds, floated to the deck amid the dust and trash also flung there.

Any theory that vibration communicated to the camera itself could have been responsible for what the films showed was disproved by the fact that the objects in view moved in disparate directions, some one way and some another. Some of them, less securely fastened, continued to vibrate for several perceptible, rapidly diminishing, cycles. In succeeding and more powerful charges some were broken clean, or their securings sheared off. At the end, there was the horrendous flooding entry of white water as the lethal charge finally breached the stout old hull. Keith and the other wartime submariners present had sat several seconds in silence after the film was over. There had been no noise, no accompanying crash of depth charges, no terror or pain inflicted. But Keith, and the others, had needed none. The view of the tortured machinery had been enough. Each had his own memories of depth chargings, and some, like Keith, would always carry in their minds the knowledge that what they had just witnessed, in the safe confines of one of the Pentagon's movie auditoriums, might have been the last thing seen on earth by their old friends and shipmates.

After the films Keith no longer wondered why it was that *Eel*'s hull had appeared to whip during depth charging, how it could be that the main engines—those huge locomotive-type diesels—had seemed to bounce convulsively on their bed plates. They had, even though no one would believe it at the time. The pictures in slow motion, taken at ten times normal film speed, demonstrated that his instantaneous impressions during the war—and those of others who had seen similar things— had not been wrong. They had not been hallucinations due to stress. These extraordinary things had actually happened.

Irrefutably it had happened to the *William B. Cushing* herself, even though the shock had been one of collision, not nearby explosion. It took the calm evaluation of all the evidence to reach the inescapable conclusion. This amount of damage could only have happened by collision with another steel hull—and at some speed.

Keith had been maneuvering his ship slowly, positioning her under the most promising frozen-over opening in the ice found so far. Originally it had been a long crack, or lead, in the ice floe. Instead of being closed by action of the wind and ocean currents it had remained open, perhaps even widened slightly, while the somewhat less saline water at the surface froze into a permanent bridge over the opening. The double echo trace on *Cushing*'s upward-beamed Fathometer indicated the thickness as somewhere between three and four feet. But the crack was narrow, less than one hundred feet in width, rimmed by old ice floes twenty feet thick or more. Seen from below, it was in shape a ravine in an otherwise fairly smooth, inverted plain of ice.

In order to break through the thin ice cover it was first necessary to position the bulbous 420-foot *Cushing* lengthwise between the two downward-projecting, near vertical ice cliffs on either side of the lead, bring her up gently and carefully, exactly midway in the thin spot. Keith, at *Cushing*'s control station, knew he was not yet at a depth shallow enough to strike the ice. His first, instantaneous reaction was that there must have been an unnoticed, disastrously deep ice pinnacle—the bottom of an unseen berg embedded in the ice floe—against which *Cushing*'s propeller, instantly stopped but not until it had turned half a dozen revolutions against whatever it was that she had struck, had received considerable damage.

But sonar, which had continuously been reporting all clear, had suddenly announced strange propeller noises dead astern in the baffles, and close aboard. Many crew members later reported having heard them throughout the hull at the time of the collision, with or without earphones, along with a cacophony of machinery noises from some other ship. The report from sonar was simultaneous with a tremendous upward heave aft which could only have resulted from something big passing underneath. Keith had just lowered his periscope, had been watching the underside of the ice through his controllable TV camera and its paired searchlights.

Hurriedly he swiveled it around to extreme horizontal train, saw bubbles and turbulent water rising around his own ship's hull.

The foreign submarine must have been traveling recklessly fast so close to the undersurface of the ice. She must surely be nuclear-powered, and she must have been running in the silent mode (which might indicate knowledge that an American submarine was in the vicinity). Coming from astern and at a somewhat greater depth, she had struck the *Cushing* right aft on a slightly divergent heading and had bumped some distance along her bottom before breaking clear. Why sonar had not previously given some warning would bear investigation, both as to *Cushing*'s own sonar and the sonar conditions themselves, but Keith was well aware of the vagaries of underwater sound transmission under the best and most usual of conditions, particularly astern, where there was a masking effect from one's own machinery and propeller. Here in the Arctic, under bumpy, fissured ice floating on a layer of brackish water, there was every opportunity for sound reception to be erratic.

The *Cushing* had not yet been quite lined up with the frozen lead when the collision took place. Keith had been maneuvering with both his main power and the auxiliary "outboard motor," the retractable emergency electric propulsion motor, when the impact came. It shoved the huge submarine ahead and sideways and changed her heading thirty degrees, by chance positioning her almost exactly as Keith had wanted her. He seized the opportunity, brought her the rest of the way up against the frozen surface, then began blowing his main ballast tanks.

Cushing's sail, specially reinforced to take the pressure, dug into the ice above and broke through with a great creaking and groaning of stressed steel, carrying a big chunk of ice "frosting" atop the black, rectangular-appearing structure. Her sailplanes, turned to a vertical position, sliced through the ice neatly and almost noiselessly on each side. Aft, the topside rudder, apparently undamaged, thrust through also, like a distant sentinel. Keith stopped blowing before the submarine was lightened sufficiently for her entire body to heave up the ice under which it lay. The three or four feet of undisturbed ice would conceal the big black hull from surface or air observation, while the narrow crevasse into which he had brought her would tend to protect her from detection underwater, should the other submarine find its way back to the place of the collision. It was almost like an underwater garage. Only the bottom portion of the missile submarine's hull would project below, visible, to be sure, to any submarine coming close enough to inspect through its periscope, but surely invisible to any sonar search. Above the ice blanket, radar might possibly distinguish the sharper outline of *Cushing*'s sail from the many rough protuberances of the ice field, but the greatest danger of detection was visual. That black rectangle and its smaller satellite, the rudder, could be seen for miles.

Keith hesitated a moment to weigh the priorities. There was something he must do before clambering out on the submarine's bridge and thence to the ice. There would be some delay, anyway, while a hastily organized working party hacked away with axes and crowbars at the huge, dripping ice cakes filling the bridge cavity. As soon as this was done they would move immediately to the area of the ship's retractable antennas and clear them for hoisting. Ten or fifteen minutes, at minimum, would elapse before *Cushing*'s radio room could begin to transmit the message he and Jim Hanson had laboriously prepared.

Encryption had been completed only an hour or so

ago, immediately after the decision that this fourth area of thin ice, frozen over as it was, was likely to be as satisfactory as any *Cushing* would find at this time of year. A message of some kind was overdue anyway. But the few minutes of delay before it could be sent were long enough to make a quick change to report the collision. It should be possible to do this without re-encrypting the entire message. Howie Trumbull would be able to take care of it.

In only one thing were Richardson and Williams wrong in their evaluation of what had gone on board the *Cushing*. Keith was not in the radio room while his first message was being sent. He had handed the quickly revised text to Trumbull and then hurried to the bridge, donning on the run a heavy hooded parka, equally heavy wool trousers and thick boots.

The hatch trunk leading to the bridge was mercifully protected by the rounded forward portion of the sail, so that there was at least some transition from the temperature inside the submarine to that of the winter Arctic. His lungs nevertheless felt as though he had suddenly drawn in a shaft of solid ice. Two breaths later (he had become more cautious, breathed more gently) he was on the bridge, fumbling with the cords so as to draw tighter the hood of his parka. There was a mild but freezing wind. He had forgotten mittens, was torn between exposing his hands to pull on the drawstrings and thus protect his face—already beginning to feel numb—and plunging them into his parka pockets to keep his rapidly stiffening fingers from freezing. He kept his head below the oval cockpit, turned his back to the wind, drew up and knotted the drawstrings, finally shoved his hands into the grateful warmth of the pockets. There he found the pair of mittens some forward-thinking parka custodian had placed in them, drew them on, and immediately shoved his mittened hands under his armpits.

It was much easier to look to leeward, but he resolutely forced himself to survey the entire horizon. The binoculars he held to his face were some protection. The month of March was at midpassage. The vernal equinox was still a week away, and the sun had not yet broken above the horizon. Instead, it traveled unceasingly around through 360 degrees, out of sight, its location revealed by a spot of extreme brightness from which rays of sunlight, broken by unseen clouds, streamed upward. The entire Arctic was a rapidly lightening semitwilight zone. This close to the North Pole, the year was divided into only the dark period, the twilight, and the daylight. In *Cushing*'s location, within 200 miles of the Pole, the nearest equivalent of "night" was when the sun was directly across the Pole, thus farthest below the horizon. In navigation parlance, the sun "dipped" when it was due north, and came nearest to the horizon when it was due south. On the twenty-first day of June, when the sun was at its most northern point, to an observer exactly at the Pole, it would be only about twenty-three degrees twenty-seven minutes above the horizon—and would appear to travel completely around him at that elevation during the day's official twenty-four hours.

There had as yet been no perceptible warming of the Arctic wastes. Winter still had the area in its grip. The temperature topside, according to a thermometer which some quartermaster had thoughtfully placed in an angle-iron recess on the bridge before laying about with a crowbar, was a minus forty degrees Fahrenheit. From somewhere Keith recalled that this point, on the Centigrade scale, also read minus forty, the only place where the two coincided. Keith had lost sensation in his cheeks. Frostbite must be near. A few feet away, four men, garbed as he was, were demolishing the last of the ice on the rounded, ice-reinforced top of *Cushing*'s sail. They had been topside far longer than he. They must be nearly frozen. The unnatural stiffness of their features and the clumsiness of their movements showed it.

One thing he could do for them, for morale in general. It might even bring volunteers for any similar jobs. He fumbled for the button controlling the bridge speaker, pressed it with his knuckle through the thick wool-and-leather mittens, spoke into it. "Control, this is the captain. The ice-chopping crew is finished and coming below. Tell the doctor to issue them a ration of medicinal spirits first thing. Also to everyone else coming down from a topside detail. It's cold up here. Be sure all hands coming topside wear face masks and full cold-weather gear." He released the button, pressed it again. "I'm going out on the ice," he said. "Send me a face mask, and keep a watch on me through the periscope."

He released the button, waited for the face mask, then began to climb over the side of the cockpit, placing his feet carefully on the rungs welded to the outside. He would inspect quickly for whatever damage could be seen from the surface. Doubtless there would be little or nothing he could see, but it would give him solitude to consider what next to do.

Keith was grateful to the supply officer whose forethought had included white paint among the special Arctic equipment with which the *Cushing* had been loaded. While he was thawing out in the after part of the warm engineroom, watching Curt Taylor and his machinist's mates as they crawled among the heavy foundations of the propeller shaft and reduction gears, another half-dozen men were eagerly earning their rations of medicinal brandy by hastily daubing a coat of white paint over all visible portions of the ship.

Damage assessment was dismaying. The other submarine had bumped and scraped some distance along Cushing's bottom and marked its passage with a series of dents visible from inside. To withstand sea pressure at depth, the pressure hull and framing of submarines, particularly the large-diameter hulls of modern missile submarines, are far stronger than comparable structures of any other type of ship. Keith was amazed at the reports of dents between frames in the Cushing's single hull section, had to inspect them himself before accepting what had been reported to him. He could conjecture what must have happened to the thin outside plating of the double hull section. The other submarine, having been struck in her upper works, must have suffered major damage as well.

Although the Cushing's hull was sound, despite the dents, the shock to her propulsion machinery had been enormous. Most significantly, her huge propeller was undoubtedly badly damaged, and the propeller shaft showed measurable travel from side to side as the electric "creep motor" slowly rotated it. When a few faster revolutions ahead and astern were attempted under turbine power, the instantaneous vibration transmitted to the whole huge structure of the shaft bearings and reduction gears was frightening. It had been intended to go up to fifty or sixty rpm, the ship still being held fast in the ice, but the shaking was so strong that Keith ordered the shaft stopped when it reached twenty rpm.

"Whew!" muttered Curt Taylor, mopping sweat off his ample face. "That's the first time I've ever seen anything like that! I wonder what's on the end of the shaft. It must be really bent out of shape!"

"It looks bad," agreed Keith, in an equally low voice. He had been listening on a telephone handset, now hung it up. "It took more steam than usual to turn the shaft. The motor was drawing more amperage, too, I saw. Curt . . ." His voice became even more grave. He drew the chief engineer farther away from the others. "Curt, we've got to hope at least one blade of that screw can still give us some thrust, somehow. The emergency propulsion motor is completely gone!"

Curt Taylor's eyes widened as he took it in. "It was rigged out, that's right! I'd forgotten—we were using it to help maneuver. What do you mean, it's gone? Is it beyond repair?"

Keith nodded. "It's gone. Wiped clean off. There's nothing left of it."

Cushing, like all the big missile submarines, had been designed with a retractable electric-powered "outboard motor," in the auxiliary machinery compartment just forward of the engineroom, which could be hydraulically extended below the keel for maneuvering in close quarters, or, if necessary, for emergency propulsion. Normally it was carried completely housed; even the opening in the ship's bottom was closed over, so there would be no break in the smooth continuity of the underwater body. Keith had been using it to help position the ship under the frozen lead, and by consequence it had been sheared off in the collision.

Her secondary propulsion having been stripped away, *Cushing* would be totally dependent on her main drive for any movement. Taylor's face showed the seriousness with which he viewed the situation. "Skipper," he said, "we had the shaft up to twenty rpm, but I don't think we could even keep that up for long. It looked to me she's definitely bent out of line. That's why it took more power to turn it. Also, there's that vibration. Whatever it was that hit us, it ruined the propeller. Who knows what we have out there now on the end of our propeller shaft!"

"If it can drive the ship at all, Curt, we've got to use it. Control reports the ship didn't even try to move in the ice while we had the shaft turning, but we didn't keep it turning very long. We'll have to give it another try. I don't want to drop out of this polynya until we're sure we can travel, or at least come back to it if we need to. Keep your boys on it. Figure out anything you can do, maybe loosen some of the foundation bolts so the shaft can turn more easily. We're going to have to get some people in the water with diving outfits to inspect—"

The telephone buzzed. "For you again, Captain," said the man who answered it, as he held out the instrument. Keith listened, put it back on its cradle with a terse "thanks." He turned back to Taylor. "They need me up in control, Curt. Do everything you can. We're in real deep trouble."

From the after end of the engineroom to the control room was a distance of over 300 feet, the major portion devoted to the sixteen silos in the missile compartment —sixteen tremendous cylinders, set vertically, extending from the bottom of the submarine through all the decks between and through the cylindrical hull on top. Strangely, despite the formidable complexity of everything about the *Cushing,* here, in the place that it was all about, where her firepower was located, there was none of the profusion of equipment so characteristic of the rest of the ship. Except for a few chests of spares ranked outboard against the curved side, and the umbilical cords plugged into each silo—reaching through to the missile at their upper end, disappearing beneath the deck at the other—the compartment seemed bare, in marked contrast to the rest of the ship. And yet, were these sixteen silos fully loaded with war-ready missiles, which at the moment they were not, they would carry within them more explosive power than the total used by both sides in both world wars!

The missile compartment, from which all this destruction could be unleashed upon command, actually presented a scene of peace and serenity. The sixteen huge vertical tubes, cork-insulated around their exterior, painted a light coral tone, had never failed to impress Keith with their total lack of malevolence. Perhaps it was that the mind of man simply could not encompass the dreadful intent, the terror, for which they had been built. Nor the fear which had inspired them.

Even now, as Keith sprinted the length of the passageway alongside the ranked missile tubes, the old philosophical reverie roused itself from some dormant part of his mind. But there was no time for contemplation today. He reached the watertight door at the end, hurriedly spun the handwheel to undog it, pushed it open. The man standing in the passageway readily understood Keith's wordless signal to dog down the door once more, and Keith continued his hurried trip past the navigation center into the cluttered open space which was the nerve center of the ship.

Jim Hanson, Keith's tall second-in-command, sprouting the red beard which would come off before return to port, was standing on the raised periscope station, facing the lowered starboard periscope. There was a look of helpless concern on his face. "I lowered the periscope, Skipper," he said as soon as Keith appeared. "There's an airplane out there, and I figured we'd be a little harder to see with it down."

"How far?" said Keith. He reached his side with a huge leap up the metal steps, aided by the handrail on either side.

"On the horizon."

"Is it coming this way?"

"Couldn't tell. It wasn't coming right at us. Yet, anyway."

"Could you see any markings?"

"Too far."

With a decisive movement, Keith shoved the hydraulic control handle, started the periscope up. "I'll have to take a look," he muttered to Hanson as the shiny tube began to rise. "It can't be one of ours, though. Do we have anyone topside?"

"Negative," said Hanson. "We're standing lookout watch on the periscope. All hatches are shut."

"Good," said Keith as the periscope handles appeared smoothly out of the periscope well. He snapped them down, hooked his right elbow over one handle, his left hand on the other, applied his face to the rubber guard around the eyepiece. "We can't dive out of this hole we're in until we know if we have propulsion," he said as he began swinging the tall, thin instrument. "We'll never get back to it, and we sure won't be able to look around for another one. Their boat must have some problems, too. It must have taken a lot of damage, considering how hard he hit us."

"You think they're looking for him?" Hanson asked the question in a low voice, standing alongside Keith as he began swiftly rotating the periscope.

"Probably." Keith answered without taking his eye from the eyepiece, leaning to his left as he let the weight of his body help spin the periscope. He stopped suddenly, straightened up slightly, began swiftly manipulating the periscope controls. Then, very rapidly, he spun the instrument around twice, stopped on the same bearing, looked for a long instant and flipped up the handles.

Jim Hanson, his hand on the control handle, pulled it toward him. "What do you see?" he asked as the periscope dropped away.

"There's three planes out there circling around something."

"How far?"

"On the horizon. Maybe a little beyond. Probably about where you saw the first one."

"You think they're looking for the boat that hit us?"

"That would be pretty fast work. Could be, I s'pose, but I'd be a little surprised if they're out looking for him this soon. We've not even got an answer to our message yet."

"Could you make out the markings?"

"No. But I'm glad we had enough white paint to cover everything that came up through the ice. I'm not too anxious for them to find us. Not yet, anyway, especially if they're out here for some other reason." Keith paused. "Listen," he resumed, "I don't want to use the periscope any more than we can help. It increases the chances they'll spot us on their radar. But we've got to keep a watch on them. So there'll have to be a topside lookout. Get a watch set up right away. He'll need heavy-weather gear, and a heater in the bridge cockpit. Also, have him keep a white sheet or tablecloth wrapped around his head and upper body."

"Aye, aye, sir," said Hanson.

Keith was grateful for the reversion to official language. Jim Hanson's questions had begun to be uncomfortable. Although Jim was his most trusted subordinate, he had known him only during the year or so of the ship's precommissioning and training period. Such questions Keith might have asked of Rich, as his executive officer, because the relationship had been going on so much longer and was so much deeper. Or, they might have been required during combat, when one of an exec's duties was to inform himself of everything his commanding officer knew and thought. Keith's eyes followed Jim as he left the periscope platform to see about organizing the lookout watch. It was the first time he could recall having been even mildly displeased with him.

And then the idea introduced itself that, for Jim, it was the nearest thing yet to a combat situation. Jim was doing exactly what Keith had done, many times before. The difference was in the nature of the antagonist. Jim's questions, in fact, were nearly the same ones Keith had asked of Rich. And suddenly Keith wondered why he had had such feelings in the first place. Could it, perchance, be the result of his own inadequacies? For he could already feel, growing within him, still held rigidly beneath the level of conscious recognition, the dread of what he was going to discover when at last the propeller could be inspected.

With the secondary propulsion system gone and the main propulsion out of commission, either with propeller blades crumpled or the shaft so far out of line that it could not be used, there would be no way of moving the *Cushing*. He and his ship and crew were trapped in the Arctic, as surely as those old wooden whaling ships! He dared not even drop out of the frozen lead in which he had surfaced, for fear of not being able to return to it!

Drafting the second message had been done with speed and urgency, yet it had taken well over an hour. And there were many discarded pieces of paper, carefully collected by Trumbull for destruction by burning. This process, too, reminded Keith of the many wartime moments when he had participated in the same thing: the drafting and redrafting; the poring over words and phrases; the painstaking distillation of every drop of meaning, accidental, possible or intended; the equally painstaking concern over how every word would—or could—be interpreted by the recipients. The effort to compress as much meaning as possible into the fewest words, knowing they would be subjected to the same process by those to whom addressed, and by many others besides.

After careful observation of the aircraft in the distance, Keith decided they were engaged in some activity centered in the vicinity where he had first seen them, not searching the area in general. There was, however, at least one plane continuously in the air, or so it seemed, for there had been only a few periods of any length during which none was visible. During the first one, a work party managed to chop a small hole in the ice behind the rudder and confirmed, from what they could see through the clear, still water, that the propeller had been badly damaged. But reappearance of a plane, albeit still on the horizon, caused Keith to countermand dispatch of the diver—the man had already gone to the bridge in his rubber suit and breathing gear—and hurriedly call back his men from the ice. Thereafter he had been more cautious. An hour later he had progressed no farther than thinking about sending out a new group when another aircraft sighting nullified the idea once more.

Timing of the second message had been exactly as Rich and Buck had surmised, planned so that it could go out while there was the best chance of reception on the east coast of the United States. The certainty that his first message must have galvanized his friends into tense attention awaiting his second had even translated into the likelihood they would try to intercept it direct, in *Proteus'* radio room. And, just as Rich and Buck guessed, Keith was in his own radio room, earphones plugged into the circuit, while his second message was being sent out. There had been a perceptible thrill as he recognized the sudden, but not totally unexpected, interposition of a new station on the circuit transmitting his own wolfpack code.

Setting up the single side-band radio was swiftly done. There was a rush of sibilant reverberation as the initial transmissions were made. Chief Radioman Melson had his fingers on the fine-tuning dial, rotated it ever so slowly. Suddenly, as though it were from a ship close aboard, instead of thousands of miles away, Richardson's voice boomed over the radio room loudspeaker. "Buck is here, too. . . . How are you, old man?" There was a nuance of meaning in the words deeper than the mere formalities. In a guarded sort of way Richardson was asking how Keith—and his ship— really were.

Keith had not thought about security. The order to go to voice communication was sufficient, so far as he was concerned, and only now, sensing Richardson's own reticence at speaking out plainly, did the possibility of interception by unwanted listeners cross his mind. They would need special equipment, able to monitor the entire frequency spectrum, but undeniably it could be done if the need had been anticipated.

Thinking fast, he said into his microphone, "This is Keith. I read you loud and clear. This is Keith. I read you loud and clear. How me? Over." He said the brief message twice. It would not do to use the name of his ship over voice radio, but his own first name would be all right. Rich had done the same.

The ship's telephone rang in the radio room. Melson picked it up, answered, held it out to Keith. "For you, sir."

"This is the OOD on the bridge, Captain. We've got a plane in sight again."

"Keep me informed," said Keith. "Be ready to submerge if it heads this way!" Keith dropped the handset. Richardson's voice on the speaker was saying, "Can you stay up on voice? Over."

"Negative, Rich. There's too much activity over the equator. . . ." Rich and Buck would understand. Maybe he was being a little coy, but there was no point in calling the attention of a chance listener to his position.

Suddenly there were two loudspeakers going at once. Richardson's next transmission was paralleled by the ship's general communication system. Jim Hanson's voice. "Captain, this is Jim. I'm on the bridge. That plane is closer than ever before. It's on a steady bearing. I think it's headed this way!"

Rich was saying something about maintaining a watch on the voice circuit. Keith had already begun a reply. Perhaps the plane had a direction finder, was homing in on his transmissions! Hurriedly he closed out the conversation, speaking quickly. His voice, he knew, would transmit its own sense of exigency. Rich and Buck, for the time being, would have to be satisfied with that.

The control room was but a step away, through a bulkhead. For the barest instant he debated going to the bridge himself. No. Jim's presence was already increasing the load up there by one. If it became necessary to dive, another extra person would slow down the process of clearing the bridge and getting everyone below. Worse, encumbered as everyone was with heavy clothing, he might be caught in the hatch trunk and jam up the process inextricably. He picked up the periscope-station mike, pressed the button for the bridge. "Jim, I'm in conn. What's it like now?" Jim would recognize his voice. No need to go through the obligatory call-up procedure.

Jim must have had his hand already on the speaker switch, automatically overrode Keith when he pushed it. His amplified voice filled the control room as Keith was uttering the last few words. "It's out of sight now. Still steady bearing, though. Maybe it's not heading this way." There was relief in Hanson's voice, and yet uncertainty, too. The plane was still some distance away, perhaps still beyond the horizon, flying low. . . .

An old memory clicked in Keith's mind. The pupils of his eyes dilated as the impact sank in. The plane was flying low. There was malevolent intent in that. It might be on an attack run! "Clear the bridge!" he yelled into the microphone, the fingers gripping it suddenly clenched, the blood driven out of his fingernails. "Take her down!"

With his other hand he pushed the handle controlling the hydraulic periscope hoist. As the bright metal tube slithered silently up from the periscope well he could sense the quick bustle of the control room crew standing up to their stations, their practiced hands waiting for the orders that would open vents, let air out of tanks and send the powerless *Cushing* deep into the icy sea.

Two blasts of the diving alarm. Jim Hanson had sounded it from the bridge after making sure the heavily bundled lookout and the OOD had gotten into the hatch trunk. He would be the next-to-last man down, would render assistance as necessary as the Officer of the Deck dogged the hatch. Already the lookout, red of face (what could be seen of it), skin puffed from the cold, bulky in the heavy clothing under his white sheet, had appeared in the control room. A quick look to his left, to the ballast control panel. Its operator was in the process of flipping the last of the switches controlling the main vent valves.

The base of the periscope appeared at the top of its well, dragging with it the big tubular radar section. Keith had chosen the radar periscope because of the superior optics its larger headsize accommodated. He grabbed the handles as they appeared, snapped them down, with a single smooth motion put his right eye to the eyepiece and swung the 'scope around to the previously noted bearing of the aircraft. The periscope height would permit him to see what the uneven ice denied to Jim Hanson on the bridge.

Just as he had thought! The plane was flying as low as it could, almost brushing the ice, lifting just enough to give clearance to occasional hummocks and piled-up drifts. It was headed directly for the *Cushing*. Its two whirling propellers were plainly visible. So was the fixed landing gear, with large broad skis instead of wheels. Fortunately, the bridge watch had been alert. Possibly the plane had been sighted before beginning its run in. Whatever the sequence of events, and their cause, now it was down on the deck, headed directly toward him. There was only one way to interpret this hazardous style of flying. The plane was trying to remain concealed. Only a professional military pilot would fly this way, and only if his intentions were not friendly!

Keith noticed that his periscope was lower, the ice surface nearer. He hazarded a swift look aft. Yes, the rudder had vanished, leaving a neat hole in the ice shaped to its cross section and the smaller hole his men had cut directly abaft it, which had not been visible as long as the rudder protrusion was in the way. He could not depress the periscope optics enough to see whether *Cushing*'s sail was still visible, and he did not try. The diving officer, or Jim Hanson, whom he could sense now standing beside him on the periscope station, would in any event report depths as the ship submerged, and he could calculate the disappearance of his sail by himself. The plane was closer, although he had been looking in another direction less than ten seconds. How long would it take to get here? How fast was it coming? How far away?

Answers to all these questions were by guess and estimation only. *Cushing,* with no way on, was dropping very slowly. During the war *Walrus* and *Eel* had customarily dived in seconds, often in less than half a minute, using the combined full diving capabilities of speed, sharp down-angle, and a boat deliberately ballasted heavy. *Cushing* was four times the displacement of *Eel,* and she had no power. Even if she had, she could not have used speed to leave her niche in the ice. She was going down excruciatingly slowly.

"What's the depth?" he snapped, without taking his eye from the periscope. He would lower it as soon as the sail was under, but now that *Cushing*'s presence had been detected he might as well use it as long as he could.

"Forty-six feet." Jim, answering instantly. He must have been watching the depth gauge. "Zero bubble. Forty-six-and-a-half—now it's forty-seven feet. Four feet to go!" Good man. He knew what Keith needed to know. The *Cushing* went completely under at keel depth fifty-four feet. Allowing for snow buildup on top of the ice, her sail would be out of sight when her keel had reached about fifty-one. "Forty-eight feet," said Hanson's voice, speaking directly into Keith's right ear.

The plane was close, now. A two-engine, propeller-driven, high-wing monoplane with fixed landing gear, rigged with skis for Arctic operations. Its presence in the Arctic could not have been spur-of-the-moment! Quickly he announced the description to Jim. "No insignia visible at this angle," he concluded. It must be only a couple of miles away.

"Forty-nine feet," said Jim quietly. The plane was clearly not a modern attack or combat plane. The apparently nonretractable landing gear—with skis, to boot —marked it as an aircraft configured for supply missions over icy terrain. But what had brought it and its two mates to the middle of the Arctic Ocean just at this moment? The idea that the Russians had been able to mount a rescue effort for their own submarine in the very short time since the accident simply could not wash. Perhaps it was a coincidence, some operation, already planned, now doubtless diverted. Perhaps—the idea struck suddenly home—the three aircraft and the submarine which had done the damage were part of a combined operation. Perhaps their presence, and the collision, were not accidental!

The plane was closer, perhaps a mile. "Forty-nine-a-half," said Jim. Its underside was more clearly visible. Keith's hand fell to the motorcycle-type elevation control, but there was no immediate necessity to elevate the periscope optics. The plane was not yet coming overhead. More of the underside was visible because it had suddenly assumed a climbing attitude. Now his angle of sight was distinctly below it. There were no insignia on the underside of the wing. A small object detached itself from the belly of the plane, between the skis, separated rapidly from it, grew swiftly in size as the plane zoomed upward.

"Sound the collision alarm!" Keith spoke rapidly. "He's dropped something! Looks like a bomb!" He turned the handle rapidly, keeping the plane in sight as the scream of the collision alarm and the deep thuds of watertight doors slamming throughout the ship reverberated in his ears. When he reached the limiting elevation he watched the plane go out of sight overhead, then spun the periscope completely around. "Put me on the reciprocal!" Jim Hanson's hands were over his on the periscope controls, shoved the 'scope to the right bearing. "Passing fifty feet," Jim said. The plane had abruptly increased altitude as it dropped its bomb, but there had been no discernible course change. It would pass over the submarine in one or two seconds and he would pick it up as it again came within his field of view.

"Fifty-one feet," said Jim as he waited. The sail must be nearly out of sight now; at least, buried in the snow and little pile of broken ice created when it pushed through. The bomb—if that was what it was—would be landing at any moment, no doubt before the plane reappeared in the periscope view. Perhaps he should have kept his eye on the bomb in its trajectory, instead of on the plane. Perhaps he should have lowered the periscope. He had consciously decided to risk leaving it up: if the bomb struck the sail, there was as much possibility of damage to the periscope whether up or down. If it missed, the 'scope was safe anyway, except for the extreme unlikely chance that the elevated portion might take a direct hit from an otherwise near miss.

BLAM! The explosion came with shocking suddenness. A cloud of white—flying snow and ice, and the smoke of the explosive charge—filled the periscope view. The rubber eyepiece vibrated against Keith's forehead, the ridge of his nose and his cheekbone. The plane had not yet come into view. Now it would be impossible to see anything for a few moments. On releasing its bomb the plane obviously had been climbing for altitude. A bomb dropped from a low-flying aircraft was often as hazardous to the bomber as to the target, because the bomb "flew" the same course and speed as the plane while dropping away from it. Its shock wave on detonation inevitably encompassed the space directly above, where, unless there were room and time to maneuver, the plane that had dropped it would be. This was why the plane had swooped upward. It had been flying too near the ice to risk the radical course change which was the normal postrelease tactic.

"Fifty-three feet." The reverberations of the explosion

had died away, although to Keith's hypersensitivity their vibrations, and the sympathetic tonal response of the submarine's huge cylindrical hull, resounded in a lengthy continuum overshadowing his exec's forced calm. *Cushing* was dropping faster, now. He had missed the fifty-two-foot mark. Most likely, despite his preternatural self-possession, Jim had missed announcing it as well.

Thirteen feet of periscope still out of water. Perhaps ten feet of it still projected high enough to be useful, above the blocks of ice thrown aside a few hours ago when the sail crunched up from below. But he could not allow the Arctic Ocean slowly to close over its extended tip, as if his ship were in an ice-free sea. There might be some tiny amount of current down below, a slow-moving, imponderable shifting of the water beneath the ice cover, enough to cause the helpless *Cushing's* great bulk to move as she descended into it. It need not be much; just enough to bring the fragile periscope tube into contact with the solid ice rimming the hole. Even though far thinner than the regular ice floes covering the area, the three-foot thickness of ice in the frozen-over lead could bend or snap off the periscope with ease. He must lower it soon, within seconds at most.

Another thought impacted into Keith's brain: barring the most extraordinary good luck in drifting under another lead, or polynya, once submerged there was no way he could get *Cushing* back to the surface again. From now on they were trapped, unable even to communicate.

"Fifty-four feet." Still impossible to see anything, although perhaps vision was very slightly improving. He dared not wait longer. Keith snapped up the periscope handles to signal for it to be lowered but he kept his face to the eye guard, his hands to the folded handles.

His knees bent slightly, preparatory to riding the 'scope down until it dropped below the floor plates. Understanding, Hanson pulled the hydraulic control handle gently, sent the periscope down at half speed. Just before he had to pull his head clear, Keith thought he saw the plane, barely visible through the thinning smoke and debris still in the air.

Afterward he could not be sure, but there was something different about it, something suddenly askew, not balanced as it should have been, something horribly wrong. On his haunches, he was forced to crane his head to the side and rear to allow the periscope to pass between his legs and descend into the well, thus did not see the wounded wing spar give way, the wing collapse and fold back upon the plane's fusilage.

Aboard the *William B. Cushing,* only the audio frequency sonar watch-stander heard the muffled crash as the disabled plane shattered itself on the ice a quarter of a mile away. The ice was twenty feet thick, solid with the iron rigidity of a century of existence and covered with a two-foot patina of blizzard-derived snow. The sound, transmitted first through the unyielding ice and then through water, resembled nothing the sonarman had ever heard. He listened carefully for a repetition, heard none, and gradually relaxed. It was a much less frightening noise than the explosion which had blasted into his eardrums only moments before. Nevertheless, the ship's standing orders for sonar watchstanders required him to write a description in his log of what he had heard, immediately following his notation regarding the bomb explosion. But the bomb explosion itself, preceded by the frighteningly unexpected collision alarm and the resulting activity, had happened too recently. He had not yet even reached for the ball-point pen with which he made his entries.

There was no further underwater noise to note, and

after a few minutes the sonarman took up his log book. It had all happened at the same time, 0612 according to the ship's clock on the bulkhead. He began to compose a single laborious entry encompassing all the events of that confusing and scary instant.

Not until the next day, in the insulated quiet of the frigid Arctic under its sheet of solid ice cover, as the submarine hovered powerless, unable to move, did the sonarman call his superior's attention to the strange crunching noise—as he had described it—which he heard just as the reverberations of the bomb explosion finally died away.

12

~~~~~~

Vice Admiral Murphy, ComSubLant, talking long distance from his headquarters in Norfolk, sounded at the moment like anything but the stodgy individual he was so well known to be. "Yes, they just brought me the message, Rich. I was about to pick up the phone to call you." The note of uneasiness in his voice was unusual. "This will have to go to CNO right away, and he'll probably take it to the Joint Chiefs this morning. The National Security Council and the President will have it this afternoon!"

Keith's message was obviously of major importance and Murphy's disquietude therefore understandable, but the idea that the very highest authority would directly and immediately become involved produced shock waves in Richardson's mind. Seconds later he was grateful for the indoctrination which had kept him silent. "How long has Leone been gone?" The admiral answered his own question immediately. "A little more than three weeks. He's been up there a week."

Rich paused a moment. Keith would have reported

any deviation from the detailed operation order. "He's been in the operating area just nine days, sir."

"Right. Umm—that's right. Maybe we should have turned him around before he got there."

"How's that?" Rich realized his own voice had risen too. It had never occurred to him to question the decision to send Keith to the Arctic.

"Probably we should have told you. This whole business has gotten a lot hotter than we thought it would. Somehow the Russians got word of Leone's mission, and they protested even before he entered the area —are you there, Rich? So, when the Joint Chiefs heard about the collision, the flap got a lot worse. That was yesterday. This second message will put them in orbit." Murphy put a characteristically drooping note to his final sentence.

"I see, sir," Richardson replied after a moment. He paused, thinking how to phrase what he wanted to say, then went on. "We had Leone on single side-band for about a minute, three hours ago." He told of the attempt at voice communication and its sudden termination. "He was right there, on the line himself, and then something happened. He had to break off, and we've heard nothing since."

"How long ago was this?" There was now a tone of acerbity and a rising inflection. "Why didn't you report it?"

"We hadn't broken the second message yet, and since we intercepted it direct, we knew your coding board couldn't have either. I figured you'd be getting it about now. The rest of the time we've been checking up on the *Manta.*" Richardson spoke carefully, sensing that in Murphy's obviously agitated frame of mind it would be characteristic of him to find fault with something relatively minor.

"Um—we didn't mind your fooling around with the

towing contraption, even though we thought you were wasting your time, but you should have asked me before trying that voice caper."

"There wasn't time, Admiral! The only way to be sure to get to him with the old wolfpack code was to break right in on the CW circuit! He'd have been gone in a minute, back under the ice or anyway shut down. Besides, it's standard operating procedure to use voice when you can. The only thing out of the ordinary was the distance." Rich saw Buck's eyes narrow. He was speaking swiftly now, still trying to think ahead carefully. "It's that towing rig I want to report on. It will work. We've tested it. I'm recommending we send the *Manta* to snake the *Cushing* out. She'll be ready to get underway tomorrow!"

Admiral Murphy was anything but mercurial in temperament, but the third change in his attitude was instantly obvious over the telephone. "Do you really think it will do the job? How do you know? How are you going to rig the towline?"

"We've been testing it for a couple of weeks. It works, all right. We get him to lower his anchor. He can do this from inside the torpedo room, you know. The *Manta* passes beneath, snags the anchor chain, and off they go."

"What if your rig doesn't make contact?"

"She circles around and makes another pass."

"What if it parts under the strain of towing?"

"The catenary drag of the chain will help take up the initial shock, and she'll be keeping a close watch on the strain gauge, so it ought not to break. That's part of what the training exercises were for. Anyway, we have two rigs, one for each stern tube. So there'll be a second chance if she does break one."

"You say you've tested this thing, Rich?"

"Yes, sir. It takes some practice doing it right, but

we're pretty sure we've got the bugs out of it and know how to handle it. We've worked it on the *Tringa* and the *Besugo* both. The *Besugo* was submerged, and that made her a lot easier to tow than the *Tringa*, once the hookup was made. Of course, the *Cushing* is a much heavier ship. . . ."

"Um . . . Umm . . . When did you say the *Manta* will be ready?"

"Tomorrow, forenoon. She's topping off provisions right now. There's a couple of adjustments still to make to the chain grab, and we decided to replace all the nylon cable with new line in case any part's been weakened."

"Okay, Rich. I'll report this to Washington right away . . . umm . . ." Admiral Murphy's voice took on its more customary phlegmatic quality. "Can you take a quick flight to Washington and be there this afternoon? The CNO may want you to brief him directly."

Going to Washington was something that had not occurred to Richardson. His instinct was against it. Thinking quickly, he said, "Admiral, I think I ought to stay here in New London and make sure everything Buck Williams needs is taken care of. He and I are the only ones . . ."

"I understand, Rich, I'll report that up the line. Maybe they'll want to call you on the telephone."

It was midnight of the same day in Richardson's combined office and sitting room on board the *Proteus* which, with the addition of extra chairs, had been converted to a small conference room. Rich had just finished describing his towing device to the small but powerful group of naval officers present. All, except Rich and Buck, were in civilian clothes. He stifled a huge yawn as he stood, pointer in hand, before the easel upon which were several poster cards with large hand-drawn diagrams of the hookup gear. He and Williams were the only two present below the rank of rear admiral. Admiral Donaldson, Chief of Naval Operations, a near legendary destroyer commander during World War II, now nearing the end of his term as CNO, had taken charge of the briefing and was asking a final question.

"Richardson, what gave you the idea to make this thing?"

"I don't know, Admiral," Rich confessed honestly. "I just began to wonder how we'd be able to help the *Cushing* if she broke down, and the idea sort of grew in my mind."

"But you couldn't have foreseen the collision. A simultaneous breakdown of both main propulsion and the secondary motor is a one-in-a-million chance."

"True," said Rich, "but a reactor breakdown under the ice cover, where Keith couldn't use his snorkle, would stop both of them." Rich was conscious of darting eyes framed in the famous pinched face of Vice Admiral Brighting in the second row.

"No reactor has ever broken down," said the monotonous, expressionless voice.

Irresolute, Richardson did not answer. The reactor in Idaho had certainly broken down. Had there not been a large group of trained men, each able to spend three precious minutes in the heat and radioactivity of the lower reactor compartment, it could not have been fixed. A slightly bigger casualty of the same nature would have required a lengthy shutdown. No mere ship, out of the resources of her own crew, could have handled the situation. It had been precisely the idea that there might be a repetition, at sea, which had been the compelling force urging him on. But the fact could not be stated in front of Admiral Brighting.

It was Donaldson, sensing the reason for Richardson's hesitation, who answered for him. "Your reactors are first-class, Martin. They've hung up the most remarkable record for reliability of any piece of machinery ever built. Not one has broken down in service yet, for any reason. They've been absolutely extraordinary. Their record for sustained performance is unprecedented in history, and the credit is clearly due to you." There was an odd twist to Brighting's mouth as he looked quickly from side to side to see how the others were taking this praise. Richardson stared at him, then deliberately dropped his eyes to the floor to mask his perception that Brighting saw nothing extravagant in the words. A glance at Donaldson: his face was impassive, guileless. Rich wondered if he were entirely imagining an undercurrent of deliberate flattery. Certainly Donaldson knew that *Nautilus* had once experienced an involuntary shutdown which took twenty-four hours to overcome, during which she had only steerageway on the surface on her diesel auxiliary engine, and that at one time or another every nuclear reactor built had scrammed unexpectedly, though usually not for serious cause. *Triton,* with two reactors, twice had had reactor difficulty during her epochal round-the-world cruise, a fact which had been kept out of the papers but had been duly reported to higher authority.

Granted, because of the intensive training both crews had received, *Nautilus* and *Triton* had been able to effect repairs themselves and had suffered no permanent disability. But the next reactor scram might be less benign. If the reactor could not be restarted, if it happened under solid ice cover, as might be the case with a single reactor ship under winter Arctic conditions, *Cushing*'s exact situation, things could become difficult.

But Donaldson was continung. "Whatever may have motivated Commodore Richardson, the important thing is that he's come up with an idea to save the situation. It was a good enough idea to bring us up from Washington for this mdnight conference aboard hs own flagship. He's the man on the spot. He's studied this more than any of us here. He's made a recommendation, and he invented the means to carry it out. The thing for us here is to decide. Sending *Manta,* as Richardson propóses, is one alternative. There may be others. What are they?"

No one spoke for a moment. Richardson waited. "We could order Leone to scuttle and send a ski-equipped transport to bring the crew back," said a voice. It sounded like Admiral Treadwell, but Richardson, who had been watching Admiral Donaldson, did not turn in time to see who it was.

"There's still a chance the *Cushing*'s propeller isn't entirely gone," said Admiral Murphy. "We should be getting another message with more information any time. Maybe he'll be able to get out on his own."

"When did your message clear, Murph?" Donaldson asked.

"About noon. I checked on it before leaving Norfolk. It's been rebroadcast three times. Leone ought to have answered before this."

"Maybe he can't. What do you think, Rich?" Donaldson turned a level gaze on Richardson. The chief of naval operations had used his nickname, he noted.

"Something happened suddenly, sir," Rich answered. "Leone's tone of voice changed right while we were talking. We'd hardly started, when he had to cut us off. Our radio room has been keeping a special watch ever since. He's not come back up on either CW or voice. That means he must have had to dive back under the ice."

"Go on," said Donaldson.

"If he's at shallow depth, up against the underside of the ice floe," said Richardson, "he can receive messages through his underwater antenna. But he can't transmit unless he can get an antenna up through the ice cover. My guess is that he can't move. If he could, he'd find another polynya and come back up."

"How long can he last up there?"

"His reactor must be all right, or he'd have said something. So he's got plenty of power. He can control his own atmosphere. Provisions are his limiting factor. Assuming nothing happens to his reactor, he can last three months. More, if he cuts down on rations."

"June or July, eh?"

"Yes."

"When is the ice at its thinnest?"

"It's supposed to be thinnest in October, but there's lots of variation. Right now we figure it's as thick as it ever gets. That's why the operation was scheduled for this month."

Donaldson nodded. "Yes. I remember. In retrospect, it wasn't too good an idea." The set of his mouth was suddenly grim. "If Leone won't transmit, we have to assume it's because he can't. Even if he doesn't get any messages, he knows we need to hear from him." His hearers nodded their assent. "So, if we don't get something pretty damn soon, we'll have to take action based on not expecting to hear from him at all."

"Yessir," said Murphy.

"The Joint Chiefs have already considered ordering him to scuttle and sending a couple of Arctic-equipped planes to pick up the crew, but we don't know yet whether they can get out of their submarine and on top of the ice. Even so, we've directed the Air Force to get two transports ready, but just preparing the aircraft to land on the ice will take at least two weeks. Maybe longer."

"We ought not to abandon the ship," said Brighting.

"That's our newest and best reactor. Scuttling should be our last option."

"We all agree on that, Martin," said the Chief of Naval Operations, "except that saving the crew is the very bottom line. Tready, you've not said a word lately. Have your New London boys come up with any more ideas? How about Electric Boat's engineers? Is there any way they can think of to fix the propeller, or replace the emergency propulsion motor?"

Rear Admiral Treadwell, in charge of the New London submarine flotilla, shook his head. "We've been brainstorming ideas all day, but we're all working in the dark. Without knowing anything about what we're up against, except that it's underwater and damned cold, there's nothing anybody can do by remote control. The *Manta* could carry up a spare propeller for the *Cushing,* all right, secured on deck somehow, but nobody can figure out a way of putting it on her propeller shaft, even assuming divers could get the damaged one off, using explosive charges or something like that. The same with the outboard motor. Who knows what damage was done to the recess it fits in. Either one of these fixes is a drydock job. Waterborne, up there under the ice, there's no way at all." He cleared his throat morosely. Murphy was nodding his agreement as he spoke.

Richardson, who had been carrying on a low-voiced discussion with Buck Williams while Treadwell was speaking, looked up and caught Donaldson's eye. "May I make a suggestion?" he asked. With Donaldson's nod of assent, he said, "There's really three things *Manta* can do when she gets up there. One is to try the submerged hookup and tow operation. Another is to serve as communications relay station. Assuming the *Cushing* is immobilized under the ice and can't transmit, if the *Manta* can talk to her through her Gertrude set she'll at least be able to relay messages for her. The third thing is that if worst comes to worst she can come up close alongside under the ice and take the *Cushing*'s crew aboard a few at a time through the escape hatches. Buck Williams has three qualified scuba divers aboard and an extra supply of scuba equipment. It will be a slow operation, hauling all that gear between ships and changing it from one man to another, but it's possible.

"The thing is, though, that it will take her two weeks to get up there. About as long as to get the planes ready. A lot could happen before then, and it might be necessary to modify her instructions, but at least it's one string to our bow we ought not to pass up. We ought to send her now, and in the meantime get the planes ready, too."

There was a glint in Donaldson's eyes as he answered. "That's a convincing argument to me, Rich. Does anyone have anything more to add? . . . Then that's the decision. Now that that's settled, can anyone enlighten me on this next item? It was handed to me just as I got aboard the plane that brought us here." He extracted a torn and folded paper from the inside pocket of his civilian jacket, put on a pair of Navy-issue glasses, and began to read:

U.S. sub shoots down Soviet research plane, claims Kremlin. (Tass) In an unprecedented action, the Soviet Foreign Office today released the text of a secret report from the commander of the current Russian polar exploration expedition, claiming that an unnamed American submarine in Arctic waters had without warning and totally without cause opened fire on and shot down a Soviet research aircraft attached to his group. Noting the presence of a foreign submarine in the area under research, the aircraft had approached to ascertain its nationality, ask if it needed assistance and request it not to interfere with the exploration and research being conducted. Instead of responding to this legitimate and civilized request, the submarine, later identified as a nuclear missile launching type belonging to the United States, opened fire with a sophisticated war weapon, one shot of which injured the plane so badly that it crashed on the ice with the loss of one of its crew members and injury to the others.

Clearly this was not the act of a single misguided submarine commander, for the fact that one of its missile firing submarines has invaded the hitherto peaceful waters of the Arctic Ocean with the intent of converting them into the front arena of threat and blackmail against the Soviet Union shows the perfidy and warmaking objectives of the United States, which cries peace on the one hand while it secretly makes war with the other.

Barbaric actions of this nature by the warmongering United States are continuing proof that she has no consideration whatever for the rights of man, human dignity or even life itself if they conflict with her imperialistic designs on freedom and peace throughout the world.

It is expected the Foreign Office will protest this outrage most strenuously to the government of the United States, demand indemnity for the injuries to persons and material, and insist vigorously that the perpetrators of this extraordinary affront be suitably and severely punished.

Admiral Donaldson clamped his mouth shut with almost an audible snap as he finished reading. No one spoke. "What do you reckon happened?" he finally said, spitting the words out to the room in general. Then, singling out Admiral Murphy, who was already looking slightly uncomfortable, "Murph, this has got to be the *Cushing* they're talking about. What do you make of it? You're not putting any new weapons on your boats that I haven't heard about, are you?" Although there was a light tone to his question, and in his voice, the look on his face had no levity in it.

"Nosir—umm," said Murphy. "It couldn't have been the *Cushing*. She has no such weapons. A couple of rapid-fire rifles, maybe. Nothing that fits this description. What do you think, Tready?"

"It probably was the *Cushing* all right," said Treadwell, "but I agree with Murphy. She could not have shot down an aircraft. It just doesn't make any sense."

"You knew the Soviets protested our sending a missile sub into the Arctic, didn't you, Tready?"

"I heard about it, yes sir. But we didn't pay any attention, absent any instructions from Norfolk or Washington."

Buck Williams whispered something to Richardson. Rich nodded his understanding. "Based on the protest," he said after Treadwell had finished, "it figures they knew a lot more about Leone's mission than this press release indicates. So it's a front job. Some kind of a coverup for something."

"Maybe they're doing the old Japanese bellytalk— maybe they are accusing us of doing what they've done," said Treadwell.

"You mean maybe they've sunk the *Cushing?* That's why they claim they lost a plane?" Donaldson laughed a brief laugh of derision. "That doesn't hang together. Murphy, what do you think?"

"Umm . . . none of it makes any sense to me, except that the *Cushing* could not have done what they say."

"Brighting?"

"I'm only an engineer. This is an operational matter.

Analytically, it seems to me the Soviets are saying they've lost an aircraft in the Arctic."

"You're right. That's the only positive statement in the whole press release," said Donaldson, "but we've still got no idea what *Cushing* could have had to do with it, if anything."

"It's all lies," said Admiral Murphy. "Umm . . . Brighting's right. They are saying they lost an aircraft, so that must be true. But also they're saying it's because of the *Cushing*. That's what's so um—um . . . weird."

"Murph, put it all in your next message to the *Cushing*. Maybe Leone'll have a simple explanation, if he can ever get clear to use his radio. We'll know in a couple of weeks anyhow, when the *Manta* gets up there. I have to go to the tank with this in the morning, so we have to compose a message to the *Cushing* before we can close off this meeting, and I'll tell the other Joint Chiefs that we'll just have to hold the fort awhile." Admiral Donaldson paused a moment, put his hands on the arms of Rich's office chair, in which he had been sitting. "Well, I guess that concludes the business we came up here for. I wonder how many people we fooled with these civilian clothes. Rich, will you have someone alert our pilot and organize transportation for us back to the airport as soon as we get the message done? Oh, wait a minute"—as Rich reached for the communication handset on the bulkhead behind his desk—"have you thought about going on this expedition yourself?"

"We had thought about it, yes sir, but . . ." Indeed he had thought about that. And he had come to know that there was nothing he wanted so much. But even as he was talking, in the middle of a very short sentence, there was an instantaneous flash of self-understanding. The days aboard the *Walrus* and *Eel* had been the high-point of his life. The single-minded concentration they demanded of him had so focused his energies that even now, a decade and a half after it all had ended, those four years loomed in his mind as the most imperative of the psychological imperatives that drove him. Being off in the *Manta,* with Buck, was the closest he could ever come again.

But it would not do to be too affirmative. This might transmit lack of confidence in Buck Williams. And he well remembered his own ambivalent reaction at taking his own old skipper, Joe Blunt, on that second, fatal, war patrol of the *Eel.* "I'm sure Buck Williams is fully able to handle this mission on his own," he went on swiftly. "He's the skipper, and he's trained both his people and himself. Having a squadron commander along would just weight him down. I'd be excess baggage. . . ." This was the speech Joe Blunt should have made, would have made if he had only known himself better. But times were different then, although perhaps there were similarities too. The prewar submarine skipper, sidelined while his juniors took to war and glory the new fleet submarines he had helped design and build, was not so far removed from himself, thirsting for one more fling at the old days with a newer and greater ship under him.

Yet it could not be the same as before. Could never be, could not even approach it. There was too great a difference in the situations, and the people, not to mention between *Manta* and *Eel.* He would not be sailing again with Keith and Buck in a well-found ship, but on an emergency mission with one of his most trusted friends to the rescue of another. That in itself was an incentive, of course, and of the strongest kind. . . .

"Your modesty does you credit, Richardson." That was Admiral Donaldson piercing through in his best Chief of Naval Operations voice, "but I'm going to have my way on this. The place for you is aboard the *Manta,* overseeing your own brainchild. I'm sure Com-

mander Williams won't agree that you'll be a weight"—
Buck was shaking his head visibly in agreement—"and
besides, I want someone up there who can take special
initiative on his own, if the occasion demands."

The eyes that returned Richardson's puzzled look
were as free of hidden meaning as a child's. Rich
wanted to pursue the matter, ask him to explain the
apparently offhand comment, but could not.

Manta's bridge was as different from *Eel*'s as it could
possibly be, narrow and streamlined for minimum underwater resistance, totally enclosed except for a tiny
cockpit just forward of the periscopes and retractable
masts, devoid of armament of any kind. The main deck,
from its flatness superficially resembling *Eel*'s, was
narrow, smooth, free of all protuberances, slick except
for a sandpaperlike nonskid surface. Its most noticeable feature, other than absolutely clean lines, was a
recessed T-shaped rail in the center, to which, at strategic points, a movable safety belt could be attached,
running its length and curving around the sail. The
mooring cleats ranged along both sides had already
been locked in their folded underway positions, showing only a smooth underside flush with the main-deck
surface. Lifelines and their stanchions had been stowed
in deck lockers. The capstans used to handle lines while
alongside *Proteus* were in the process of being de-
mounted and likewise stowed for sea as the submarine
proceeded slowly down the Thames River.

Richardson, a useless extra number on the bridge
beside Buck Williams, savored the cold morning river-
mist despite two nearly sleepless nights in a row. He
had become well acquainted with it during the past
weeks. The only difference was that he had been less
fatigued, and this time, instead of a short jaunt a few
miles to sea for testing, *Manta* was setting out on a

long voyage thousands of miles to the north. At its end, trapped under the Arctic ice cap, lay a crippled submarine unable to communicate, whose only chance for survival rested in the efficacy of a pair of new and untried (though well-tested) devices loaded in *Manta's* two stern torpedo tubes. That, and the ability of the people on board to cope with the extraordinary and unexpected conditions they were sure to encounter.

A couple of hours' sleep had partly alleviated the need which Rich recognized nevertheless as just over the horizon, waiting to claim him as soon as the heightened excitement from getting underway had worn off. Buck, he knew, was not much better off, except that he had had no last-minute personal preparations to make before departure. A system which demanded so much of its principals just before sending them on special missions ought, somehow, to be improved—a mental observation Rich was oblivious of having made at least a dozen times.

The Thames River air was bracing: cold, but not chilling; mist rising off the water, diffusing the angular outlines of the ancient buildings lining its banks on both sides. A broad waterway to adventure, between the great industrial complex of the General Dynamics Electric Boat shipyard to port, on the Groton side, and old Fort Trumbull to starboard, on the New London side, which now housed the Navy's underwater sound laboratories. Farther downstream the vista softened, became less industrialized, with pleasant riverfront homes on both banks, broken only by the refinerylike complex of the Pfizer pharmaceutical laboratories. *Manta* was the only ship underway in the channel, slipping quietly and effortlessly at slow speed through the placid river water.

No roaring diesels spewed a mixture of water and smoky exhaust through mufflers beneath the main deck aft, no open induction valve in the after part of the sail sucked in a torrent of air to supply demanding engine air-intake blowers. Astern a purposeful current surged backward, frothed with white edges against the undisturbed water on either side, burbled under the thrust of two deep-lying propellers—and inside *Manta*'s smooth-lined hull a torrent of steam was spinning four deceptively small, heavily insulated turbines, two connected to each set of micrometer-matched speed reduction gears. All this had been brought about by raising control rods built into the top of her reactor: a great, inverted, stainless-steel jug in the bottom portion of which, in carefully configured geometry, lay the active nuclear material that provided the heat, and thus the power. This was the product of that strange, difficult, gnomelike man, Admiral Brighting, who, because of his intransigencies, his temper tantrums and his disregard of the human qualities, had made himself hated in the U.S. Navy even as that same Navy, at the same time, acknowledged the incomparable debt.

There had been an extraordnary change in submarining since the war. Had the Navy possessed but a few vessels equivalent to the one Rich now rode, and dependable torpedoes to match their performance, the entire course of the Pacific war, and possibly of the Atlantic as well, would have been different. For one thing, no submarine skipper would have feared any enemy task force, nor been forced to give over pursuit and impotently watch it pass by out of range. The strenuous and dangerous (when there was possibility of enemy air cover) surface "end-around" to reach an attack position ahead would have been unnecessary, replaced by a straight-out submerged chase from which no merchant ship and only the fastest warships could escape. ComSubPac's problems would have become much more heavily weighted in logistics than they had been anyway, to keep those few extraordinary submarines supplied with the torpedoes they would have needed. If the torpedoes had worked properly, as they finally did, the Japanese would have been driven from the sea in a year. And, on the other side of the coin, there would have been no water mole, nearing exhaustion of its already depleted battery, writhing in the agony of repeated depth charges, groping blindly—and so slowly—to avoid the threatened dissolution, the terror of the crushing death or, in shallow water, the more generous, if slower, suffocation as the air gave out in an immobilized steel tomb.

Being at sea in a nuclear submarine always caused Richardson to think this way, but as squadron commander there had been little opportunity to leave his desk except for the occasional underway inspection of one of the boats in his squadron—until the near daily series of test runs in *Manta,* for which he had somehow been able to free himself. Now, what he had wanted most of all, a long cruise to savor the nuclear changes fully, was beginning. There was guilt mixed with the pleasure, however, for the mission on which he was embarked was a desperate one. Yet the pleasure was undeniable. He willed himself to concentrate on Keith, and the ship and crew whose lives hung in the balance —and found himself instead thinking of Admiral Donaldson with gratitude and uneasiness combined.

"When Southeast Ledge Light is abeam, go ahead standard and set a course for the Race, Deedee," said Buck to his OOD, a lieutenant named D. D. Brown, whose title on board was the anachronistic "gunnery officer." The lighthouse, a solid, square structure, built of brick on a rocky outcropping almost in midchannel, could have passed without much notice in any town or city, except for the unusually thick walls which made its windows resemble the gun embrazures of an old fort. There had been a time when keepers would wave to the submarines as they entered or left the Thames River, but no more. The light on its roof had been on automatic for years. "Topside is secured for sea, Commodore," said Buck, "and the ship is rigged for dive. We'll be securing the maneuvering watch after we round the Ledge."

"Very well," said Rich. He put down the binoculars with which, from habit, he had been inspecting the lighthouse, settled his parka hood more firmly around his head. He and Buck had been standing on opposite sides of the bridge cockpit, on folding metal steps which lifted them a foot higher above the bulwarks. Buck stepped down at the same time Rich did. At higher speed a little more protection from the cold wind would be welcome. The move brought the two men shoulder to shoulder against the after edge of the cockpit.

"How did you leave Laura, Skipper?" asked Williams. "Short notice for her, wasn't it?" The question was part of an unofficial conversation, not meant, as the previous exchange had been, to be heard by others.

"Oh, she was caught by surprise, of course, but she took it in stride. She knew something was going on, especially with that late-night session aboard the *Proteus*. Also, she's guessed it has something to do with Keith, and that's got to be nothing but a woman's intuition."

"She couldn't be your wife all these years and not know when something big is going on, Skipper. You've not had much sleep the last two nights, there was that thing in the paper about the *Cushing,* not that it had anything correct, and now you're suddenly taking the *Manta* off on a long cruise. I was bushed, myself, when I finally rolled into my bunk down below, but I was way better off than you because I'd already moved aboard. She's got to have guessed something's up." Buck made no effort to stifle his huge yawn.

"I suppose I could have done some better planning," said Rich. "Anyway, I'll have plenty of time to get rested before we hit the ice. Except for thinking about what Keith and his crew are going through, I could be a passenger. You're the one who's going to have to do all the work." He put his binoculars to his eyes, and Buck knew he did not wish to pursue a discussion of last night's events.

"There's an emergency on," Laura had said, "and it's got something to do with Keith. It's all over the base, and all over New London too." She had been asleep, but had slipped on a robe to help Rich throw together some changes of clothing to take with him. When Rich did not answer, she went on, "Peggy called a couple of hours ago. She's hysterical."

"What about?"

"Oh, everything. Sometimes I worry a little about her. If there's any gossip or rumor floating around about anything or anybody, she's heard it. She's a regular dirt hound, and it's practically an obsession with her. Right now there's a lot of loose talk going around about the *Cushing,* and I'll bet Peggy's heard it all. She's found out about that big secret conference you've just come from. Says it has got to be about the *Cushing,* and that the big Navy brass came up here in civilian clothes and went straight aboard the *Proteus* to talk to you about it."

"Is that why she's hysterical?"

"Partly, I think. The rumors are about Keith, this time, even though they're not personal, and she's finding that hard to take. What set her off, though, was a telephone call from a newspaper in Washington."

"What did the newspaper want?" Richardson paused

in the act of selecting the right khaki shirts, turned to face her. "When did they call?"

"She called me right afterward, so it was just over two hours ago. Mainly, the man only asked if Keith was skipper of the *Cushing,* and when they had left New London. Where they were bound for. That sort of thing. In her frame of mind that would be enough to get her upset right there, but then he came on with something about Keith being mixed up in some kind of a fracas with the Russians, and that really scared her. I promised I'd call her back as soon as I'd had a chance to talk to you about it."

"There's nothing I could tell her," said Rich. "Was it the reporter who told her about the conference? They ought not to be allowed to do that kind of thing. Calling up a skipper's wife with this kind of rumor . . ." He left the sentence unfinished, threw the shirts roughly into his suitcase.

"Maybe, I don't know. I heard about it earlier, though. A big Navy airplane landed over at Trumbull Field, and three Navy sedans were waiting for it and took everybody to the *Proteus.*"

"Well, you can't call her back," said Richardson.

"Come on, Rich. Of all the things she's asked me for lately, this is the most legitimate. She's sitting by her phone right this minute. It's her husband. She's worried silly, and she needs help. I promised I'd call as soon as I'd talked to you. What can I tell her?"

"Well—okay. But you have to say that you don't know anything about any conference, one way or the other. So far as you know, Keith's all right. So's the *Cushing.* She's not to pay attention to any rumors about her. The *Manta*'s going on routine training exercises."

"Then why are you going along, Rich? She's going to ask that just as soon as she finds out you've gone, and that's going to be later on today sometime."

"Tell her . . . tell her . . ." Richardson struggled with the words but more, Laura could see, with himself. "Well, all right, but you've got to make her swear to secrecy. I'm giving the *Manta* an Operations Readiness Inspection, an ORI. Got that? An ORI. It'll take a month, and Keith's going to be all right. That's the second point. Keith's going to be all right, but she's not to talk about it to anyone."

"That sounds pretty mixed up to me," said Laura, "but I'll try to put it across. You're giving the *Manta* an ORI, and somehow Keith's going to be okay. She'll know either the ORI's a fake, or else you're not doing anything for Keith. Besides, who ever heard of a month-long ORI? She won't buy that story."

"Look Laura, whose side are you on? Just tell her what I said. You don't know what I'm doing either, do you? You don't know if this sudden trip has anything to do with Keith or not. We're doing everything we can. You just keep saying that I said Keith's going to be okay, and not to talk to any reporters. They don't know anything, and they'll just get her upset."

There was unaccustomed asperity in Richardson's voice, which he instantly regretted. Laura compressed her lips, said nothing. "Look, Laurie," He said after a moment, coming around the bed and sliding his arms around her waist, "we're getting underway tomorrow, and I'll be gone for quite a while. And I can't tell you anything, even though I know I can trust you all the way. But we don't trust Peggy, do we? Whatever you or I tell her is as good as broadcast all over town. Besides, I don't want to think of her right now."

Laura's face was close to his, her eyes wide open. She nodded her head against his. Her mouth parted slightly, and he could feel her body coming closer. Her arms moved against the small of his back, and then he was kissing her, pushing her down crosswise on the bed alongside the suitcase, fumbling with the buttons of her robe.

Later, lying clasped together in the delicious rumpled aftermath, he said, "Go ahead and call Peggy. Right now, if you want to. Tell her to keep her shirt on, and if she gets any more calls like that to refer them to Admiral Treadway. But don't get into any long talk with her at this time of the night. Just say she should keep her faith in the U.S. Navy. Then hang up and come back here."

Laura rubbed her nose languidly against his cheek. "Aye, aye, sir, Commodore," she said, "if you think you're up to it. But what do I say if she asks me if I've got my shirt on?"

13

~~~~~~

The trip northward in the *Manta* was totally different
from any submarine voyage Richardson had ever experienced. It was the first time he had embarked for
such a long time and for such a distance in a nuclear
submarine. At the beginning he had, of course, known
what to expect. Diving was effortless; the diving alarm
was apparently sounded more for the sake of tradition
than to alert the crew. There was none of the old hurly-
burly, no necessity for split-second timing to get engines off the line, exhaust valves shut, huge air-intake
pipe sealed. The people on the bridge were allowed to
get below with some dignity and without emergency; if
one of them was held up for some reason, clothing
snagged somewhere or some last-minute function that
needed doing—such as securing a collapsible step
against rattles during a prolonged submergence—time
could be made for it. When the bridge hatch was
closed and the lookouts had taken their seats at the
diving controls, the diving officer ordered the vents
opened, told the planesmen the depth he wanted, and
Manta gently angled downward without missing a beat

in the even rhythm of her turbines. The initial course
led directly off soundings, and as the bottom fell away
the planesmen gradually increased depth until they
were holding her steady—and stationary, from all sensation that anyone could observe—at the ordered cruising depth of 500 feet.

There was no feeling of motion, no feel whatever for
the sea. The interior of the ship was a quiet, cylindrical
cavern, full of controlled efficient activity, but they
might as well have been buried in the earth, locked up
in a cave somewhere. Of forward motion there was
no indication whatever, except for the changes in the
regular Fathometer readings which were constantly
plotted on a chart of the ocean-bottom contours, the
single clocklike hand of the electronic log indicating
Manta's speed as a fraction over nineteen knots, and
the fact that the slightest motion of bow or stern planes
was instantly reflected in the depth gauges.

The silence was of course not as real as the senses
indicated, for everyone had from the beginning been
attuned to the sibilant hum of the ventilation system
and relegated it to the nonaware background of consciousness. Occasionally there was a gurgle of the hydraulic machinery, the swishing of confined oil under
pressure, a repressed whistle of compressed air, each
individual noise telling of some small operation helping
to keep the *Manta* on course, speed and depth. Yes,
despite these communications of the submarine's own
inherent being and function, and despite, also, the concentration of the men at the diving stand—two planesmen and the diving officer of the watch—there was no
feeling, no forced awareness, that this minute fragment
of the world was moving at all.

Immediately aft of the control room, in a sealed compartment beneath the deck, *Manta*'s heart was pumping
out an unceasing supply of steam which passed into

the engineroom in two great insulated, convoluted pipes
leading to four turbines, two turbo-generator sets and
the auxiliary steam line, and finally entered the con-
densers as fully expanded steam from which all the
work had been extracted. The steam provided all the
energy for the myriad pieces of machinery which made
up the enormously complex synergistic whole and then,
in the form of water, was pumped back into the steam
generators to repeat the cycle. There, instead of from
combustion of oil, gas or coal, heat was returned to it
from the pressurized water of the reactor primary loop
—water under such great pressure that it could not
flash into steam even under the tremendous, controlled
temperature of nuclear fission. Here was the secret, for
the nuclear power plant needs no combustion anywhere
in the power cycle, and the fuel, built into the reactor,
lasts for several years.

But as every man aboard the *Manta* well knew, the
power of the atom is not released easily. Tremendously
large, extraordinarily designed main coolant pumps cir-
culate the pressurized water constantly from reactor to
steam generators and back again. Equally unusual drive
motors raise and lower the control rods which increase
or decrease reactivity within the reactor. Extraordinary
and unusual, because no leakage can be permitted; there
can be no joint, no bearing or seal ring through which
a drive shaft projects, no contaminating lubrication, no
physical contact between driving agent and the driven.
No leakage of any kind, not even an infinitesimal
amount, can be allowed in the primary loop; for not
only would radioactive contamination result, the pressure could not be maintained and the system would
not function.

Over it all, monitoring every pressure, every temperature, every device, every important circuit and
function, was one of the world's most detailed and

complex instrumentation systems. And over the instruments the most highly selected and trained crew the Navy could put together maintained constant surveillance.

Pumps throbbed, generator sets hummed, turbines roared and reductions gears whined; in the engineroom there was purposeful movement and noise aplenty. But everything was nevertheless static. Every piece of machinery stood in its appointed place, delivered its product through shafts, cables, pipes or air lines, and reported its performance in gauges mounted nearby. Only the blurred revolution of two propeller shafts in the lower level of the engineroom evidenced movement— and even this was hardly visible, for the perfectly balanced shafts, turning at hundreds of revolutions per minute, seemed to be standing as solidly still as everything else around them. Just as the men were.

Throughout the engineering spaces, men stood, or sat, before their machines, watching them attentively, occasionally making a tiny adjustment, carefully ministering to their needs, rooted to their duties for four hours at a time, eight hours out of every day.

But no one, encased in the elongated steely cylinder of which he was a part, hurtling northward through the Atlantic Ocean, was unaware of the sea, even though he might pretend to ignore it. Not with the sea pressure of 500 feet of submergence squeezing the steel bubble enveloping him. The sea was unfelt physically, could be joked about, was taken as a matter of course. But not ignored. No matter where one was it was never far away. In some cases only inches. And, like all implacable fluids, it needed only a single entry point to begin its deadly work.

Manta's annunciators had been placed on Ahead Flank even before clearing Montauk Point, and remained there twenty-three hours of every twenty-four.

Her course, decided in advance, had been set on a broad, looping curve that would sweep her around Nantucket, the Grand Banks and Iceland before finally settling on due north. Day after day she burrowed through the North Atlantic, her sonar searching actively ahead and to both sides, her Fathometer continuously recording the depth of water beneath her. Her whole being was concentrated on but a single objective: to reach, as soon as possible, the vicinity of position Golf November two-nine on the polar grid.

Once a day, however, she slowed to come to periscope and snorkel depth. Since *Manta,* an earlier submarine than the *Cushing,* had no apparatus for making oxygen from seawater, nor its complement, the carbon dioxide removal equipment, she routinely conserved her supply of compressed oxygen by periodically exchanging her internal air with the atmosphere. Usually this would be done in anticipation of a prolonged submergence, and thereafter every twenty-four hours whenever possible. After a full day, oxygen depletion was noticeable, and the instant restoration of vitality when the snorkel could finally be opened and fresh air drawn in became one of the pleasure points of the ship's routine. Other than the steady changes made in her great circle course, to bend it more and more toward the north, this was the only variety in her day-to-day existence.

After a few days, Richardson noticed that the same group of off-watch crew members seemed to be lounging around the control room during the periods of periscope depth, occasionally asking for a look at the sea and sky, volunteering to take a turn at periscope watch, generally contriving to make themselves useful. Both periscopes were kept up continuously during the hour or so it took for the routines associated with free air and low sea pressure: charging air banks, expelling garbage, blowing sanitaries.

"We call it 'periscope liberty,' " said Buck. "It didn't happen during our day trips out of New London because we never stayed out long. But it goes on all the time when we're at sea like this, and it's the same gang. Not all of them always ask for a look every day, either. They listen to what's said by those who are on the 'scopes. They get some kind of a lift just being where someone can see out. We let as many as possible have a turn on the 'scopes, so long as there's nothing special going on."

"Still tied to the surface, eh? Maybe you-all aren't a 'new breed' of sailor after all." Richardson and Williams were having a leisurely second cup of coffee in Buck's relatively spacious stateroom while the steward's mates were clearing away the wardroom after the evening meal. Rich had refused Buck's offer of his own cabin, had taken instead the top bunk in the executive officer's room. Even so, Rich had the uneasy feeling that some more strenuously employed younger officer had been evicted to make room for him. Besides, Jerry Abbott, the exec, had another roommate in addition to Richardson, and his cabin was about half the size of Buck's. Almost automatically, Rich had taken to spending some of his leisure in Buck's room while, at the same time, guiltily trying to avoid interference with Buck's own needs for it. Now, with the air in the ship recently renewed and the day's work and drills done, Buck was tilted back in his straight-back aluminum desk chair, while Rich sat on the bunk, propped up on the triangular plastic-covered pillow with which it was provided.

"That 'new breed' stuff is all newspaper hokum, Skipper," answered Buck, "and I know you think so too. It's not even relevant. There's no difference be-

tween submarines of today and sixteen years ago when
we brought the *Eel* back from the war. We used to
have the same kind of fellows wanting to come up to
the bridge for a breath of fresh air every time the *Eel*
surfaced, remember? It wasn't really the fresh air. With
our ventilation system there was always plenty of fresh
air when we were surfaced. In the enginerooms there
was a darned cyclone. Fresh air was an excuse, and it's
the same with our 'scope liberty."

"I guess it's pretty normal," said Rich. "They obviously can't go topside, so the control room is the next
best. This certainly is a relaxed way to travel." He was
enjoying the desultory conversation. There was no pressure on him. Buck and his crew were, of course, busy;
but there was nothing Rich could do until *Manta* arrived
in the area where *Cushing* lay disabled. One might as
well enjoy the enforced ease, making sure only that all
would be as ready as it could be when the big effort
began.

Buck was taking a deep swallow from his cup, savor-
ing it on the back of his tongue. "I've no doubt," he
said, "and that's one thing where we're far better off
and at the same time less well off than in the old diesel
boats. Look at the way we're making this transit.
There's no pitching, no rolling, no concern for the
weather, no worries about another ship running along
without a proper lookout. Our own lookout is electronic, or sonic, which is the same thing. The old
Manta's plugging along at full flat out, and you'd think
we were sitting alongside the dock in harbor somewhere.
Everything is so well organized there's no challenge.
The wheels are spinning back aft and everyone goes on
a watch in three, gets his three squares, sees a movie,
turns in and gets up to go through it all again. I'm not
saying we're idle, because there's always ship's work to
do. In fact, nearly everybody works at least four hours

in addition to his eight hours of watch. But it's always the same. Our variety is when we have a field day, or some drills for a couple of hours, or when we come to periscope depth to see if the world is still there. It affects different people differently. Being in the control room at the right time can become important to some of them."

Richardson nodded, smiled as he finished his coffee, then sobered slightly. "We'll have variety once we get near the *Cushing*. There'll not be much complaining about boredom then. Speaking of drills, it seems to me you've sprung just about every kind of emergency there is on your boys. Are you planning any ship and fire control exercises?"

"Yes, sure. I thought we ought to get the emergencies smoothed out first." Buck was suddenly on the defensive. "Why? We can have some tomorrow, if you want."

"Anytime is fine with me. We can't practice the towing operation, but there's no telling what else we might run into up there."

"You're not expecting any more collisions, hey?" Buck grinned. "If so, though, we'll give a good account of ourselves. During our overhaul last year a complete icebreaker superstructure was built on this old bucket. It added tons of weight, and every bit of our reserve lead ballast had to be taken off. Our bow is like the ram bow of an old battleship, and so's our sail. EB swears we could cut our way up through ten feet of solid ice."

"Sure, I know all about what EB did to your old tub. But how would you cut through ice that thick? Not by blowing tanks?"

"No. We might be able to break through four or five feet by blowing ballast and coming up flat," said Buck as he tipped his cup back for the last delicious drops of hot black liquid. "For thicker ice we'd have to hit it from underneath with speed and a pretty steep angle so as to slice through with our bow. That's what the Electric Boat design shop says, anyhow."

"Has the *Manta* done much steep-angle work?"

"Whenever there was a chance, or a good excuse. We all do, these days, ever since the first guppies showed what you could do with big angles. Besides, it's a great way to keep your crew on their toes, and it makes everybody keep loose gear stowed right. Come to think of it —I'd forgotten—you're the one who started the steepangle dive business, back during the war. I remember how you used to make us dive the *Eel* at fifteen degrees, out there in the area. I can see why you're interested."

"Fifteen degrees used to get us down a lot faster, all right, and once in a while we were mightly glad, but after the war some shippers went a lot steeper. The *Amberjack* used thirty degrees regularly, both up and down, and turned in reports about the tactical benefits. It got so people called them '*Anglejack* reports.'" Richardson put his empty cup on the desk. "The *Pickerel* is supposed to have surfaced from deep submergence with a seventy-two-degree angle, once. She came half her length out of the water." His relaxed position on the bunk had not changed, but he was thinking of something. There was an air of greater attention about him, Buck noticed.

"I remember those reports," said Buck. "I think I read every one. The *Amberjack* was one of our first guppies, and they claimed that with all the new speed and maneuverability the way to change depth in either direction was to use angles and get moving, the same way aircraft do. It's old hat, now. Did you hear they once put forty-two degrees on the *Triton?* It was last year. Some kind of a test Brighting wanted."

"I heard about it in the Pentagon. Some of us thought

it was a bit much, especially with a ship that big, but it was a one-time thing, done very carefully. One thing it showed, though. If that monster can go to an angle that big, even for a special occasion, all the smaller boats should be able to. It's just a matter of training, and being accustomed to handling your boat that way."

"Ship, boss. We're trying to inflate our importance a trifle."

"Ship. Right. It's about time, especially for the nukes. I was just thinking about what we might be running into, and it struck me we ought to have steep angles in our bag of tricks," Richardson said. There was seriousness in his words, and again Williams felt himself somehow on the defensive.

"Well, we've done a lot of it," Williams said. "We're rigged for angles this very minute. It's part of our rig for sea. It's not something anyone makes special reports about anymore. But we sure haven't practiced breaking through any ten feet of ice cover with any seventy-two-degree angles, if that's what you're thinking of!"

Richardson was instantly contrite. "I didn't mean to sound critical, old man. I'm sorry. I was just being curious." He waved his hand across his face in a gesture of friendly understanding. "Submarining has gone so far these days it's like a whole new science, with all new boats and equipment."

"Ships. But I'll bet it didn't seem so on the new *Trigger* when she made that famous—or maybe I should say infamous—shakedown trip to Rio," chuckled Buck, trying in his turn to ease the moment. "She was the first of the postwar boats to be completed, and her diesels were a fiasco. That wasn't all, either. Her evaporators were no good, and neither were her periscopes. Her skipper caught hell for saying so, too."

"Later on, a couple of that class had to be towed back to port, one all the way from England, so he was sure right," said Richardson. "The Navy made it up to him with the *Triton*." He was gladly following Buck's lead, glad of a safe refuge—relaxed professional conversation—from the danger he had nearly fallen into. "You know," he went on, "giving him the *Triton* was completely old Brighting's doing. Sometimes some of us have wondered if he wanted to prove a point and figured this might be a good way to do it. When the *Triton*'s shakedown cruise took her completely around the world, submerged and nonstop, without any serious mechanical trouble whatsoever, you had to admit he certainly did prove something. As far as I'm concerned, he proved that his ships were the best there could be, anywhere. You've got to say there could not possibly be a more demanding test of a brand-new ship!"

"Admiral Brighting sure is a strange one, boss. Do you remember that time in his quonset out in Idaho?"

"I was just thinking about it," confessed Rich. "He may be a tyrant, but he certainly gets results. The tests and training he puts his people to, and the government contractors he deals with also, are so far beyond what everyone's been used to that they're like a new technology. The *Trigger*'s shakedown compared with *Triton*'s makes a good illustration. The *Triton* could have gone on another round-the-world cruise the next day, while they doggone near had to tow the *Trigger* back from Rio. It was a perfect example of the difference between lousy engineering by committee and the kind of good engineering Brighting does by himself."

"He didn't add much to the conference in the *Proteus* the night before we got underway."

"He couldn't. As he said, he's an engineer, not an operations type. But he did come up with the salient point about the Russian press release. They've lost an aircraft in the Arctic under strange circumstances.

Strange enough for them to blame it on Keith. And Keith's second message said there were military aircraft searching in his vicinity. They must have been up there before he arrived. It all hangs together. Something big's going on." Richardson's forehead had been creased in thought often since their departure, Buck had noticed. It was wrinkled now.

"There was one other thing Brighting did," Buck said. "You know that piece of paper he handed me at the airport just before they took off? All covered with pencil notes and figures?" Williams was looking at Richardson in an odd way.

"Yes. Some new settings for your power plant, he said."

"Yes. The reactor control officer's been going over them, and tonight he said he's ready to put them in. Know what they do?"

"No," said Rich, his keen interest evident in the narrowed gaze he leveled on Buck. "But I was a bit curious when I heard Harry Langforth report to you."

"Brighting's authorized a reduction in our thermal margin and increased the allowed temperature difference between the hot and cold legs of the primary loop. The rest of the figures are the new alarm points for the instrumentation."

"He handed all this to you on a piece of paper?"

"In pencil. Right off the top of his head. He must carry all those numbers in his mind. I rode to the airport in the same car with him, and he was writing in the back seat. So some of the figures are a little hard to read. He said to check them out and then put them in effect."

"Has Harry Langforth given you an estimate of what the change does?" asked Richardson.

"It adds twenty percent to our reactor output. Harry figures we'll make about three more knots at full power. Brighting said the new settings might be useful." The odd look was still on Buck Williams' face.

"Three more knots! That'll give us nearly twenty-three at flank speed!" The furrow was still on Richardson's brow, now more accentuated. "You say he told you the increased speed might be useful?"

"He didn't say anything about speed."

"But that's what he was talking about, all the same! What a foxy old devil he is! I take back what I just said about him."

"What's that?"

"That's he's only an engineer, not an operations type. He's handed us something that might make all the difference in this caper of ours. Who says he's not operations oriented!" The frown cleared, was replaced by a grim smile. "We were talking about *Triton*'s shakedown cruise. This one we're on is a lot more than any shaketown. It's going to be the toughest test the old *Manta*'s ever had, and Brighting thinks there may be more to it even than anyone is anticipating. He's famous for looking at the possible dark side ahead, you know.

Buck tipped his chair upright, pushed the coffee cups aside, cleared a space on the writing surface of his desk and pulled a pad of lined paper toward him. "You're another, Rich! I've seen you from way back, and I've got a feeling you're thinking we may have some need for all that new horsepower. We'll have the new settings in place by tomorrow morning. What sort of ship and fire control drills would you like to start with?"

Richardson's mind had suddenly wandered to the private conversation he had had in the lead car with Admiral Donaldson. Strange that Donaldson and Brighting should think so much alike, and from such dissimilar backgrounds! Resolutely he shook his head to clear it, hunched forward on the bunk so that he also looked over the writing surface, and the two friends lost themselves planning the exercises.

Cindy Williams was tall and angular. There was a strength about her which entirely belied the sensitive vulnerability of her mouth and the sympathetic set of her eyes. She was fully as tall as Buck—taller when she wore heels—and her calm, thoughtful personality was the perfect complement for Buck's more volatile, crisp makeup. At least, so Laura had always thought. Cindy was not beautiful the way Peggy Leone was beautiful, and occasionally, not today, her grooming was somewhat casual—a fault Peggy would never have been guilty of. She was a sincere person, devoid of self-consciousness. Laura had liked her from the first time she saw her.

Now Cindy and Peggy sat on opposite ends of Laura's sofa, while Laura faced them across the low coffee table in her living room. On the table stood the remnants of afternoon tea, and alongside the tea tray was an opened bottle of dry cocktail sherry. A half-empty wineglass stood before Cindy on the low table.

Holding her own glass lightly by the stem, Laura sipped the amber liquid. She was glad she had thought of bringing it out, though it had not been in her original plan. It had provided her with an opportune interruption and might smooth the remainder of the afternoon.

A long obligatory telephone conversation with Peggy, late on the morning of the *Manta*'s departure, had fully discharged any further duty to her; that and the previous, much shorter call she had made, with Rich's reluctant approval, very early the same day. There was nothing more she could do for her. She would try to avoid an open rupture, but she had not been successful with any of her previous plans for controlling the grow-

ing situation. Now she was more than ever determined
somehow to escape further embroilment with this fret-
ful, tiresome woman.

Perhaps Cindy had also had experience with Peggy's
obsession. Perhaps she sensed Laura's reluctance to go
into it with her yet again. Laura was sure of it when
Cindy adroitly deflected Peggy the first time she tried
to steer the conversation toward Keith. "I know both of
your men have been away on long cruises from time
to time," Peggy had said, "but somehow Keith seems
to draw the longest trips, and the most frequent ones,
too. It's been nearly a month, now, that he's been gone."

"Buck had a skipper once," Cindy interjected, "who
said at least once a day that 'the place for a young man
is at sea and away from all ba-a-a-d women!' Buck used
to imitate him for my benefit. He had all sorts of little
sayings like this, and I think Buck had every one of
them memorized, with gestures and facial expressions."
She had turned toward Laura as she spoke, and Laura
had the distinct impression of having had the ball tossed
to her.

"I know who that was," said Laura, picking up the
thread "That was Dan Backus. He was a well-known
character. He had a big family, and when he wasn't
pretending to knock them he was bragging about them.
Will you have lemon or sugar, Peggy? This tea is
straight from China, and is already rather sweet. You
can smell the jasmine in it. I think it's half flower
petals."

"Sugar, please," said Peggy.

"Is one enough?"

"I like it sweet. Can I have two lumps?"

"Of course. And take a couple of these little biscuits.
They're supposed to be Chinese, too, but they're made
right here in Connecticut."

"Thanks. I will. They look delicious. With my sweet

tooth Keith says I'm lucky I don't look like a balloon."

"All the girls in the squadron are just green over you, Peggy," said Cindy. "I wish I were petite like you and didn't have to worry about gaining weight. A horse must have made faces at Mother about the time I was born."

"If all your worries are only about gaining weight, you're lucky." Peggy had the characteristic petulance in her voice which told Laura she was about to revert to her favorite subject.

Quickly, Laura said, "Tell us about that school you've just put Ruthie in. What's its name—the Thames Valley Junior School? From what I've heard, they have a very advanced curriculum for the youngsters."

Peggy could not resist the bait, even though she suspected the subject might have been raised to keep the conversation in a different channel. For half an hour, interspersed with interruptions for more tea, she expanded upon the virtues of the newly formed school and its highly touted program for preschoolers. Finally, however, the teapot was nearly empty, its contents no longer hot. Sensing that Peggy could not be further denied, Laura had the inspiration to suggest sherry. This gave her an excuse to go to the kitchen for a few moments. When she returned she deliberately made small talk about the wine until all three had their wineglasses and had sipped from them.

The wine was of excellent quality, straight from Spain, a gift from one of Rich's friends who had just returned from there. It might ease the strain for Peggy a little. After all, she had a right to be worried about her husband. But Laura was beyond hoping there could be any permanent adjustment in Peggy's attitude toward the Navy. She would help her over the present situation as well as she could, but that would have to be the end.

Peggy, in the meantime, perhaps not appreciating

that Laura was quietly arranging the best atmosphere possible for what was bound to be a difficult and perhaps painful discussion, chose the moment to discard all subterfuge. "I want to talk about Keith," she said bluntly, putting down her wineglass and including Cindy and Laura in her tense two-handed gesture.

Laura caught Cindy's quick look of sympathy. The thought projected across the space between them without need for words. Laura must know far more than Peggy. Cindy probably did, too. Peggy was worried, most understandably so after the unusual events of the past week. She had every right to Laura's counsel. But what could Laura tell her?

Most of what Laura "knew" was actually only surmise. But she was in a far better position than Peggy to draw accurate deductions. She had indeed had more and better inputs than Peggy. How much could she tell of what she knew, or guessed? Would she thus be violating Rich's confidence, even though he had carefully not confided in her—perhaps in anticipation of this very situation? She was his wife. She knew better than anyone else what was motivating him, what he was thinking. She was better able than anyone to divine what was going on. He knew it, had warned her that Peggy could not be trusted with a secret. But he hadn't told her anything. Whatever she thought was strictly her own creation. Peggy had come for help. Her hysteria about Keith must be about to crest again. Laura had to try to do something.

"I can't stand it anymore," Peggy said. "Every time Keith leaves it's worse, and this time it's worse than ever. I'm always afraid for him, and I'm afraid to be left alone with Ruthie, too. I swore I'd never go through that again, and now look."

"It's never for so very long, Peggy," said Laura

soothingly. She realized she was using the same voice she might to a child.

"Yes, it is, too! It's always too long! Nothing is ever settled in our lives the way it should be! Now I'm sure he's in danger!" Peggy's voice broke. "What am I going to do?" she wailed.

Laura swiftly skirted the coffee table, perched on the arm of the sofa and leaned to put her arm around her. Cindy, she saw, had uncrossed her legs as if to get up also. "It's especially rough for you right now, Peggy, but it's only a guess about Keith even being in the Arctic. Maybe he's nowhere near where the Russian plane got shot down."

"If a plane did get shot down," said Cindy. "Maybe none of it's true."

Peggy had her tea napkin to her eyes. "I just know it's Keith they're talking about," she sobbed. "That must be the *Cushing* up there under the ice. I'm scared. Maybe the Russians will attack her for shooting at their airplane. Maybe I'll never see Keith again!"

"Remember what Rich said to tell you before he and Buck got underway," said Laura swiftly. "He said to keep your faith in the Navy. Remember?" She squeezed Peggy's shoulder as she spoke.

"That's easy for you to say, Laura," said Peggy, her face working. She looked belligerently at her. "Keep your faith in the Navy, Rich says! What faith?"

"The faith all of us have."

"I have faith, all right! That's all I've got! I've got faith that the Navy will never back its people up in a tough spot! It will always look out for itself, all right, and the trade-school boys will look out for themselves. They always put people like Keith in the most danger, and then they go off and leave them to face it alone! Faith in the Navy? Faith in nothing! That's a laugh!"

Peggy's voice had risen. Her overwrought emotions boiled over. She almost shouted the last few words.

"You're upset, Peggy, and that's not surprising. But what you're saying isn't fair, and it's just not true." Laura spoke quietly, though it took an effort. She wanted to shake her, shout some sense into her. But Peggy was not rational. The thing to do was to calm her. "Do you think the Navy will simply abandon a brand-new and very valuable ship, and its crew of a hundred and twenty-five men? That doesn't make any sense! It's never been done. Not in our whole history. It's contrary to naval tradition, too."

"Well, why don't they do something, then? Why don't they tell me something?"

"Peggy, they can't. If the Navy makes any sort of announcement, even privately to only a few people, that's practically the same as telling the Russians too. If things are as bad as you fear, do you think that sort of thing will help Keith?"

"They've not helped me much!" There were both a whine and a snarl in Peggy's voice. "I told you I can't stand it anymore! The Navy's never done anything except make me miserable!"

Cindy said, "You've got to think of it from Keith's point of view, too, Peggy. What he thinks must mean something to you."

Laura said, "Keith has put his trust in the Navy, Peggy. If he could, he'd tell you so right now."

"No, he wouldn't! I wouldn't let him! I hate the Navy! Even when he's home I hate it, because he's never there long. He's always planning that next trip, and it wasn't any better when he was on duty in Washington. He was in the Pentagon all day and all night too. I counted his hours; some weeks he was in the Pentagon for eighty hours and even ninety hours. It's just not fair!" The cocktail napkin was twisted into a sodden ball, clenched in her hand. She waved it wildly as she spoke.

"It's true the Navy asks more of its conscientious people, like Keith," said Laura. "But that's why he's had such important assignments. Rich says he's a couple of years ahead of his contemporaries right now. The Navy asks more of him because he's one of the best officers it's got."

"That's so! The Navy's using him for a patsy. It always has. I know. I've seen it too many times!"

"Is that why he's got the best and newest ship in the Navy, right now?"

"That's why they've sent him out on this dangerous mission. It's obvious! That's why!"

"Peggy," Laura said as calmly as she could, although she could feel herself tensing and knew she could not keep her rising reaction totally under control, "both Rich and I have been trying to convince you that's not true. This assignment he's on now, whatever it is, is due to his reputation as one of the best skippers in the Navy. It's an honor for him."

Laura's arm was still draped over the back of the sofa, not quite touching Peggy. Nevertheless, Peggy peevishly brushed it away. "No kidding!" The sarcasm in her voice was heavy. "They always send Keith off on the big risks! Don't tell me they don't! And I know why they pick him. Send one of our boys on those tough jobs? Oh, no! Send Keith Leone. He's not one of ours. He doesn't count."

Laura could see Cindy's eyes narrow, then widen. Perhaps she had not heard this portion of the litany of complaints. "Don't be silly," Laura said, still in the quiet tone. She was about to go on, say something more, but Peggy continued talking.

"You, of all people, ought to know what I'm talking about, Laura! Your first husband didn't go through the trade school either, did he?" Peggy accentuated the words "trade school." "Have you ever thought about that?"

"Nobody cared where Jim Bledsoe's diploma came from! He was one of the best sub skippers we had!" Laura spoke sharply, with anger. She herself was surprised at the way her words came out. The mention of Jim had caught her unawares. She had not spoken of him for years, rarely thought of him these days. The memories flooded in on her. It was the first of the war years, and they had been married only five days, during which Jim worked fourteen hours a day on board the new *Walrus,* getting her ready for the trip to the Pacific from which neither returned. It was not long enough to build a marriage, although she had tried her amateurish, insufficient best.

The hurt came slowly, the days in succession dawning with hope, passing with a slight deepening of the growing disappoinment. She wrote two long letters a week, setting aside the time necessary to do so even when the long silences and sparse replies made continued cheerfulness a misery. Jim was at war. His ship was at sea, fighting. He rarely was in port long enough to answer letters. Then came the day when she met Cynthia Schultz, wife of the ship's engineer, happily carrying a handbag full of thick envelopes—when she had only two thin ones. The worst was when Jim took the *Walrus* to Australia, where he was lionized as a brilliant combat submariner. His exploits, camouflaged and censored though they were, filled the news. Friends called to congratulate her, strangers spoke of the pride she must feel, and she had been forced to smile gratefully through her shame, for there were no letters at all in her purse. Once, a mortifying memory, she had pretended in a desperate moment that a letter from someone else was from Jim.

But that was all long ago. Now, every time she thought of Jim, a deeper understanding drifted into her consciousness. Perhaps their marriage might have survived, might even have been good had it not faced the insuperable handicap of the war, and what war did to people. She was even able to recall without squirming the intimate, demeaning little artifices she had employed in some of her letters—how pathetic, how much in the realm of fantasy, yet all she had to work with, for the memories were so few—and how hopeless she felt when his short replies showed none of the spark she was trying so anxiously to keep alive. She knew, now, that her own inadequacies as a young war bride, for which she had blamed herself in the beginning, were not at fault. Neither was Jim's neglectful correspondence, nor his infidelities with Joan and with others. These she had managed to understand even at the time, even with the hurt she then felt. She had not blamed Joan. Joan, too, was a child of the war and, like any of the men, had her own private needs. But it was terribly painful, all the same, and there were days when she could hardly face the thought of yet another of the same empty nature. Finally, it was Rich, who came to seek her out after it was all over, who restored her self-respect, and (it seemed at the time) her sanity. She had been astonished how quickly the world turned right again and over the years had learned why that had been inevitable.

No. As to all this, she was now invulnerable. Her only vulnerability was for Jim himself. She was proud of him, proud of his record, and of his great sacrifice. Proud of her own offering too, if that was the right word, for the death of that marriage—separate and distinct from Jim's own death (she recognized this now)—had been a sacrifice also demanded by the war. The pain and anguish were far in the past. Now there were only warm memories of Jim as he had been. She would defend him fiercely, almost as a mother might the child of her youth. For Jim would never grow old. Through the years he would become younger, until he would be almost as her own child. She was all he had. He had no family, had left no one behind but her. She would protect him, and his memory.

Laura's flash of anger left her as quickly as it came. For a few seconds no one said anything. Even Peggy was still. There was an oasis of stillness.

When Laura broke the silence, her voice was low and soft again, but it contained the faint vibration of an emotion she could remember at times hearing in Rich's when he spoke of the *Walrus,* or of some friend, like Stocker Kane, also lost in the war. The emotion was for far more than one man lost at sea, or a husband of a few days forever deprived of his right to the promises life had made to him. Jim had at least been able to taste of them. He at least had had that. She was glad she had helped, had been his wife, even if for only five days. Implicitly, she felt love, and sorrow, and limitless compassion for the countless young men who had marched to the altar of war through the ages, casting all their youth, and all their plans, and all their hopes, into that pitiless cauldron. Some had been maimed, like Rich, who carried an ineradicable scar on his soul, or devoured, like Jim. They had been so brave. All had been touched, somehow. None had escaped. "He's still out there, you know," she said, her quiet, almost reflective voice like a solitary cloud drifting through an open sky. "He's forever there, with his ship and his crew, and forever young. Most of his crew were in their early twenties. Did you know that? He was the oldest man aboard, and he was only twenty-nine. Once a year there's a ceremony in Pearl Harbor for the boats still on patrol. That's what they call it. 'Still on patrol.' For some, like Rich, it's a very sentimental occasion. The *Walrus* was his old boat too, you know." Tremulously, she smiled a tiny smile. The memories were deep. Cindy, she saw, understood. Her eyes blinked away the tiny moisture that had gathered there.

But, again, it was a mistake to think of Peggy as a normal person, with normal perceptions. She saw her chance, leaped at it. "Jim was the same as Keith, only from Yale. So they took Rich off and gave the boat to Jim. They should have sent the *Walrus* home for a while, for an overhaul, which she needed, but instead they sent him off to the most dangerous area, and he got sunk! *Walrus* was due to come back to the States for a six-months overhaul, wasn't she? You'd have had six months together at Mare Island or Hunter's Point. But instead, the Navy sent him out again, and you never saw him again. That's why he's still on patrol! That's not going to happen to Keith, I can tell you!" She looked triumphant.

Cindy and Laura were both on their feet. The blow had been below the belt, and it was a telling one. Cindy spoke sharply. "That's not fair of you, Peggy! It's not true, either! Rich was in the hospital with a broken leg. The whole sub force knows the story of Jim Bledsoe and the great patrols he made before he was sent on that last one! It also knows how Rich and the *Eel* wiped out the Japanese ASW force that caught him!"

"That didn't help Jim much."

"It showed what Rich thought of him!"

Laura tried to retain her carefully recaptured calm, but she knew the smooth articulation that came out of her held the edge of a barely contained fury. She hoped Peggy would not notice, for the thing to do was to get her into a more productive frame of mind. For this, she would have to exercise self-control, for Peggy was clearly in no condition to do so herself. "None of any of this concerns Keith," she said. "If there's anything Cindy or I can do that will help you, or Keith, we want to do it. The first thing is to know what we can do. There's no use wasting time on things we can't influence, or being upset because the Navy isn't telling us everything it's planning or thinking."

Cindy was nodding her head in agreement, her eyes fixed on Peggy, almost as though she were mentally sending a signal to her. Peggy, however, sensing her momentary advantage, paid no attention. Perhaps she really did not know what she was saying, perhaps didn't care. "I told you what I'm going to do! I'm not going to let anything like that happen to Keith if I can help it!"

"Peggy, you've got to stop thinking you can have any effect on what happens to Keith! You're just driving yourself and your friends up the wall. That's all you're doing. The way you're acting right now does no one any good whatsoever." Cindy spoke warmly and directly, but her eyes were flashing.

"Yes, it will! I know what I'm doing! He's been gone a month, and now maybe he's in danger! There's always some emergency. Nobody tells me anything, and I'm about to go crazy!" (I think you already have, thought Laura and Cindy simultaneously.) "The Russians are probably looking for him!" (Laura felt a tremor go through her body.) "I'm sick of being scared to death, and sick of nobody telling me anything, and sick of what the Navy puts you through in general! As soon as Keith gets back from this trip I'm asking him to put in his retirement papers!" Her hand trembling, Peggy downed the remaining half of her sherry, reached for the bottle uninvited, refilled her glass, took another deep gulp.

"You can do that, now that Keith has his twenty years. Of course." Laura found the strength to keep her voice steady. "But please, don't set your mind in concrete until you can talk to him. You owe him that much."

"I don't need to talk to him," cried Peggy. "I tell you, I've had it. If Keith won't see it my way, Ruthie and I are leaving!"

Laura could feel Cindy's cool eyes focused on her. She glanced quickly at her, turned back to Peggy. "Peggy, dear," she began, "we—that is, I—"

"Don't you or anyone 'Peggy dear' me! I'm sick of being patted on the head and told not to worry, or that the Navy will do my worrying for me. What does the Navy think I am? I don't have to take this, you know."

"We understand, believe me," Laura began again. "This whole thing has been awfully hard on you, but you've got to lay your feelings aside, at least until Keith is back home with you. Things will look a great deal different by then." Part of Laura's mind told her that Peggy had a right to be agitated, that it was her own duty to try to help at this difficult time, despite the exasperating nature of everything else about her. She was crying again, crying for help as much as from self-pity. What to do? How to help her? Laura had the sensation of diving headfirst into a pit of quicksand. She drew a deep, lung-expanding breath before she went under. "Listen, there's one thing I can tell you that might make you feel a little better about everything . . ."

Another deep breath. She didn't really know anything for sure, but it was a good guess based on what she did know. If it made Peggy better able to face what she must face with a little more equanimity, it might be worth it. She hoped Rich would forgive her for what she was about to say. "This is confidential, now, but anyway the Navy isn't forgetting Keith up there in the Arctic. There's been all sorts of conferences on what to do." (Peggy certainly knew about the conferences;

so did the rest of the submarine base, most probably. And, yes, almost certainly the *Cushing* was in the Arctic. Saying so could not be a security breach. The newspapers had published it.) "They've sent Rich and Buck to join him. That's what Rich meant when he said you should keep faith in the Navy." The quicksand closed over her. She felt herself suffocating.

A smile of relief on Peggy's face, or was it one of gratification? More worrisome, Cindy gave her a startled look. But there was no turning back.

"Our three men served together during the war. That's why Rich is out with Buck right now. This is all very secret information" (God forgive her!) "and I shouldn't be telling anyone, but you two are married to the two skippers involved, and if anyone has a right to know, you do. Anyway, that's why all the mystery. Please don't say a word about this to anyone. Anyone at all. You've got to keep it to yourselves, because I wasn't supposed to tell anyone either. Nobody knows what's really going on" (this, at least, was completely true) "but you can bet on one sure thing. Before long, Buck and Rich and the *Manta* will be there too!"

Cindy's expressive eyes were turned full on her. Laura could sense the disapproval issuing from them. No doubt Cindy, too, had her own ideas about her husband's latest mission. Perhaps Buck had told her more than Rich had told Laura. If he had, he must have sworn her to secrecy. In any case, she had kept silent. Now she would believe Laura had confirmed her surmises, or revealed what Buck had cautioned her not ever to speak of—whichever—and in the process, because Peggy would not keep quiet, had thereby increased the danger to be faced by her own husband.

No help for it. It had had to be done. Perhaps Laura could later explain it all to her privately. Cindy was saying something. Were her lips a shade more compressed than usual? Laura could not be sure. "Peggy," Cindy said, "all of us have to be realistic. Now of all times. We've got to remember that our three husbands have gone through a lot together. Whatever's going on, if Rich and Buck are in it too, you can be sure Keith could have no better help anywhere. If he had his choice, this is exactly what he would want."

"Realistic, you say! Realistic!" The word had triggered something, the wild irrationality Laura had already sensed. "I'm the one who's realistic! I'm sick of everything about the Navy, I tell you!" Peggy rose to her feet, face flushed, hands clenched at her sides. "I'm not part of it, and Keith's not part of it either! It does anything it wants to you. Anything!" Her eyes were glaring, her breath came in short quick pants through reddened nostrils. "I hate it, I tell you! And I hate both of you, too! You're both part of the clique that's running things. You've had your own way too long! I know all about that patrol on the *Eel* when old Commodore Blunt was killed, and I know all about the Lastrada dame, too. She had a much bigger piece of Jim than you ever did, Laura, my dear. She serviced half the men on Oahu at one time or another. She had a piece of Rich, too, before you got him. She was screwing him every night for a while! There's a lot more to that story than you know, I guess!

"And Rich should never have brought old Blunt back to Pearl Harbor in a torpedo tube. He should have dumped the body at sea, the way they do everyone else. The Navy docs tried to cover by saying he died of a brain tumor, but they never explained that broken neck he also had. . . ."

The livid, twisted look on Peggy's face was positively leering. Her mouth held a distorted, exulting expression. Laura stood rigid, her hand an inch from Peggy's shoulder. For an insane instant, there was the temptation to smash her across the face with open palm and every bit of strength she possessed. Instead, she steeled herself to speak coldly, contemptuously. She pronounced each word distinctly, knowing that doing so helped her retain that shred of control which alone kept her from succumbing to the tearing outrage within her. "Peggy, that is absolutely unforgivable. There is nothing more I can do for you. You are unwelcome in my house. Please go away. Now."

Cindy hustled Peggy to the hall closet, draped Peggy's coat around her shoulders and threw on her own, and then, nervously but determinedly, led her out the door.

Alone at last, Laura found her hands trembling as she carried her tea tray back into the kitchen. They were trembling only partly in suppressed rage, for even though she knew she was privy to no secrets (thank God Rich had protected her) she had come perilously close to saying too much to a woman she did not trust.

www

Unlike Keith, Rich and Buck planned no ceremonial inspection of the edge of the ice cap. *Manta* simply remained deeply submerged and at high speed, aware of the approximate location of the southern boundary of the cap from ice patrol reports, and specifically, as she passed under it, from her upward-beamed Fathometer—and went immediately from the domain of light and air to that of darkness and ice. Henceforth she would be confined to her stored oxygen and waste removal capabilities. After a final recharge of air from the surface, a regular schedule was begun of bleeding oxygen into the ship from her storage bank of compressed oxygen and eliminating carbon dioxide and the sinister carbon monoxide through absorption and burning. The daily slow depletion of oxygen, causing lassitude and discomfort during the couple of hours preceding the snorkel period when the air was changed, became a thing of the past. "We're keeping the oxygen above twenty percent by volume, and we figure we can stay completely submerged for thirty days," said Buck. "After that, we might have a problem. We could stretch things some by bleeding good air out of one of our compressed air banks while we're pumping it down with our compressors into a different one."

"You trying to teach me some new submarining, old man?" Rich grinned at Buck over their afterdinner coffee cups. "Seems to me, in the dim dark ages of the diesel boats, we used to do that to save the compressed oxygen. We had to pay for oxygen out of our ship's quarterly allotment back then, not like now. You modern submariners don't know what it was like, in the bad old days."

"You go right straight to hell, Commodore. We're doggone glad we don't. And so are you, very respectfully, sir, and all that." The best part of the day was at hand. The strenuous and sometimes ingenious drills were over, the air in the confined hull was sweet and invigorating, the evening movies were being set up in the wardroom and crew's mess hall. Everything was as it should be. The entire calculations of strain on the towing gear, from initial contact to the steady-state towing phase, had been gone over. The devices themselves had both been inspected, their few moving parts lubricated, the strain gauges tested. They had suffered no deterioration from their week in the slimy cold of the stern torpedo tubes, were as ready as they could be.

To the gratification of Rich and Buck, the new settings on the reactor controls had worked out to twenty-three percent increased power, and with everything wide open the *Manta* had actually logged almost twenty-four knots, beyond the capability of the electronic log to measure. Speed had been computed from propeller rpm. Following the test run, however, and except for short periods during certain of the new drills, they had decided to continue at the old speed and keep the new power in reserve for use when and if the situation demanded it.

By this time, *Manta*'s course was due north. There were less than a thousand miles to go to reach the *Cushing*'s estimated position at grid Golf November two-nine. Tomorrow Buck would shift navigational plot and the inertial navigation system to the polar grid.

"We're nearly there, Buck," Rich said after a moment, the easy smile on his face fading slightly. "We should be making contact with Keith within forty-eight hours. I've got to admit the whole thing's beginning to build up in my mind. It's been a great trip up to now. . . ." He paused. His face grew more serious. "I mean, it's been really relaxing. But do you feel like a movie tonight? I sure don't."

"Me neither," said Buck, "but I wasn't going to say so. We'll be trying this thing out for real day after tomorrow. But we ought not cut the wardroom off from movies just because we don't want one—why don't we get another cup of coffee, and I'll tell them to go ahead without us."

Prior to *Manta*'s departure from New London, a carefully drafted priority message had been sent to Keith via the special low-frequency station in Maine in the hope that even though unable to transmit, *Cushing* was still able to receive signals through her underwater antenna. At Donaldson's insistence, Rich himself had drafted the message. Coded in Washington before transmittal (in deference to the hour, the CNO had offered to have this done by his own coding board), the message conveyed the purpose of the *Manta*'s voyage, details of the submerged hookup, and the procedures required of the *Cushing*. On the day of *Manta*'s projected arrival, *Cushing* was directed periodically to echo-range on her active sonar, blow a police whistle on her underwater voice communication set or release an air bubble through her main ballast tanks, all in a complicated time sequence. She was to keep this up, precisely as specified, until further instruction.

In the meantime, with her receiving senses at maximum alert, *Manta* would patrol the vicinity of *Cushing*'s last known grid position and home in on the noises: a combination of locating device and recognition signal. Once the two submarines were at close range, conversation was authorized over the UQC in plain language and at minimum volume. Keith was to have ready and transmit directly to Rich, by voice, an already enciphered message stating his condition and, most specifically, any information he might have regarding the aircraft the Russians claimed to have lost in his vicinity. Then, before doing anything else, the *Manta* was to seek a polynya in which she could surface to relay the message.

Not until then would *Manta* be free to begin the hookup and extraction operation. Although acting as a radio relay link had initially been Rich's suggestion, he had privately argued strenuously against requiring the additional delay the message would involve. "If the *Cushing*'s in the shape we think most likely, without propulsion but otherwise okay, there'll be a good chance of getting both ship and crew out of there. If that's true, and nothing else is changed, then the idea of abandoning ship and scuttling her will be put on standby, right? Then why waste time? If there's any kind of skulduggery going on, as soon as whoever's doing it realizes there may be a chance of our getting them out . . ."

But this argument he had lost. Admiral Donaldson shook his head, interrupted him. "I know exactly what you're saying," he said, "but I've got my orders, too. This came right from the National Security Council to the Joint Chiefs. This is an affair of state, now, and they want answers just as soon as they can get them.

Sorry, Rich, but that has to stay in the message, and it's a direct order to you."

"Don't they see this puts Keith and his crew in even greater jeopardy?" Rich said desperately, momentarily forgetting he was speaking with the Chief of Naval Operations, the highest officer on active duty in the Navy. He was thinking only of the possibility of the lengthy sonar or radio transmissions being overheard, of their arousing curiosity (he almost said "the enemy's curiosity") and then allowing time for possible inimical reaction. He recovered himself in confusion. "Sorry, Admiral, But look. Whatever happened that made Keith go off the air so suddenly came right after his long second message. Direction-finding is a fact of life in radio communications. We've got to figure they have the capability, whoever they are. They could have DF-ed him and homed in on him. Maybe they even homed in our single side-band talk, but that was so short it's less likely, especially with the frequency shifts we made. Now we're telling him to make a long transmission on the UQC, the most easily detected sonar there is!"

Admiral Donaldson was listening gravely, nodded slightly as Richardson spoke.

Encouraged, Rich continued with even greater urgency. "If they pick it up, they'll know there's another sub there. And then the *Manta* has to go find a thin place in the ice cover, break through, and repeat the same thing on the air. Even if they don't pick up the low-power UQC, there's nothing secure about our ship-to-shore frequency. If they DF-ed him then, they'll DF us too. We've got to expect they've got a direction-finder. Either way, they'll know another sub has got up there, or else that the *Cushing* has repaired things enough to do it herself. They'll be alerted that something's going on. If their sub is still around, and if the collision was no accident, it will join the party for sure!" Richardson suddenly realized he had raised his voice, dropped it precipitantly. Thank God they had closeted themselves privately to compose the message!

"I know it, Rich," said Donaldson steadily. "Don't apologize for telling me what you think. I was in the war too, remember, and we had to think this way all the time. If I can get the JCS to lift the requirement, I'll get a message off to you right away, but for now this is the way it's got to be."

But no message had ever come. Without doubt, Donaldson had made the effort. He must have been turned down. The information must be considered vital. Rich could not help wondering if the NSC planning-group functionary who had demanded it had any concept of the cost it might exact.

Richardson said nothing to Buck of his misgivings, nor did he mention his private protest to Donaldson on the subject. With the slow fading of the hope that a message would arrive negating the requirement, he realized he must try to dismiss the problem from his mind. All the more so since there was nothing he could do about it. He concentrated on the pleasure of being at sea on an extended voyage, on the companionship of Buck and his officers, on the sheer joy of seeing a magnificent combination of men and machinery running faultlessly, apparently effortlessly, doing the daily drills demanded of it with precision and élan. He concentrated also on the necessity of keeping every sense alert, every possible situation analyzed in advance, every conceivable contingency prepared for, in anticipation of the trial that lay ahead. It had been difficult at first, but he had managed it.

Then gradually, as the magic of the submarine and its extraordinary capabilities—so different from those he had been accustomed to for so many years—enfolded him, the tension evoked by the interview with Donaldson drifted away. Not entirely away, but into the recesses of consciousness. There it remained, only occasionally to be brought out and examined. Donaldson was not given to unconsidered, impulsive action. At least, not in these later years. Why, then, had he contrived to make it seem as though sending Rich along with Buck had been an afterthought, almost a whim of his own? And if, as Rich now had begun to suspect, Admiral Donaldson had intended to do this all along, there must be some important function for Rich to perform.

But what? He had received no instructions whatever, unless those strange words the admiral had used on board the *Proteus,* later reinforced by his additional comment in the Navy sedan as the two rode to the airport, were to be so considered.

Finding the *Cushing* proved not an easy task. She was not where she was supposed to be, not at Golf November two-nine—at least, according to the *Manta*'s navigation, checked and rechecked. It was necessary not to alert the Soviets, if their submarine happened still to be in the area, or if they were listening in another way. There was, too, the worry about collision with the other sub or, for that matter, with the *Cushing,* if somehow the notorious capriciousness of sonar expressed itself at just the wrong time and in the wrong way. One could not simply go blundering ahead at full speed.

Keith almost certainly had not been able to move his ship. Without propeller or emergency propulsion, she must be immobile under the ice, probably resting with the top of her sail against the underside. If she was not in the position reported by Keith, it must be because of drift due to currents and ice movement. She could not be far away. A few miles at most.

Manta began circling the datum, plotted at *Cushing's* position as last reported, at slow speed, listening intently at the designated times for evidence of her presence. She made two complete circles two miles in diameter, then slowly changed the circle into an ever enlarging spiral, at maximum submergence depth.

Richardson was beginning to curse himself for not having selected a signal frequency at least twice as rapid when, at long last, the first faint beeps on the active echo-ranging sonar were heard. "He wasn't on for long, only about three pings," Jeff Norton reported, breathlessly. "I was right there in the sonar shack. It was right on time, but we didn't get a good bearing because he quit too soon."

"What's the approximate direction?" Buck asked the question quietly, well aware that the primary requirement he had laid on his sonar crew had been to obtain the bearing of anything they heard. He had not directed Jeff to be in the sonar cubicle, but was not surprised that *Manta's* communications officer, also sonar officer, had taken it on himself to be present at that critical instant. Buck's astonishment was over the fact that an accurate true bearing had not been obtained.

"Southwest. But the three beeps came in so fast and were so faint that we hardly heard them. We could barely make them out on our scope. I'm awfully sorry, Captain. They definitely were from the southwest quadrant, but that's all I'm really sure of." Norton was clearly abashed by his failure, and by his skipper's disapproval.

"Maybe he's a lot farther away than we thought," Rich muttered. "That would account for their faintness and missing a couple of pings."

"Make your course southwest by grid," Buck said to the OOD. "Increase speed to ten knots. In half an hour we'll be five miles closer to him." He consulted his watch. "The next signal is air blowing. It's due in thirty-two minutes and will last ten seconds."

Nothing was heard at the appointed time, nor at the next, twenty-seven minutes later, when the police whistle was scheduled. "We'll continue as we are for the next period," Buck said. "That will be another fifteen minutes, and we'll be twelve miles nearer to him, if that was Keith we heard. Then we'll circle again, if we don't pick up anything." Rich was nodding his approval. The next signal scheduled was the whistle again, but the one following that, in forty-three minutes, was to be echo-ranging at long scale, five pings at maximum gain.

It had been assumed that the pings of the active echo-ranging sonar would most likely have the greatest range, be heard from the greatest distance. On hearing them, *Manta* would send her own ping simultaneously with the termination of *Cushing*'s fifth, beamed in the direction from which that signal had been received, and start a stopwatch the instant the transmission was cut off. *Cushing* would have started a stopwatch with the cutoff of her own fifth ping, would stop it with receipt of *Manta*'s, and transmit a single short sixth ping to stop the *Manta*'s watch. Sound travels 1,600 yards per second in water. Since a round trip by sound was involved, the time in seconds on their stopwatches, multiplied by 800 yards, would give each submarine the approximate distance to the other. Once bearing and distance had been determined, closer approach would be facilitated by air blowing or the whistle, until finally the *Cushing* would "talk" the *Manta* into close proximity.

With forty-three minutes to wait, again Richardson's impatience caused him to curse the long time delays he had built into the system, forgetting the purpose: to make their function less obvious to a chance listener. At minimum speed, *Manta* slowly described several complete circles in the water. She was as though suspended in space. Above, below, in all directions, nothing but water. Hundreds of feet above, a solid, impervious sheet of ice, twenty feet thick or more, but irregular, some places thinner than others. Below, thousands of feet below, the floor of the Arctic Ocean, slimy with the primordial ooze of aeons, split into two deep basins by the Lomonosov Ridge. North, east, south or west, whether on polar grid chart or any other, an area the size of Australia, or the United States. *Manta:* a tiny blob of life, of protoplasm, the size of a particle of dust, or sand, launched into an olympic-sized swimming pool in search of another dust-sized particle of life.

When there were only five minutes left to wait, Buck, Rich and Jeff Norton all crowded into *Manta's* cramped sonar room, leaning over the operator's shoulder, trying not to press into his needed working space. Norton held a stopwatch in his hand; the sonarman, Rich noted, held another. Rich and Buck stared at their wristwatches. "Half a minute," said Buck. There was a twenty-four-hour clock attached to the sonar room bulkhead. It had been synchronized with the ship's chronometers, as had the watches worn by Rich, Buck and Jeff Norton, and carefully reset to Greenwich Mean Time. It had been necessary to hold the clock mechanism so that the second hand would also be on GMT, and now the benefit was apparent. Keith would also have done this, would probably start his pings on the second.

Norton made a snapping motion with his forearm precisely as the twenty-four-hour clock reached sixteen hours, twenty-eight minutes and zero seconds, started his stopwatch. The second hand crawled slowly around its dial. Rich had stopped breathing. So had everyone else in the tiny compartment. The second hand was at seventeen when a spoke of light appeared on the dial of the sonar receiver. Norton stopped his watch, and simultaneously a faint but clearly recognizable ping filled the compartment.

"Seventeen seconds and a fraction," said Norton. "Make it seventeen and a half."

"Sh-h-h-h; don't talk!" whispered Buck.

The spoke had vanished, leaving a decaying fluorescence where it had been on the tube. Then it reappeared, along with the amplified but still faint ping, reinforcing and brightening the same spoke, went out again, came on again. Rich could see the sonarman orienting his transmitter, softly fingering his hand keying button with his right hand, holding the stopwatch in his left. Simultaneously with the cessation of the fifth ping, and its light-spoke, he punched his hand key and started his stopwatch. A brilliant white spoke in the dark red sonar scope dial overlaid and dwarfed the dimmer one from the distant station. The receiver had been automatically blanked while the signal was being sent, but its reverberations filled the room the moment the key was lifted. One could hear the sound signal beaming out, traveling 1,600 yards per second toward the source of the five sequential incoming pings.

Jeff Norton had reset his watch, started it again at the same time as his sonarman, was figuring on a scrap of paper. "If Captain Leone had his watches zeroed on GMT the way we did," he said, "and if he sent his first ping out exactly on the dot, he's twenty-eight thousand yards away; fourteen miles."

Buck smiled at him, nodded. "Good thinking, Jeff. We'll be able to check it when we hear his sixth beep." Deep feelings of relief were stirring within him. There had been only five pings. The other station—other submarine, it *must* be, could only be, another submarine— had stopped with five. It must be the *Cushing*. Keith.

And he must have received the message, therefore knew they were on their way, was expecting them, was therefore okay. Rich, standing there so impassively, must internally be feeling the same. How could he keep such a poker face?

The sixth ping from the other ship would certainly identify her as the *Cushing*. It came. "Thirty-six seconds," said Jeff. He consulted the watch held by his sonarman. "He's got the same. Thirty-six seconds—they lost one second somewhere. That's twenty-eight thousand eight hundred yards, just under fourteen and a half miles."

"Close enough for government work," said Buck genially, wanting to make up somewhat for his earlier rebuke. "Maybe he sent his first ping half a second early. That would do it, wouldn't it?"

"Yessir."

Richardson was already leaving the sonar room. Buck began to follow, turned back. "Jeff, that was real good work. And Schultz"—he clapped the sonarman on the shoulder to attract his attention away from his dials and earphones. Palmer Schultz, a freckled "middle-aged" youth, anywhere from twenty to thirty-five years old, twisted the near earphone, with its covering of soft rubber and sound-absorbing fiber away from his left ear, half turned toward Buck. "Beautiful job, Schultz. We're going to close him now. That's the *Cushing,* we've no doubt. I want you to log everything you hear from that bearing as we go on in. But keep your regular search all around going, too. I need to know everything that happens in the water. Do you know what you're supposed to hear from the *Cushing,* and when?"

The Chief Sonarman nodded assent, his eyes straying back to the darkened, hooded instrument which was *Manta*'s ears and, sometimes, her only link with the whole universe outside the machinery-crammed cavern of her hull. Norton also nodded, several times, well realizing Buck's words were meant for him as well.

"All stop!" said the OOD. "All back one-third—all stop!" The bow planesman twisted the annunciator knobs in the console in front of him.

"Answered all stop, sir," the bow planesman reported, adding after a moment, "I have no control on the depth, sir. She's not answering the bow planes."

"That's as it should be," responded Lieutenant Tom Clancy, *Manta*'s engineering officer, at the moment on watch as officer of the deck and diving officer. "Speed indicates zero. Stern planes, do you have control?"

The stern planesman, seated beside the bow planesman in front of the diving console, pushed his control lever all the way forward, then brought it back into his lap. "No, sir," he said as he returned it to the center upright position. "She's not answering stern planes."

"Put your planes on zero," ordered Clancy. "Report depth changes every foot. Chief Mac"—addressing the grave chief petty officer seated to his left before a five-foot-long array of gauges, switches, dials and machinery controls—"I want to stay at this depth, one hundred-fifty feet, zero bubble. Operate your ballast control panel to hover, reporting each one hundred pounds of ballast change."

"Aye, aye sir," said the chief, whose name was McClosky. He flipped one of the tiny levers on the panel, waited a few seconds while he scrutinized one of his dials, flipped it back. "Flooded two hundred pounds into auxiliary," he said. "Trim looks good. Fore and aft trim looks right on."

"It ought to be," Clancy answered. "We worked on it enough." He turned around to face Richardson and Williams, who were watching from the periscope station behind him. "All stop, Captain," he reported.

"Speed zero. I think we have a stop trim. Depth, one-five-zero feet." There was a suggestion of professional pride in his voice. The newer attack subs, and all the missile submarines, were fitted with automatic hovering gear. With *Manta,* it had to be done by hand. Doing it well bespoke someone who knew his ship, and his business.

"Good, Tom," answered Buck. To Rich he said, "I guess that's it, Commodore. By plot we're within a quarter of a mile of the *Cushing.* The Gertrude's turned all the way down. You should be able to talk with Keith now, but she shouldn't carry over a mile or so. I'll keep the 'scope up while you do, and if we drift any nearer maybe we can see her. If she's up against the ice there'll be plenty of clearance to pass right under her, even with the 'scope up."

Richardson held the UQC microphone in his hand, at the end of a short extension cord. He fingered the button on its side. So much depended on what he would find out in the next few minutes! He raised it to his mouth, pressed the button, spoke into it. "Keith, old man," he said, unconsciously speaking softly. "This is Rich. Do you read? Over." He let go the button, could hear the reverberations as his voice was carried by the sound waves. There was a rushing noise, as though there were something being physically dragged through the water. In a sense this was true, for the slow-moving sonar transmission left echoing reverberations throughout its passage. The UQC was omnidirectional; that is, like an ordinary radio broadcast station, whatever transmissions it made were in all directions all the time. There was no security in it, and no directivity, but under the circumstances it was the best medium for communication.

Perhaps he should have used the *Cushing*'s official voice call (Northern Lieutenant) and the *Manta*'s (Flat

Raider). He had decided against them as unnecessary. Were there some fleet operation involved, with other ships also needing the UQC, they might have been. Without deliberate intent, he had leaned his head against the UQC speaker, mounted on the after bulkhead of the periscope station, was concentrating his attention on the answer he was willing it to give. Thus, when it came, sooner than he expected, the clipped semimechanical voice which sounded so much like Keith's spoke loudly right into his ear.

"Rich! Skipper! It's so good to hear you! I read you loud and clear, how do you read me? Hello to Buck, too. Thank God you guys have showed up. We're about to go stir crazy over here! Over!" There were worlds of relief in Keith's voice, distorted and mechanized though it was by the less-than-optimum reproduction of the speaker. No doubt it was matched by every man aboard, as many as possible of whom had probably congregated within hearing distance of *Cushing*'s UQC.

Buck's broad grin of happiness must be mirrored by his own, Richardson felt. He could not see much of it— just the lower part—for Buck's forehead and eyes, the entire upper portion of his face, were covered by the rubber eye guard of the periscope, as, his shoulder muscles bulging, he slowly turned it around. The rest of the control room crew, Tom Clancy, Chief McClosky, the planesmen, who had dared a quick glance over their shoulders, several others, not on watch, who had found an excuse to be present, all had glad expressions on their faces.

Soon the work of making the submerged hookup would begin, but first it would be necessary to carry out the preliminaries so specifically ordered. "Keith, obviously you received the message from ComSubLant. Do you have the one from CNO? Do you have your message ready?" Again the sensation of his words traveling slowly through water, dissipating rapidly in the vastness of the ocean.

"Affirmative to both, Skipper. Our message is a long one. Two hundred sixty-three groups. Can it wait till we're out from under the ice? We've hardly been able to budge since the collision, and we're pretty itchy. Over."

"Sorry, Keith. Orders. But if you couldn't budge, how did you get so far from the reference position? Over?"

"We tried some gliding and made a few miles, I guess. It's all in the message. You'll break it, won't you? Over."

"Affirmative. We'll relay it just as you give it to us, but in the meantime we'll be breaking it too. Are you ready to pass it over?"

"That's affirmative, boss. Stand by to write."

"Standing by." Richardson closed a small switch which had been taped to the side of the UQC speaker. At Jeff Norton's suggestion, wires had been led to *Manta*'s radio room and a spare speaker put in parallel with the UQC. The switch merely turned on a small light near the extra speaker. The two radiomen on watch had been instructed to copy everything they heard on their speaker whenever the light was on. They had, of course, been avidly listening already.

A new voice took over the UQC, Howie Trumbull, according to Jeff, reading in measured cadence the gibberish of the encoded message. Each letter was spoken phonetically, as were the numerals and letters of the heading. To guard against errors, Jeff Norton was then required to fetch the message from the radio room and read it back, using the same slow voice procedure. During the whole of the laborious interchange, Rich and Buck listened to it from the periscope station in the control room.

The entire exchange took two hours to complete.

*   *   *

"This is crazy," grumbled Buck. "Here we've been half a day looking for a lead or polynya to break through—with shallow enough ice, that is, so it won't be an all-fired emergency—and all we've seen is solid ice cover, twenty feet thick. We can go anywhere we want, in any direction, so long as we don't try to go too far down, and not too far up. We've got a seven-hundred-foot layer of clear water to roam around in, and we've found the *Cushing* but we've not found a way to get that message relayed. Everything is go to try to snake her out of here, but we can't because of that dumb message! There's nothing in it that's so damned important it couldn't wait. We could have made the hookup and have her twenty miles away from here by now!"

"Ours is not to reason why," said Rich.

"Tennyson also said someone had blundered, right?"

"Yes, back in Balaclava or wherever it was. But they didn't know in Washington what we know now. In fact, they don't know yet. It's important for them to know about that plane and the bomb, and that some kind of long-planned operation is going on up here. Also, remember how ComSubPac had all the subs report in right after the cease-fire in 1945? That was so he'd know for sure who was still okay as of then. One reason was to make any possible Japanese skulduggery a little tougher to do. So, this message tells Washington the *Cushing* is still alive."

"Okay, sure, Skipper. But all the same, I'd feel better if we were on our way with her. That Gertrude is the most easily detected sonar there is, even with the gain way down. If the Russians were smart enough to lower a good sonar set through a hole in the ice, even from pretty far away, they might have picked up something. And then when we open up on radio, if we ever get to, they'll know for sure something's cooking."

"Can't help it, Buck. But aren't you the one who

made me a speech about the Arctic being a free ocean, so we shouldn't worry about what anyone else thinks or wants?"

"That was before we knew the Russians had really tried something. That bomb was not very friendly."

"Neither was the collision."

"Do you really think that was deliberate?"

"No way of ever telling. They'll always claim it was an accident. Keith was smart, and damned ingenious, to get as far away from the scene of the crime as he did."

Buck grinned a worried grimace. "Ingenious is right! Who ever thought you could glide a submarine?"

"Well, it's no way to move very far. Not for a submarine as big as the *Cushing*. But one of the little research subs was designed to travel that way. It had big planing surfaces, of course. So far as I know it's never been built, but the theory sounded as if it might work. It's amazing, though, how far Keith managed to move that big boat of his."

"Ship."

"Ship."

After spending several hours in the control room, hoping, perhaps rather naïvely, that a usable polynya would turn up quickly, Rich and Buck adjourned to Buck's stateroom, leaving a special watch on the ice detector, with specific and careful instructions. Two changes of watch later, with the idea beginning to intrude that perhaps at least one of them ought to try to get some sleep, they felt the ship heel suddenly. Buck had already reached for the telephone handset on the bulkhead over his bunk, when the call bell rang. "Captain? This is Jerry. We've just passed under a possible. I've marked it on the DRT, and we're turning now to go back to it."

"We'll be right there." Buck replaced the telephone

as Rich got to his feet, and the two walked swiftly to the control room.

"It's the best one I've seen," said Jerry Abbott, "but it's not all that good. Here's the Fathometer trace." He was holding a piece of paper just removed from the ice detector. Buck and Rich scrutinized it closely. "About six feet thick," said Abbott. "As a guess, the thin spot was about an eighth of a mile long along our track."

"Yes." Buck looked up. "We heading back for it now?"

"Yessir. I made a Williamson turn, and we've slowed way down."

"Good," said Buck. Turning to Richardson he asked, "What do you think, Commodore?"

"This is the first reasonable opportunity, isn't it? Maybe, in the next couple of days, we might find a better one, but I'm with you. I'd like to get this message off and go back to the *Cushing* as quick as we can. Did you tell me your sail can push up through six feet of ice?"

"That's what the Electric Boat Division designers say."

"The *Manta*'s your boat, so it's your decision, Buck. But if you're asking me, I say let's give the EB designers a test of their product."

"Good!" said Williams. "I say the same." Abbott had been an interested listener. "Do you have the conn, Jerry?" Buck asked.

"Affirmative, Skipper."

"All right. Put us right under the polynya at all stop, dead in the water, and catch the best trim we can get. I'll take over the conn when you're ready, and we'll bring her right on up."

"Tom asked to be called if we're going up, sir. He wants to take over the dive."

"Okay. Call him. Also alert radio, and have the top-side crew get ready with ice-clearing tools. Be sure they're dressed for the cold."

The routine regularity of the submerged watch gave way to an orderly bustle of preparation. In a very few minutes movement stopped and quiet returned. Buck, looking through the periscope, maneuvered into the center of the thin-ice area, using *Manta*'s propellers sparingly and methodically, taking his time. Finally ready, he looked inquiringly at Richardson, who had stood quietly watching nearby, received his quick nod of assent, spoke to Clancy. "Tom, blow forward and after groups slowly. Bring us up flat. Remember, there's probably a layer of fresh water under the ice, so we'll be losing buoyancy as we get closer to it. Try to keep us moving upward at the same rate."

"Aye, aye, sir," said Clancy, who had already been thoroughly briefed on the vagaries of specific gravity of seawater under the polar ice cap. He turned to Chief McClosky, who also had come on watch for the oc-casion, said, "We want to keep the bubble on zero as we come up, Mac. Blow forward group. Blow after group." The chief flipped the two toggles, kept his hands on them. There was the sound of air blowing into tanks. Clancy and he huddled together watching the gauges. "Secure after group!" said Clancy. McClosky, anticipating the order, instantly moved the left toggle to the shut position. Another second, two seconds. "Secure the air!" McClosky snapped shut the other toggle. The submarine had assumed half a degree down angle, but the bow now was rising faster and she was on an even keel again. "Ninety feet," called out Clancy, vectoring his voice in Buck's direction. "Zero bubble."

Buck was still watching through the periscope. "Looks good, Commodore," he said. "I'll drop the 'scope at eighty feet."

"Eighty-five feet," said Clancy. "Rising steady. Zero bubble. Eighty-two feet. Eighty-one. Eighty feet."

"Down 'scope," said Buck, folding up the handles. The quartermaster on watch hit the periscope hoist control lever, and the precious instrument dropped into its well. "It looked about ready to hit the ice," said Buck with a grin, "but I knew we had at least ten feet of gravity. It was kind of scary, though. Busting the 'scope against the bottom side of the ice would be a little hard to explain back in New London."

Rich's answering smile was testimony to his full appreciation of the situation, as well as his confidence in Buck.

"Seventy-five feet," said Clancy. "She's going up a little faster, now." Perhaps a little more air had been used than absolutely necessary. The air bubbles in *Manta*'s ballast tanks would expand with the reduced pressure due to decreasing depth, and their resulting buoyant volume would increase. Simultaneously, the reduced salinity would have a contrary effect. Balancing the two opposing factors was a nice exercise in judgment.

"We'll hit the ice at around fifty feet," said Buck. "With six feet, maybe more, to break through, we'll feel it. It'll be a pretty solid jolt."

Tom Clancy was calling out the depths. "Sixty-five feet," he said. "Sixty feet."

"Rig in bow planes," ordered Buck. Unlike the *Cushing,* whose sailplanes could not be rigged in and consequently had been designed to elevate to ninety degrees and slice through the ice as the ship came up, *Manta* had the older design of bow planes in the forward superstructure which were always housed when the ship was on the surface. Were the entire superstructure of the submarine to break through the ice, a distinct possibility if its resistance proved to be less than expected, the planes would almost surely be damaged if they were rigged out and struck the underside of the ice flat.

"Bow planes rigged in," reported McClosky.

"Fifty-five feet," said Tom Clancy. "Fifty-four. Fifty-three. Fifty-two. Fifty-one. *Fifty* feet!"

Crunch! A tremendous washboiler sound of suddenly stressed metal. *Manta*'s deck seemed to drop away from them, her sturdy hull twanging, the myriad gauge dials in the control room vibrating in jangled disharmony. There was squeaking and moaning of steel girders, a heavy scraping noise, the sound of huge fingernails scraping a rough surface.

"Fifty feet," said Clancy, reading from the large-scale depth indicator on the diving stand. "Fifty feet . . . just under fifty now . . . she's going on up now . . . forty-nine and three-quarters . . . forty-nine, forty-eight . . . she's moving right on up now, Captain. Forty-seven, forty-six, forty-five. Top of the sail is through, sir. Permission to blow all ballast?"

Buck, who with Rich had been following Clancy's depth reports on the small-scale depth gauge in the periscope station, was hastily putting on cold-weather gear. "Blow all ballast!" he ordered, echoing Clancy's request. "Let me know when the upper hatch is clear."

"No way I can tell you that for sure, Skipper," said Clancy with a grin of satisfaction. "We could have scooped up a tubful of ice on the bridge. It could be packed tight. I'll tell you when it's out of water, though."

"Are all diving officers as persnickety on details as mine?" Buck asked Rich with a relieved grin of his own. Successful passage of *Manta*'s first test in the Arctic ice had infected him too.

"I sure don't know as to that," answered Richardson with mock gravity, "but I can remember a certain torpedo officer who was every bit as persnickety. How he ever got to be skipper of a nuclear boat I'll never figure out!"

"Now, Commodore, you please be quiet about that pore ole nuke skipper, you hear? Can't have my boys getting the wrong idea, you know!" The success of the moment was to be savored, even though fleetingly. Buck adjusted his face mask, spoke hurriedly to Jerry Abbott, stepped to the ladder leading into the hatch trunk, squeezed his bulky garments through the opening, began to climb through the lower hatch.

"Skipper," said Buck savagely, "do you know how much good useful time we've wasted getting that damn message off?"

"I know."

"Just about a full day. More than twenty hours! First we couldn't find a thin place to break through. Then when we finally got up, there was so much ice driven down into the openings on the top of the sail that the antenna couldn't be raised. But before we could get someone out there to work on it, we had about an hour's chopping of ice on the bridge to clear away that huge chunk of ice on top of the sail so that a man could even reach the place. Then, when finally we got the antenna up, we couldn't get anyone to answer our call-up. I got so cold waiting up there I couldn't take it anymore and had to send for Jerry to take over. You'd have thought ComSubLant or somebody would have had every shore station in our whole system alerted!"

"It probably wasn't ComSubLant's fault, Buck. Radio conditions were bad, that's all. Probably because the sun's above the horizon now."

"Maybe it wasn't his fault. But then when we *finally* got Radio Guam to answer—think about that one, Guam!—they said we'd have to wait with our message because it didn't have enough priority!"

"That was our own fault. We should have raised Keith's priority. We did, after we got the word."

"Well, okay. But we shouldn't have had to do it. If Keith's message was so important, better arrangements should have been made to get it by those who wanted it. Anyway, after three more hours fiddling around poking up through the ice like a damn black lighthouse, beating our brains out on the radio, sending repeats over and over again, finally we get the receipt and can go back down and begin what we came up here for."

"I don't blame you for feeling frustrated, Buck," said Rich. "I feel the same way. I tried to argue Admiral Donaldson out of making us do this, but I couldn't. It was a JCS order. Anyway, now it's done. They've got their message, and we're free to do our stuff."

"I suppose I should look at it that way too," said Buck morosely, "but I'll feel better after we've got the *Cushing* out of this place. Whatever goes wrong I'll blame on this delay, I know that."

www

"Keith," said Richardson over the UQC, speaking softly with the transmitter set at minimum gain, "do you
have our dispatch about towing procedure? Any questions? Before trying the hookup we want to look you
over through the periscope. What is your heading and
exact depth, and where's your anchor?" The words
reverberated out along the carrier wave, could be heard
dying in the distance.

"Affirmative on the dispatch, and three cheers, no
questions. We're against the ice. Depth seven-three feet.
Anchor's housed. Ship's head one-two-eight," responded
Keith Leone's voice seconds later.

"Okay, old man. Just keep a zero bubble. We'll pass
under you with the 'scope up and take a good look.
There's enough light coming through the ice."

"Roger. We'll keep our anchor housed until you give
us the word to lower away."

"Roger. This won't take long. Out." To Buck, Rich
said, "Finding Keith the second time was a lot easier
than the first time. It helped a lot that he thought of
reactivating the homing signals."

"That's true, Skipper," Buck muttered, "but still this whole thing took too long. All together, it's more than twenty-four hours now. You and I've been up the whole time. So have a lot of others. We're already beat, and our real job's just beginning."

"Can't be helped, Buck, but we'll all get some rest once we have Keith moving out of here. What depth do we need so as not to hit him with the 'scope up?"

"The high 'scope will just graze him at one-three-five feet, if we go right under him. Recommend we make our first pass a few yards abeam at a hundred forty feet, and check for anything dangling below his keel. I'd sure hate to hit a piece of debris hanging there."

"That sounds like good sense to me. Set him up on the TDC and conn us under him parallel and off to the side at minimum speed. If it looks clear we'll go closer the second time, and then right under, if necessary. Once we get a good feel for it, we'll try to hold in position for a careful look at that wrecked propeller."

Manta slowly positioned herself in line with the *Cushing*'s heading, from ahead, as it turned out, this being the shortest distance, in the meantime rising to the prescribed depth. "The depth is critical, Tom," said Buck to his engineer. "It'll be tough to stay right on at the slow speed we'll be making. Be sure we have experienced men on the planes and the ballast control panel—and maybe you ought to stay here in the control room yourself."

"Aye," said Clancy. "Deedee has the dive. Want me to relieve him? He's about due for relief anyway."

"Yes. We'll be making only about one-knot speed; so you'll practically need a stop trim."

"Aye, aye. I'll take over. Stop trim it will be." Clancy conferred briefly with Deedee Brown at the diving station in the control room's forward port corner, then

announced to Buck at the periscope station and everyone else in the control room, "I have the dive."

With Clancy making tiny perfecting adjustments to
the trim, her propellers turning at creeping speed and
Buck and Rich manning both elevated periscopes, the
Manta swam slowly toward and beneath the *Cushing*.
Raising the periscopes out of their wells against the sea
pressure of only 140 feet had been a slow and laborious
process for their hydraulic hoists, for they had been
designed with periscope depth, less than half that, in
mind. Great care would have to be exercised in lower-
ing the periscopes when the inspection was completed;
the pressure would drive them down correspondingly
fast, with possible damage on bottoming. Both were
much more difficult to turn than at normal depth: pressure was driving them hard against their support bearings in the hoist yokes.

Sonar and the TDC continuously reported bearing
and range. Slowly the range shortened. The *Cushing*
was nearly dead ahead. They would pass almost directly under her. "Losing her forward," said Jeff Norton
on the speaker from the sonar room. This was to be
expected; the sonar transducer was located under
Manta's forefoot. "Last range, one-four-oh," said Jeff.
"Ten degrees off the port bow."

"That checks, TDC," said Deedee Brown from the
starboard side of the control room, drinking deeply
from the mug of coffee which was all he had permitted
himself before manning his battle station. "Now it's
one-three-oh."

"I figure we should see him in four minutes, Commodore," said Buck, mindful that everyone in earshot
was eagerly listening. Richardson did not answer, for
the same reason. His own estimate was more nearly
five, to allow for the additional distance from *Manta*'s
bow to her periscopes.

"One hundred yards," announced Brown.

"I wonder if sonar can hear any of his machinery noise, Buck," said Richardson, his face still pressed against the rubber buffer of the periscope eyepiece.

"Ask them, Jerry," said Buck, likewise immobilized against his own periscope. "Also ask the *Cushing* if they can hear us."

Both heard the answers to Abbott's questions directly. "Affirmative," said Jeff Norton, using the ship's intercommunication speaker from the sonar room. "He's quiet, but we can hear a steady hum. We've had him ever since a thousand yards."

"Affirmative," said Keith over the Gertrude set. "We can hear you very loud. One pump especially. Sounds like your condensate pump."

"Fifty yards," said Deedee Brown. "Twenty-five yards. Ten. Five, four, three, two, one, mark! We should be passing under him now."

"You must be about to pass under us," said Keith's familiar yet distorted voice over the UQC.

Suddenly, shockingly, a tremendous black mass swept into view, dead ahead. Startled, Williams grabbed for his periscope hoist control lever, nearly jerked it toward him, recollected himself just in time. "Wow!" he exploded, with a nervous expulsion of breath, returning his face to the eyepiece buffer and swiftly manipulating the hand controls.

To Jerry Abbott and the other anxious watchers in the vicinity, it was clear that both Rich and Buck had had a scare. The huge bulk of the other submarine, appearing so suddenly directly in their fields of view, must have seemed about to strike them, the mathematical calculations notwithstanding. But now both men had recovered, were tugging at their periscopes, operating the motorcycle-type controls in the handles, shifting from high-power magnification to low- and back again, elevating and depressing their angles of sight.

"Say, this is interesting," said Buck Williams. "Keith's sail is painted white! It sure wasn't that color when he left New London! Wonder when he did that?"

"There's a scratch!" said Richardson. "It's a dent. A small one."

"Where is it?" asked Abbott swiftly, pencil poised over the clipboard prepared for notation of observations.

"After end of missile compartment, port side, halfway between keel and waterline!"

"There's the EPM! It's dangling on a bent girder about fifteen feet below the keel!" said Buck. "It's really mangled, too! Good thing we didn't pass directly under—it could sure wreck a periscope!"

"Here's another dent! A big one! Ten feet below the waterline, middle of the engineroom, I'd estimate! No doubt she was hit from the port side!"

"Right!" exclaimed Buck. "I can see a lot of dents all along the port side, from here on aft!"

Jerry Abbott was writing rapidly. "Can you see the propeller?" he asked.

"Here's the port stern plane! It's really bent! Folded right up against the side like an aircraft wing on a carrier hangar deck!" Buck's excitement had transmitted itself to everyone in the control room. Only Tom Clancy and his diving station crew kept their eyes rigidly on their instruments.

"The rudder looks okay," said Rich, "from here, anyway—no, it's bent to starboard. The top rudder is okay. It's got a lot of white paint on it, too. The lower rudder is bent to starboard, but maybe it's still operable. The propeller is total. It's a mass of twisted junk. Even if he could get the shaft turning, it wouldn't give him

any thrust at all. I've never seen one as bad as that!"
He drew back from the periscope, saw Buck Williams
looking at him contemplatively. "I'd like to go back
and hover near the propeller and stern control surfaces," he said. "Do you think we could balance right
off her stern for a closer look, perhaps from right aft?"

With Buck's nod of comprehension, he went on. "I
don't think there's anything more to be gained by looking over the rest of *Cushing*'s underwater body, but
we ought to have as good an idea as we can of how
the situation is back there. Especially whether Keith
can steer or not. Towing him will be a lot harder if
he can't. While you're maneuvering around, I'll get on
the underwater telephone with Keith and tell him what
we're up to, and ask him to try to operate the rudder
while we're watching. Stern planes too, although that
looks pretty hopeless."

"Keith," Rich said a few moments later into the
Gertrude mouthpiece, "we're dead astern of you. How
do you read?"

"A little mushy, but clear enough, Rich. How does
it look?"

"Not good. Several big dents, your port stern plane
is folded up against the side and the rudder is bent.
The propeller is useless, I'm afraid. We're closing in
for another look at your stern. Can you operate your
rudder?"

"Affirmative. It moves slowly and we can't go as
far right as we used to, but I think it's usable."

"Good! That's very good news. How about the stern
planes?"

"We have a little travel in them before they bind,
but not much. We can go from five degrees rise to three
down."

"Good," said Rich again. "When we get into position I'll ask you to operate the rudder and stern planes and maybe the propeller shaft. Can you do that?"

"Affirm. We know the shaft's bent out of line. Max rpm is about twenty."

"Roger. Back soon."

"Roger."

"Well, what do you think, Buck?" Rich and Buck were again at their periscopes, with *Manta* now balancing at a slightly shallower depth than before, directly astern of the *Cushing* so that the tips of her extended periscopes appeared to be only a few feet away from the mangled propeller of the disabled submarine.

"Nothing anyone can do for that eggbeater out there, but maybe they can work the rudder and planes."

"That's what I think, too. Have Jerry ask them to work the rudder."

"Wilco," said the Gertrude set, and the rudder began to move.

"Nothing much wrong with that," said Richardson with satisfaction. "At least Keith can steer! Now tell them to secure the rudder and go to the stern planes."

Through the periscopes, both men saw the halting, painful movement of the horizontal control surfaces. "Tell him to secure that. The port plane is striking the hull, and that's the most he's ever going to be able to move it."

They waited as Abbott transmitted the message and the movement ceased.

"Now tell him to try the propeller, building up slowly to whatever speed he wants." The crumpled mass of bronze, once a beautifully curved, delicately balanced example of shipbuilding art, slowly began to rotate, and in the process its center could be seen describing an arc inches in diameter. "Tell him to stop!" said Rich.

A moment later, speaking on the UQC himself, he said, "Keith, your propeller shaft is bent at least six inches out of line. I could see it making a foot-diameter circle as it went around."

"I understand," said Keith, after the barest suggestion of a delay.

"We're going to get clear now and prepare for towing. We'd like you to drop down to one hundred fifty feet and hover there. Lower your anchor to the fifty-fathom mark and set your brake, but not too tight. We want it to slip a little as we take you in tow to help ease the initial shock. Be ready to tighten the brake as the pull begins, and secure it with everything you've got as it approaches the eighty-fathom mark."

"Wilco," said Keith.

"Let us know when you're ready."

"Wilco," said Keith again.

To Buck, Rich said, "The only difference between what we're having Keith do and what the *Besugo* did is that she had to rig her anchor from the forecastle before submerging and therefore had to set the brake tight at the beginning. This may help make up for the *Cushing* being three times as big."

"Roger," said Buck, looking steadily at his superior. Both of them knew the exchange was entirely for the benefit of their crew, for the procedure had been discussed in private many times.

"His anchor will be at four hundred fifty feet. We'll make our depth five hundred, so there'll be no chance of hitting it."

"Roger, Commodore. When do you want to go to towing stations?"

"Whenever you're ready, Buck. Which side do you want to use?"

"Makes no difference. Port side."

"Very well."

The stilted, official conversation was necessary for one reason only: Richardson and Williams had decided to make the real thing as nearly like the drills as possible. Chances of error would thereby be lessened, and crew confidence increased. Now Buck picked up the hand microphone for the ship's general announcing system, spoke into it. "All hands," he said, "rig ship for towing. Port side." He hung the mike back in its bracket, turned away, then turned back and picked it up again. "This is the captain," he said. "This time it's for real."

The only change Richardson saw in personnel stations was the arrival of the ship's best helmsman, and separation of the wheel and annunciator controls from the bow planesman's station to which, in the cruising condition, they had been cross-connected. Doubtless there was not a person on board for whom Buck's final admonition was needed. Nevertheless, Rich was instantly aware of its effect. He himself felt like cheering.

Manta had departed from New London with her two sets of towing gear stored in the after torpedo tubes. The inner doors of both tubes had already been replaced by anchor billets. Getting ready to tow involved only opening the outer door of the designated tube, number eight, and ejecting the contents, a metal canister filling the entire tube, by a short jet of high-pressure air through a fitting on the anchor billet. The canister, merely a large galvanized iron can, slid out, split open and sank, releasing the paravane. This immediately began to rise toward the surface, carrying with it a short section of heavy chain on the near end of which was a large steel hook. The other end of the chain terminated in a swivel, from which extended a long length of beautiful white nylon hawser, now being dragged outward and upward from the open tube. The inboard end of the hawser also held a swivel, followed by another section of chain which entered the open torpedo tube door and was firmly attached to the anchor billet.

Several refinements had been added to the original device during the course of testing it: strain gauges had been the first; a large bolt in the billet, when unscrewed, now allowed the chain and hawser to drop clear, thus permitting the outer door to be shut and the tube to be restored to its original use. Most recently, the hook had been modified to slide easily down the anchor chain of the ship to be towed until it fetched up on her anchor, where it would snag fast, and an additional UQC had been installed on *Manta*'s stern to facilitate communication abaft the propellers. Just before departure, the hooks for both devices had been checked by actually testing them with a chain and anchor identical to the *Cushing*'s, intended for an identical submarine still under construction.

While the football-shaped paravane was deploying upward and to port, where its vanes kited it, Buck was maneuvering the *Manta* into position two miles astern of the *Cushing,* waiting for the ready signal from her. It came in half an hour, about when expected, and Buck set the course. As before, the TDC and sonar were used to establish the proper relationship to the *Cushing,* so that *Manta* would pass parallel to, but not directly beneath, the disabled missile submarine. Calculations and drill both had showed that at three knots the paravane streamed, as planned, about one hundred feet above and fifty yards off to the side of the towing submarine. *Manta* was programmed to pass fifty feet below and one hundred feet abeam of *Cushing*'s anchor, so that her diagonally dragged hawser could not fail to intersect the vertically hanging anchor chain of her quarry.

"We'll be abeam in five minutes, TDC," said Deedee

Brown. "Checking right in there, about thirty-five yards on her starboard beam."

"Come left one degree," said Buck to his helmsman. "Steer one-two-seven."

"One-two-seven, aye aye" said the helmsman from his post a few feet forward of the raised conning station. His movement of the wheel was barely perceptible. An instant later he announced, "Steering one-two-seven, sir!" He had not taken his eyes off the gyro compass repeater in front of him.

"Mark your depth!" said Buck.

"Five hundred feet. On the nose!" This was from Tom Clancy.

Buck picked up the general announcing mike, waited, looking at the clock mounted nearby. "All hands," he said finally, speaking deliberately into it, "we should start feeling it five minutes from now! Mark your clocks!"

Richardson glanced at his wristwatch. It was an involuntary movement, one he had made at precisely this point during each of the drill exercises. But his mind hardly registered the positions of the hands on its dial.

"One minute until abeam, TDC," said Brown. "Thirty yards."

"That's about what I wanted, Skipper," Buck said quietly. "She's a fat ship and I want to be sure there's plenty of overlap across her chain."

Rich, sitting on the stool which had automatically been his station since the beginning of the drills, nodded his agreement.

"Two minutes till we might feel the chain!" Buck announced over the mike, looking at the bulkhead-mounted clock. To Clancy he said, "Remember, Tom, the chain will begin by pulling us up by the stern. Keep a zero bubble and let her seek her own depth. But when she starts taking on the weight of *Cushing*'s anchor gear back there, you're going to have to pump out a lot more water than for the *Tringa* or *Besugo*. Don't let her get an up angle, and don't let the depth increase."

"Roger," said Tom Clancy, wondering why it seemed necessary to repeat these already well-rehearsed matters.

"Abeam to port! Twenty-eight yards!" announced Deedee Brown. "That checks with sonar," he added.

Buck grabbed the mike, announced immediately, "We're abeam! We'll begin to feel the chain one minute from now!" Speaking quietly to Richardson he said, "Do you suppose there's any chance Keith won't realize he'll have to flood forward trim when we take the chain, and that we want the *Cushing* to increase depth some?"

"That's all in that long dispatch we wrote for Com-SubLant to send. Anyway, he'll know what to do while his ship is being towed. The *Cushing*'s not going to tow quite like the *Besugo,* you know. Setting up steady-state conditions will have to wait until we've got him hooked and underway."

There was a tight grin on Buck's face. "I know all that, and I'm damn sure Keith knows how to handle his ship. I guess I'm getting wound up a bit."

"I know. It wouldn't be natural if you weren't."

"One minute since abeam," said Jerry Abbott.

"Silence throughout the ship!" ordered Buck on the speaker system. To the helmsman he said, "Stand by!"

The silence reminded Rich of a submarine during the war rigged for silent running and expecting the initial salvo of depth charges. In a way, it was an apt comparison, for the tenseness of the moment was equally great.

"Mark! A minute thirty seconds since abeam," said Abbott, nearly whispering.

Rich knew that the first faint rubbing contact might be felt anytime after the one-minute mark, depending on the accuracy of the estimated distance to the anchor when passed, but most likely not until nearly two full minutes had passed. Indeed, the first contact, when the nylon cable would be merely rubbing against *Cushing*'s chain, might not be felt at all. More pronounced, though for a very short period, would be the links of the two chains rattling against each other; most noticeable of all would be when the hook had engaged the anchor chain and was beginning to pick it up. By careful calculation and actual experience, this must happen exactly two minutes thirty-six seconds after the anchor was passed abeam, although there might be a few seconds more before it was noticed. But if the hook did not engage the chain at that point, it would pass it, necessitating another try.

Buck, trying to look confident, was succeeding much better than his slight, taciturn exec, Rich noticed. It might not have been the height of wisdom on the part of BuPers to put two such similar nervous-energy types in the same sub—but then no one had ever accused Buck of being taciturn, and he did have a sense of humor which Rich had not yet noticed in Jerry. He wondered how well he was concealing his own nervousness.

"Two minutes!" whispered Jerry, holding up the same number of fingers.

Sitting on the stool, Rich tried to keep his emotions contained. This was, of course, the moment of truth, but as had happened occasionally, something might have gone wrong. Well, if so, they would try again, passing nearer to the anchor, and there was always the other rig, unused, in number-seven tube. Perhaps, because of the ever melting layer of ice on its surface, the Arctic Ocean salinity was less than that off New London, even if Tom Clancy hadn't noticed it, and therefore the paravane might have less than the calculated buoyancy. But Tom *would* have noticed the difference in *Manta's* own trim. In fact, come to think of it, he had reported the need to pump out several tons of water from the trimming tanks, but no one had felt it was a really significant amount. . . . Still, if the paravane floated noticeably lower, the nylon hawser could conceivably pass under the anchor. . . . But this was absurd. It could *not* be that much lower. The nylon itself floated. If anything it would bulge upward, instead of down.

"Two minutes thirty!" Jerry whispered, with a look of doom. Buck, Rich noted, was again eyeing his own stopwatch. Good man! At the thirty-six-second point he intended to stop, as planned, regardless of whether the chain had been engaged or not.

But all of Richardson's worries were forgotten at that instant, when sonar reported on the speaker, "JT hears the chains!"

"All stop!" barked Buck. The helmsman twisted his annunciators to Stop, watched the follower pointers from the engineroom match him.

"All stop, answered!" he said.

Again, the wait, but now it was for realization of, and reaction to, the next step. The hook would begin to drag the chain, in the process initially seeming to lift the *Manta,* and then at some point, having led the chain forward of the *Cushing,* the hook would begin to slip down toward the anchor. The noise of this would be very clearly heard, even though it would be happening in the sonar baffles dead astern. Somewhere in this process, perhaps not until the hook had engaged the anchor itself, *Manta* would begin to feel the weight of *Cushing's* anchor. *Cushing,* at the same time, would feel the loss of weight. Keith must, nevertheless, permit his ship to drop down to approximately *Manta's* depth, whatever that turned out to be, and *Manta* must be allowed to rise even as she picked up the added weight.

"Speed through water?" Buck demanded.

"Two and a half knots," said Jerry. "Dropping fast. Now it's two knots. One knot. Touching zero."

Buck had the mike in his hand. "Maneuvering, make turns for two knots!"

"Maneuvering, aye, aye!" said the speaker.

"Conn, sonar," said the speaker. "JT reports hook slipping! We can hear the links!"

"Great!" said Buck. Jerry Abbott, typically, said nothing, but the grin on his face did it for him. Everyone in the control room wore a broad smile.

"*Cushing* should be feeling it by now, don't you think, Skipper?" said Buck, forgetting his protocol. "Permission to try them on the after Gertrude?"

"By all means," answered Rich, letting his own gladness show.

Buck flipped a toggle switch under the UQC set mounted nearby along with a profusion of other instruments, put the mike to his lips, said, "Northern Lieutenant, this is Flat Raider, submerged tug, at your service, sir. Do you feel my pull?"

Instantly the speaker came back. Keith's voice, as before, lacking something in the quality of the reproduction, but unmistakable. "This is Northern Lieutenant. Affirmative your last. You're wonderful! We're watching the brake and our trim. Over."

"We're going to build up to three knots for starters," said Buck over the mike, "and try for a steady-state pull. Course-, depth- and speed-changes will be very gradual, and announced in advance. The first thing is to get a common depth, maybe three hundred feet. Once we get settled down we'll increase speed to four knots, or even five if the strain gauges show the rig will take it. Probably you should tow a little above us because of where your chain is, but the main thing is to get to a 'hands off' condition where that big fat tub of yours will just follow along naturally. Over."

"We roger for all that and your insults, you little pip-squeak, but we're cheering for you all the same. Listen!" Rich and Buck could hear the sound of cheering over the speaker. "You guys have no idea how tough it's been just sitting here for weeks like this. Thank God you've come! And super thanks to whoever it was invented this towing idea!"

Buck was about to speak, glanced inquiringly at Rich, who make a cutting motion across his throat. "That's about all for now, Keith. Talk to you later. Out."

"You and your crew were absolutely marvelous, Buck. Here we are at last, towing the *Cushing* at four and a half knots, safe and sure at four hundred feet, and we haven't a care in the world. We could even probably speed up over five knots, but I agree with you, what's a few days more now that everything's going so well. Once we snake them out from under the ice, we can come to periscope depth to send our message, if we want to. ComSubLant might send a regular tug and bring them in in the normal way, but he won't need to. It's a lot easier to tow submerged. We may as well bring them all the way home, and I think that's what I'll recommend."

Rich was having dinner in *Manta*'s wardroom, surrounded by most of the officers. The feeling of success, the gladness and pride of achievement, were everywhere. In celebration of the occasion, the cooks had prepared the best meal of which they were capable, and a holiday spirit prevailed throughout the ship. In the crew's mess the same meal was being served, and similar happy sentiments were being voiced. Doubtless the same thing was happening aboard the *Cushing*.

"I know you've been up a long time, Commodore," said Buck, "and I'll bet you'd like to turn in. So would I; but do you think before you do, you could go back aft and say a few words to the crew? I know they'd appreciate it."

"You just bet I will, Buck. When do you want me to do it? Right now?"

"Finish your dinner first. But maybe after coffee."

"Fine. Maybe you'd better brief me on who your special people were, so I'll not pass up anyone who really made a big contribution."

"Well, there's the sonar gang, you know about them. Especially the JT operator. Incidentally, they came up with an idea why we didn't hear the chain and hawser rubbing. The *Cushing*'s a new submarine, so her anchor chain was new and freshly painted. It didn't have anything like the resistance of the old rusty chains of the *Tringa* and *Besugo!*"

"Well, I'll be damned! That might have made the difference, all right! We should have thought of it!"

"And, of course, there's the torpedo gang. Deedee Brown's people on the TDC, and particularly the men in the after torpedo room. Matter of fact, they've got the biggest job, because they've got to monitor that strain gauge from now on, all the way to Connecticut."

"Yes."

"And the engineers. The throttlemen have been controlling speed ever since we got to the steady state. They've got a special telephone hookup with the after room lads, and they'll slow down without orders anytime the strain exceeds the reading we've set for them."

"Yes," Rich said again, but he was beginning to think that Buck's enthusiasm would result in his citing the entire ship's company. At this moment, however, the arrival of a messenger from the OOD changed everything, and it was never the same again.

"There's a sonar contact!" the young lad said.

"The JT picked it up first," said the scared-looking sonar watchstander. "He had it on sonic. Then it came in closer, or got louder, and I could hear it on the big set, the BQR. It's staying on a steady bearing, a little abaft our starboard beam."

"What's it sound like to you?" asked Buck.

"Can't tell, sir. Sounds like a ship is all I know. JT thinks so too. That's why we reported it."

Decisively, Buck seized a pair of shielded earphones hanging above the sonar receiver, plugged them into a spare jack. His face contorted as he listened, then, without a word, he handed the earphones to Richardson. As soon as he adjusted the earphones over his head, Rich could hear it. Distinct machinery noises; the sound of a pump running, gear whine—that would be the reduction gears—the sibilant swish of water past an unyielding hull.

"It's louder now than when we reported it," volunteered the sonarman.

"How does it sound on JT?" asked Rich.

By way of response, Buck reached for a hidden switch on the bulkhead. The sound of muted machinery noise filled the tiny sonar compartment. "That's what he's hearing up forward with his sonic ears," Buck said.

"Is it only on that bearing?"

"Yessir! I was searching all around, like Mr. Norton told me. I can hear the *Cushing* back aft in the baffles. She's pretty faint, but I can hear her. Everything else is all clear all around." The sonarman was torn between fear of his superiors, whose grave demeanor might mean they blamed him for not detecting the contact sooner, and fear of the unknown contact itself.

"I wonder if Keith has this same contact," said Richardson.

"We can ask him on Gertrude."

"Can you give it to him on your wolfpack code?"

"Yes. I'll get the book." Buck dashed forward, snatched the pamphlet from his desk safe after failing the combination the first time, ran back to the sonar room.

Richardson had switched off the sonic sound repeater. "What does QS SS mean?" he asked. "First he sent RI KE—that means Rich from Keith—then QS SS."

"It means Rich from Keith, that's the first part, all right," said Buck, almost breathlessly, flipping the pages of the thin booklet. "Where did that come from?"

"From the *Cushing,* just now, on the UQC. He sent it in Morse, with his whistle."

"It means, 'Sonar contact to starboard, believed to be submarine.'"

"That's what I think it is, too, Buck. It's a ship, all right; so it's got to be a submarine!"

"What's it doing?"

"Nothing. Just keeping up with us. Maybe it's closed in some, because the sound's a lot louder than when sonar picked it up."

"Could it be the same sub that rammed the *Cushing?*"

"Whoever, it is, Buck, he's looking us over. That seems pretty clear. What he might do about it is something else."

"We're stuck, too. Towing the *Cushing* like this, we can't change speed or course, at least not fast enough to mean anything. How far do you think he is?"

"I asked that while you were getting the code book. We've had the sonar in the passive mode, so it's not been echo-ranging. As a guess, he's within a couple of miles."

"Shall we take a ping range?"

"Wait. He doesn't know he's detected yet. Did Keith tell us how much chain he has out?"

"Yes. Seventy fathoms."

"Have somebody break out that set of his general plans you were smart enough to bring along, and figure out the exact distance between his sonar head and ours."

Buck's face showed instant comprehension. "Right! Our JT head is a little aft of the BQR 2, so I'll get both numbers!" He left the sonar room, was back in minutes. "Jeff and Tom are getting both plans, ours and the *Cushing's*, and laying the whole thing out on the wardroom table. We can tell Keith to give us his bearings in the wolfpack code!"

"That's lucky. Our friend over here is listening to us. He probably knows everything that's gone on up to now."

"Yes. God damn him anyway!" Buck swore with deep feeling. "I was afraid we were talking too much. It's all because of that message we had to send! If they were monitoring the area by sonar they heard it once that way, and then a while later they heard us send the same message by radio. So they had to know another sub's arrived up here, and this bastard was sent to investigate. He's probably recorded every Gertrude transmission we've made!"

Richardson had put down the earphones he had been wearing since entry into the sonar room. He and Buck were hunched in a corner of the room, their heads together, their voices lowered. The sonar operator, heavy sponge-rubber earpieces over both ears, was seated at his console, oblivious of them. Rich glanced

down at him uneasily, then, reassured, turned back to
Buck. He moved his head closer to him, spoke in an
even lower tone. "I'm afraid you're right. I don't like
this at all. Keith obviously doesn't either. That's one
reason he used the wolfpack code and the whistle instead of talking."

"I thought of that, too, Skipper. At least, we've not
been blathering like idiots over the phone. I guess both
of us figured to save that until we were more clear.
Good thing, too."

"The cat's already out of the bag, but anyway, you'd
better give instructions that no one, OOD or anyone
else, should use the UQC without permission. Keith's
probably doing the same thing."

"I have already. I was going to tell you."

"Good. Maybe he's only watching us to see what
we're up to. When he realizes we're hauling the *Cushing* out of here, he may go away."

"I sure hope so!"

"In the meantime, how do we tell Keith what we
want him to do?"

Buck fished the little code book out of his pocket.
"Easy. We start with his initials and yours, his first,
this time. Then we send the group for triangle or tri-
angulation, and then the one that means, 'Request
enemy bearing.' Keith will know exactly what we're
doing. We can send him the bearing from us in the
code, too, but there's no way we can tell him the baseline length."

"Let's give him the bearing anyway. He might know
where your sonar dome is, and that message from
CNO tells him the towline length. When we give him
the range he can work the problem backward, and that
will correct his baseline if it's not right."

"Gotcha, boss."

* * *

For two more hours the Russian submarine (for such it could only be) remained in the plotted position: approximately 5,000 yards, two and a half nautical miles, on Keith's starboard beam. Then it grew more distant, and finally faded out altogether. With almost a corporate sigh of relief, for Rich and Buck soon realized the entire ship's company had become very much aware of the situation and its possible implications— magnified, no doubt, by their imaginations—a gradual but sweeping course-change was executed. As an additional precaution, silent running for both submarines was ordered, with particular attention to the condensate pump, and then Rich and Buck gratefully climbed into their bunks for their first rest in nearly thirty-six hours.

Still uneasy, however, or perhaps because he sensed that the situation had not come to any definite conclusion, Rich flopped on his bunk fully clothed, only removing his shoes for greater comfort. He was instantly unconscious.

The ventilation blowers had been turned off in the silent condition, and he was perspiring heavily when he awoke. Jerry Abbott's clock told him he had been asleep for about five hours. Something was not right. Something was permeating the boat, an aura, a feeling that something—an emergency—was afoot. The cobwebs in his brain were only peripheral. Groggily, he searched for his shoes, put them on, but all the while an instinctive part of his mind was probing, gearing itself. There was a quietness, an atmosphere of worry, even of dread, permeating the ship. It could only be one of two things: either there had been some casualty —to the *Cushing,* the towline or the *Manta*—or the Russian was back.

He stepped quickly across the passageway, looked quietly into Buck's room. It was empty. So was the wardroom. He started for the control room, had to wait for an instant because the control room messenger was coming through from the opposite side of the bulkhead door.

"Commodore! I was sent to get you, sir! There's distant pinging, coming closer!" The young sailor's face was flushed, his eyes showed white completely around the pupils. There were beads of sweat on his cheeks and upper lip. Of course, it had been hot in the control room without the ventilation. . . .

"Thanks, son," said Richardson, trying to demonstrate a calm he did not feel. He ducked through the watertight door, headed for the sonar room.

Jeff Norton and Buck were already in it, as was the chief sonarman. Tom Clancy, Deedee Brown and the chief of the boat (now called "chief of the ship"), Chief Auxiliaryman Mac McClosky, were standing in the passageway outside the aluminum-framed door. Those in the passageway made way for Richardson, but there was not room to enter the sonar room. He stood in the doorway, craned his neck into the darkened space, listened.

"I heard distant pinging first," the sonarman at the console said. "So I reported that. Chief Schultz came running in, and then Mr. Norton, but by that time it was already getting louder. He was pinging all around. I think he was searching. Then he started to beam it right at us. I think he got contact right then. That's about the time you came in, Captain. He's pinging right on us now, on long-range scale. He's not searching anymore."

"That's right, sir," said Palmer Schultz, serious-faced. "When I first heard it, the pinging was sort of general, all around his dial. While I was here I heard him bounce a real solid ping right off us, and that was the ball game. He's got a solid contact now. He's too far for us to hear any screw noises, but he's not getting louder quite as fast as he was. So I think he's slowed down."

"Does JT have any engine or screw noises?" Buck asked.

Schultz spoke softly into a microphone. "Do you have anything besides pinging on two-two-eight?"

"Affirmative," said the JT speaker. "I hear distant machinery noise. It just started to come in. I think he's pinging, too. I can hear the clicks."

"Okay," said Schultz. "We've got it here, too. Keep on it and report any changes. Get us a turn count as soon as you can hear the screws."

"Okay," said the voice.

"Did anyone get the commodore?" Buck asked, without turning his head.

"I'm here, Buck."

"Put the BQR return on the speaker, Schultz. We may as well all hear it," said Buck.

The pings transported Richardson backward in time. They were exactly the same as they had been during the war, with but a single difference. The intention behind them was unknown. There was also another noise, a high hum, emanating from the same bearing. "I think we're beginning to pick up his machinery," said Schultz. "Pretty soon we may hear his screws." He spoke into his mike. "Can you hear his propellers yet?" he asked.

There was no answer. Schultz gently replaced the mike in its cradle.

"Turn count, one-two-oh!" said the speaker suddenly. "It's a single-screw ship!"

Helplessly, the crowd around the sonar shack heard the alien submarine close in and resume its former station. "He'd never get away with that if we weren't immobilized with a tow," said Buck angrily. "What does he think he's doing, anyway?"

There was no answer. After a minute, Buck spoke

again. "I don't like this at all, Commodore. I think we should go to battle stations."

"I think you should, Buck," said Rich, steadily. "Does your code have a signal for telling the *Cushing* to do the same?"

"We can tell Keith that we're doing it. We never thought of putting anything in the code for telling another skipper how to run his ship."

"Well, tell him we are. He'll know what to do."

"Jerry," said Buck, "are you out there?"

"Right here, Skipper," said Jerry Abbott's voice behind Rich.

"Sound battle stations. Here's the code book." He slipped the book out of his pocket and held it behind him. "Use the whistle at minimum gain on the after Gertrude. At least that one's partly directional because of the baffles. Tell her we're going to battle stations."

"Wilco," said Abbott. Rich took the book from Buck's hand, passed it behind him, felt it taken from him. In a moment the musical chimes sounded through the general announcing system. It was the first time in sixteen years that Rich had heard them except in drill, and again he felt himself driven backward in time. They ceased, and Rich could hear the whistle slowly and precisely sending the Morse code letters AS. The letters were repeated twice, but they were less audible over the bustle of the crew dashing to their stations.

www

"I think he's closing us," said Schultz from the sonar console, where he had taken over his battle station. "He sounds louder, and the decible meter is reading a little higher."

"Get another bearing from the *Cushing,* Jerry, and pass him ours when we get it. Schultz, give me a good solid center-bearing thirty seconds from now." Buck was waiting the agreed-on interval so that his and Keith's bearings would be at approximately the same time. "Stand by. . . . Mark!"

"One-four-seven by grid," said Schultz. Jeff Norton wrote the number on two scraps of paper, handed the first to Deedee Brown at the TDC and the second to Jerry Abbott when he came by for it.

Approximately a minute afterward, Brown returned. "Thirty-two-fifty yards," he said. "Jerry came in the wardroom while we were plotting it; so I guess he's checking with the *Cushing.*"

The darkened sonar room was dominated by the sonar console, in the center of which lay, at a convenient angle for viewing, a circular glass-faced tube dimly backlighted in red. The center of the tube was dark, but greenish-white flashes emanated regularly from the four-o'clock sector, halfway to the edge, and each flash coincided with a reverberating ping which jumped from the three pairs of earphones listening to it and bounced around the metal walls of the tiny compartment. Richardson wondered why Schultz, Norton and Buck Williams were not deafened by the piercing, high-frequency echo-ranging signals sent by the other submarine.

He had to tap urgently on Buck's shoulder to get his attention. "We may as well go active ourselves. He's not being very polite, and there's no point in our being polite either. I'll tell Keith to do the same. Go on short scale at full gain, and aim it right into his receiver, but wait one minute before you start so Keith can go off with you. Does your code cover this?"

"Not all that, Skipper."

"All right, I'll tell him on Gertrude." Grim-faced, inwardly seething and at the same time worried, Rich walked the few steps to the periscope station, vaulted to the elevated platform, picked up the UQC microphone. "Keith," he said without preliminaries, "this is Rich. We're going active, and I want you to do the same. Short scale at full gain; aim it right at him. He's closing in on us. Maybe this will make him be a little more circumspect."

"Wilco, boss," said Keith's voice. "Do you want to start right now?"

"In fifteen seconds. Ping for exactly one minute, then stop. We'll do the same."

"Roger!"

Back at the sonar shack, Rich was gratified to see by the sonar console that both submarines blasted forth their beams of concentrated sonar energy at nearly the same instant. The spot on the scope occupied by the stranger was bathed in a rapid succession of flashing pings, and the corresponding echoes were loud and precise. The intruder, as seen on the scope, seemed to have an unearthly, eerie glow, and Rich could have sworn that he could discern, for an instant, the actual shape of the underwater craft.

Schultz positioned the range marker over the spot, read the range. "Thirty-two hundred yards, right on," he said. "He's still closing us . . . no, now I think he's stopped closing. The range is opening slightly. It's stabilized on thirty-two hundred."

Williams gave a coarse laugh. "That barrage slowed him down a little!"

"Maybe, Buck," said Rich, with the same grim look on his face, "but I wouldn't bet on anything permanent. My main idea was to show him that he's fooling around with a couple of United States men-of-war. If he's a Soviet Navy skipper, that will mean something to him."

Suddenly, all echo-ranging ceased. There was nothing on the screen. "He stopped too, sir!" said Schultz in a surprised tone. Then he grunted vindictively. "I'll just bet you there's a couple pairs of stinging ears over on that sub. They probably had their gain way up, the same as we do when there's nobody pinging on us. Serves the bastards bloody well right, too. I hope their eardrums are busted good!"

Rich and Buck were again in their somewhat sequestered corner of the sonar compartment. "Skipper," Buck said in a low tone, "have you any guess at all why he went away and then came back the way he did?"

"I've been thinking about the same thing, and the only idea I've come up with is that he shoved off to ask for instructions. How long was he gone? You must have it in the sonar log and the quartermaster's notebook."

"I already had Jeff look it up. It was five hours forty-three minutes from when we heard him turn away until we heard his echo-ranging when he came back."

"Then I'd have to guess that he went somewhere within about a two-hour run, got his orders quickly and tore back looking for us. In the meantime, we covered about twenty miles, though it might not have been directly away from his base, whatever that was."

"True. Besides, we made a ninety-degree course change right after he left, remember. So if we were going directly away from him one time, we couldn't have been the other."

"That's right. Did we log the bearing we picked him up on?"

"Sure. At least, the quartermaster's supposed to. Why?"

"Buck, could you have your plotters assemble every scrap of info they've got on that sub, and plot it? See if we can figure out what direction he departed in, and what direction he came back from. And see if your code lets us ask Keith the bearing and distance of the spot where he was rammed, and even the estimated location of the position those planes seemed to be operating around."

"Glad to. But what good will that do us now?"

"You never know, old friend. But the more you find out about your enemies, the more you're apt to luck into something you can use. And I don't mind telling you one thing, very confidentially. Down deep, I'm scared. This whole situation stinks. If our friend yonder decides to play it rough, there's damned little we can do. We're on steady course, speed and depth, and he knows exactly what those are."

"Not depth, exactly."

"Don't kid yourself! We'd have had it figured out by now, and you can bet he has, too!"

"But what can he do? What could they be wanting?"

"For one thing, they'd love a sample copy of our latest model Polaris missile submarine. They'd give a lot for that."

"Keith would never surrender his ship."

"Agreed. But what if he got into absolutely desperate straits, and only the Russians knew where he was, or could help him. They claim he shot down one of their aircraft, remember! What if the price of saving the lives of his whole crew was for Washington to order him to surrender and let the Russians cut a hole in the ice to get them out?"

"Couldn't Keith be the last man out and open the vents behind him?"

"With the whole crew hostage? By that time Washington would be running the show, not him."

"What if a whole bunch of airborne troops landed at just the right time . . ."

"And at just the right place, which wouldn't be at all where we thought they were, ready for a mini-war in the snow and to sacrifice about as many men as they'd likely rescue . . . no sir, Buck, the Soviets had us over a barrel when there was only the *Cushing* here, and they knew it. At least, they thought so. It would have been so easy just to wait. They could even have had that sub checking the *Cushing* every once in a while. Keith was mighty smart to move her the way he did, even though he didn't get far. Not many skippers would have thought of that. But they probably knew exactly where he was anyway, all the time. Maybe he'd have been smartest if he'd simply hovered at maximum submergence, letting himself drift wherever the deep currents took him. They'd have had to come looking for him by echo-ranging, then, and at least that would have warned him. With luck, they might not have been able to find him."

"So, the *Manta* . . ."

"Exactly. We're the fly in that ointment. They don't need us or even want us. It's the *Cushing,* a brand-new missile sub, that they want. But we're the motive power that's snaking the prize out from under their nose."

"You think we're the target?"

"If they decide to play real rough, we are. On two counts. One, we're the motive power. Two, if we disappear, their hardball diplomacy is actually strengthened."

"Then"—Buck had lowered his voice to a whisper—"you do think the collision with the *Cushing* wasn't an accident! But how could they do something that risky deliberately? Their sub could just as well have been the one sunk."

"She hit him from aft, and Keith thinks he was on a nearly parallel course. Also, she was running silent. Otherwise, he'd have heard her. If they'd have had any advance warning he was on his way, it might not have been too hard to fix one of their nukes with some kind of steel girderlike protection, or even some sort of projecting ram to stick up against a revolving propeller. We have a pretty tough ice suit built into the *Manta,* you know. At least, you were bragging to me about it. Why couldn't the Soviets do the same thing, but skewed slightly?"

"It still sounds farfetched to me. Even if such a sub could wreck Keith's propeller, he couldn't be sure of getting the emergency propulsion motor too."

"He did, though. Didn't he? Did a really superb job. Got them both at once. I'm guessing that was fortuitous. Most likely the scheme was to disable the main propeller as though it were an accident, as though the *Cushing* had hit some hard ice. And then, while she was creeping home on the EPM, they'd have plenty of time to clip that off somehow."

"If all your guessing is close to right, that Russian sub skipper must be a pretty doggone experienced one. And pretty doggone tough, too. If his mission was to disable Keith by ramming him with his own sub, he still was taking a hell of a chance that he might have been the one disabled."

"We took a lot of chances a few years ago too, Buck. Ramming is not an unknown naval tactic, especially if your ship's built for it."

"They must know an awful lot about our subs, how they're built and all that," said Buck pensively.

"Don't you think they do?"

"I suppose so. But they couldn't have had that sub just hanging around up here waiting for someone maybe to show up. They must have known Keith was coming. Pretty far in advance."

"Not possible?"

"He didn't even know himself until a few weeks before!"

"Sure. I didn't either, till a week or so before he did. But the thing had been planned a long time. They could have been watching construction of the *Cushing*. She's the only missile sub built with an ice suit, you know. She's the only one we could have sent. When did you find out her sailplanes could be elevated to ninety degrees?"

"Quite a while ago. It was all over Electric Boat because there were so many design changes needed." Rich said nothing, and after a short pause Buck muttered, half to himself, "I see what you mean. The *Cushing* was the boat for them to watch."

"Ship. That's your line."

"Ship."

The sonar room was almost silent. Buck and Rich had unconsciously squeezed their heads tightly together in their darkened corner, above and to the side of the sonar console. The tiny compartment, the ship, the orderly quiet of the men at action stations, the tension of readiness for immediate emergency—all had temporarily fallen away from their consciousness. At the same time they were at the spot where the crisis would be first recognized, ready to take instant action even prior to the startled report from the sonarman.

Schultz, wedded to his precious sonar set, was unconscious of the low-voiced conversation two feet above his head. His head half-covered with huge, sound-insulated, sponge-rubber-covered earphones, reaching from behind his eyes to the curve of his neck behind his ears, concentration upon the information conveyed to him by the electronic instrument in front of him was total. He had already decided to call attention to the slightest deviation in the Russian submarine's movements simply by striking out with his left hand. He would not have to distract his own attention by speaking. He would hit something, someone, and bring them over to him. More, as a man at the top of his profession, wise in the down-to-earth practicality of submariners, with perhaps his own life and those of all others aboard depending upon him, he knew this was exactly what his superiors would have expected. His own instructions to the operator of the sonic JT set, sitting on a stool with a similar set of earphones in the forward torpedo room, were to stand on no protocol or ceremony, to report anything he heard, or thought he heard, instantly via the special speaker circuit between the two stations.

There had been a pause in the conversation between the two officers. Both felt their senses acutely tuned to the limitless medium through which their ship was passing. Above them, not far away, was the nearly impervious ice cover; below, very far below, the rock basaltic plates of two of those slowly drifting crusts on the earth's mantle which, in the Arctic Ocean, had by their confluence ages past created two huge basins, thousands of fathoms deep. Between the two limits, and further limited by the maximum depth to which *Manta*'s strong shell could descend, there was complete freedom to move in any direction her masters willed, as fast as they willed, up to the top power her nuclear reactor could deliver and her turbines receive.

Except that *Manta* was not free. She was a prisoner of the towline, constricted to move only slowly, steadily, constantly, in a single direction. Slight, and only very gradual, changes could be made in speed; changes in depth and direction could be made only very slowly, with the greatest of care. Violation of any of these rules would inexorably rupture the thin, weak thread that held out hope to Keith and his crew of 126 men.

"I think I'll go start Jerry on that plot we want," said Buck. "Back in a minute. We'll have to use the UQC to get the information we need from Keith. Okay?"

"Got to," said Rich.

When he returned, rather more than a minute later, for he had made a quick head call, Buck found Richardson and Schultz huddled over the sonar display. "He's begun echo-ranging again," said Rich. "And he's begun to move out ahead of us. He's up to something!"

"If he shoots a torpedo, I'll have to maneuver to avoid. The towline will break."

"I know, Buck. We'll have the other one to hook up again with, if we get the chance." Then a thought struck Richardson. "Don't you have a couple of decoys up forward?"

"Yes."

"Have them get one ready for firing. Quick, man!"

Buck did not even answer. He picked up the telephone handset, spoke directly into it, gave the order. "They'll have to haul out one of the fish and load the decoy into the tube. They're pretty fast, especially with all the extra men up there on battle stations. Three minutes, they told me."

"God, we should have thought of this before," muttered Rich. "That's one string to our bow we should have had ready!"

"I should have thought of it," said Buck. "After all, I'm skipper of this craft." He was silent for a long, thoughtful minute. "What kind of fish do you think he's likely to have?"

"Some straight running, for sure. The question is whether he can set them to run this deep. Besides that, probably some kind of target-seeking torpedo. Since they're antisubmarine, most of them can be set for any depth a sub's likely to be, and when they detect a sub they'll go after it, whatever the depth. If he shoots one of those, we've got to make it think the decoy is us."

"That's what the decoy's for, all right. But where do we go after we shoot it? There's not much maneuvering we can do."

"If you stop your screws, put her in full dive and flood negative, the *Cushing* will coast overhead. You could even back a little, when you're deep enough. If you're lucky, you might not even break the towline."

"We should warn Keith, shouldn't we?"

"We should; but if that sub's really up to something, he's monitoring us with every resource he's got. We'd better not take the chance. Keith will know something serious is going on, and will cope."

The telephone gave its characteristic squeak. Buck snatched it, listened. "Four and a half knots," he said.

"Forward room wanting to know what speed to set on the decoy, eh?"

"Yep. They're about to shove it in the tube."

"Good. That was quick work."

"Thanks." Buck picked up the telephone again, said, "Tubes forward, you got that loose fish secured for angles? Good! Good work up there!" Hanging up the phone he said to Rich, "We're always supposed to be ready for steep angles, but that torpedo was hanging in midair while they hauled it out of the tube, so I thought I'd check to make sure it was secured. It's secure, all right. The chief even pretended I hurt his feelings by asking."

"His feelings weren't hurt. He's proud of his work, and he's pleased with you for giving him a chance to show it."

Buck felt an elbow in his middle. Schultz was pointing to the illuminated spot on his dial where the enemy submarine was indicated. It had drawn well ahead, and echo-ranging spokes were no longer coming from it. Simultaneously, both officers noted the unexpected lengthening of the silence since the last ping.

"What's he doing?" said Rich. "Could he be getting ready to shoot?"

"Echo-range, Schultz! Full power and short scale!" Buck ordered. There was savagery in his voice. Grabbing the phone, he said, "Tubes forward, set the decoy for short-scale pinging. Then flood the tube and shoot it! Let me know when it's away!"

"Good for you, Buck," said Rich quietly. "If he shoots now, it's likely a quiet, fairly slow torpedo, programmed to finish its run by homing on noise. That must be why he shut off his pinging. So as not to confuse it. If he plans to shoot he'll do it now while we're pinging, so that his fish can home on it."

Buck still held the phone to his ear, did not answer. Suddenly he said sharply, "Secure pinging!" Schultz flipped a switch on his console as Buck thrust past Richardson, stepped into the passageway outside the sonar room. "All stop!" he called peremptorily. "Tom!

Flood negative! Twenty degrees down angle! Make your depth seven hundred feet!"

There was a clank of mechanism beneath their feet, the sound of water rushing through a large orifice, a huge whoosh of air and an increase in pressure on the eardrums. *Manta* began to incline downward with an ever increasing angle.

Buck had run across the control room, was talking to Tom Clancy. "Start blowing negative and zeroing the bubble at seven hundred feet, Tom," he said rapidly. "I'm going to have to back then, and you'll have your hands full keeping control. Use a bubble in bow buoyancy or main ballast if you need to. When the *Cushing*'s about overhead we'll go ahead again. You'll have trouble with your weights aft, too."

"Maybe you'd better let her drift down an extra hundred fifty feet, Skipper, seeing this looks like an emergency. *Cushing*'s got her anchor at seventy fathoms, and she's at three hundred feet right now. So that's four hundred twenty feet added to whatever depth she winds up at when she starts feeling that extra weight. We don't want to bump into that big iron mushroom of hers down there!"

"Right, Tom! Make your depth eight hundred fifty!"

"Also, you know there's going to be a hell of a lot of pressure in the boat when we vent off all that air we'll be using in negative tank!"

"Can't be helped, Tom. Do it slowly. When we get a chance to, we'll pump it back down with the air compressors."

The deck had begun to incline quite steeply. The depth gauge was already registering five hundred fifty feet as Buck struggled across the control room to the sonar room. Three hundred feet to go! And, of course, he would have to allow for the angle in calculating where *Manta*'s stern was.

Schultz was saying, "Looks like there's another sub-marine out ahead of us! It's pinging just like we were, and I can even hear machinery noises."

"How about the Russian? Do we know for sure he's fired at us?"

"We think so, Buck," said Rich. "The JT reported something in the water, some faint swishing noise, out ahead of the Russian. We can't hear it here. It's too bad they didn't think of putting the JT controls in the sonar room too."

"The later boats have them that way, you know. What's the Russian doing now?"

"He's just stopped. Hovering, I guess, waiting for us to catch that fish of his."

"Would you authorize shooting one at him?"

"If he's really fired at us, I'll sure think about it!"

"We'll know if our decoy gets sunk!"

"That's what I was thinking!"

All three men in the sonar room had to brace them-selves against the steep downward inclination of the submarine. Now there was the sound of air blowing, and Buck heaved his head out the doorframe. He stepped out, holding to the frame for support, stretch-ing his hand in front of him to the stacked motor-generator sets across the passageway. He skidded for-ward, holding to the rail around the periscope stand, reached the diving station. "Tom," he said, "we may not need to back. Take her on down anyway, and I'll give you two knots in a couple of minutes. Get us a zero bubble as soon as you can."

"Thanks, Skipper! With no speed and all this chang-ing of weights, I've got all I can handle today!"

"We might be firing a torpedo or two forward, Tom, to make it a little less boring for you. He's already shot at us!" Buck left Clancy staring at him, started back to the sonar room. The angle already had lessened and the climb took only moments. "How's it going?" he said.

"Our decoy's out about a thousand yards ahead now, still sounding like a great little old submarine, and JT reports he thinks that thing the Russian shot, whatever it was, is about to merge in with it."

"Schultz, what do you think?" Buck had to lay a hand on his shoulder to attract the sonarman's attention.

"There was something out there all right, coming closer. It was on a steady bearing with us for a while, but then when we slowed down it started to pass ahead. Maybe it had a steady bearing with our decoy." The chief sonarman had laid back one earphone. "Now it's mixing in with the decoy, sniffing around it, like."

"Has it passed it, or is it about to?" Buck asked.

"It should have passed it by now, but it hasn't. It's still sniffing."

The angle was rapidly returning to normal. Abruptly, Williams picked up the phone. "Maneuvering! Make turns for two knots! Control, report that to Mr. Clancy and the helmsman!" He was returning the telephone to its bulkhead cradle when suddenly Schultz ripped off his headset with an exclamation. "Ouch!" he said, massaging his right ear, but neither Buck nor Rich heard him, for the sonar room was filled with the reverberations of a sharp, distant explosion.

The surprise with which Rich and Buck stared at each other was real, even though the explosion had not been entirely unexpected. "How long do we have before he realizes he didn't tag us after all?" asked Buck rhetorically.

"A couple of minutes, maybe. The longer we stay in *Cushing*'s sonar shadow, the longer it will take him to figure out what's happened," said Rich.

"What about Keith?"

"He'll realize we're close aboard, and will guess we fired the decoy."

"I'd like to shoot one of our Mark Forties at that bastard!"

"Buck, I'm in command of this force. I order you to return the fire. See that my specific order is entered in the log!" Buck Williams stared at his superior. The look on his face, the determined fury in his eyes, were clear, and all too familiar. Richardson was glaring at him unblinkingly. "Put it in the log, Buck," he said softly. "If you do not carry out my order, I shall relieve you from command!"

Buck was puzzled for a fraction of a second. Then his brow smoothed, and he knew what to do. He knew Richardson meant precisely what he said, and he had thought of the reason why. "Aye, aye, sir!" he said. He picked up the phone. "Tubes forward," he said, "the commodore has ordered us to return the fire. Load the other decoy in the empty tube. Prepare one Mark Forty for firing! This is a war shot. This is not a drill!"

Backing out of the sonar room, Buck took three steps forward and to the right, where Brown and his fire controlmen were standing at their stations. "Deedee, have you been keeping the setup on your TDC?"

"Affirmative, Captain."

"Very well." Buck knew that some of Richardson's suddenly icy demeanor was infecting him too. "Tubes forward have been ordered to prepare one Mark Forty war shot for firing. Set your inputs accordingly!"

"Aye, aye, sir!" Brown was tall, blond, sensitive. His blue eyes were shouting the questions in his mind.

"Quartermaster!"

"Here, sir."

"Enter in your rough log as follows: 'The intruding submarine has opened fire upon us, and is identified as an enemy ship of war. The explosion just heard was an attempt to sink the *Manta*. The squadron commander has put this ship on a war footing and has directed *Manta* to return the fire.' You got that?" Buck was speaking slowly and precisely, waiting for the quartermaster to scribble the words as he dictated them.

"Yes, sir!" said the man, his eyes widening.

More rapidly, Buck went on, "We're already at general quarters. Do not sound the general alarm. Have the word passed by telephone to all compartments!" This, perhaps, was not necessary, for all hands would have the information within seconds anyway. Probably they already knew, for at battle stations all compartments automatically manned all telephones.

He turned back to Brown. "How are you doing, Deedee?" Buck could see the men industriously turning dials, making entries into the complicated instruments arrayed against the curved skin in the ship. Deedee Brown himself was busily transferring figures from a plastic card inserted in a receptacle on the face of the TDC into the input section.

"Ready in a minute! We need a good range and the depth of the target."

"You'll have to use three hundred feet for depth; that's the best I can give you. When you're ready to shoot, we'll get you a ping range. As soon as you have that in the fish, we'll let her go!"

Brown stepped close to Buck, whispered, "What was that explosion we heard just now? Did it have anything to do with our decoy?"

"Yes, it did, Deedee. It destroyed it. If we hadn't slowed up and sent the decoy along our track in our place, we'd all be dead right now!" Buck felt a sardonic satisfaction in telling Brown. Someday he'd be a submarine skipper, and it might be well for him to remember this day. Suddenly Buck was recalling certain experiences of his own, and then he realized that another such experience had occurred less than a minute before.

Buck turned away, returned to the sonar room. For the moment, sonar was the center of information. He would fire the torpedo from there. Swiftly, he explained his intention to get an accurate range with a single ping just before firing. Schultz nodded his comprehension. The single-ping range was a standard prefiring procedure.

Rich, also nodding, said, "We've got to do it, all right. We can't tell from the sonar what his course or speed is, or if he's got way on at all. I hate to, though, because it will alert him that much sooner."

"Me, too," said Buck, "but there's no way out of it. Deedee has the best bearing Schultz can give him, but the Mark Forty has to have a range to know where to start its search. We're pretty close to the *Cushing*. Maybe he'll have us both merged in his sonar and will think the *Cushing* did it."

Brown appeared directly behind Buck in the sonar room doorway. "We're ready," he said. "Tube's flooded. Outer door's open."

"All right, Chief; get a single-ping range. Get the best bearing, too. Feed 'em both automatically to the TDC." A single white spoke lashed out from the center of the sonar dial, impinged directly upon the faint dot representing the enemy sub. He heard the squelched transmission signal, and the clear, solid echo which returned.

"Thirty-eight-fifty," said Schultz. "Bearing zero-three-seven and a half, relative. TDC's got them both, sir!"

Despite his statement to Brown, Buck could not remain in the sonar room. He leaped out the door, heard Deedee call out loudly, "Set!" Rich, he felt rather than saw, was right behind.

"Fire!" cried Buck sharply. Brown, his finger poised

on the firing key, punched it hard to the left. He stepped
back, waited, eyes on the indicator lights.

"Torpedo started, ran out normally," said the telephone talker. Brown was watching his fire control panel
carefully, nodding his head. "She's away," he said.

Back in the sonar shack, Schultz was watching the
path of the torpedo. It had curved to the right, was
speeding toward the spot occupied by the enemy submarine. It would run at high speed into the general area,
then slow, make a circling search, finally go back to
speed and home in on magnetic attraction. It was the
best torpedo the U.S. Navy had, the product of years
of research. Its record of successful firings was outstanding. It was fast, nearly silent, and almost 100-
percent deadly.

"Good shot, Buck," said Richardson. "I think he's
a dead man!" But as they watched the sonar scope,
suddenly the spot the Russian submarine occupied became suffused with its own white light, a light which
persisted. The speeding trace of the torpedo entered
the enlarged spot and vanished. Disbelievingly, the
three men in the sonar room watched for an appreciable
time, but nothing happened. The large white spot died
down, disappeared, leaving not even the original indication of the presence of another submarine.

"I think I saw him take off," said Schultz, by way
of possible explanation. "He was making knots, behind
all that white, and he went right off the scope!"

"At least, you scared him silly, Buck. Maybe now
he'll leave us alone!" But the grim look on Rich's face
showed he did not believe his words, nor did he expect
Buck to. "How fast do you think we can tow Keith?"
he went on.

"Maybe six knots, or a fraction more," said Buck.

"Make another radical course change, away from

the direction he went, and go as fast as you can. Run up close to the ice, too, as close as you dare. That will confuse his sonar. We've got to take this opportunity to lose him. I'll explain it to Keith. On our third day with the *Besugo,* we ran overloaded for several hours. Can you find those strain-gauge readings?"

"They were all logged. I'm sure we can."

Despite Buck's misgivings, resuming towing resulted in only a few bumps as the towline was again stretched. Once a steady towing condition was achieved, he gradually increased speed until both ships seemed fairly flying along, close under the ice pack. They might have been able to go even faster than the seven knots shown on the log had it not been necessary for Keith to maintain a small amount of plane angle because of the *Cushing*'s tendency to tow a few feet above the *Manta.* After three hours, Buck was contemplating ordering his crew off action stations, and slowing to conserve the strength of the towline as well as to reduce his noise level. But this was the moment sonar chose to pick up contact once more.

It was Schultz, still religiously maintaining his solitary watch, who was forced to bring the bad news. "Sonar contact," he announced in a heavy voice over the speaker system. Rich and Buck crowded into the sonar shack. "It's him again!" said Schultz. "No doubt about it anymore. I'd know that signature anywhere!"

"We have to break the towline, Buck! We'll have to fight this guy on even terms! If he sinks us, Keith's done for anyway. We've no hope at all if we stay tied to him!"

"I've been thinking the same! Shall I do it now?"

"Yes! I'll go tell Keith!"

As Richardson picked up the UQC handset, he heard Buck order, "All ahead full!"

"Keith," Rich said in the low tone which had become habitual, "that fellow is back again, and we're going to have to break the towline. After we dispose of him we'll be back to pick you up with the other tow rig."

"I understand," said Keith's distorted voice, and Rich knew he did, fully. He quickly described his own already laid plans for this contingency, and then said, "If we get a chance to, we'll try a Mark Forty on him ourselves. We still have a few strings left. And, Skipper," Keith's voice deepened, took on an expression of determined will, even under the poor reproductive quality of the equipment, "whatever happens, we'll never give up this ship. Never."

It was Richardson's turn to say, "I understand." He followed it with, "If we don't make it back, wait him out at test depth or below. I doubt he can follow you down there, nor can his fish!" As he said the words he found himself wondering what good that could possibly do, for without *Manta, Cushing* was dead too!

And then the nylon line snapped with a shuddering flip, and Buck sent *Manta* sliding down into the depths. The last thing Rich heard was Keith's quiet "Wilco!"

"It's us he's after; so it's us he'll chase, Buck. We've got one decoy left, and we've no idea how many fish he's got, nor how many of those defenses against the Mark Forty."

"It didn't make any noise, at least nothing we heard. Maybe it's not a weapon he shoots at all," said the disconsolate Buck.

"You mean, some kind of a magic energy device? Inexhaustible, maybe?"

"All I mean is he might not have to shoot a piece of hardware. So it wouldn't be something you could count, like our decoys. But maybe he wasn't all that sure it was going to work either. He sure ran off in a hurry.

If he'd only run a little longer, we might have shaken him!" Buck spoke morosely. His disappointment was keen.

"True, old man, but right now our problem is to kill him before he kills us. We have six Mark Fourteens and five Mark Forties left forward, is that right?"

"Plus two Mark Forties in the skids in the after torpedo room. I've told Deedee to unrig the after room for towing and load both of the Forties he has back there."

"The Forty is a single-shot fish. You shoot it very carefully, one at a time. You can reload one quicker than you can fire a second shot. So if you have one of them and our remaining decoy loaded, you can also have a salvo of four Fourteens in the other tubes forward."

"You don't expect him to let us get within range of an old Mark Fourteen!"

Buck's exhaustion was showing in his slowness at picking up the idea, Rich decided. "Maybe this magic energy thing you thought up can stop the electric motor in the Mark Forty, but if that's what it does it won't faze an old straight-running steam fish," he finally said, and was secretly delighted when Buck's eyes lighted and he gave the necessary orders.

The *Manta* had separated from the *Cushing* only a short distance, contrary to Rich and Buck's first intention to go many miles away. As had become virtually a necessity during the past few encounters, they were in the darkened sonar room, awaiting developments which could only be seen, and that poorly, in the sonar equipment. And yet, there must be instantaneous response. Awareness of the enemy submarine's whereabouts must be constant, and careful evaluation of any change or movement, immediate. She had approached to a distance of about a mile and had apparently stopped.

Doubtless she had silenced herself as much as possible. Even so, she made a faint but definitely discernible note. It was this tiny noise level, which Schultz and the JT operator were so strenuously keeping in their earphones, that created the spot on the sensitive scope.

The *Cushing* was not visible on the tube, nor could the JT hear her. She was somewhere overhead, resting against the ice with all machinery stopped. Lighting was minimal and on the storage battery; there would be no cooking; all unneeded personnel had been ordered to their bunks. In this condition, her cavernous interior had ample air for forty-eight hours and there was stored oxygen sufficient for many more days. Her battery was her limiting factor. Keith could remain in this condition for seventy-two hours, he had said, before his battery would be too low to restart his reactor.

Buck had also stopped every piece of nonessential machinery, including his primary loop main coolant pumps, but had kept his heaters on and the reactor functional in the newly developed natural circulation mode—a low-power condition from which restoration of full power could be accomplished in minutes. Under Clancy's skillful hand *Manta,* too, was stopped, hovering on a fortuitous thermal layer at the 300-foot level.

For the time being, it was a standoff. "I'll bet he can't see *Cushing* either," said Buck. "Maybe he's even lost us, if we're quieter than he is. We ought to be. So he must be making up his mind whether to go active with his sonar."

"When he does, he'll find us both, and he'll know the one against the ice cover must be the *Cushing.* Also, she'll give the bigger echo."

"We could try keeping our broadside to him. Unless he happens to get both of us broadside, our echo will be about as big as Keith's."

"If we ease up against the ice ourselves it will confuse

him even more," said Rich, thoughtfully, "but then, sound is so funny we might lose contact on him ourselves. Or, we might hear him better."

"We can always come back down again, boss. Let's try it!"

And so Tom Clancy blew some air into his tanks, and the *Manta* slowly drifted upward until she bumped gently against the solid ice, her side turned toward the intruder. True to the well-known vagaries of sound, contact remained, and ten minutes later the tiny luminescence that was the enemy lashed out with six strong rapid pings.

"He can't hear us!" Buck chortled. "He can only see us by going active!"

"Right," said Rich, "and unless Keith was also broadside to him, by accident, the echoes he got must have been nearly identical. So, right now, he can't tell which is which. We ought to be able to use that, somehow."

"Shoot our last decoy?"

Rich snapped his fingers. "Get it programmed so it simulates us trying to get away. Then get two Forties ready. Back out a Fourteen. They can reload it later. Can the wolfpack code tell Keith to get some fish ready?"

"That's one of the things it was made for."

Preparations were going forward when Schultz made the signal Rich and Buck had learned to anticipate, and the sound of inimical pings filled the compartment. "I think he's getting ready to shoot," said the sonarman.

"How do you know that?"

"Don't know. Just feel it," said Schultz. "There!" He pointed to a wispy, wavering discontinuity in the smooth blankness of the scope. "There again! There's another! He's still pinging, and he's fired twice!"

There were two discontinuities on the sonar scope emanating from the enemy submarine, one diverging

COLD IS THE SEA

slightly across its face, the other coming in steadily and remorselessly toward its center. "He's fired at both of us!" said Buck.

"Buck!" There was a decisive snap to Richardson's voice. "If he can't hear us, he must have fired on active sonar bearings and ranges. Set the decoy to run in circles under us! Maybe that will attract the fish! I'll tell Keith to do the same. Hope he can!" Rich dashed away, returned a moment later. "He's going to try," he said. "These are pretty slow-running torpedoes, so there may be time. Also I told him to shoot his Forties with us. Is our decoy away?"

"Affirmative!"

"There'll be a minute or so more before his fish gets here. Time to shoot ours!"

A quarter of a minute later, a thin streak arrowed on the scope toward the Russian, traveling much faster than the weapon he had fired, passing it close aboard on the sonar scope. As before, a brilliant white phosphorescence bloomed over the spot where he was, and there was no explosion.

"He's still there, I think!" said Schultz. "He didn't run this time! The *Cushing*'s fired too!"

A streak similar to that made by the *Manta*'s weapon, which could only have come from the *Cushing,* drew itself swiftly across the scope. Rich, Buck and Schultz were watching it with consuming interest, to the exclusion of all else. The Soviet sub's reaction to this second shot would show whether she could remount her antitorpedo protection quickly. Then a violent explosion shook the *Manta*'s sturdy structure. The resounding roar, reverberating through the sea and inside the submarine hull, blocking out all sound save for itself, threw clouds of dust and paint particles into the air. On the sonar scope there was nothing to be seen; only the startled, white, almost alive reaction of the scope as it attempted to reproduce electronically what it had heard through its audio senses.

"All compartments report to control!" Buck shouted into the telephone, looking, at the same time, at the sonar scope. The whiteout was receding, the Soviet submarine reappearing, surrounded by a fading halo of phosphorescence.

"He can't keep this up!" said Rich. "That must be a whale of a lot of energy! Shoot again! As soon as you can!"

A third swift streak raced toward the enemy submarine. Jerry Abbott appeared at the sonar room entrance. "No damage, Captain," he said. "It was close, though. Must have gone off right under us!" A distant explosion filled their consciousness. "Get a report from Leone!" snapped Richardson. Abbott darted away.

Again the halo effect enveloped the enemy. Again the speeding Mark Forty torpedo, the U.S. Navy's best, entered the immune area and disappeared.

"Cushing reports she's been hit!" gasped Abbott.

"Cushing's fired again!" said Schultz.

"Are you reloading forward, Buck?" asked Rich.

"Affirm. Two more Forties."

"Shoot again, as soon as ready!"

In all, six Mark Forty torpedoes, from two different locations, converged in succession on the intruder. In succession they ripped into the area where the sonar scope showed her, into the halo effect which seemed almost to have developed pulsations, so fast was it going on and off—and disappeared.

There was a cry from Schultz. "He's fired again! He's fired at us! It's coming this way!"

"You'll have to try to outrun it, Buck!"

"Coolant pumps in high speed, maneuvering!" ordered Buck on the telephone. "How much speed can you give me?" He listened anxiously. "Not enough!"

he said. "Use all the steam that you've got in the generators! Override the low-pressure alarm and the high temperature-differential scram! Keep those rods up! Get us rolling!"

He shouldered Rich aside, stuck his head outside the sonar room. "All-ahead emergency," he called to the helmsman. To Clancy, across the control room, he yelled, "Two hundred feet!" Back inside, on the telephone, he said, "Don't wreck the reactor, Harry! We'll still be needing it. But if you can't give me speed, right now, it won't make any difference! That first explosion was meant for us, the *Cushing's* been torpedoed, and there's another fish headed our way!" Turning to Rich he said, "They'll do it! Harry Langforth's with them, and he'll build up faster than this old reactor's ever gone before!" Suddenly he grinned tightly. "Wish old Brighting could see us! Where are all those reactor safeguards now, hey?" He darted out into the passageway again, called, "Left full rudder!" To Rich he said swiftly, "What's the course dead away from that fish?"

Richardson had been anticipating the need for this information. "Three-four-five on the grid!" he answered.

"Make your course three-four-five, helm!—Jerry!" he barked. "Stay here on the control station and relay for me!" He returned to the sonar console. "Where's the fish now?" he asked.

"I'll lose it when we get it astern," said Schultz anxiously, beads of sweat all over his face. "It's about half a mile away right now!"

"Do we have any speed estimate on it?"

"It took about three minutes from the time he fired until he hit our decoy. That's thirty knots, Buck!" The look on his superior's face had never been grimmer.

"This old bucket's never gone that fast in her life, but she's sure going to try now!" Buck thought. He picked up the telephone. "Harry? The fish chasing us can make thirty knots. How bad do you guys want to live, back there?"

Hanging up, he said to Rich, "They won't have to gag the safety valves, like in the old days of steam engines, because they'll be using all the steam as fast as our two kettles back there can make it, and the pressure's going to drop. But everything else, they'll do. What we need, right now, is pounds of steam per minute. More pounds of steam through those steam generators than they ever made before!"

Richardson nodded quietly, as Jerry Abbott called in, "Steady on three-four-five. Depth two hundred. Speed twenty, increasing!" Incongruously, his mind traveled backward many years, back to a submarine-school qualification exercise in his first command, the old *S-16.* The old destroyer *Semmes,* acting as target, had nearly rammed the *S-16.* By swift action, in analogy not far removed from that just taken by Buck, he had managed to avoid the disaster. Through it all, Tex Hansen, submarine-school training officer, two years senior to Rich, had not said a word, even though his own life, too, hung in the balance. Once in a while, over the years, he had wondered how it felt to contain one's self in such circumstances. Now he knew.

Strange that in the face of mortal danger, with total and terrible dissolution perhaps only moments away, he could feel so calm, so detached from it all. It was almost as though he were somewhere else, someone else, contemplating it, even enjoying the heightened sensation of it, but not affected by any of it at all. He had felt this way before. Very much this way. And he knew, without any doubt whatever, that Buck was experiencing precisely the same emotions, probably the same thoughts. His asides during the emergencies which had flowed upon him, one after the other, proved it.

"The fish is pinging!" Schultz murmured, sweating

heavily, his shirt suddenly dark with moisture. How could he hear, with the tumultuous wash of *Manta*'s frantically whirling propellers exactly between his sonar head and the target-looking torpedo? It figured, of course, that if anyone could hear through all the turmoil, he could. He was the most expert, the most experienced, sonarman on board.

So the fish was pinging. It must be close, close enough for the last-stage target-searching cycle to have been activated. It would home in on the echoes, drive in with the full speed of its little motor, until fatal contact was made. What was Buck doing?

"Twenty-six knots! Increasing slowly!" called Jerry Abbott.

"Open vents! Blow main ballast! One-minute blow, wide open!" Buck's orders reminded Rich of a time, under very similar circumstances indeed, when he had issued the identical command. Perhaps it would have the same effect.

The clank of the nearby vent opening. The noise of blowing. "Speed now twenty-seven!" said Jerry Abbott. "Still increasing very slowly."

"It's still pinging astern!" Schultz.

There was that tight grin on Buck's face. "Here we go, Skipper. The last maneuver!" He leaned out of the sonar room door, called, "Right full rudder! Leave it on! Thirty degrees down angle! Make your depth nine hundred feet! All hands stand by for steep angles!"

At twenty-seven knots, the *Manta* pitched into the curve like an aircraft doing a spiral dive. She listed twenty degrees or more into the turn, her bow swept downward, her gyrocompass repeaters began to spin like so many tops. Rich could feel the centrifugal forces on his body, and the slippery angle of the deck beneath him. Hanging on to the motor-generator stand outside the sonar room, he heard Abbott, gripping the rail a

few feet above him, say with forced calm, "Speed nineteen. Passing five hundred feet. Two complete circles."
There was a roaring somewhere in the water. Rich
could sense the furiously flailing screws stirring it up
in a way no submarine had ever stirred it up, spraying
a screaming froth of cavitation in all directions, a veri-
table column of violently disturbed water, a spiral,
vertical column 500 feet in total height, a corkscrew of
turbulent currents, upright in the sea, tight with the
tiny diameter that only a high-powered nuclear submarine could achieve, impervious to sonar, filled with
its own sound and its own echoing defiance.

"Eight hundred fifty feet! Leveling off!" said Jerry.

"Rudder amidships!"

"Rudder is amidships!" cried the helmsman, throwing his weight into the effort, supporting himself against
slipping by hanging on to his steering wheel, yet stopping the rudder exactly on center. *Manta's* deck flattened out with a smooth snap roll.

"Nine hundred feet!" called Abbott. "Speed increasing rapidly! Twenty-one . . . twenty-three . . . twenty-
seven . . . increasing slowly now . . . twenty-eight-a-
half . . ." Relieved of the slowing effect of the hard-
over rudder and planes, *Manta* was bouncing forward
almost as if shot from a bow, rocketing through the
sea depths with a reckless abandon as her powerful
heart rammed the superhot pressurized water—her life-
blood—through her steam generators.

"Mark your head!" said Buck.

"Mark your head!" shouted Jerry Abbott.

"Three-zero-four!" said the helmsman.

"Three-zero-four!" reported Jerry.

"Let her go three-one-zero!" said Buck. He picked
up the handset. "Maneuvering? Harry? How are you
doing back there?" He put it down, grinning that same
tight grin. "Rich, Harry says he's broken every operat-

ing rule old man Brighting and his engineering boys ever thought of, except one. He's still got a working reactor. But everything's heating up back there. Bearings and such. He can't go on indef—"

BLAM! A loud, somewhat muffled, strangely reverberating bang. Close, but not intimately close. "All ahead one-third!'" ordered Buck. "We beat it the hard way, Skipper!" He grabbed the handset again. "Harry, you did it! Cool her down gently back there, and treat her like the queen she is! May Martin Brighting live a thousand years!"

"Go to silent running, Buck! Shift to battery. Stop all machinery. *NOW!*"

Williams gave the order, then he demanded the customary damage reports. Midway through them, the puzzled look on his face suddenly vanished.

~~~~~~

"Buck, that was simply beautiful!" said Richardson. "That vertical corkscrew you made in the ocean must have seemed like a solid wall to the little fellow's sonar. So it drove into it and set off the detonator. Whatever made you think up that maneuver?"

"Maybe the air blowing was what actually did it, boss. We'll never know. I vaguely recall somebody showing me how to do that when some bad guys were after us, a long time ago, on some old sub the name of which I now forget."

"It was your spiral dive, Buck. That was what did it. I never saw a submarine handled that way before!"

"Actually, we'd practiced it. I was saving it to pull on you sometime," said Buck, pleased. "But we never did it with that kind of speed before, nor with this good an excuse to show it off!"

"Well, it sure saved our bacon, old man!" Richardson put his hand on Buck's shoulder. Then his smile faded. "How much farther to the *Cushing*'s plotted position?"

"Three miles by the dead-reckoning tracer. Good

thing we marked the DRT and set it on automatic when all this started. You should see what it looks like!"

"I've looked at it. It's wild, all right."

"I wish we could go faster."

"We mustn't be detected."

"I know. Do you really think the Russian may think we're sunk?"

"I'd bet on it, Buck. The last he saw of us was when we took off with his fish in hot pursuit. He must have heard all that noise you put in the water, and right after the fish exploded you slowed down to nothing. It's not like the two times he hit our decoys. So now he's waiting there, taking stock. If Keith's sunk too, we'll hear him start up and go away; if not, he'll be taking his time nosing around, because the *Cushing* would still be dangerous."

"And we're sneaking in, on the battery, running silent and at deep submergence, waiting for some kind of a false move."

"We can't leave Keith till we know for sure."

"Agreed. I'm trying to think of what to do if we find our other playmate again."

"The first thing is to find him before he knows we're still alive. The second thing is to kill him." Richardson's words were said without expression, almost as if he were referring to a routine happening. But Buck knew better.

A slight reduction in the urgency of *Manta*'s situation was recognized by the two mugs of black coffee they held. Schultz, who must have lost ten pounds in unevaporated perspiration, had refused relief and was still at the sonar console. A large towel, with which he repeatedly wiped his face, lay around his heavy shoulders. Neither Buck nor Rich noted the fact that they were in a nearly identical condition. Buck had tucked the end of his towel under his belt. Rich's was stuffed behind a wire cable in the corner of the sonar room.

The sonar room ventilation had been planned for only a single occupant, the man on watch. Apparently no one had considered that a skipper, accompanied by whatever superiors might be aboard, might choose to conduct vital ship control functions there also. Not that there was greater comfort anywhere else in the ship at this moment, for *Manta* had been running for several hours with all ventilation, and even the air-conditioning, shut down. The atmosphere inside the submarine was fetid, the heat unbearable, or nearly so. It *was* unbearable in the engineroom, where the temperature had at once risen to 150 degrees, and men had passed out. That compartment was now cooling, however, for its outer skin was not insulated. In the meantime an extra supply of salt tablets had been sent to the few men required to remain inside.

All metal portions of the submarine which in any way communicated to the sea outside were alive with condensation. It dripped off everything: pipes, stanchions, instrument foundations, light-fixture brackets, bulkheads. Everyone had sweat bursting out of his pores, even those few fortunates privileged to lie down somewhere for a legal snooze, and the puddles of condensed moisture on the decks made footing hazardous on the once polished linoleum.

But there were far more important things to think about, the primary one being how to remain alive.

Neither Rich nor Buck said anything for several minutes. Schultz brought both to his side with a simple factual statement: "I'm hearing something!"

"What's it like?"

By way of response, Schultz flipped a switch, spoke into a microphone mounted on the face of his console. "JT, do you hear pounding on the port bow?"

"Affirmative! I was just going to report it!"

"Well, don't you let me beat you to it again! You're supposed to hear sonic noises before I do!" Turning to his skipper, Schultz said, "Pounding, forty port."

Buck was already adjusting the spare set of earphones. Clamping them on his ears, he frowned with concentration and nodded his head at Rich. "Here!" He detached the left phone, handed it to Rich. Through it Rich could hear rapid intermittent blows of steel on steel, rhythmic for a short period, then spasmodic, then a flurry of hurried blows again. "Frantic" was the word that instantly came to Richardson's mind. Several more blows, then silence.

"I'd say that's someone hammering something with a hammer or mallet," said Rich. "Fairly close aboard. He sounded in a hurry to get it done."

"Repairing something, maybe?"

"My guess is it's Keith."

"Why not the other?"

"Keith was damaged. Neither sub would want to alert the other one. He might have had to do it."

"What do we do now?"

"Nothing. We wait. If it was Keith, the Soviet will come over to investigate. Maybe we'll be able to hear him."

"Schultz," said Buck, lifting one of the sonarman's earphones, bending to speak directly into the exposed ear, "any estimate of the distance to the pounding?"

"Close," said Schultz. He flipped his switch to activate the microphone connecting him to the JT sonic head. "JT, how far to the pounding?"

"Close. A mile, maybe. Sounded like it was being reflected from the ice." The JT man's answer came only into the earphones. Schultz had not activated the sonar room loudspeaker. Buck saw Richardson smiling at him.

"It could be Keith," Rich said. "If we've ever been quiet and listening, now's the time!"

Buck spoke softly into the telephone handset. "Silence, all hands. Absolute silence!" To Schultz he said, "Chief, we'll make a slow circle to clear your baffles aft. Search all around for any other noise, and check the bearing of this one whenever you can." Replacing the earphone, he felt, rather than saw, the short jerk of the sonarman's head which was supposed to pass for a nod of understanding.

Again, the deep silence of waiting. Slowly, *Manta* described two complete circles. She was at maximum depth, far below the authorized test depth, as deep as Buck dared take her, sweating figuratively and literally both in her own hull and in the persons of her crew. The squeeze of millions of tons of Arctic seawater— over 300 tons on each square foot—pressed upon her body. All her machinery was stilled. Her battery, which kept her sonars functioning, her planes operative and her two propellers slowly turning, was totally silent. The occasional splash of a drop of condensate, too heavy to remain on the surface where it had congealed, was loud. The silence was that of death. An apt similitude, for death would probably come out of it. For someone.

The third circle was nearly finished. "We'll steady on the bearing where we heard the pounding, run about a mile, and circle again," said Buck.

"Right," said Rich, indicating by his expression that he could think of no better action.

Manta slowly swam on the ordered course, began to circle, in the opposite direction. "For variety," said Buck, with the familiar tight smile. For more than an hour, switching occasionally to relieve their arms and hands, Rich and Buck had held the spare set of earphones to their ears. They were beginning to think of themselves as Schultz, long since, must have subconsciously felt of himself. They were large, amorphous beings, spread-eagled in the ocean, with antennas stretching in all directions; antennas floating into the infinite reaches, gathering in all the droplets of information, of sounds modern and primeval, listening with every sense of their beings, waiting. Waiting with limitless patience. Waiting for some sign.

All three men heard the report from the JT receiver when it came. "More pounding. Quiet like. It's above us, I think." Schultz nodded vigorously, pointed to his own earphones. He, too, had heard something, although neither Rich nor Buck had noted it.

Buck flipped the switch Schultz had been using. "What's it like, JT?"

"Sounds like a rubber hammer hitting something. Not iron. Maybe it's hitting wood."

"Keith!" said Rich. "He's okay! They're making repairs! It's got to be him!"

And then Rich felt a blow on his hip. Schultz was pressing both earphones against his head. He was gazing at his sonar scope, but his eyes were far away, far out in the ocean, which, for him, was totally represented by this circular fluorescent tube.

"What do you hear, Chief?" But Schultz could not hear the question. They waited, agonizing, wanting him to speak, not willing to break into his concentration. Finally he put his finger on his scope, tapping it gently with the fingernail.

"I hear something," he said. "About here!"

"Is it the Soviet sub?"

"I think so. It's getting louder, but it's still faint."

Coached by Schultz, Rich and Buck were soon able to hear the noise themselves, and finally there came the verdict which made all the waiting, and worry, and discomfort, of the past few hours worthwhile. "It's him. That's the same signature we've been hearing."

"Skipper," said Richardson, "I'd give my right arm to be able to see up!"

"So would I, boss," returned Buck, unaccountably pleased with the unexpected salutation. "We'll raise the 'scopes as soon as the hoists can lift them against sea pressure."

"Have you calculated the extra stress?"

"Yes. It's well within the tensile strength of our hoist rods. The problem is that our hydraulic hoist cylinders don't have the area to overcome sea pressure at our present depth. They can't lift them below about two hundred feet. Maybe not then."

"Well, it sure would be good to do this deeper, but let's stop our rise as soon as the 'scopes can lift. I'd like to be under both subs, with them silhouetted against the light coming through the ice cover. If we can only see what we're doing, we might be able to figure out something. We'll only have one shot, you know!"

Buck knew very well. Once the enemy realized he had been fired on by the submarine he thought he had eliminated, there would not be another chance. Without speaking, Buck reached for the periscope hoist controls, put them both on Raise.

Plot and the DRT both indicated they were under the calculated position of the immobile *Cushing,* and Tom Clancy had been directed to bring *Manta* upward very slowly. A small air bubble in safety tank had started the ascent, and now he was judiciously venting it inboard—into the interior of the *Manta*—so that no betraying air could escape into the water. The enemy submarine, estimated to be a mile or so away, was approaching cautiously. A Mark Fourteen torpedo salvo, judged to have the best chance of being immune to whatever exotic defense system he had, nevertheless required point-blank range and a positive depth determination.

The torpedoes themselves had been modified to accept depth settings of up to one hundred fifty feet. A minimum setting of ninety feet would guarantee safety of the *Cushing* resting against the ice, even if she happened to be in the line of fire. But the vertical dimension of the enemy sub, except in the small conning tower and bridge area, might be as little as thirty feet. The depth setting chosen would have to be within this thirty-foot spread. And, of course, the torpedoes would have to be correctly aimed.

Manta had passed the two-hundred-foot mark before Jerry Abbott, at the periscope station, called his superiors from the sonar room. " 'Scopes starting up!" he reported.

"Holding her at one-eight-five, Captain!" called Clancy. Jerry Abbott quietly slipped into the sonar room as Rich and Buck took his place at the periscope station. Both 'scopes were rising slowly.

"They'll be mighty hard to turn when they're up, Skipper," warned Buck.

"Can't be helped," grunted Rich impatiently. He grasped the hoist rods with both hands, tried to force his periscope to rise faster. It did no good. The progress of the bottom of the periscope out of its well was excruciatingly slow. With his hands on the barrel or the hoist rods, he could feel the movement, but there was hardly any way to discern it in its shiny steel surface, which was the same from top to bottom. Lights had been dimmed in the control room because of the limited illumination expected in the water. Looking down into the well, Rich was gratified to see faint light shining out of the exit pupil, striking the oily surface of the

narrow steel well. At least it appeared there might be
enough to see by!

Buck had the shorter periscope, as was his right because its eyepiece would be the first out of the well and
it had the greater light-gathering power. He fixed himself to it as soon as it came above deck level, slowly
rose with it. Heaving it around with difficulty he said,
"The bottom of the ice is almost white. It's translucent.
But there's no black hull anywhere!"

One minute later Rich duplicated Buck's action. It
was much easier to swing the periscope while it was
rising than after it had reached the top of its ascent.
"The same," said Rich. "Nothing in sight!" It was a
disappointment, but Richardson told himself they
should not have expected to see the *Cushing* immediately. Now would be the time for Keith to do more
pounding, but they had not been willing to risk calling
him on the underwater telephone. Either the intruding
submarine or Keith's would come into view sooner or
later. Patience!

After two hours of lugging on the periscope handles,
Richardson's arms were sore. He suspected Buck's were
too. He would have liked to give up his vigil to someone else, Jerry Abbott, for instance. But he could not,
would not. Neither would Buck, he knew.

A thought struck him. Not knowing *Manta* was there,
if Keith were to get an unexpected sonar contact he
might shoot a Mark Forty at it. Well, this risk would
have to be accepted. Keith would not shoot unless sure
of his target. He would keep on hoping *Manta* had survived, would know his friends would return if able,
might even divine their stratagem. Because it was what
he would have done. Then Rich's thoughts took another
tack. *Cushing*'s sonar was at least as good, and a great
deal more modern, than *Manta*'s. If *Manta* could hear
the approaching enemy, the *Cushing* should also—un-

less, this time, sound conditions right up against the ice were poor.

"I'm having Jerry swing us around to put our bow on the noise," said Buck's voice in his ear. "He's drifting slowly right. Plot calls his speed at four knots, range no more than half a mile." How could they know that? It must be a sheer guess. It did make sense—maybe because he wanted it to. "Jerry says Schultz gives it half a mile also." Now, that was good news. Schultz, at least, had something to go on, and to him the sonar was an extension of his senses. Half a mile away, a thousand yards. How far could one see horizontally? Not far. A ship would have to be almost directly overhead for its hull to be outlined against the dull light through the ice. Where the devil was Keith? Why didn't he start pounding again? And had he hauled up his anchor? If not, the chain would present an additional hazard.

Another hour passed; an hour and a half. Rich's shoulders were aching with his unaccustomed straining. Following Buck's instructions, Jerry had been slowly traversing the area where *Cushing* should be, keeping *Manta*'s bow whenever possible on the bearing of the enemy to reduce the possibility of detection. The Soviet submarine, also, must be searching. Probably in much the same way, and with no more to go on.

And then Jerry Abbott suddenly jumped on to the periscope platform. "He's pounding again!" he whispered. "Very close!"

"Bearing?" said Buck.

"No bearing! Schultz says it's right overhead! He and JT hear it all around the dial!"

"Even if we don't see Keith, Buck," said Rich, "that will bring our playmate over here."

"We're ready!" said Buck. "But we have to be sure which is which before we shoot!"

"What do you think I've been thinking about!"

Both men had kept their eyes to the eyepieces, faces pressed tightly to the face guards of their respective periscopes. And then Buck saw the *Cushing*. "I've got Keith in sight!" he said. "Bearing, mark! Almost straight up! As high as you can elevate!"

"Two-four-eight," said the quartermaster, who had been hovering nearby, almost totally idle, for hours.

"Put me on him!" Forgetting he was not the skipper of the submarine, Rich had barked the order as if he were. No one seemed to notice, or think anything of it. He felt someone's hands, the quartermaster's, helping swing the heavy periscope. It was already at full elevation.

There, in silhouette, surprisingly near and quite distinct in outline, was the unmistakable shape of a U.S. missile submarine! He was looking from beneath, saw a fisheye view, but there could be no mistake. He searched the bow section, saw the thin line of the anchor chain hanging vertically down. Keith was snug against the underside of the ice pack. He might even be under a relatively thin place, for there seemed to be considerable light around him. Now where's the other one? As he thought the question, he heard Buck ask it, and Abbott's answer.

"Very close! On zero-two-three, coming in slow!"

"We may see him in a minute, Buck! I hope he's shallower than we are!"

"He will be, boss! He won't be able to raise his periscopes any deeper than we can. Probably not as deep. He'll be coming in to look Keith over!"

"That's the way I figure it, too. He'll be checking for the damage his fish did.' '

"You know what he'll do if he thinks it'll be too big a job to bring her in, don't you?"

"There's no doubt what his instructions are." Rich

spoke very quietly. The thought had been growing in his mind for the past several hours. Dead men tell no tales. Enough of life, treasure and national prestige had been risked in this operation already. A negative decision on the part of the foreign submarine skipper would dictate another torpedo, and one for the *Manta,* too, once her continued existence was inevitably revealed. The silence of the sea would claim yet two more victims, and no one would ever know what had happened under the silent white overlay which had, since before history, sealed the mysteries of the Arctic.

Some portions of the U.S. Navy, aware of *Manta*'s rescue attempt, would assume that it had gone too far, had been too unorthodox. Ergo, it must have resulted in disaster to both submarines—a comforting thought for the mediocre mind, illogical though it might be. Poorly informed speculation, nonetheless articulate, would suggest dozens of ingenious solutions of the mystery, some of them ranging into the occult. Some would even have both submarines transported through time warps, or black holes in space. Nowhere in the West, probably, except in some secret drawer of the U.S. National Security Council, would there be an accurate appraisal of what had most likely actually occurred.

Rich and Buck had kept their periscopes trained on the bearings given by Schultz, relayed by Jerry Abbott, and they saw the enemy submarine simultaneously.

She was moving very slowly, with three periscopes up, passing between the *Manta* and the *Cushing* at a depth roughly halfway between them. She had a very large bulbous bow, a small bridge structure well forward, a conical stern section and a large single propeller, barely turning over. She was larger than the *Manta* but considerably smaller than the *Cushing.* As she came into view what instantly struck both Americans was the strange structure wrapped around her bridge and forward portion. It looked almost like an afterthought to her design and added greatly to the outsize bulge of her bows. Massive, heavy, askew, deformed even—and then Rich realized what it was. Great steel beams and thick protective plates, built around the sleek basic form. The askew condition was due to some strong force that had bent and twisted them out of their original shape!

"That's the damage he took when he hit Keith," said Rich.

"Right, boss! I was wondering. That's got to be it!"

"What depth do you figure him at?"

"He's looking her over through his 'scopes. So he must be at about the same depth we were when we did. Keel depth a hundred forty or so. Thank goodness we're well below him. It's dark below. There's no way he could see us." Buck spoke rapidly, in a low tone suited to the dim light in the control room and the secrecy of their effort.

"Hear us, either, the way you've got this boat of yours silenced."

"Ship. We've got her pretty quiet, all right. Damn good thing!"

"Ship. I was estimating his depth as a hundred thirty feet. We can hear him plain. Keith should, too."

"Yes, but he's been tied up with those emergency repairs."

Rich and Buck had become growingly conscious of the noise level of the enemy submarine. Schultz and Abbott had been hearing it for a long time through the sonar equipment. So had the JT. The enemy skipper had evidently shifted to the silent mode, but he had his reactor running—heavy machinery of some kind, anyway—and there was a strong hum, a whine of high-speed gears, which was what Schultz had heard at first. Now, at close range, the sound of the gears was coming directly through the water into *Manta*'s hull, where it could be heard by all hands. The eerie feeling associated with the foreign noise, the noise which had done its best to destroy them, affected everyone.

"Keith's bound to hear him now, but the bastard's too close to shoot. When he moves off a bit Keith may try a shot. That's a chance the Russian knows he's taking, but he's still got that thing that stops electric torpedo motors, and by now he knows it works. We don't have it, and we'd better be on the other side of the *Cushing* when Keith shoots!"

"Listen!" A series of short, staccato whistles came over the Gertrude speaker. "Keith's sending RI KE! There it is again! RI KE! He wants to know if it's us!"

"Well, we can't answer him! Not yet, anyway."

Rich had been gradually training his periscope to the left, following the enemy submarine. So had Buck. He could feel Buck's nearness, the smell of his sweat, the occasional foot in the way of his own. The intruder was slowly passing beyond the *Cushing*. Soon he would turn, probably, for another pass on her other side. "All right, Buck. I think this is our chance. You know what to do!"

The *Manta* swam slowly, silently, in the opposite direction, turned. Buck was using as much speed as he dared. At the depth, her screws were silent.

"We're ready forward," said Deedee Brown. "Depth set, one-two-oh feet. I need a range and bearing!"

"He's turning toward," called Schultz in the stillness, shouting from the sonar room. "He's swinging to the right! He's broadside to us right now! Shoot him! Shoot him right now!"

"Make haste slowly," said Buck. "Make sure we don't miss. Deedee, set in starboard ninety. He'll go ahead emergency as soon as he hears us, so spread the fish forward to cover a ten-knot speed increase. Schultz"

—he raised his voice to be sure the sonarman would hear—"can you separate the *Cushing*'s echo from the target's?"

Jerry Abbott jumped back into the sonar shack. Unnecessarily. "Yes, sir!" Schultz, beseeching: "I've got them both! He's the far one!"

"Very well," said Buck. "Get me a single-ping range and bearing!"

A wail from Schultz. A cry of pain. "He's fired! *Cushing*'s fired!"

"He's not shooting at us!" Buck's voice was loud in the dead silence. "Single-ping range! Now!"

The ping went out instantaneously, so loud that everyone jumped a second time. "We're on automatic to Deedee!" assured Abbott.

"Set!" said Brown.

"Fire!" said Buck Williams. The word was an expletive.

Unlike the new torpedoes, which swam out of their tubes silently on their own power, the older ones had to be expelled, shot out by a blast of water. In the forward torpedo room the firing ram slammed back and forth four times, resounding loudly, masochistically, throughout the interior of the ship. Four massive waterhammer jolts shook her hull, ten seconds apart. Four times the compressed air returning the ram to battery snarled and snorted through its control valves and the vents at the end of the stroke. Four old Mark Fourteen torpedoes, each following ten seconds after its predecessor, evenly diverging to the right, roared out of their torpedo tubes. They headed directly for the *Cushing*. A few hundred yards beyond her was the enemy.

"He's got his halo up!" Abbott, calling from the sonar shack. No pretense of silence now. There was noise in the water. Lots of noise. *Manta* had suddenly transformed herself into the noisiest submarine ever in the Arctic Ocean. She would have made a huge spike in every sonar within miles. And four old steam-driven torpedoes, lovingly overhauled but roaring like banshees because that was the way they had been built, were driving madly through the sea, their single-stage turbines blaring at high, clattering pitch. *"Cushing* fired a Mark Forty! It's gone into the halo! . . . And, that's it! It's stopped! We heard the motor stop!" Jerry was at last excited. He could be forgiven. So could Schultz, after twelve hours of steady concentration on his sonar, watching an underwater game in which his own life was one of the pawns.

"That shot from Keith was his way of telling the Russian something," said Rich. "Keith was hoping he wouldn't have time, with the short range, to get up that halo defense of his."

"At least, now Keith knows he's not alone around here!" said Buck.

The enemy submarine's captain heard the single-ping range being taken, instantly knew what it portended, instantly ordered emergency speed. The whine of her adversary's madly cavitating propeller filled *Manta's* sonar shack. Schultz later claimed he had also heard her rudder slam hard over against the stops. As it did so, the thin fan of torpedoes, now covering a spread of two ship lengths, passed under the *Cushing,* kept on going. . . .

The intruder heard them coming, heard their roaring grow suddenly much louder when part of it was no longer screened by the helpless bulk of the big missile submarine. Her screw had begun to bite. Maybe she could get clear. She was moving ahead, but slowly, so slowly, and the torpedoes were so close. . . .

The first torpedo, aimed to hit amidships in case the

enemy did not move, missed astern by a large margin. The second missed by only a few feet. The fourth and last inevitably missed ahead, for the third one struck home, and exploded.

Whatever their shortcomings of modernity, Mark Fourteen torpedoes packed far more explosive than the newer, far more exotic, antisubmarine torpedoes. Their mission, after all, had been to sink big surface ships. For this, hundreds of pounds of the most powerful explosive were needed. If possible, the bottom of the target should be beaten in, her keel shattered, or her whole side torn off, from turn of the bilge to the main deck. By contrast, only a small hole, merely big enough to let in the sea, is needed to upset a submarine's delicate submerged buoyancy and send it to the bottom forever.

Assisted by the rigid incompressibility of seawater and the poised pressure ready to squeeze everything together, invade every opening, the detonation of 800 pounds of torpex was cataclysmic. The entire middle of the enemy submarine disintegrated, blown into thousands of pieces, many of them tiny shards of metal with razor-sharp edges, all of them hurled with bullet-like velocity in all directions. Steel bulkheads—or portions of them still remaining—were penetrated by them. No life could exist near them; but all life anywhere near had been obliterated already. And the grenadelike fragments themselves did not travel far, for the waiting sea, in its instantaneous rush resembling a bomb exploding inward, swallowed everything up.

The two halves of the submarine, the propeller still spinning rapidly on the cone-shaped stern, were driven apart by the explosion. Then they upended and sank separately to the bottom of the Fletcher Abyssal Plain, 12,000 feet down.

* * *

"Keith," said Buck softly on the turned-down UQC, "it's Buck. Do you read?"

"Affirmative, old man. What a relief to hear your voice! I'll never in my life forget that uproar when your firing ram started cycling over there behind us! I thought I'd faint! And then when we heard your fish coming right at us, well, I kept thinking it had to be you, but I had heart failure anyway, all over again!"

"Sorry we couldn't warn you in advance. We had to let him keep thinking he'd sunk us. But how're you doing? The boss wants to know."

Keith's exuberant voice dropped. "Not too good, Buck. That last fish of his hit in the double hull section, back aft. That was lucky because we're not taking water very fast. But we can't stop the leak. I've had to abandon the auxiliary machinery compartment. We've got everyone forward and the compartment's pressurized. For now we can hold her by pumping our variable tanks, and then we'll hold her with the main ballast tanks. But the leak's in the overhead, and we can't stop it with air pressure or anything! I'm afraid we're done!" Keith had evidently placed his hand over his mouth so that his words would not be overheard.

"What's the time, Keith? Rich is right here. Do you read me?"

Again the muffled voice, hand still guarding it. "I get you. We can hold out for two or three hours more, I guess. Not much more. I'm putting a down angle on her right now, to get the stern up and reduce sea pressure. But that can't last. The ballast tank around the compartment is wrecked, too, of course. We're running the drain pump but the water's gaining. Finally we'll be hanging on our forward ballast tanks with an up angle, and when she gets heavy enough she'll drift away from the ice."

Richardson and Williams conferred hurriedly, then

Rich picked up the mike. "Keith, how many wet suits have you?"

"Four, I think—yes, four."

"We have six. Three qualified scuba divers. How many do you have?"

"Two. Some others have done it for recreation."

"All right. Listen. Stand by to transfer your men to the *Manta* through the escape hatches! Get your scuba experts suited up, and one of the amateurs. We'll do the same. Our boys will bring our extra suits and tanks over to you. Buck is bringing the *Manta* up alongside you right now. We'll rig a line between us, as close as we can snub it. The divers can guide the men across the line and into our hatch, and then cycle the gear back to you. First thing you do is rig one of your deck cleats, and then rig your forward escape chamber so you can use the lower hatch and keep an air bubble inside. Can you handle that?"

"Affirmative! You bet!" Keith had taken his hand away from his mouth. He was letting everyone in the control room hear. "Our heading's two-eight-three on the grid. We're steady, not drifting. Been like this since we stopped coasting. That was quite a ride you took us for just before the line broke, by the way. We coasted for nearly twenty minutes! I'll start briefing our people right away. Be ready for you as soon as you can get alongside!" There was a pause, then Keith said, his voice again muffled, "You sure you can do this okay? That's taking a big risk with another sub to bring it alongside in midocean submerged like this!"

"We'll worry about that, Keith! Don't you bother! The water's still, here under all that ice, and we'll come up real slow and easy, until we're floating against the ice too. It's worth a few scratches and dents if we touch. Go and get your crew lined up. Four men at a time will take a while, and the scuba men will have to be changed off, too."

Tired as they were, Buck Williams' crew showed their professionalism by the way they handled their submarine. Buck positioned her exactly where he wanted her, assisted by periscope angles, Schultz on the sonar, and even an extraordinary solution done on the torpedo date computer—which, however, came too late for use except as a check. Then Tom Clancy and his diving control group caused her to rise slowly and gently, adjusting for gradually reducing salinity of the water as he did so. The *Cushing*'s underwater television camera, with its lights, illuminated the entire scene and enabled Keith to help by coaching Buck.

When it was finally necessary for Buck to house his periscopes for fear of striking the ice, the two submarines were on nearly opposite headings, bows overlapping by some fifty feet and twenty feet apart. *Manta,* because of her smaller size and the missile submarine's down angle, came to rest with her deck about ten feet higher than the *Cushing*'s, but that was of little moment. As soon as all relative motion ceased, the hatches on the two submarines opened, and a black-rubber-suited figure with silver tanks on his back appeared on the deck of each. Each man had a line attached to his middle, which he clipped to the safety track on deck, and another on the large deck wrench he carried. Someone inside the open hatches of each ship was assisting, and after some difficulty, in both cases an extra man had to swim out to assist with the cleats. In their condition of near weightlessness it was impossible for a single person to place sufficient leverage on the wrench, a situation anticipated by the experienced divers.

Then a heavy line was brought out from the *Cushing,* fine four-inch white nylon, weightless in water and strong. The eye spliced into one end was looped around the opened cleat in *Manta*'s forecastle, the standing part snubbed securely and then belayed to the one on *Cushing*'s rounded bow. Buck had maneuvered the *Manta* so that the two escape hatches were virtually abeam of each other. Then one of the *Manta* divers carried a sack of scuba equipment over to the *Cushing* and handed it into the open hatch.

"Our men say two will be enough to monitor the transfers," said Keith. "That will give us more suits, and we'll be able to transfer more men per group."

"Maybe, but we still have to carry back the empties to you. The extra scubamen can stand by, over here, and we'll shift them when they get tired. Let's start with three monitors," said Richardson. It was a conservative decision he was later to regret deeply.

Slowly, seven men at a time, the transfer began. Seven men, with their tanks, filled the *Manta*'s escape chamber to capacity, or nearly so. Then it was necessary to close the outer door, quickly release the pressure, and open the lower door into her forward torpedo room. The procedure was speeded by permitting great quantities of water to dump into the room instead of the more tidy, but slower method of draining it through the drain valve, and aboard *Manta* there were many hands available to strip the newcomers of their scuba equipment, bundle it hurriedly into sacks and prepare it for the return journey to the *Cushing*.

The water was cold, several degrees below the freezing point of fresh water, but not uncomfortable with the suits on, the *Cushing* men said. Not, certainly, in comparison with the discomfort in store for them otherwise! The regular scubamen, trained and aware of what to expect, said only that it was "not too bad." Enthusiasm for the work they were doing, frequent forced rest stops inside a relatively warm rescue chamber while the next transfer was being readied or suits being switched around made it easy, they said. Whenever feasible, they took another turn on the rope stretched between the two ships, to keep it taut and to prove that moderate effort, extended over a reasonable period, could actually move something as big as a submarine.

Rich finally had to order the divers to shift their jobs after an hour in the water. This was the limiting time according to the instruction manual, and he also had them stop pulling on the line between the ships. *Manta* had rigged in her bow planes, so there was no danger to them from possible contact with *Cushing,* but there was no need to force the two ships to touch when things were going so well.

But seven men per transfer, opening and shutting hatches, and changing equipment for each group, took time. One hundred twenty-seven men, *Cushing*'s actual complement counting her skipper, would take eighteen trips, with one man left over. At ten minutes per group, the fastest time achieved, eighteen transfers would take three hours. A nineteenth transfer would be necessary for the one man still aboard the *Cushing.* Richardson knew well who would be that last man.

Nor would he ever be able to forget the sinking feeling in his chest when one of the resting scubamen reported the *Cushing* to be higher in the water, her bow now conveniently level with the *Manta.* This could only mean that she was no longer able to maintain the down angle Keith had programmed to reduce the water pressure, and hence the force of the leak, in the damaged compartment!

Eleven transfers had been made. On the UQC Rich told Keith to hurry, that he would authorize eight men per trip, with only two monitoring topside. Keith's voice told him what he was afraid to hear: the ship would not last more than half an hour longer.

Then more disaster. Two of the scuba tanks ran
out of compressed air. They were recharged immediately, but it took time. Then one of the mouthpieces,
too anxiously taken from one of the transferees,
dropped and was damaged. Unusable. More time lost.

"Boss," said Keith over the underwater telephone,
"we have a full outfit of regular escape breathing gear,
with hoods. If we leave off the tanks, we might be able
to reduce the suiting-up time."

"Try it with half of the men!" The stratagem was
successful, the men with the hoods being helped by the
others, and the next time all but two used hoods instead of tanks. But now *Cushing* was floating with a
noticeable up-angle, and its gradual increase could be
seen by the scubamen topside.

"We can't hold her, boss! Depth's increasing! I'm
going to let out a group without waiting for the wet
suits!" Richardson and Williams, without the underwater TV, could only imagine the scantily clad men,
wearing nothing but their regular clothing, a breathing
bag with oxygen, and a yellow, Plexiglas-faced hood
over their heads, being herded out of the *Cushing*'s
airlock. The scubamen would help them to the now
tightly stretched nylon line which was beginning to
take some of the negative buoyancy of the missile submarine, and along it into *Manta*'s airlock. The change
in procedure caught the operating crew in *Manta*'s torpedo room as they were opening the lower escape
chamber hatch, getting the previous group out of the
chamber. The instructions received only minutes before
had been to bundle the suits quickly into sacks, forgetting the tanks, and give them immediately to the waiting
scubaman, who would take them back into the airlock.
Not till then would the lower hatch be closed. Of
course, the upper one could not be opened for the same

period. A small confusion, quickly straightened out—but at the expense of another vital minute or two.

The men came in, nine of them, faint with the cold, gasping, but alive.

"Twenty-three men left, Rich! We're putting ten of them out this time! It's all our hatch can hold! Stand by to grab them!"

There was no way to communicate with the men topside, except through a hastily generated system of pounding on the hull. The situation had been explained, however, the last time a scubaman appeared in the escape trunk. The number of bangs on the hull indicated the number of men to be found in *Cushing*'s trunk when the hatch was opened. As the tenth bang resounded, the rope connecting the two submarines was extending downward at an appreciable angle. The action of the line was causing the sinking *Cushing* to drift slowly under the *Manta,* or pulling the *Manta* over her, which was the same thing. The line was stretched to its uttermost, a fact the divers recognized. Hurriedly, they urged the men onward and up the line. The escapees pulled themselves up rapidly along it. Then, near the *Cushing,* but with a snap audible also inside the *Manta,* the line broke.

The released nylon snapped backward like the rubber band it had virtually become, but the vicious whiplash was subdued by the water. Even so, the short end of it struck the scubaman on the missile submarine's rounded foredeck, knocking him off. At that instant the two submarines touched, *Manta*'s keel scraping across the bullet-shaped bow of the *Cushing*. Pulling himself back by his safety line, the scubaman found to his horror that the line was jammed in its slot on *Cushing*'s deck, where the *Manta*'s scraping passage had crimped the recessed track. He could feel the pressure rapidly increasing in his ears. Frantically, he struggled with the belt around his middle. It seemed jammed too. He let out all his breath, tried to force the heavy web belt over his hips. It would not move. The buckle was suddenly too complicated to operate. Desperately, he tried to shove it over his shoulders, but this, too, was impossible. He had forgotten about the tanks on his back, and now he had lost his mouthpiece. A huge dark shadow, the *Manta,* and safety, was just above him. He could almost reach it with his hand! He grabbed for his mouthpiece, found it hanging down on its hose, jammed it into his mouth. His lungs were tight. There was pressure on his chest. No air in his lungs. No help for it; he would have to inhale water, swallow it. Then he could get air! But instead, a violent coughing fit seized him. He lost the mouthpiece again. He could not release himself from the *Cushing.* With a last convulsive effort, he managed to yank the toggles which inflated his life jacket. The rubber-impregnated fabric closed around his chest, lifted him to the limit of the tether still connecting him to the sinking submarine. But now he could not move. He was like a kite on the end of a string, floating above the slowly descending *Cushing.* Despairingly, he saw the shadow of the *Manta* receding. He reached for it with both arms, and knew that he was doomed.

Three of the ten hooded men had got into the *Manta*'s rescue chamber before the line broke. Two more were nearly there, managed to get in on their own. The remaining scubaman got two more in, but three floated away, lifted up against the ice cover by the air in their hoods. Heedless of his instructions, he released himself from his safety line, swam after them. Grabbing the nearest one, he motioned downward. Seventeen feet below, the submarine's dark upper works were visible. The man nodded, tried to paddle down-

ward in a vertical, upright position so that the air
would remain in the hood. He could not. The scubaman squeezed the hood, forced a bubble of air out, but
it immediately expanded again with air from the breathing bag. He tried wrenching the hood off, tried impro-
vising instant buddy-breathing technique with his single
mouthpiece, but the man could not, or would not,
understand.

Anxiously, the scubaman swam down, tried to enter
Manta's rescue chamber. It was closed. The men inside
were transferring into the interior of the sub. He
banged on the deck with the hammer tied there for the
purpose, heard the answering sledgehammer thump.
The door opened after an interminable time, and he
entered. Minutes later, he emerged again, this time
with an assistant, not dressed, who would remain in
the airlock. He carried a length of line with a buoy
on the end. Swiftly he knotted the line outside the open
outer hatch, released the buoy, followed it up, riding
with the line under his arm. He was not far from the
men in the hoods, who were floating quietly with their
heads against the underside of the ice. He reached the
nearest, gripped his arm—and recoiled in horrified dismay. The arm floated downward limply, remained hanging at a small angle with the rest of his body. The man
was dead.

So were the other two. But as the scubaman was
investigating them, two others appeared, and then four
more, floating up swiftly from below the *Manta*. Rapidly he swam to each, dragged him to the buoyed line,
indicated he should haul himself down it. Gratefully,
worriedly, they obeyed. The next to last got only partway down, then stopped, his hands and feet desperately
gripping the line. The man above was forced to stop
also. When the scubaman finally was able to turn his
attention away from the others to go back and clear

the tangle, he had to pry both bodies free. Two more
yellow hoods appeared below him, coming from deep
beneath the *Manta*. Helplessly, fatalistically, he let go
of the stiffened body in his arms, let it float away,
lunged for the newcomers. He intercepted one before
he had reached the ice, was able to get him to the
buoyed line, start him down. The other hit the ice,
but he was able to get the buoy to him, and he accompanied him partway as he haltingly pulled himself
down.

There were five dead bodies floating in yellow,
Plexiglas-faced hoods, up against the ice. The scubaman swam to each, felt him carefully, then on to the
next, repeating the procedure. Finally he left them and
swam down to the submarine. The two men he had
just sent down were holding the knotted end of the line
near the closed hatch. They were still alive, moving
feebly. They could not last long in this temperature.
He banged on the hatch, banged again. Finally an
answering thump, and a minute later it opened. By this
time both men were unconscious. He shoved them inside, yelled to the suited diver waiting for him with
head above the waterline in the chamber, "Watch for
more guys coming up! I'll be right back, but these guys
may have had it!" Then he pushed him out and shut
the door.

He was in time, *Manta*'s doctor assured him, though
barely. But when he got back outside there was no one
in sight except the scubaman who had taken his place,
and the five hooded bodies above, against the ice. In
vain they searched for the missing diver who had been
on the *Cushing*'s deck. He was an experienced, qualified
scubaman. He would not have panicked, would have
found means to free himself from the sinking missile
submarine's deck. But he was nowhere to be seen. Ten
minutes, fifteen, they waited. No more yellow hoods

came up from the depths below. No welcome dark-suited comrade appeared. The five bodies overhead stood watch, dangling upright against the ice, their hoods slightly flattened against it, their bodies hanging loosely, limply, arms slightly away from their torsos. They had so nearly made it! Their heads were on the same level as the top of the *Manta*'s sail. One could so easily swim the few yards up to them, grab their feet, and pull them down. . . .

Disconsolately, the two scubamen reentered the escape trunk, closed the door, and made ready to report that there was no further action topside.

"Rich," said Keith, speaking over the UQC in a quiet, yet tense voice, "we got everybody out but four. Jim Hanson and Curt Taylor are with me still, and chiefs Hollister and Mirklebaum. I'm afraid we're going to have to ride her on down, boss. I hope all the others made it!"

"Five, Keith. You didn't count yourself!"

"That's right, five. Did you get all the rest?"

"I'm sure we did, Keith. We're still taking a muster with your list. Howie Trumbull is in charge. And I have your ship's log and your unfinished report. You can rest easy. All your men are okay!" Richardson was far from sure of the truth of this, for although he could not see, he had been receiving frequent reports and had an excellent idea of the struggle taking place outside the hull, only a few feet from where he stood in *Manta*'s control room. "Is there anything at all you can do, Keith?" he could not refrain from asking. "Is all your variable water out? Safety and negative and everything? How about your anchor and chain? Could you try a big bubble in main ballast? Couldn't that boost you up for one final escape? One more time would do it."

"Come on, old man, we've done all that. We all tried to pile in the hatch the last time, but the ship

upended, and everybody fell down against the bulkhead. They were trying to make it back up, but there
wasn't time, so I had to slam the hatch on the two that
were in already. Now we're at two hundred feet, and
I'm back in the control room sitting on the bulkhead
to reach the UQC. It's down between my feet. We can
hear the air bubbling out of number-one main ballast
through the flooding holes. We're making our last dive,
and it will be a deep one."

Richardson felt something salty in his face. More
than one submariner in a sinking submarine had closed
the hatch that might have led to escape over his own
head, thus closing the trap upon himself as well as the
shipmates trapped with him. This was precisely what
Keith had done, with life prolonged at his option, with
two men, destined for survival, already in the escape
chamber and waiting. Rich knew without its being said
that Keith had been handling the lower hatch himself,
had had it yawning open above; or perhaps, since *Cushing* had upended, was now vertical in the water, it had
been by that time alongside of him—and had consciously chosen not to enter it. In fact, since he had
personally shut the hatch himself, he must actually have
entered the escape chamber, taken hold of the hatch,
and pulled it shut behind him as he backed out! Captain
of the ship, he could not leave so long as there were
men for whom he was responsible still aboard. Faced
with his life's climactic decision, and only seconds to
make it, he had chosen instantly. Or, possibly, he had
firmly made up his mind before.

What to do? What to say? What to say to one's own
deep, personal friend, now about to be stilled forever?
Rich felt his eyes stinging. There were tears there. His
nose hurt. There was a knot at its base, at the top of
his mouth. He gripped the mike to control himself,

strained with both hands to squeeze it away, finally said in a voice he could not recognize, "We understand what you're saying, Keith, old friend. Buck's here too. All that we've heard will be reported fully, and believe me, there's going to be some truth told when we get back. We're sorry, Keith. Believe me, we're so terribly sorry. What can we do for you and the fellows with you? Tell me. Anything. It's a promise!" Something like a vise was closing down Richardson's throat.

"Tell our wives that we love them. No, Stew Mirklebaum says he's divorced. The rest of us. Mirklebaum says to find Sarah Schnee—Schneehaulder"—Keith spelled the name—"one of the fellows you've picked up will know who she is. Tell her he's thinking of her. Jim Hanson wants you to tell Mary he loves her and little Jimmy. Larry Hollister sends love to Eleanor and says not to forget they'll meet by the first bloom of the lilac tree. Curt says Suzanne know he's always hers. And tell Peggy and Ruthie for me"—here, Keith's steady voice broke for a moment—"tell them I love them, and would like to have been able to get Peggy that little garden in the picket-fenced yard that I always promised her. Someday we'd have had it, too. Tell her the Navy didn't let me down. It did all it could, and so did you and Buck. There's nothing more anyone could do than you did for us. Tell her we're not suffering, and aren't going to."

The stricture in Richardson's throat threatened to suffocate him. "I've got it all, Keith. I promise, and so does Buck," he choked out. "And there'll be a full report on how you carried out the best and finest traditions of the United States Navy, and how you told that foreign submarine, Soviet or whoever he was, by that last torpedo of yours, that you weren't about to give in to him or anyone. And we'll also tell how you stayed with your ship to the very last, giving your own life to save your crew and making sure they escaped, even though you couldn't."

"I'm not the last, Rich. There's Jim and Curt and Larry and Stew, and we're all together now. Passing three hundred feet."

Silently, Buck handed Rich a piece of paper. Richardson looked at it, frowned thoughtfully, did not speak for a full fifteen seconds.

"Rich, are you still on the line?"

"Rich, here. Yes, Keith. We've just got a report on your muster. For a minute I thought of lying to you, but I can't. All of your crew is accounted for except five. They didn't make it. They were in the last two groups, and didn't have the wet suits. Jim Baker, Howard McCool, Willson Everett, Abe Lincoln Smith and John Varillo. I'm sorry, Keith. They got up all right, but they died in the water before we could get them in the chamber. Also we lost one of our divers when the line carried away."

"I'm dreadfully sorry, Rich, and Buck too. I meant to tell you, I saw him carried over the side through the TV when the line parted, but I thought he'd have no strain getting back on deck with his safety line— what was his name?"

"Cliff Martini."

"I'm sorry, Buck. Tell his family for me. We're going down faster, now. Just passed four hundred feet. About the five of our men who died, they were all good men. John was a fine young officer and would have been a credit— I understand he was engaged to be married to a girl named Ellen Covina. She lives in New York. Look her up for him, will you? And also the next of kin for the other four— I don't know all the details—oh, we know. McCool's family is in Groton. So's Abe Smith's. Everett lived in Waterford. Baker was born and brought up in Norwich, Larry says. Passed five hundred while I was talking."

"Okay, Keith. We've got it all. Wilco on all of it, old friend."

"We're nearing six hundred. Mark, six hundred. I'll try to keep giving you the depths. That will be something the designers might like to know." Keith's voice was growing fainter, and with the last speech he must have raised the output gain control. The time of transmission of his voice from the sinking submarine was lengthening.

Rich raised his own gain to full. What could he say to help Keith over these horrible last few minutes? What could anyone do? "Keith, remember our second cruise on the *Eel?* Remember how you rescued me from that fake sampan, and that sadistic character, Moonface? I'll never forget how you burst out of the water with our old ship and impaled that wooden tub on her bow buoyancy tank. That was beautiful!"

"Thanks, Skipper!" Keith's voice took longer to reach him. Perhaps he had not answered immediately. "I've often thought of it, too, and wondered how you managed to keep from finishing Moonface all by yourself when we got the upper hand."

"I've wondered myself. It was partly because of Bungo Pete, I guess." (There, the name was out again. Rich sensed Buck looking strangely at him.)

"Seven hundred! Forget Bungo, Rich! You've paid for that too many times! I'd have done it, too, and I'd not have worried about it after, either. What about this guy you and Buck sank today? He probably had a wife and kids at home, and so did Bungo, most likely —and so did I. Eight hundred!"

"I understand what you're trying to say, Keith, and I'll try."

It took appreciable time for Keith's voice to make

the return trip. "You've got to promise me, Rich. Don't let me down now. Don't let any of that stuff throw you. Put it behind you. No matter who comes to you with it! No matter who! I mean it, Rich. Haven't been able to think of the words to say, got to try to get it in." Keith's voice had risen in pitch, and was louder. "Buck knows what I'm talking about. Tell Peggy I love her, and for her to take the insurance and get that house and garden, far away from New London. But don't you talk to her, Rich. Not unless there's someone with you. Ask Buck! This is going to throw her, and sometimes she's— Passing a thousand feet. Missed the nine-hundred-foot mark. Sometimes she says things she doesn't really mean, or doesn't really know about but makes you think she does. Don't let her upset you, Rich. She's my wife, and you're my best friend, and I love you both, and it tears me to think of it. Be sure Buck or Laura is with you! That's all I can think of to say. The others are over in the corner talking by themselves. They said they don't need to talk to anyone. Eleven hundred. Going fast, now. I can hear the internal bulkheads squeezing. She'll last a bit longer, but not much. Twelve hundred. I can smell chlorine. The battery's spilled for sure. Took a long time, though. It's a good design. Thirteen. We're off the deep gauge. Give it to you in sea pressure. Where's a sea pressure gauge? I'm disoriented. Here's one. I can barely read it from where I'm sitting to get to this mike. It should be built with a long cord, instead of fixed to the bulkhead, which is now the floor—the gauge is showing seven hundred pounds. That's more than fourteen hundred feet. Now it's nearly eight hundred. I'll hold the mike button down with my foot and maybe I can stand up partway to read it—it's eight fifty. I'm shouting. Can you hear me? Don't answer. It doesn't matter, but I'll keep trying. . . ."

Keith's voice was changed with the distance and with his attempt to shout from a position closer to the sea pressure gauge. But it was still intelligible, still Keith. Rich felt Buck's arm around his shoulders, put his own arm around Buck's neck. Subconsciously, both of them felt the presence of other men, other members of *Manta*'s crew, many members of the *Cushing*'s crew. Rich felt Buck's quiet, shaking grief, knew his own was communicating itself to Buck. There were soft noises of anguish from others in the control room, but otherwise silence, except for many men, breathing as quietly as they could. Never had the silence been so absolute. Never had a packed control room, packed with the crews of two submarines, been so still. Even the breathing was stifled, muted, kept shallow so as not to bother anyone. In the distance, a far corner, someone let out a tiny wail, "Oh, God—!" It might have been a prayer. It was savagely shut off. A vicious elbow in the ribs, or a firm hand over the mouth.

Keith had said not to answer, but Rich had to say something in the momentary silence of the UQC. He cleared his throat, swallowing the lump that was in it. "Keith," he said. He had to force his voice to work. By sheer will he overrode the clutch in it. "Most of your crew is here with me. They're all blessing the best submarine skipper they ever had, and the best friend they ever had. Their hearts and minds are with you at this time. Those who traveled in deep waters with you are with you still." He released the button, heard the strange traveling sound of the carrier beam as the message went out, attenuating, in all directions. But also down.

". . . hundred pounds. That's amazing, Rich! Eleven hundred! Who could have thought—twelve hundred! Tell Peggy I love her! Tell Ruthie the last thing her dad did was to think of her. Thirteen hundred! Something's given way down aft! I think she's going! Good-bye! Thanks for all! Fourteen . . ."

A smashing roar came over the UQC speaker—Keith had been holding the button down—and then it was silent. But everyone in the *Manta* heard the awful, shattering, crushing implosion when the fantastic sea pressure, at whatever depth *Cushing* had reached, burst the stout, unyielding, high-tensile steel into smithereens. Embrittled under pressure, yet standing rigid, firm against millions of tons of overpressure, when finally it gave way the thick, armor-quality steel split into thousands of pieces, ranging in size from tiny fragments to tremendous solid plates weighing tons, all of them driven inward with velocity beyond comprehension. And the sea followed instantly, with a voice like thunder, compressing the air to one one-hundredth of its previous volume and raising its temperature high into incandescence.

Keith, Jim, Curt, Larry and Stewart did not suffer, nor did they even feel pain. Awareness ceased instantaneously, when their bodies ceased to exist.

Great sections of steel curved in various shapes to fit the exigencies of *Cushing*'s designers, now broken in every conceivable way but still curved, fluttered down through the black water like leaves falling from a tree in autumn. When they came to rest they covered a wide expanse on the bottom of the Fletcher Abyssal Plain. Under them, deeply buried in the ancient ooze of the bottom, were the resting places, for all time, of the two halves of the Soviet nuclear submarine *Novosibirsky Komsomol,* and the *Cushing*'s reactor, which sank swiftly in one piece because of the immense pressure it had been built to contain.

ww

There was a new compulsion in the *Manta* as she raced for the edge of the ice pack, where the ice would be thinner, the probability greater of being able to break through to send a message. For the better part of a day, Rich and Buck labored over its wording. They must report the loss of the *Cushing,* give the names of the men lost with her, tell of the battle with the intruding submarine, and describe their suspicions that there was some sort of a Soviet base, not far away, near enough for the submarine they had sunk to have gone there for instructions. The *Cushing* might well have been originally very near it, since Keith had reported seeing aircraft apparently orbiting just over the horizon, and landing and taking off.

The message, encrypted in the highest classification code available on board, ended with terse naval jargon. UNODIR PROCEEDING RECON GUARDING VLF ONE HOUR NOON GREENWICH: Unless otherwise directed, *Manta* would try to locate the base and discover its nature and purpose. Once a day, at noon Greenwich Mean Time, she would come to as shallow a depth as possible, at minimum speed, to listen to the very-low-frequency radio circuit for any instructions. Otherwise, the *Manta* would most likely be at deep submergence and unreachable by any means of communication.

Thirty hours were required to find an area where the ice cover was thin enough to break through. Buck directed his course to pass as nearly as possible through the same spot where the relayed message from the *Cushing* had been sent, but it was not found. Doubtless they passed within a short distance of it, but there was no indication of any thinning of the ice pack on the upward-beamed Fathometer, nor any sign of discontinuity of the ice pack as the *Manta* cautiously circled the area with her periscopes up. Finally, it had been necessary to punch through ten feet of cover with the submarine's bow, elevated at a steep angle so as to take the shock of the contact with her strongest icebreaking capability. Then *Manta* came back around and, more gently this time, shouldered her way through the shattered slot in the ice with her sail. When the message was at least cleared—it had carried the highest possible priority prefix—she went deep and headed toward the place indicated on Jerry Abbott's plot.

Buck Williams, sitting at the head of the wardroom table, was wagging his head. He and Richardson had adjourned there to study Jerry's work, leaving the exec free to continue the incredibly complicated task of organizing living, sleeping and messing arrangements for an influx of nearly double the crew of the *Manta*.

Jerry had plotted backward every known movement of the enemy submarine, as Buck had instructed, but he had had to make a number of assumptions, some questionable at best. And there had been no opportunity to get anything from Keith. Fortunately, Keith had given an estimated position of the aircraft he had seen in his last message, the one transmitted via the

Manta. How long ago had that been? Less than two days. A decoded copy lay on the table.

"I hate even to look at this," growled Buck, clutching one hand into a fist while he tapped the paper with the other. "This little piece of paper cost Keith his life! I hope they choke on it down in Washington! Do you really think Admiral Donaldson will get it across how much this has cost? Will he ram it into the people responsible?"

"If I know him, he certainly will. The lives of eleven damn good men, not to mention a brand-new submarine, is a stiff price tag. He won't let that pass easily. But, of course, all they can do is be sorry."

"The very least they could do is send the people who insisted on this message up to New London when we hold the memorial service! They ought to be made to sit in the front row!"

"They'd better be incognito and sit in the back, as far as I'm concerned." Rich paused. "But right now we've got to figure out what's going on up here. Those guys are no little exploration party on the ice! There's a lot more than that going on!"

After several hours of study, frequent interrogations of Jerry Abbott and many cups of coffee, an "indicated circle of probability" was decided on. It was twenty-five miles in diameter, circular since it was only the locus of centers of possibilities. As soon as it was reached, a slow, methodical, crisscross search of the circle would be begun, with both periscopes up looking for anything unusual. The area of practicable view was so tiny that Rich and Buck quickly realized they could pass nearly directly under the spot they were seeking without seeing it. Active sonar, which might increase the size of the area being searched at any moment, was ruled out.

"I don't think we should echo-range," Rich told

Buck. "They could be listening. There could be another sub around. Anything."

"We really don't have any idea of what we're looking for," grumbled Buck, as the second day of fruitless search drew toward its end. By agreement, he and Rich were alternating periods of wakefulness, except that both found themselves haunting the radio room during the daily VLF listening stint, and both enjoyed the afterdinner coffee hour, now reconvened in Buck's cabin.

"The main thing that worries me, Buck, is that for some reason we'll be ordered out of the Arctic, or run out of oxygen or CO absorbent. With all the *Cushing* people aboard, that's going to be a problem very soon. We'll find out what's going on if we're able to look for a while. We just have to have enough time."

"Do you think Washington knows what we're doing, Skipper?"

"They're just as curious as we are. If they call us off, it will be because they have to. That's what I'm worried about."

But no orders arrived. Cutler, which could be heard clearly, carried only a single message for them. Prosaically addressed to ComTaskGru 83.1, it merely acknowledged receipt of Rich's previous message and added the perfunctory, "Submit written report upon arrival Conus."

The place was found by an unexpected means, by the sonarman on watch, midway of the third day. "I think I'm hearing a beacon," he reported.

Schultz, instantly on the scene, confirmed it. "It's very distant. It sounds like one of those homing beacons divers use. It's a standard intermittent buzz. You can only hear them a mile or so!"

"It's for that sub to home in on!" said Buck. "He navigates to a mile or so of this place, picks up this little thing, and homes in on it!"

"So will we, after we've made a couple of complete circles around it. After that, I want to pass under with the periscopes up, starting as deep as we can use them. Now that we've found their base of operations, whatever it is, it's up to us to find out everything we can about it!" Rich's logic was unassailable, and Buck found himself apologizing for hinting at a shortcut.

Moving slowly and deliberately in the dead-silent condition, *Manta* made not two but three complete circuits around the sound source, at different depths, plotting and recording every scrap of information that could be obtained. Finally, with Rich's approval, Buck ordered her two periscopes raised and told Tom Clancy to gradually increase depth to 185 feet. "Any deeper, and the hoists won't hold them up, boss," he said. "They'll still be hard to turn when we get down there, but at least we'll not have to wait while they creep out of the wells."

Rich smiled morosely as he received the report. Neither he nor Buck was far from the memory of Keith's last moments, which hung, cloudlike, over everything.

Nor, for that matter, was anyone else aboard. Merely the fact of the *Manta*'s extraordinary crowded condition was a constant reminder. Jerry Abbott had made the fairest possible division of sleeping spaces, eating schedules and "standing hours." Since a man occupies less useful space in the vertical posture, everyone was required to be physically on his feet twelve hours out of every twenty-four. Whenever possible *Cushing* crew members were put on watch with their opposite numbers in *Manta*'s crew, again only to reduce congestion. But there were many, the missile department crew for example, who had no counterparts in the *Manta*. And all of them, despite sincere effort, were constantly in the way. Not that anyone complained. Men had died to make their safety possible.

Manta's control room, at least, was kept moderately clear, most particularly in the vicinity of the sonar shack, the periscope station and the diving station. With extra personnel available, there were two quartermasters on watch with a third detailed to maintain a most complete notebook log of all activities. One quartermaster was assigned to assist at each periscope. "How much longer to pass under?" asked Buck, without taking his eyes from the eyepiece.

"Two minutes fifteen," said his quartermaster. "Dead ahead. A hair on the port bow."

"Tell Mr. Abbott to pass directly under, if he can."

"Aye, aye, sir."

". . . How long now?"

"Ninety seconds . . . sixty . . . thirty . . . twenty, fifteen . . ."

Richardson had no idea when it was that he first realized he was looking at something. Though clear, the water was dark, for there was very little light penetrating the ice cover, and out of the deep formlessness of the shadowed water, solidity slowly emerged. It was the color of water, bespoke regularity, and rigidity, a gradual gathering together of vague nothingness in the sea until there was something, square and angular, huge and sinister. And close. Very close! Rich realized he was looking with his line of sight elevated, quickly swiveled it downward, saw what he took to be a square bottom, flipped up the handles, reached for his periscope hoist lever.

"Down periscope!" rapped out Buck, snapping up his control handles. His startled tone caused his quartermaster to jerk the hoist lever, and his periscope shot downward. The man managed to push the lever back toward Raise, to brake the fall, barely in time to bottom the periscope without damage.

Rich's "Down 'scope!" was almost simultaneous with Buck's. As he instinctively grabbed for the lever, he felt his own quartermaster already there, pulling it for him, getting the heavy tube down swiftly and safely.

"Left full rudder!" shouted Buck. "Take her down fast!" The whoosh of air and the rush of water into negative tank pervaded the control room. He made a show of wiping the sweat off his forehead. "Did you see what I saw, boss?"

"I think so. What do you think it was?"

"It was mighty big, that's all I can say!"

"I think we'd have passed under it, but it sure scared me," said Richardson. "Damn good thing we were going so slow!"

"That's for sure!"

"What was it, Skipper?" asked Abbott, standing on the main deck outside the periscope circle rail. "An iceberg?"

"No. Too regular for that. Something straight up and down in the water!"

"That's what I saw, too, Buck! I thought I could see the bottom of it, though—could you?"

"Negative, I had my 'scope turned up. All I saw was something suddenly awfully big and awfully close!"

"The bottom looked squared-off to me. It was man-made, all right!"

"Did it move, or look as if it could move?"

"Passing three hundred. Give me a depth, Captain!" said Clancy, calling from the other side of the periscope station. "I need speed, or permission to blow the tank."

"Blow negative now, Tom," said Buck swiftly, "and vent the pressure easy. Try to hold whatever depth you can stop her at."

The noise of blowing air. Then the flood valve clanked shut, and a great quantity of air, at pressure corresponding to the depth of water, began to vent into the ship. Rich and Buck had to swallow several times before their sinus passages felt normal. "I don't think that thing was mobile, Buck. That was no seagoing shape. Let's come on around and ping on it. We'll have to chance nobody will hear us. Maybe that will give us an idea of what it is."

At half-a-mile range and depth of three hundred feet, *Manta* made several complete circuits of the strange object, pinging first strongly, then progressively less so. Finally Schultz had his equipment down to minimum power, the ping barely perceptible as it went out, almost inaudible when the echo returned. And gradually, the outline of what they were looking at so painstakingly came clear.

Rich recognized it first. "It's a cylinder, Buck! Four cylinders, rather, fastened together in some way and standing upright in the water!"

"That's what it looks like, all right! I've never heard of anything like this! Have you?"

"No. Not ever. It must be floating in the sea, but it doesn't look as if it were intended to be mobile."

"Not with that shape," said Buck. "How big do you make it?"

"No idea—yes, we do too have a guess. If the bottom really was a little above the tops of our periscopes, that would put it at a hundred twenty feet or so. From the sonar picture it's about two-thirds that in width."

"And the top's got to be frozen in the ice pack! If it can't move, it's got to be!"

"That makes sense, Buck. But what is it?"

"Let's close in again till we can see it, boss," begged Buck. "Maybe that will give us the clue. Besides, if anybody heard us pinging, the quicker we get this over with, the better."

"Agreed!"

The water was remarkably clear, but the dim light filtering through the bumpy underside of the ice pack was barely sufficient to outline the huge structure. The control room had been darkened, leaving only red lamps glowing at the important stations. Buck and Rich kept their faces firmly pressed against the rubber buffers at the periscope eyepieces, the better to acclimate their eyes to the tenebrous half-light. Forty feet above them, at the tops of the periscopes, they turned their two glass orbs from side to side, elevated and depressed the prisms inside, and gradually the amorphous thing took shape. There was an impression of massive strength, vertical steel solidity held together with an intricate interlocking of rugged girders, combined with a much more delicate tracery of smaller lines running in every direction. At several places steel ladders could be distinguished. The entire structure—or structures, for there seemed to be four principal elements of equal size—was painted sea gray. It was relatively new, for as yet there had been very little growth on the surfaces. Here and there black lettering could be seen featuring the occasional "reversed" characters of the Russian alphabet. Other areas, irregular in shape, were most likely merely abrasions, or rusted places.

As the *Manta* crept slowly around the complex, rising nearer the surface and then descending to inspect its bottom, its dimensions were determined to be approximately 120 feet in depth, roughly 80 feet in width overall. In composition it was four huge vertical cylinders, each some 35 feet in diameter, attached together by steel girders. Where it encountered the ice overhead, three sides of the square were evidently frozen into it, for there was no visible demarkation above, except that light came through the ice and not through the metal. But on the fourth side there was a large opening in the ice, in length and width many times the size of the two cylinders touching it, through which bright sunlight streamed in stark contrast to the dimness everywhere else.

"What do you think, Buck? Ever see anything like this before?"

"The only thing I can remember that looked like this was the grain elevator in my hometown. It has six silos, sort of roofed—silos! *Silos! Could* these be missile silos?"

"Missile silos, floating in the Arctic Ocean! By God, that's what they could be! Then that little polynya would be a resupply dock! Imagine the trouble they're going to, to keep it ice-free! Buck, I think you hit it! This is the headquarters of that Soviet polar exploration expedition they were talking about in that lousy press release, and it's really an intercontinental missile base! I'll bet you five there's an ice runway alongside it, too!"

"We've got to report this as soon as we can, boss!"

"Just as soon as we can. But we've got to be sure first. If we're right, this will really shake up the powers down in Washington!"

"This must be where that submarine was based, and we know he's not coming back. Maybe we can ease on up and take a careful look! Then we'll know!"

"And take a batch of pictures through the periscope, too, to prove it! Our intelligence boss will love us for that!"

"We'd better go to battle stations, boss. Whoever these people are, their history shows they'll resent strangers taking pictures through the periscope!"

"I was about to say the same, Buck. But don't sound

the alarm. Pass the word quietly in case they've got a
sonar watch on."

Positioning the *Manta* in the center of the artificial
polynya was easy; it was more than twice her length in
both dimensions. The difficulty lay in bringing the submarine up slowly, using buoyancy only—with no way
on she got no benefit from her control surfaces—and
stopping her ascent at exactly the right depth. The
periscope itself could be varied in height from the conning station deck to the overhead, thus giving the diving
officer a few feet of flexibility in case *Manta* began to
rise or descend unexpectedly. A person using the periscope could do it either lying on his stomach or standing, or anywhere in between so as to expose only the
desired amount of the instrument. The big job was
Clancy's, for it took consummate skill to hold the great
steel bulk of the submarine within five feet of the desired depth without motion of any kind.

Tom Clancy was fortunately entirely equal to the
task. With Buck at a half-crouch, the tip of *Manta's*
high periscope came one inch above the mirrorlike surface of the artificial lake. Buck spun it around swiftly,
dropped it two feet below the surface. "I didn't see
anyone looking," he said, speaking quickly, "but there's
a lot going on. I could see cranes, a hangar and several
huts, all painted white or covered with snow. Quite a
few people wandering around, too."

"Can I have a look?" Rich could not keep the eagerness from showing in his voice.

"That's what we're here for! That and the camera!"

Through the tiny prism at the top of the attack periscope, Rich was first conscious of the height of the ice
all around: nearly ten feet above the surface, he estimated, high above the minimal periscope height he and
Buck had determined was all they would risk. This was

not an ordinary floe. The ice must extend five times that far below the surface. The Soviets had preempted an ice island for their missile station! Then he saw the hangar, a large, white, arched-roof building vaguely resembling the quonset hut which had been their quarters in Idaho. The elevated white booms of two large cranes were promiment against the sky.

He was dictating his observations rapidly to two quartermasters and two yeomen as he swiftly traversed the periscope. Near the hangar he thought he could distinguish an aircraft, though of this he could not be sure for the height of the ice interfered, and it would not be wise to raise the 'scope higher for a better look. The structure enclosing the tops of the silos, white like all the other construction, apparently even with the ice surface, formed a portion of one side of the polynya. One silo door was open; he could see the twin halves standing vertically, parallel to each other. Extending for some distance below the water surface, and in the air up to the level of the ice ledge, the two silos nearest him were covered with metal siding, again white, but artfully camouflaged where it entered the water. At a distance it resembled the edges of the polynya. The smooth steel glistened in a non-icelike manner, however, and from nearby it looked more like the side of a ship, painted white, without portholes.

Alongside the shiplike siding, mooring cleats—they could only be for submarines—had been built. They too had been painted white, but there were dark rope burns which proved they had been used. And, as Buck had said, there were numbers of people to be seen, all dressed in heavy clothing.

Rich dunked the 'scope several times as he made his methodical traverse, and he maintained a constant monologue dictating his observations. The necessity of maintaining no more than an inch or so of periscope exposure in the calm waters of the artificial polynya caused him to vary his attitude from standing fully erect to squatting on his haunches, once lying flat on his stomach to bring the eyepiece of the periscope as near to the deck as was possible while Tom Clancy fought to keep *Manta*'s 3,000 tons of steel from drifting higher.

It was with surprise that Rich noted, when he finally dunked the 'scope a little farther than usual and turned it over to the camera party, that he had been using it less than five minutes. The camera party itself, with four cameras ready and the arc of interest carefully defined, accomplished its mission in half a minute.

Buck retrieved the periscope, spun it twice rapidly as he bounced around on his haunches, once inspecting the sky, then dropped it to the bottom of its well.

"This has been mighty well done, Skipper," he heard Richardson say, more loudly than necessary, so that he would be overheard by nearly everyone in the control room. "Now let's get away from here and get off that message!"

Rich might have gone on, was, in fact, preparing to say a few words in specific praise of Tom Clancy and his diving team, when all thought was abruptly reoriented by a thunderous crash! *Manta*'s deck seemed to buckle, then straighten. Richardson felt himself flung into the air, saved himself from falling by grabbing the guardrail around the periscope station, found it vibrating madly. Buck had also nearly been thrown off his feet, he noticed, and several of the men in the control room had truly been knocked down. The atmosphere in the control room was alive with particles of paint, dust and cork. *Manta*'s entire interior resounded like a huge steel drum.

"All compartments report!" said Buck urgently to the battle stations telephone talker a few feet away.

Rich found himself blessing the foresight which had led
them to order the ship rigged for depth charge and the
crew at action stations beforehand. Then the second
depth charge arrived, if anything, closer than the first.
And then a third, and a fourth, and a fifth. . . .

Nikolai Konstantinov Shumikin, commander of the
First Soviet Arctic Free Missile Base, was seriously
worried. For a time things had been going so well, and
now, ever since he had sent Zmentsov back to prevent
escape of the damaged American missile submarine, the
sixth sense which had always served him had not been
functioning. Number one, there had been a second very
recent transmission in undecipherable code from somewhere nearby, and for this last one there was no clear
explanation. Grigory Ilyich Zmentsov, skipper of the
Novosibirsky Komsomol, had suggested the one before
it must have been from a submarine sent from the
United States to render assistance to the one they had
so cleverly immobilized. The trapped vessel, the newest
model of Polaris missile submarine, must not be permitted to escape. The Americans had no right to attempt to make the Arctic Ocean into a place from
which they might shoot Polaris missiles! His own top-
secret missile base, of course, was a very different thing.
It was more like an extension of Russia's land mass a
little farther into the sea: perfectly legitimate, even if
subterfuge had been necessary because of stupid
treaties. But not a missile submarine! That was too
much!

His first report, praising the *Novosibirsky Komsomol*
and her commander for so brilliantly carrying out his
instruction to damage the American submarine in an
apparent accident, had resulted in deserved praise for
himself as well. It had been an extraordinary stroke of
luck to have been forewarned of the expected appear-

ance of the enemy sub, and to have had Grigory Ilyich
and his specially configured *Novosibirsky Komsomol*
ready. Reporting the loss of one of his aircraft as due
to a weapon fired from the damaged submarine had
given the Kremlin an excellent pretext for the decision
to take the damaged vessel into custody, and it had also
camouflaged the bombing run he had ordered. That
had been necessary to prevent the enemy submarine
from escaping. The intent, after all, had been only to
drive her back under the ice once more, so that she
could not further communicate with her headquarters,
and this had been achieved. It was simply unfortunate
that she had managed to surface and get those two
initial messages off.

Indeed, that had been the beginning of the bad luck
that, somehow, had dogged him ever since. The second
submarine had undoubtedly come in response to the
call for help, but had been stupid enough to advertise
her presence by sending a long message herself, from
not many miles away. By great good fortune, Grigory
Ilyich had actually been in Shumikin's office when the
radio messenger arrived to report interception of the
transmission, and he had immediately ordered him to
investigate. The Americans were really astonishing. Grigory had returned with the extraordinary report that
somehow the second submarine, a smaller, older model,
had actually managed to rig a towline to the first one
and was even then in the process of extracting her from
under his very nose! There had been no time to radio
for instructions. He had had to make the decision on his
own, and it had been a most difficult one, but it was the
only one possible. It would not have been necessary to
order the second submarine destroyed, had it not interfered by taking the first one in tow. He regretted the
necessity of rewarding such ingenuity with death, but
there had been no alternative.

Grigory Ilyich had departed immediately, but he had not yet returned. That was four days ago. It was inconceivable that anything could have gone seriously wrong! Grigory himself had assured him that the towing sub was helpless to defend itself, and furthermore could not have that recent triumph of Soviet technology, the new force-field antitorpedo system which made all Soviet submarines practically immune to attack. Perhaps they had gotten farther away than Grigory had expected, or perhaps some other difficulty was holding him up. Submarines were delayed more frequently than other ships because of some unexpected problem. One had to be respectful of the implacable power of the sea, especially if one operated beneath its surface. All the same, it had begun to be worrisome.

Three days ago the second of the two recent American messages had been brought to his office in the hangar, and this had caused Shumikin extreme concern. The direction-finding people had said it had been sent from farther away than the previous one. Perhaps the Americans had gotten much farther—had towed faster—than Grigory Ilyich had predicted they could. Perhaps they had actually given him the slip. But Grigory was persistent. He would continue the pursuit. He would find them eventually, even if he had to track them out past Greenland! But, then, how had the American submarine managed to break through the ice to send a message if it was still attached to a towline? And what was Grigory doing? Why had he not reported back? By this time he must have found them. He must be returning soon. The underwater beeper had been going continuously. He would have no difficulty homing on it. Where in the devil was he?

For three days there had been a close watch kept on the lagoon. Shumikin would be informed the instant Grigory's periscope was observed, or his sonar heard.

It would be only a few steps from anywhere in his base to the silo-pier, and he could be there before the *Novosibirsky Komsomol* completed surfacing. Then he could set his mind at ease. Probably the delay was nothing important.

He was still in this frame of mind when, late on the fourth day since Zmentsov's departure, the expected messenger came. But the initial delight at seeing him instantly gave way to dismay. The man was excited. "There is a submarine! But it is acting strangely!" Shumikin had to force himself to walk to the observation post. He would have covered the short distance at a run, but it would not do to let his men see that he was anxious. On the way he learned that echo-ranging had been heard, but the vessel had seemed to become more distant instead of coming closer. Perhaps Grigory Ilyich for some reason could not hear the beeper and therefore was searching the sea by sonar. This had happened once before, when the beeper had broken down, but that was not the case today. Now, the periscope had been sighted in the lagoon, but instead of rising high out of the water, as was Zmentsov's custom, it remained very low and could be seen turning in all directions as though it were inspecting the place. At this point, the puzzled watch officer had sent for his superior.

In the observation post, fortunately built for just this contingency, Shumikin was able to inspect the waters of the polynya through binoculars without himself being observed, and what he saw increased his apprehension. The periscope was indeed acting most strangely! It was going up and down at short intervals, turning in all directions and never exposing itself more than an inch or two above the water. When it was lowered beneath the clear surface he could see the tapered end, only a few feet under, poised, waiting, and then in a moment it would rise again to repeat the process. Nikolai Konstantinov Shumikin was no submariner, but the entire performance was disquieting. Grigory Ilyich would not behave like this unless something were seriously wrong! And then the full implication struck him with sledge-hammer impact. Savagely, he turned on his officer of the watch.

"Why was I not informed of this sooner?" he demanded in a fury. "Why was this submarine permitted to echo-range without my knowing of it?"

The man was unable to answer. He had been expecting the *Novosibirsky Komsomol,* knew nothing about the possibility of another submarine being in the vicinity, had not been overly disturbed by the slightly different pattern of the echo-ranging, had not, in fact, become concerned at all until he had seen the periscope. Shumikin stamped his foot in rage, continued with the same furious anger. "Sound the alarm, you dolt! This is an enemy! Release the ready depth charges!"

Twenty depth charges, in camouflaged racks at the far side of the polynya, could be released electrically. They had been carefully set deep enough so that the explosions would not damage the silos, nor the ice above them, hence they could not harm an interloper at shallow depth. A far more potent weapon lay in the torpedo room, built in the base of the mooring pier. There were two torpedo tubes, and a supply of the latest target-seeking torpedoes, similar to those carried by the *Novosibirsky Komsomol.*

With the sounding of the alarm, furious activity struck the missile base. There had been planning, and drills. Now the base commander was thankful for his insistence on them. Other depth charges would soon be ready to be rolled into the lagoon, and the cranes could swing still others almost into its center. Numerous small guns and two large 100-millimeter anti-aircraft rifles would also be manned, although they would be useless unless the strange submarine surfaced. Most important of all, the torpedoes could be brought into action in three minutes from a standing start.

At least a minute had elapsed since the first depth charge. They had all been set deep, but nevertheless the surface of the polynya was roiled with disturbed water, and the periscope had disappeared. Shumikin grabbed the observation post telephone. "Sonar!" he barked, "Where is that submarine?"

"It's going away, Commander! Right after the depth bombs we heard it speeding up!"

"Well, keep the contact! It was your negligence that let it come up on us without warning! You should have reported at once on the battle intercom! Don't repeat your error or it will go very hard with you!"

"We guarantee it, Commander! The error is regretted, but we did not know—" Shumikin banged the telephone down with irritation. He was in no mood to listen to excuses, especially when his subconscious told him there might be a certain amount of justification to them.

He pushed the call for the torpedo room. "Torpedo!" he shouted in the same tone. "When will you clowns be ready with those fish?"

"About a minute, Commander! We're going as fast as we can!"

"Very well! Hurry!" He slammed the phone into its cradle, leaped out of the observation post and ran toward the hatch leading down into the torpedo room. He was almost in a frenzy. He knew well what the strange submarine was up to. He knew as soon as he realized it must be an American. Already he regretted the depth charges. They had only alerted the enemy. It would have been better to surprise him with the torpedoes. Having detected the silo base, perhaps even having photographed it, the American submarine commander was undoubtedly hightailing it to find a place from which to inform Washington. This must be prevented at all costs! If these torpedomen were ever to beat their three-minute record, now was indisputably the time!

By his presence in the torpedo room he hoped to galvanize his men into even greater effort. But in this he was disappointed, for even to his nontechnical eyes they were working as rapidly as possible. Shumikin had the good sense to desist from his exhortations as soon as this was clear to him, and finally there came the moment when both torpedoes could be fired, fortunately at a still well-defined sonar target. He congratulated himself also on having acceded to the demand of the senior torpedoman that there be a suitable wait, more than half a minute, before firing the second torpedo. Else they might interfere with each other, the man had said, rendering both of them harmless. How nearly he had come, in his impatience, to overriding the torpedoman's obvious professional training! But now both torpedoes were on their way, and at least one of them, most likely both, would certainly home on the target. Sonar should shortly hear two muffled explosions, and he would then know he had at least protected the grave secret entrusted to his care.

As for Grigory Ilyich Zmentsov and his ship, the heroic *Novosibirsky Komsomol,* it was too bad, but a painful duty now developed on him. He would spend all day composing a fitting epitaph in the form of a message describing how they had sacrificed their lives in the service of their country. He would begin this difficult chore immediately, with the highest personal priority, as soon as sonar reported the two explosions. . . .

Walking deliberately, Shumikin left the torpedo compartment and went down another hatchway leading to the sonar room. It would be good to be there in person, both to ensure the highest performance of its personnel,

whose attainments he had had reason to doubt recently,
and to be able to report that he had personally witnessed the results of the initiative he himself had been
forced to take in performance of his duty.

The depth charge meter in *Manta*'s control room had
gone wild, but it had also indicated that all the depth
charges were at some distance below. Not many in her
crew had experienced depth charging. The ship's hull
vibrated resoundingly, despite its extraordinarily solid
structure. The noise was tremendous. Pipelines, frames,
cableways, even the very bulkheads with their great
watertight doors shook spasmodically with every explosion. Buck Williams, after a quick reassuring look
at the depth charge meter—the tests, months ago, had
convinced him the gadget really worked—took a per-
verse pleasure in the initiation his crew was getting.
Cushing's crew too, for that matter. He, at least, had
experienced it all before.

So had Rich. Buck had felt actual pleasure carrying
out Rich's order to stay at periscope depth despite the
shattering, smashing blows being inflicted, the dust
storm raised inside the ship, even the knowledge that
somehow one of the charges might be set shallow
enough to do actual harm. It had been his evaluation,
concurred in by Richardson and substantiated by the
depth charge meter, that the Soviets would have to set
the charges deep. Otherwise they would risk unaccept-
able damage to their own installation, in particular their
precious silos. The guess had proved correct. And then,
when the last of twenty explosions had died its reverberating death, he was able, with the greatest composure,
to seize the temporary cessation of the attack to order
depth increased and the reactor to deliver power to the
waiting turbines.

It had all been too easy. First the inspection of the

missile base. Then, the depth charge attack had removed
any doubt of Soviet intention to safeguard knowledge of
its existence in the Arctic, even at the cost of direct,
hostile, military action. Now no power on earth could
prevent the *Manta* from making known what she had
discovered. Buck heaved a deep sigh, and at that moment heard the scream from Schultz, ten feet away in
his sonar room. "Torpedo!" Schultz shouted the word,
shouted it with all the force and all the voice at his
command.

Buck did not wait for the sweeping motion of Richardson's hand. "All ahead emergency! Take her down!"
Instantly he could feel the tilt of the deck, the bite of
the suddenly accelerated screws. Tom Clancy at the
diving station and the engineers in the maneuvering
room were slamming all their pent-up tension into
execution of the order. But there was too little time.
The range was much too short. Even as the air vented
from the negative tank, adding its whistle to the now
silent compartment and its quota of air pressure which
he could feel on his ears, there was a vicious jolt, a
violent resounding blow, and the high-pitched sound
of an explosion combined with rending metal. Buck
could hear something, metal fragments, rattling on the
hull.

Simultaneously, steady, fantastically heavy vibration
began to be communicated to *Manta's* rugged structure.
Buck and Rich were both looking at the annunciators,
when, unbidden, the starboard annunciator turned to
Stop.

"Starboard shaft is stopped! Maneuvering says the
starboard shaft is damaged! They've stopped it because
of heavy vibration!" The telephone talker stuttered in
his panic.

Buck snatched the nearest handset out of its cradle.
"Maneuvering, Captain here. How bad is it?"

"That explosion must have been right on the starboard propeller, Captain! She started vibrating like crazy right after! I had to stop it, sir!"

"Are you taking water? How's your shaft seal?"

"The engineroom's okay! We're checking the stern room now!" Buck held the instrument to his head while he waited. "The seal's been damaged, Captain! The stern room's taking water! Request the drain pump on the stern room bilges!"

"Tom! Take the angle off the boat! Start her back up! Stern room, open your drain-pump suction! We'll put the pump on as soon as she's lined up! Maneuvering, get some men back aft and tighten the gland! Where's Mr. Langforth?"

"He's just run back there! So did Mr. Steele."

"Good! Keep me informed about the leak!" Buck turned to Abbott, who was gripping the other side of the periscope-stand guardrail, staring at him. "Jerry! Get on aft as fast as you can! We've got to know how bad we're flooding!"

To Clancy, Buck said, "Tom, how are the stern planes?"

"They're moving slower than before, but I think we've still got them, Captain! We're taking the angle off now!"

"Have someone check the hydraulic pressure, and get a report from the after room on how the stern planes are operating!"

"Aye, aye, sir—passing five hundred feet! Twenty-five degrees down, decreasing!"

Buck and Rich could feel the angle lessening as Tom Clancy followed instructions.

There was another cry from Schultz. "Torpedo! Another one!" His scream was of pure terror.

Manta was still in a headlong dive, her port engine still racing. Buck did not hesitate. "Right full rudder!"

he ordered, his tense voice sharp with urgency. "Tom, keep the angle on!"

Manta rolled to starboard, leaning into the turn like a rollercoaster car. Her gyrocompass repeaters began to spin. She had almost reached full speed but had slowed markedly with the loss of one engine, and now even more as the rudder drag took effect. The whirling port propeller, driven with the maximum output of the reactor and steam generators, was cavitating heavily because of the increased hull resistance. Its noise came clearly through the hull. Richardson's face was immobile. Buck suddenly had the impression that he was not there at all.

"This is it, Skipper," said Buck softly. "Just like the last time, only we've lost half our power. It's all we can do!" He spoke almost with resignation.

"What's our depth now, Buck?" asked Rich, not stirring from his position, braced against the double angle on the ship.

"Passing six hundred feet. We'll have to take the angle off her pretty soon, even if we can contain the leak!"

"Buck," said Rich, speaking somberly and slowly, "Keith did one thing for us that we didn't appreciate at the time. It's almost as if I could hear him all over again. Do you remember the depth the *Cushing* reached?"

"Yes. He told us fourteen hundred pounds sea pressure. That's over three thousand feet!"

"If the *Cushing* could go that far below her design depth, so can we, Buck! Even with a bad leak. But that torpedo won't! It's our only chance! Tell Tom to keep the angle on and level her off at fifteen hundred feet!"

Buck nodded shortly, his eyes wide as he took it in. The memory of Keith's last moments was strong in him as he deliberately gave the orders. There was silence in the control room, and in all the other compartments.

The silence of men who realized the risk but who also understood the necessity for it. If ever they were to put their faith in the men who had designed and built their ship, who had given it a marvelous power plant and a magnificent hull to go with it, now was the time. Damaged or no, there was no other choice.

One thousand five hundred feet was far below *Manta*'s designed depth, yet far short of the depth sustained by the *Cushing*'s stout hull before its inevitable and catastrophic collapse. The *Manta* was there in slightly more than a minute, and as Clancy began to level off, the immense pressure of the sea was already obvious. During the descent there had been creaks in the solid structure, as the implacable squeeze drove everything inward upon itself. Light partition bulkheads were bowed, drawers and sheet-metal doors were jammed shut. Even some of *Manta*'s steel interior decks were curved upward or downward, where their girders were compressed lengthwise. All depth gauges had reached their limits and had been secured, the valves communicating to the sea closed tightly. So had most of the sea pressure gauges, only a few of which could register the 670 pounds per square inch the depth produced. A special watch had quickly been set up on all sea connections, throughout the ship, with special emphasis on the periscopes and propeller shafts. Most particularly on the port shaft and its thrust bearing, now also taking increased pressure from the depth as well as the drag imposed by the dead starboard shaft. As expected, its oil temperature had immediately begun heating up.

Everyone aboard was subconsciously aware of an unwonted rigidity in *Manta*'s heavy framing. Flecks of paint popped off as the squeeze minutely compressed the steel, and it seemed to settle itself, almost as though with flexed muscles and a look of defiance, at holding back the malevolently waiting sea. Steel shapes cannot be alive, and yet there was the indisputable aura of elemental struggle about them as they held fast.

Manta's speed on one shaft had been reduced to fifteen knots with the rudder hard over, and the overloaded propeller was thrashing loudly. Buck left the rudder on for one more full circle to render the disturbance it made in the water as nearly impenetrable as possible, then put the rudder amidships and let her steady on a course away from the polynya. Resistance eased, the furiously cavitating screw became more quiet, but not completely so, and *Manta*'s speed increased to nineteen knots.

The real battle, as everyone was well aware, was taking place in the stern room, where the inrush of water must be somehow contained, where Tom Clancy's two assistants and the entire engineering department, backed up by Jerry Abbott, were at full stretch. There were no illusions about what was going on. The water must be spurting in with maniacal force, sufficient to break an arm or rip off clothes and skin. The proper treatment for any leak is to reduce the pressure behind it—exactly opposite to what they had done. With the damaged shaft stopped, the seal where it exited from the *Manta*'s hull could be clamped down tightly by its huge peripheral bolts, but to do this under the best of conditions men would have to reach into nearly unreachable places, jammed, confined, with hardly the room to swing a wrench. Only now they would also be confronted with a roaring spray with the force of fifty fire hydrants issuing from behind these same bolts. But no news, in this case, must be good news. They must be coping with the leak, somehow.

Jerry Abbott was undogging the door leading aft to the reactor compartment, was returning to the control room. He left a trail of water dripping on the deck behind him, and a large puddle began swiftly forming

under him as he stopped, facing Buck. He was soaked
through and breathing hard. "We can't hold her at
this depth, sir," he said rapidly. "We've got the packing
nuts as tight as they'll go, but the water is coming in
so hard that two of us had to hold a piece of sheet
metal to deflect it so that one man could reach the
gland nuts. We'll have to pressurize the compartment!"

"Is everybody out of there?" asked Buck.

"Not yet. Harry Langforth and Whitey Steele and
our three best men are still working on the gland, but
there's not much more they can do. The leak's still a
bad one. The drain pump's taking a suction, but it
can't pump very fast at this depth. The water's gaining
fast, and I'm afraid the rest of the seal might blow out
with the pressure!"

"We've got to stay down here for a while, Jerry,
until that second torpedo either runs down or collapses.
Have them abandon the stern room and start putting
air in it. That will help the drain pump, and also cut
down the rate of the leak!"

Abbott said, "Aye, aye, sir!" and ran aft. As he
passed through the watertight door he heard Buck
order, "Port ahead two-thirds!"

"The best thing we can do is slow down, Skipper,"
said Buck to Rich. "If they've got another fish ready
we're still making so much noise it might be able to
follow us! Everything else is silenced except the propeller!"

"Right!" It was not necessary to mention the fact
that, in her present condition, *Manta* dared not slow to
such a degree that she could not carry the increased
weight. Buck would otherwise have ordered one-third
speed. A glance at the diving station verified that Clancy
had already begun to use angle on the stern planes to
hold the stern up. More would be needed as speed
dropped, as well as a large bubble of air in the after

group of ballast tanks. They could hear the hiss of air as Abbott began to follow his orders at the stern room bulkhead.

Chief Sonarman Schultz finally made the report that had been so anxiously awaited. "When we quieted down I could still hear the torpedo pinging somewhere astern and above us," he said. "Then it sort of petered out and stopped. I think it finally ran down!"

Clancy had been adding air for several minutes to the ballast tanks aft to compensate for the weight of the water in the stern room, and the anxious looks on his face and on those of his diving crew testified to their realization that the total cubic capacity of all of *Manta*'s air banks could only expand six times against sea pressure at the 1,500-foot depth—far from enough to empty the after ballast tanks. A silent cheer went through the control room when Buck gave the order to bring the ship up.

"It's obvious we'd not have been able to stay down much longer, Commodore," said Buck. "Jerry says there's five feet of water in the stern room. It's still coming in fast, but with the shallower depth and air pressure in there, he thinks we can cope with it." Then he went on, speaking more slowly, with a certain deliberate formality in his words. "Commodore, this illegal base has opened fire on us without cause, and it has damaged us. The submarine based here sank the *Cushing* and caused the loss of eleven good men, one of them our close friend. I request permission to return the fire!"

Williams saw once again the faraway look in the face and eyes of his superior. Rich spoke quietly, almost pensively. "No, Buck. We're not at war, and we'll not attack in cold blood. I killed a man that way, once, during the war, and I vowed I'd never do it again. Shape your course away from here at shallow depth, and we'll let Washington handle it when they get our message!"

"My God, boss! What do you mean, 'cold blood'? After what they've done? This ship is a man-of-war! They can't shoot at us without getting shot back at!"

"They can't hurt us now, Buck. And Bungo Pete— I mean, Captain Tateo Nakame—couldn't hurt us then, either. I drove him to shooting with his rifle when he saw what we were doing to his lifeboats!"

Buck's arm around his shoulder was almost like a blow. "Skipper!" he hissed, "stop it! You heard what Keith said, and I've been saying the same thing! Stop it! You hear me? Okay, we'll not try to get even with these bastards, but you've got to promise me to stop it!" Both hands were now on Rich's shoulders, gripping them.

Jerry Abbott, coming on the tableau, ever afterward puzzled over the meaning of what he saw. Nor did he have any way of realizing that it was he who at that instant changed the entire complexion of the private talk between his skipper and their admired, but unaccountably suddenly irresolute, squadron commander. "Skipper!" he said to Buck, "we've got to surface! We can't stop the water! We'll have to get the stern as high as we can and remake the seal with flax packing! The graphite seal is completely shot, and it's getting worse fast!"

"How long can we hold out the way we are, Jerry?" asked Buck.

"Who knows? The seal might let go any minute! A couple of hours, no more. With air pressure in the stern room, I mean. We'll have to let it off to go back in there, and there's no telling what will happen then!"

"How long will it take to make the change once you start?"

"About an hour. It's a big job, but we have every-thing we need to do it, once we can stop the water from coming in like this!"

Richardson, listening, knew that Admiral Donald-son's cryptic words aboard the *Proteus,* and in the sedan returning to the airfield in Groton, had at last achieved their full meaning, even though neither he nor anyone could have anticipated the situation. "The United States needs someone who can make the right decision at the right time, and take the responsibility for it, Rich. That's the main reason you're going along on this trip. You may run into a lot more up there than we expect!" Aloud, Rich said, "There's only one place around here we can bring her to the surface, Buck!"

"How are we——" Buck began, but Richardson inter-rupted him.

Speaking loudly, so as to be overheard, Rich said, "Buck, enter in your log that because there is only one place to surface, which is occupied by a hostile force that not once but several times has endeavored to de-stroy this ship and all on board, and has now seriously damaged her so that the lives of all hands depend on her coming to the surface to make repairs, the com-mander of Task Group 83.1 has ordered destruction of the offensive power of the said base so that *Manta* can surface unmolested!"

"Aye, aye, sir!"

"I will sign the entries in the quartermaster's note-book and the official log to attest to their accuracy. And now, make ready the torpedoes!"

Nikolai Konstantinov Shumikin, finally relaxed at his desk, was beginning to be pleased with himself. No matter how you cut it, no matter that the American missile submarine had got away, or that the *Novosibir-*

sky Komsomol had been unaccountably and unfortunately lost, the American submarine which had had the temerity to lift her periscope in the middle of his own artificial lagoon was now also resting on the bottom of the Arctic Ocean. He himself had heard the torpedo explosion which had killed her, and he had heard some of the desperate moves she had made to save herself. With her had died the possibility of premature revelation of the existence of his missile base. This the Kremlin intended to announce at the appropriate and propitious time, as the many briefings he had received had made clear. His primary responsibility was to safeguard its secrecy until then, and he had succeeded. It had been at some cost, but he had been successful.

He would compose a priority message explaining that a number of exotic weapons had been used against him, all illegally and all unsuccessful, that Grigory Ilyich Zmentsov and his whole crew in the *Novosibirsky Komsomol* had died heroically defending their country, and that his own inspired crew had finally sunk the American submarine responsible for it all. Having the trapped missile submarine slip through his fingers, for there was no way to find her now, was a misfortune, but it would have to be accepted. Certainly that had been through no fault of his. On the contrary, it was he who had taken the decisive action which had nearly captured her after all—and, in any case, she could know nothing about the existence of the missile base.

Loss of the *Novosibirsky Komsomol* would be the hard thing to explain, but surely the Naval Ministry knew they were taking this risk when they fitted her out for her special mission. Nevertheless, he would have to provide sufficient detail so that a plausible announcement as to the circumstances could be made. He was beginning to grapple with the problem, had decided he would have to send two messages, one in language proper for public distribution, the other a more private, more accurate explanation for official use only, when suddenly the alarm bell jangled. "Torpedo fired!" shouted a hoarse voice over the command intercom.

Shumikin leaped to his feet, pressed the button overriding the sonar room. "What do you mean, 'torpedo fired,' " he snarled. "Who ordered it?"

"It's not us, Commander, It's that submarine! We heard it firing! There's two torpedoes, now! We can hear them! They're coming this way! Very noisy! They're big torpedoes!" The voice rose in a shriek, then was cut off.

A tremendous geyser of water and explosive gas burst out of the open silo, rose high above it and, descending, drenched everything within several hundred yards. Nearly simultaneously, a wracking, explosive BOOM shattered the calm atmosphere. A plume of gray smoke shot high above the ice, then lazily drifted away in the still air.

The ruined silo, instantly filled with angry water, jerked sideways, hanging from the heavy steel foundations built into the ice and from its moorings to the other three. The ice cracked on the far side of the hangar, and the water level rose several feet up the steel facing of the *Novosibirsky Komsomol*'s mooring pier.

The second torpedo struck a silo diametrically opposite the one first hit. Its exit doors burst open. A second geyser of water, mixed with smoke and gas, shot into the air. This time it was followed by a streak of white-hot fire from the ruptured fuel section of the missile recently lowered into it.

The silo complex, which had begun to list to one side, straightened. It had been built with tremendously strong and wide underpinning in the ice itself, firmly planted into the rigid crystalline structure and then "cemented" in place by water. Its designer had proudly stated that it would continue to float, and remain operable, even if two of its silos were damaged or destroyed, and this had, by consequence, been written as one of the operational requirements. Now he was proved wrong, for the weight of the two flooded silos dragged down the entire structure, the whole section of the ice island into which it had been built, to within inches of the water level in the polynya. Seawater began to trickle around the hinges of the missile exit doors of the two undamaged silos, and into the long, narrow, unsealed cracks separating their halves.

The personnel of the undamaged silos needed no encouragement to evacuate. They had already been severely shaken by the two heavy explosions they had felt, and all electric power had cut off. Candles and battery-powered lights only heightened their appreciation of danger. When one of their number frantically reported that water was only centimeters from the portals of the crew entry hatches, they unceremoniously started up the interior ladders to the top level and ran out. They were barely in time, for great cracks had begun appearing in the laden ice. Water was coming through them, collecting on the surface, everywhere. Within minutes, a stream of water was running down the personnel hatches. The base commander, confronting the men as they ran, furiously ordered them back to their stations, but they stood stolidly, affecting not to hear him, not daring to obey.

By this time the burning silo had begun to resemble a missile trying to drive itself farther into the ice. Violent, rocketlike flame was erupting from the exploded silo doors, reaching, like a searing blade, a hundred feet into the air. From there it gradually turned increasingly deep shades of red until finally the fire cone petered out, some six hundred feet above the ice, in a plume of jet-black smoke.

It had been a mistake to tie in the aircraft hangar's services with those supporting the silos. The designer had used the opportunity to include its foundations with theirs also, and the whole ice slab, with its network of steel beams, insulated conduits, pipes and cables, had been laid out with great engineering skill and frozen solidly together. It cracked in several places, but the steel links in the ice held firm, and the entire camp area began to sag. Then, with a great smashing of ice, groaning of tortured metal and snapping of steel reinforcements, along with a continuous popping of burst rivets, stretched hoses, broken pipes and tangled utility lines of all kinds, the hangar, silos, cranes and all equipment in the vicinity slowly began to descend into the sea.

Or, rather, the sea waiting underneath simply poured up through the cracks, and out of the lowered edge of the polynya, to inundate the space recently occupied. A huge slab of ice cracked free from the rest of the ice island, just beyond the hangar, and irresistibly was dragged down by the weight of two full silos and two more filling rapidly.

Sensing the danger from the suddenly slanted footing and the water creeping ever farther over familiar environs, everyone in the camp began to run toward the only undamaged area, the aircraft landing strip. Nikolai Shumikin, despairingly recognizing the inevitable, could do no more than follow. The last man out of the ruined missile base, he stepped reluctantly off the sinking ice and the shattered remains of his command, stood on the edge of the runway, on the good ice.

His mind was still numb as to the magnitude of the disaster, but he knew that full appreciation would come in time. Everything was going straight to hell! And he would not be able to escape blame. Everything had gone wrong, beginning with the time that American missile submarine had arrived in the Arctic! He was furious with himself, furious with Grigory Ilyich, in a rage against his watch officer and the sonar watch-standers who should have heard the submarine return-ing. The fact that there might have been nothing to hear did not even enter his head. They should have alerted him!

He shaded his eyes as he looked into the low-lying sun, and with despair saw the hangar, with one plane inside, both cranes, the other aircraft which had been temporarily parked outside the hangar, the radio hut and his two big anti-aircraft guns, flanking their com-bined ammunition magazine, gently dropping out of sight, following the already vanished silos.

For a long time, Nikolai Konstantinov Shumikin stood looking at the scene of his disaster. That it was a personal as well as an official one could not be doubted. And then he saw a strange periscope rising out of the once again smooth waters of the much en-larged polynya. It was club-headed, with a large glass window—two glass windows, in fact. And it kept rising, higher and higher, until the black foundations under-neath also broke water, and then the entire hull of a submarine.

It was a strange submarine, one he had never seen before. And it seemed to surface in a strange way, somehow oddly tilted, with the highest exposed portion of the hull at the point farthest away from the periscope. No men were to be seen. No one came on deck, or into what he assumed must be the bridge area, near the base of the periscope, although he could hear some noises of concealed activity apparently from that vicinity.

The periscope itself, he could tell from the glass windows at the top, was in nearly constant motion, although frequently it steadied for long minutes during which he felt it was leveled exactly at him. He felt distinctly uneasy at such times, as though he were in personal danger, but there were men watching him from the runway, and he stood his ground.

After about an hour, air bubbled from around the hull of the strange submarine, and it slowly descended back into the water and disappeared.

19

〰〰〰〰〰〰〰〰〰〰〰〰〰〰〰〰〰〰〰〰〰〰〰〰

"This is Joan Lastrada, Laura. I'm in New London for a few hours. May I come over?" Laura recognized the infrequently heard voice instantly.

A Navy sedan dropped her off and departed. Pouring coffee, Laura looked at her visitor with warmth. Joan was still slender, still had the heavy black hair coiffed with just the right nonchalance. The strong bones beneath her dark eyes accentuated the slightly concave cheeks. Her complexion was smooth, understated; perhaps a bare touch of makeup. Was that a gray hair over one temple? No matter. Laura, too, once in a while used some coloring. Women could appreciate the necessity for these things.

Joan's gray suit was exactly right to set off her hair and eyes. Laura could feel the strength in the long, tapering fingers when they shook hands. Joan shook hands firmly, almost like a man, she thought.

"It's so nice to see you, Joan," Laura began as she offered the cream and sugar. "Neither? No wonder you're so stylish! It's been almost a year since we've talked," she went on tentatively. "I don't think I ever adequately expressed how very much I appreciate what you did. Rich mustn't ever find out, though, because you know how Navy men are about official business. He was very clear that I was never to bring the subject up with you, but he couldn't forbid you to call me. All the same, I couldn't even call back to find out if you'd been able to do anything. But I knew you must have been the one responsible for old Brighting's change of heart. It was great of you to do that, Joan."

Joan waved aside Laura's apology. "Don't worry about that. All I did was make him see that Rich wasn't involved in Scott's plan for BuPers to take over selection of nuclear trainees." She hesitated. Her eyes flickered, then steadied honestly on Laura's. "Besides, I guess you know I used to be very fond of Rich—long ago, during the war."

"Yes, I know. . . . I know he thinks a great deal of you, too." Now it was Laura's turn to try to convey, without saying the words, that, to her, Rich's wartime relationship with this still extremely attractive woman was no longer a threat to her marriage, but a bond between the two women, something she welcomed.

"That's awfully nice of you, Laura." Was there the very slightest emphasis on the conventional words? "But I agree, we can't tell Rich anything about this. Even the strongest men—like Rich—would find that hard to take."

Laura sat silently for a moment, sipping her coffee. Enough had been said. Probably she and Joan would not ever be intimate friends—perhaps that was in truth impossible, given the situation—but they understood each other. Joan's integrity would always match her own. She put down her cup. "What brings you to New London, Joan? You're still in Brighting's office, aren't you?"

"Yes, I'm still with him. But I came because I wanted to see you."

"That's awfully nice for me. How long will you be here?"

"I flew up this morning on Navy business, and I have to leave in a little while. The car that brought me will come back to take me to the airport."

"That's a fast trip."

"I'm still in Naval Intelligence you know."

"Still?" Laura's voice rose in surprise. "Rich said you were, during the war, but I didn't know you still were. I thought you were just a regular WAVE officer."

"Well, I am. I'm in ONI—that's Naval Intelligence— and I'm assigned to Admiral Brighting's office. But I'm leaving next month."

"Oh, really? Where are you going? I'll bet it's some exotic place!"

"Oh, I'll be staying in Washington. What I meant was that I'll be leaving the Service." There was a glow in Joan's face and an anticipatory look, as if she expected and even welcomed the next question.

"Leaving the Service?" Laura was genuinely surprised. "Why leave it now?"

"Martin Brighting and I are going to be married!" Joan's face was radiant.

Impulsively, Laura leaped to her feet and embraced Joan. "How marvelous! How stupendous! What stunning news! Rich will be thrilled too! Oh, I'm so happy for both of you! We all pictured the admiral as remaining a confirmed bachelor after Marilyn Brighting's death. How wonderful that isn't so! How marvelous for both of you! Can we come to the wedding?"

"Well, no. Not actually. I mean, we're going to be married very quietly by ourselves, and then take off for a honeymoon in Jamaica." There was a hint of

pride in the smile on Joan's face as she added, "It will
be Martin's first vacation from the Navy in years. He's
promised not to mention business even once! But the
next time you're in Washington, you and Rich must
visit us!"

"We will! We would love to!" said Laura enthusiasti-
cally, and then stopped, bewildered, as she looked at
Joan.

A transformation had come over her visitor. The
look of happiness on Joan's expressive face had changed
to one of deepest sorrow. There was the glint of moisture in the large eyes. "Why, what's the matter?" Laura
asked.

"There's something else I have to tell you. I really
had no right to come here and be so happy. It's terribly
sad. You'll have to help all you can. No, this has nothing to do with Rich," she added quickly, as Laura
stiffened with alarm.

"What is it, then?" Laura asked, almost in a whisper.

"Laura, this is completely unofficial. I ought not even
to be here, according to all the rules, but Martin insisted on it and Admiral Donaldson agreed. But I can't
tell you anything more. You'll know soon, but please,
when you do, don't say anything about this visit. Don't
ask me how I know this—it's part of the business I'm
about to leave—but we know you've been having
trouble with Peggy Leone. She's going to need your
help, Laura. Lots of help, and soon. You've got to do
what you can!"

"Joan, I can't. Peggy would never want my help.
You have no idea of the things she's said to me!"

"I know what she's like. I could probably repeat
nearly every word to you. She said a few untrue things
about me, for example. And poor old Captain Blunt,
too. We know she's behaved very badly. But she's going
to need you. She'll need help very much. She's alienated

nearly everyone around here, you more than anyone, I'll agree, but you're the wife of Keith's squadron commander. You have a duty to her."

"Joan! You're telling me that something's happened to Keith! You can't mean——!"

"I can't tell you anything. I'm only saying you've got to help Peggy, no matter how you feel about her. She's always been terrified of the Navy. Did you know she's been going to a psychiatrist? We've talked to him. This morning. We knew he wouldn't discuss his patients, but he managed to convince us she should not be alone even for a minute, once this thing hits her!"

"You're saying Keith's dead! Joan! I can't believe it! How can it be? What happened?" Laura put her hand to her face in horror. Something was grabbing her intestines. Her flesh felt dry, her body rigid. She clutched at Joan with the other hand.

"I can't say anything more," said Joan uncomfortably. "Whatever you're guessing is only a guess. And keep it all inside you. Don't show, and don't tell." The look of inexpressible sadness was unmistakable. "You've got to be with Peggy when the news breaks. Admiral Treadwell will tell you when. Nobody else can handle it. Will you?"

"What dreadful news!" Laura felt as if her mind were flooded with emotion. "Of course I'll be there!"

The good-bye handshake turned into a fond, sad embrace, and Joan was out of the house and into the car, which had arrived unnoticed. When she was gone, Laura stood leaning against the door she had just closed. The enormity of what she had heard was shattering. Poor Keith! What could have happened? She visualized him at the bottom of the sea, entombed in the steel prison of his submarine, suffocating slowly and horribly. Rich had many times said that dying from lack of oxygen was not unpleasant. One merely went

to sleep. But the thought was a frightening one, nevertheless. Why did it have to happen to Keith, Rich's best
friend in the Navy? Then another idea seized her. Rich
and Buck must have failed in their mission of rescue.
But, at least, they would come home safe. Keith would
not. His death, however it had happened, would soon
be made public.

And what about Peggy? Laura's personal dislike of
her had vanished. Joan had been exactly right. She
was simply terrified of the Navy. Was that wrong?
Especially when her fears had proved justified in the
most devastating way? Like her or not, one had to
admit she had been right to be afraid. The poor thing!
How cruel! How dreadful for her! And how awful, too,
for poor little Ruthie!

Laura would have to make plans. She would need
help. Cindy would have to relieve her occasionally, and
Nancy Dulany too. She would probably have to sleep
in Peggy's house for a few nights. Provisions would
have to be made for Jobie. At fourteen, that would not
be hard; he was already showing his father's indepen-
dence. Perhaps Peggy's telephone should be discon-
nected, or perhaps made to ring somewhere else, in
Admiral Treadwell's office, where someone could be
on duty to take messages. Food would have to be
organized. Someone would have to make sure Ruthie
was properly fed, taken to school, and fetched home
again. Peggy must be allowed to cry. She would be
hysterical. But she should be encouraged to do as many
of the ordinary routine things as possible, as were
within her strength, simply to keep her sanity. Poor
Peggy! That was, of course, the essence of the problem.
How much could she take? Even a perfectly normal
woman would need help at a time like this!

No matter what happened, it would be imperative for

Laura to keep a cool head. Peggy would be very hard
to handle.

Laura pushed herself away from the door, went to
the dining-room table. She took a piece of paper. She
would make a list of things to do, and plan some dis-
creet phone calls. She would know how to handle this.

She knew she would not fail.

Dell Bestsellers